Praise from Her Peers

"Through the eyes of a sensitive ten-year-old, Elizabeth Evans takes an unblinking look at some of the intimate secrets and desires that subvert and upend the American dream of the perfect family. Set in a posh midwestern suburb in 1959, *The Blue Hour*, with its **chilling portrait of an era**, lingers on."

> —Alix Kates Shulman, author of *Memoirs of an Ex-Prom Queen*

"The time is 1959 and an American family is evoked in all its tricky, tainted innocence. **A wonderfully engaging and surprising novel**, part mystery and part cherished recall."

> —Joy Williams, author of *Escapes* and *Breaking and Entering*

"*The Blue Hour* is about an America we all remember, the pain we all wish to deny, and the exquisite, expensive habit of familial love. Elizabeth Evans recalls the intimate negotiations of family with such care and intricacy that one feels anew the wonder and the terror of being a child and having parents."

> —Robert Boswell, author of *Mystery Ride* and *The Geography of Desire*

"What **an enthralling book** this is—about eruptive sexuality, men who are at once commanding and childish, and daughters whose eyes are opening into stunning clarity."

> —Bonnie Friedman, author of *Writing Past Dark*

"**A powerful and moving** study of family life. Elizabeth Evans writes, with Jamesian precision, from the narrator's childhood and adult points-of-view simultaneously so that the reader feels, remarkably, the emotions of the growing girl and the grown woman both at once. **I am thrilled** by Evans's taste and tact, as much by her large talent."

> —Frederick Busch, author of *Closing Arguments* and *Harry & Catherine*

Also by Elizabeth Evans

Locomotion, Short Stories

ELIZABETH EVANS

THE BLUE HOUR

1995 / ALGONQUIN BOOKS OF CHAPEL HILL

Published by
ALGONQUIN BOOKS OF CHAPEL HILL
Post Office Box 2225
Chapel Hill, North Carolina 27515-2225

a division of
WORKMAN PUBLISHING
708 Broadway
New York, New York 10003

First Front Porch Paperback Edition, November 1995. Originally
published in hardcover by Algonquin Books of Chapel Hill in 1994.

LIBRARY OF CONGRESS CATALOGING-IN-PUBLICATION DATA

Evans, Elizabeth, 1951–
  The blue hour / by Elizabeth Evans.
   p. cm.
  ISBN 1-56512-124-4
  1. Married people—Illinois—Fiction. 2. Family—Illinois—Fiction. I. Title.
  PS3555.V2152B58 1994
  813'.54—dc20   94-19749
                                                         CIP

10 9 8 7 6 5 4 3 2 1
First Edition

Special thanks to my editor, Shannon Ravenel, and to Mary Elsie Robertson, Jonathan Penner, Buzz Poverman, Michelle Bernard, and, especially, Steve Reitz.

For my father,
who taught me the art of storytelling,
and for my mother,
who encouraged the storyteller in me.

Hansel and Gretel sat by the fire, and when the noon came, each ate a little piece of bread, and as they heard the strokes of the woodaxe they believed that their father was near. It was not the axe, however, but a branch which he had fastened to a withered tree, and which the wind was blowing backwards and forwards.

"Hansel and Gretel"
The Brothers Grimm

CHAPTER I

Some people complain because they can't remember things—say, the name of the couple who once lived next door, or even the order in which events in a life began to go wrong. But I remember: not just names and sequences, but the lush depths of a chinchilla coat as it hung in cold storage, my father's hands rising off the steering wheel, even the optimistic green and white of the amphetamines a certain doctor prescribed for my mother halfway toward the end of everything.

Which is why I also know that the very first glimpse my family had of the Bishop house included Channing Bishop—tan, tall, suddenly *right there*, bolting out the grand front door and into the summer rain at the precise moment our realtor lifted his finger to the bell.

"Well, hello, there!" my father said—a friendly man, laughing and smiling, he stepped to one side of the walk to clear a path for Channing Bishop. My shy mother—a little nervous—backed into a clump of wet evergreens. She raised her fingertips to the plastic rain bonnet covering her bun. A thing decorated with little balloons of red and yellow and blue, that bonnet had come as a premium with a loaf of bread. She raised her eyes towards its transparent roof, murmured to my sister, Nancy, and me, "I bet I look snazzy."

How much does it matter that the year was 1959? Is it more important that it was 1959, or that it was early June, the wet trees and lawns throwing off a swarm of enchanted green light?

While my mother struggled with the ties of the bonnet, Channing Bishop paused to yank a windbreaker over his head. "Enjoy yourselves," he said, then rushed off down the walk—like no one answering a door in our experience, no, like some cool TV detective giving the slip to farcically inept cops.

I was ten at the time, and no sophisticate. But I felt certain my parents would take Channing Bishop's breezy exit as a snub, and my heart ached for them when he bolted through the opening in the handsome stone wall at the top of his walk, sped off in the silver sports car parked at the curb.

If my father felt bad, however, he didn't show it. "Man, oh, man! That's some car!" he cried, while Nancy—thirteen, clawing her way towards glamour—whipped her eyeglasses from her skirt pocket in order to watch Bishop zip down the street.

Nancy was full of contempt for the stuff of our lives, and, in general, I considered her arbiter of all action; on this occasion, however, I meant to show the world that I couldn't be even *slightly* impressed by someone who'd been rude to my parents. Along with the realtor—tall, beefy, butch haircut so short it was transparent—I turned away from the street and helped my mother out of the bushes and onto the walk once more.

I can't remember a time when my mother didn't struggle with her weight, and when she was particularly heavy, as she was that summer, her broad-cheeked face had what I thought of as an oriental character, stereotypically placid, inscrutable. She had other sides, of course. In the company of certain girlfriends, she was often giggly and given to making odd noises to suggest delight, horror (*Oh, poo! A-yee-yee!*). Still, that day, before our arrival at the Bishop house, she'd worn only the inscrutable face, and I was surprised by the change that swept over her as she stood looking into the Bishop foyer: something to do with the lift of her chin, a brighter eye, animal alertness.

"Now, just remember, we're only looking at this house for the *experience*," she said. "It's not for rent, and it's way out of our league." She looked at Nancy and me as she spoke, but I sensed she meant her words for the realtor.

"That Chan!" the realtor boomed. He winked at my mother as if he knew her to be a woman accustomed to rude young millionaires. "You'll get to know him once you settle in Meander, Mrs. Powell! Quite a guy, really! You've no doubt bought Bishop Meat: you know the products if not the family!"

My mother didn't respond to the realtor's words, only stared ahead into the twilight interior, and I glanced at my father to see if this would suffice:

No.

At that time in his life, my father's main business was asphalt, and years of hopping out of his car to nudge along his crews had left him with a ruddy face and hands. Still, while he stood outside the Bishop house, watching my mother—waiting impatiently for her to say something to the realtor—the color in his cheeks rose as steadily as some well-fed flame.

"Dotty? Chuck was speaking to you? About Bishop Meat?"

For my mother to show even the slightest disregard for what my father wanted made goosebumps of alarm rise on my arms. She adored him, I was proud of how much she adored him, it seemed to make us royalty. "Mom." I tugged on her arm, prompting her. "We always buy Bishop's hot dogs, don't we, Mom?"

"What?" She gave me a brief, annoyed glance, then turned to the realtor. "So this is *that* Bishop?"

It would seem comical to most people, I'm sure—how grand and intimidating Meander, Illinois, with its fifty thousand people, seemed to us after Dolores, Illinois, with its seven thousand. But there was the uprooting of it, too. My father had assured us we'd love Meander, we were going to grow rich there; even so, Nancy had slammed doors, broken things, worked out a scheme to stay on in Dolores in her friend Trudy's old playhouse. Then my mother had turned deadly serious and warned Nancy, "If Dad feels the move's important, that's that."

We were moving because my father planned to start a door factory in Meander—aluminum doors, screen doors, garage doors. Until we reached the Bishop house, we'd looked only at rental properties. We'd live in a rental until my father got his factory running; after that, he'd build what he always called "Dotty's dream house." He'd already bought a wooded lot, had an architect draw up plans. The memory of the blueprints and drawings he scrolled out across our kitchen table still fills me with nostalgia: rooms seductive as glades, rooftops dappled light and dark by the foliage of pen-and-ink trees somehow more dreamily beautiful than any tree ever was in real life.

"Help!" The realtor laughed as he groped in the dark main hall for a light switch. The rest of us still stood in the foyer. Nancy's long, thin nose sniffed at the masonry tang of the house as if it released deep instinctual warnings. Nancy was sensitive to decay, odors of the body. She went pale and fainted with some regularity. "This place may be famous," she whispered, "but it smells like the underground lavatory at the park!"

The agent laughed. He was jumpy with laughter, and as he laughed, he patted at his big belly as if it were a faithful pet. I liked him, but suspected I should beware any and all of his noisy charms. Earlier that morning, during our drive over from Dolores, my mother had mentioned that her phone conversations with the agent had given her the clear impression he considered us "a bunch of hicks."

"Hicks" had been a mistake on my mother's part.

"Hicks!" my father had cried, and lifted both hands from the steering wheel, as if to prove himself shocked beyond concern for our safety. Which wouldn't have surprised me in town, at safer speeds—I knew his theatrical bent—but, at that moment, we were rushing down a country road. Wet gravel popped loose beneath us. One bad bump would have sent the car on a roll into a ditch, through barbed wire and fields of corn. Nancy and I shrieked. Our mother closed her eyes—she looked as if she were going to sleep, had already accepted our doom—a gesture almost as awful as the way we drifted to the left just before my father lowered his hands to the wheel once more and declared in a voice both brittle and damp, furious and pained, "*Hicks*? Why, you don't know beans about what that man thinks, Mother!"

In the sudden blaze of the Bishop home's front-hall lights, however, it did seem as if none of us fit properly into our clothes. And our clothes were the wrong clothes, too, weren't they? One of my father's socks had slipped into the heel of his shoe, exposed his pale ankle. My mother was weary. The little hitch in her step left from a childhood bout of polio showed more than it normally did. Her linen suit—though she continued to bestow upon it the honorific "good"—that old beige suit had grown too small in belly and bust, and, after the damp day in the car, its fabric had the rusty, wrinkled look of rags hung up to dry beneath our kitchen sink. As for Nancy, though I usually considered her the epitome of teenage glamour, that day the hard crest of hair she'd sculpted above her forehead gave her face the startled look of the bats caught by camera flash in my *Encyclopedia of the Animal Kingdom*.

And myself: Today, I hope I'd look at myself with greater charity, but at that moment, in the Bishop hall mirror, I saw only a skinny kid, dishwater-blond hair whacked to within an inch of its life, dress so large I might have been the clapper inside a bell, practical eyeglasses, teeth bucked as a mule's from years of finger sucking. It occurred to me that I resembled those children the social service agents sometimes brought to my grade school: scrawny kids who weren't sure what last name to use this month, kids we all understood would be gone in a few weeks, never seen again, so why make friends?

The agent threw more switches. More lamps blazed, spot-lighting the staircase, the ceiling of the landing and hallway high above our heads.

"Aha!" my father said approvingly.

My mother smiled at his pleasure, then lifted her eyebrows at Nancy and me to let us know that we should smile, too. Her lipstick was the bright red of those days, and, considering how shy she was, it always struck me as brave of her to wear such a decided color.

"Eighteen inches thick!" With the butt of his palm, the agent thumped the walls of the Bishop house. "Imagine!"

We took turns thumping a wall papered in what my mother assured us was real grass cloth—apparently a good thing. *And* in keeping with the taste of the home's famous architect, the agent added. My mother nodded. Clearly, she wanted to say something, and the struggle between her ambition to speak and her shyness turned her cheeks pink. Such moments always made me nervous—both that she would speak, that she'd lose her chance to speak—and I took refuge in a pointed examination of the front door's panes of glass, each one swirled with caramel, the dreamy, creamy stripes of agate and horn. My heart beat hard. My mother's opportunity was passing, it was too late, the agent began to turn towards the entry to the living room.

"Oh!" Her hand flew up like the hand of a schoolgirl. With a little gasp, she said, yes, she was familiar with the architect's work. Prairie School. Oriental influences.

My father jingled the keys and coins in his pants pocket, and when she finished, he smiled, said, "Hmm! Is that right, Mother?"

The agent smiled, too, then went on to recite certain facts about the house, its use of local limestone.

"Mm-hmm." Though deep-chested as a pigeon, my father stood just five foot six, and, consciously or not, he'd developed a posture for talking to taller men: head held down, hands in his pockets, every now and then offering up a little nod. In this way, he managed to look polite, but also preoccupied; confident, even wily, instead of small and deferential.

"Next!" said the agent, and ushered us into the buffered green light of the living room.

Except for a grand piano, the living room stood empty. Its drama was heightened by the way in which the house perched on an incline; we'd entered at street level, but the living room was two stories up, and looked out into leafy branches of hackberries and elms and acres of bright rain-drenched grass that ran down to a creek backed by buff and gray cliffs.

"Gosh," I murmured.

Behind me, the agent laughed: "That's what I say, Penny! *Gosh*! What do you think, Bob? Bet your dad'd get a kick out of seeing you set up in a house like this!"

My mother dragged her fingers along a black marble fireplace mantel, her face looking both strained and giddy. "How's he know Grandpa Powell?" I whispered to her.

"Farm sales through the bank, honey"—"the bank" meaning the one owned by my grandfather in the little town of Lamont.

"What a fellow!" Like a bird who wets his whistle before song, the agent dipped his head, raised it. "I suppose he's awful proud of you, Bob, with all *you've* accomplished!"

As was his nature, my father waved off the compliment, then launched into a story about my banker grandfather: how one morning he'd grabbed a push broom to sweep up his bank's parking lot, and along came a fellow new to town, someone ripe for teasing.

In imitation of an older man, my father squeezed his voice higher, exaggerated the dramatic pauses both he and my grandfather used in speech: "'Oh, those bankers inside are awful nice! They pay me a quarter an hour to do odd jobs! Even let me come in for coffee when the weather gets cold!'"

My father laughed. "Apparently, before Dad was through, he had this poor fellow so worked up, nothing would do but he go into the bank and complain: 'Why, it's a *crime* for you wealthy businessmen to abuse that elderly gentleman!' and so on."

The realtor laughed so hard at my father's story that he had to take out a handkerchief, mop his eyes. I laughed, too, but apart from my father's imitation of my grandfather's voice, the grandfather in the story didn't sound anything like *my* Grandfather Powell. My grandfather was a man who always kept his gray fedora on his head, as if pressing business might force him to leave any minute now. In the middle of Sunday supper or Christmas dinner, he thought nothing of interrupting all conversation to rap his knuckles beside my father's plate, ask of the farm he'd given him years before, "Bob, what sort of return did your tenant tell you he got on your beans?" Or, it might be, "Bob, what's this I hear about you starting up a *pizza* restaurant?"

"Say!" The realtor raised his hands in front of his face, snapped his fingers—an odd, abrupt gesture that made him appear both hypnotist and subject. "Dotty, Bob! You got yourselves a lovely lot, but don't forget: you planned on *building* before you knew Bishop's place was coming on the market. You know I sold this Welshman of yours his new spot, Bob?"

My father nodded pleasantly. The "Welshman" would be Archie Jones, the soft-spoken, silver-haired gentleman whose sad but morally invigorating tale had convinced my father to start up the door factory in the first place. Archie was a crackerjack salesman, my father said, a self-made man, a genius with numbers—

"Say," my father grinned at the realtor, "have you seen that car of his, Chuck? Great big Lincoln convertible?"

"It's a beauty all right, Bob! And we found him a lovely house here, too. At a heck of a price."

"I haven't seen it, but I understand he's pleased."

The realtor made a face of happy surprise. "Why, say, I'd be happy to drive you by!"

"Oh, no, no," my father said, then added in the cheery whisper he used for most confidences, "over the years, I've learned not to mix business with pleasure, Chuck."

"And if it ain't broke, don't fix it, right?" The agent grinned. He touched the high keys of the Bishop piano, rapped out a happy tinkling noise: "Anyway, from what I hear, you two are going to give St. Louis Door a run for the money!"

"Got to get the factory up and running first!" my father said, but from the way he straightened, rose up a little on his toes, you could see he was pleased that good news about the factory had circulated around Meander. I felt a surge of happiness myself, and turned to smile at my mother. She worried, I knew, about how much time my father would have to spend starting up the factory. Summers, my mother and Nancy and I always moved to our cottage in a little resort town named Lake Bascomb and saw my father only on weekends. That summer, with the work on the door factory, we'd seen him even less than usual.

"Just between us kids, though," my father told the realtor, "it'd be a wonderful thing if we put St. Louis Door out of business! The bastards moved Archie all the way from New York and, six months later, they gave his job to some dumb bunny of a director's son!"

"Bob," my mother murmured in response to "bastards." Nancy and I exchanged a quick glance of pleasure and surprise. We'd never heard our father use that word before. Would "bastards" be part of his vocabulary in Meander? "Bastards" sounded a little like "buzzards," a little like a foreign word, something that might have been said by an uncensored version of that lazy landowner, Don Diego—in truth, the valiant masked man and friend to those in need: Zorro!

And see how my father flicked away my mother's objection! Zip, zip, zip went his hand, like Zorro's sword as he made his mark: "I don't mean to apologize one minute, Mother! Those fellows at St. Louis Door are a mean, mean bunch!"

"You're just calling a spade a spade," murmured the agent.

"That's right!" My father frowned at the agent, but his frown was a frown of camaraderie; he went on to explain how Archie Jones came from the part of Wales that our Powell relatives had fled years before. Archie's slate-mining father was so poor that little Archie had to rise at dawn to gather horse dung from the roads to sell to local gardeners. "Poor fellow! Going to school all mucked-up and all! And then to come to America alone!"

I'd seen my father excited about his business partners before but never so *touched* as he was by Archie Jones of the Welsh lilt, the breath that labored as he reached across his vast stomach to jot down calculations at our dining-room table.

And Archie: the day that Archie and my father had signed their partnership papers, Archie had said to me, "I hope you know your father is a great man, Penny."

"No, no," my father had objected, "we're just doing what's right, Archie. We're just going to show the big guys what a couple little guys can do when they put their heads together!"

That had been in Dolores, sometime in the early spring, maybe three months before our house-hunting trip in Meander. We'd just come through a period when my father walked the floor until dawn, hands in fists on top of his head. He'd backed a subdivision for a Leon Cottrell who turned out to be lining his and his suppliers' pockets with my father's money. To clear certain loans, my father had had to sell the colonial he'd built as a wedding gift for my mother, and move us into one of the subdivision's little ranch-style houses.

"Your father is a great man," Archie repeated. Then he and my father shook hands as they stood in the doorway to the living room where my mother and I watched *Queen for a Day* and folded laundry. Because the ranch-style's living room was too small to hold the couch from our colonial, my mother and I worked, side by side, on the love seat that had formerly sat in the colonial's front hall. Even now, I can almost retrieve a sense of her soft hip against mine, the startling but not unpleasant smell of laundry bleach on her hands. At that moment, I understood I had a double job to do: say something that showed that I both appreciated Archie's compliment to my father *and* knew it to be no more than the truth. Usually, my mother would have helped me, supplied me with words, but that day she stared straight ahead at the TV. A lank-haired woman was explaining to the MC and his audience that what she needed most of all in the world was an iron lung for her teenage son. Tears began to spill from my mother's eyes. They hesitated on the broad bones of her cheeks, then slipped towards her jaw where she knocked them off the way someone might knock off a row of icicles—with the back of her hand. Those tears were not in response to the TV show, I felt certain—my mother hated the way it made suffering into an entertainment—and so I assumed she was moved by Archie's kind words about my father. Kindness often made her cry, and, if my mother cried, I inevitably cried, too—which usually made her stop and try to bring me a smile. But not that day. That day, she got up and left the room and didn't come back again until long after Archie Jones had driven away.

"So what do you think, Dotty?" The realtor hesitated, then—looking mischievous—bent down, lifted an edge of carpeting in the Bishop den. Beneath the carpet lay old tiles: tiny hexagons of white, black, maroon. "I'd show them off, wouldn't you?"

My mother's nod of approval was modest, but it was plain to see that house had her by the throat; try as she might to conceal her interest, it fanned behind her eyes like a fish glimpsed through dark water.

"Of course, this isn't the sort of home you usually find on the market. Chan's still crazy about the place—you'd have to be crazy *not* to be crazy about it! He's only selling because"—here the agent lowered his voice into some temporary, gloomy region—"well, the wife ran off with his best friend, this Danny Mott. Took the kids. Chan—doesn't feel comfortable here anymore. You understand."

A television-sized picture took immediate shape in my head: Chan Bishop's ex-wife and Danny Mott engaged in some violent sort of tango. I pictured Mrs. Bishop with plunging cleavage, cotton-candy hair, long, long nails. Except in the news and on detective shows, I'd never even *heard* of a woman running off and leaving her husband. Since infancy, Nancy and I had been made to understand that everything our parents did was for our benefit. The idea of adults pursuing happiness at the expense of their children shocked me in the same way that news of murder and mayhem did; horrible, but also distant, and, hence, tantalizing, too. And the poor little Bishops: in my scenario, their noses ran unchecked, they waited around on unmade beds in hot desert motel rooms, eating dry cereal from the box. I felt so sorry for them, my eyes began to tear, but then my father cried out, "Poor little kiddies!" and—just like that— the weight of his sympathy pressed down on mine until it changed into ugly envy.

"Well, yes, it's a darned shame," the agent said. He seemed a little startled by my father's outburst. "Now, here"—he hastily pointed to a chipped spot on the wainscotting—"the wood's solid walnut under here. And this"—he switched on the chandelier—"good as they come: Waterford crystal."

THROUGH ALL of this, Nancy had looked slightly bored, held her nose at such a lofty angle it looked like a hatchet she meant to drop—chop!—but when the agent started us towards the stairs to the bedrooms, she yanked on my arm, whispered a fierce, "*Wait.*"

I waited. Everything about Nancy struck me as fascinating, the way her long nose went white at its tip when she was angry, the way her allergy to the rubber bands on her braces left her with tiny tabs of white skin on her lips.

"So. . . ." She brought her face close to mine as the adults moved off. I could smell the butterscotch Life Saver in her mouth, and I regretted that, as usual, I'd wolfed down my roll of candy within minutes of getting into the car—crunch, crunch, crunch—so eager to extract the most intense sweetness that I'd denied myself longer pleasure. "So, didn't you think Mr. Bishop was attractive?" Nancy whispered.

"Attractive" felt odd to me; it was the sort of word our parents used about people they knew. "Well, not *handsome*," I said.

"Oh, *handsome*." Nancy's eyes were bright blue, full of intelligence, some natural superiority I could never fathom. She sounded now as if she dismissed the idea of "handsome" as childish, though only the week before, with the help of our mother's "summer girl," she'd made an album of TV stars, catalog models, the man with the eye patch in the Arrow shirt ad.

"Why'd I ask you, anyway?" she said, and then, before I could dash upstairs, she gave me a pinch on the arm that I vaguely supposed I deserved.

The hall at the top was gloomy, and bigger than any bedroom in our ranch-style. I found my parents in a bedroom that matched the size of the living room below. It, too, stood mostly bare: a mattress on the floor, a telephone.

"Chan and this Mott owned a *plane* together!" the agent was saying. "The families vacationed together, for crying out loud! You can imagine the shock."

From the doorway, I watched my mother watch my father. If he smiled, she smiled. If he frowned, she looked concerned.

The agent tapped a finger against his temple. "Chan was *crazy* about her," he said. "Crazy."

My father and mother both smiled at "crazy," shook their heads, but the word made a shiver roll up my spine and down. As far as I could tell, to drive men crazy was the goal of a girl's life. I wanted to be in love's crazy thrall myself—no kid stuff for me, thanks. Give me broad-shouldered Richard Egan fighting to keep his hungry hands off Debra Paget in *Love Me Tender*—

"Penny." Spying me in the doorway, the agent signalled me over to the window to look at the view. It was the same view we'd seen from the living room, but now the rain had stopped, the sun shone, a cinnamon and white pigeon flapped its wings to brake its flight, then disappeared into the limestone cliffs.

"You see that old dam across the creek down there, Penny? That's what's left of the mill they named this neighborhood for."

"So we're"—my father lifted his face, began to sing—"'Down by the Old Mill Stream'!"

The realtor laughed, then added, "And if you need proof Chan still likes the neighborhood, those footings across the drive, there, that's where his new house is going up!"

While my parents looked out the window and remarked over the pentagonal outline of the future house, the realtor gave me a wink, stuck his hand behind the curtain, and drew something off a hook: a mask imitating "made-up" feminine eyes (one closed and winking, one open and screechingly blue, both decorated with a spidery fringe of plastic lashes). The realtor grinned, lifted the thing to my nose. "It's for a sunlamp, to protect your—" He turned to my parents, tapped his eyelids. "Must have been Haldis's: the wife."

"So was this fellow she ran off with Mott of Mott Construction?" my father asked.

"His family, yeah."

"Gad!" My father squeezed his eyes shut tight, laughed. "And he left all that for some—tootsie-belle?"

"Well, there are tootsie belles"—the agent grinned—"and then there are *tootsie-belles*. But, say, Bob, can we admit this is a once-in-a-lifetime house?"

Nancy didn't even glance our way as she passed through the bedroom, disappeared into a smaller room that was apparently part of the master suite. That was how separate from the rest of us Nancy could be. My mother, on the other hand, kept watch on my father and the realtor as intently as if they held the flag that would start a race in which she meant to run.

"But what about our lot?" I whispered to her. "How can Dad—"

She gave me a quick, pleading glance. "Sh! Don't spoil things for me, Penny!"

I never wanted to spoil things for my mother. On the contrary. Stung, I went to look for Nancy. The room she'd found was what the realtor later told us was "the lady's dressing room," and there Nancy turned in gloomy circles in front of a bank of mirrored closets. "Look at my ankles!" she demanded. "Why don't *you* have ugly ankles, Penny?"

"Your ankles *aren't* ugly," I said. "They're cute."

Nancy made a face. That summer, following the lead of our summer girl, she'd developed a beauty regime that included washing her face three times a day with Noxzema, followed by Ten-O-Six on cotton, then Clearasil ointment. Each night, she washed her hair, applied green goo to it, and rolled it up on wire and mesh appliances that kept her face several inches off the pillow. Nancy doubted her charms, while I, in much the same way that I believed my family would go to Heaven—anything else was too awful to contemplate—I *had* to believe that both Nancy and I would, like the Ugly Duckling, grow up to be beautiful.

"Here they come," Nancy whispered, and then the adults appeared in the doorway. My father was saying something about Mott Construction—what'd this Mott do now, if he'd left the family business?—but he paused in mid-sentence to register the dressing room's bank of mirrors, all of us doubled there:

"Say, now!" His voice rose. In crept a hint of my grandfather's faint brogue. He gave my mother a pat on the hip and chuckled as he eyed her reflection. "Say, now, that's an awful lot of woman, there, isn't it?"

One of his standard jokes about my mother's weight: a lot of woman. I glanced at Nancy. She looked embarrassed and angry. I didn't know what to feel. I was certain we were meant to be amused, to treat the comment as if it were to the point, but harmless, and *witty*, too, because it was the sort of thing someone *might* say as a compliment. And there was even more, wasn't there? We were to take his remark as a display of affection, something along the lines of: mustn't he love her if he doesn't like the way she looks but he puts up with it anyway?

I didn't want the agent to laugh, but also prayed that he would. Because suppose he *didn't* laugh, and my father felt foolish; or suppose he made a joke about my father's own thick waist? The agent was no fool, of course. He hooked a thumb into his belt, squinted at the mirrors. "Say, *my* profile sure ain't what it used to be!" he said, and then, miraculously, he delivered the laugh my father sought, but not at my mother's expense; and, somehow—though my mother's face looked a little waxy—he got us moving again.

More bedrooms, more baths, then down two flights of stairs to the red-tiled basement where a towering lady in grimy knee pads cried out, "Don't step on that floor! We just got it waxed!"

The realtor turned on the stairs to smile up at my family. Behind him, a teenage girl appeared in a door leading to what seemed to be the basement's recreation room. The girl stood even taller than the woman and wore her meager hank of hair drawn back tight by a rubber band. She gave us all a half-smile, revealing teeth so crooked they looked as if they'd been knocked out and now she held them in a jumble on the tip of her tongue.

"Guess Mr. Bishop didn't tell you we were slaving away down here?" the girl asked.

"Paula," the woman said. From the similarity in their heights and complexions—their skin had the mottled surface and sheen of headcheese—the two were clearly mother and daughter.

The realtor laughed. "We'll just head back upstairs!"

To the custom kitchen with the toaster that sprang from the wall, shelves that rolled out on ball bearings. Four faucets, gas *and* electric ranges, twin ovens, a brick barbecue grill with a copper hood big as a sports car, and—set into the counter—a square of stainless steel that, with a flip of this and that, became the base for a host of appliances: blender, mixer, juicer, can opener.

Down in the basement, the teenage girl sang a hit of a few summers before, Billy Williams's "I'm Gonna Sit Right Down and Write Myself a Letter." Nancy groaned in protest, but the adults laughed, so I did, too.

"Now that you've got background music, why don't you just wander around a bit, folks?" the agent said. "I need to sneak off, make a call. Maybe that floor'll dry in a bit!"

As soon as he left the room, my mother—pale, rubbing her temples—hurried to the sink. She took aspirins from her purse and downed them with water cupped in her palm.

"You getting a migraine, honey?" my father asked. To my relief, he moved in close, began to navigate his hand across her back in circles of apology. Though she didn't answer right away, he wasn't deterred. Once, when I was older, his big sister, Fran, told Nancy and me how our father—the smallest boy in the high school—wore metal taps on his shoes so people would notice when he came down the hall; as a grown-up, he still held his self-consciousness at bay with fillips of flamboyance. In the Bishop kitchen—I couldn't remember the last time he'd done such a thing—he suddenly scooped me up, threw me over his shoulder, declared I was a bag of beans, look, Nan, Dotty, think we ought to trade this one off to the Indians?

I laughed. I wanted everyone happy, I liked the way my blood rushed to my head as he tipped me forward, but my mother and Nancy looked away as if we did something shameful.

"So, Dotty." My father swung me down to the floor. "So, Chuck thinks it's a once-in-a-lifetime house."

"And it is," she said.

He bounced his pockets' collection of coins and keys, a sweet maraca sound. "So, you like it?"

I followed her gaze. Out the window, on the terracing between the Bishop house and its neighbor, a silver-haired woman wedged small flowering plants between the limestone flags that formed the retaining walls on the sloping property. The woman wore a garden smock and green rubber boots and, from a distance, at any rate, she seemed to have achieved the sort of finely tuned old age that advertisers use to promote elixirs and ointments. Had my mother been in a good mood, she would have declared the silver-haired lady "handsome" or "inspiring," something like that; but now she said only, "Don't tease, Bob."

"Don't tease!" He leaned against a counter. He rubbed his eyes with his knuckles, yawned like a child actor waking into a dream. "So you don't think it'd be too show-off?"

I understood the cautious, slightly blank look on my mother's face. It was important that she *not* act as if she believed in what might turn out to be a joke; that she *not* hurt his feelings by making him think she believed he might give her something he had no intention of giving.

"The old girl imagines I'm pulling her leg," my father said, with a wink. He looked like a beginner when he winked, like a boy trying to figure out how to make his way in the world, and this lack of expertise tore a sweet, predictable rent in my heart.

"Dotty." He brought his face close, lowered his voice. "Sweetie, if this house'll make you happy, dear, it's all yours!"

She shook her head. "But we can't, can we?" She started to cry, and then I did, too—as I said, we were a terrible bunch of criers, even Nancy couldn't help joining in, though anyone could see how furious this left her. Crying because your mother cried! Crying at the same time as your little sister!

From the doorway, the realtor boomed, "How's it going, folks?"

Shoulders bobbing, my mother turned away. Even my father's eyes had misted at her happiness, and he touched his fingertips to their inner corners. "Well, Chuck!" He shook his head, but couldn't quite answer. "Well!" The word slid out from beneath the burden of his emotion like a groan. "If I can just get an answer out of Dotty, here, I'll tell you!"

She reached a hand behind her back, made a weak fanning motion, wait, just wait.

The realtor nodded happily. All traces of funereal compassion now gone, his voice grading into jazzy conspiracy—quick, not missing a beat—he said, "Bob, this Bishop's got more money in the bank than—well, confidentially, he can *afford* a loss."

My father kept his eyes on my mother. He smiled as she turned around again. She took a handkerchief from her purse, and laughed a little at her tears—though her efforts to control them contorted her face, made her look like a person in pain.

"Frankly speaking, Chuck," my father said, "frankly, I had *that* kind of luck."

Which just then sounded so silly, so *untrue*, it made us all laugh. Anyone could see we were lucky from the way my father grinned, the way he held up his palms like a farmer feeling the first drops of a long-awaited rain.

CHAPTER 2

Recently, two boxes of photographs, stored away for over thirty years, arrived at my house. One of the boxes—a Lord Calvert carton—was marked "Powell." The other—a Sun-Maid Raisins box—was marked "Matsons."

As it turned out, almost all of the Matson pictures were of my Grandmother Matson. Multiple copies, multiple poses in the same situation. Grandmother Matson—then Mary Hannigan, age eighteen, nineteen—picnics with friends who capture Mary hiking up long skirts and petticoats to step over a log. Age ten, Mary in a studio portrait featuring fancy hat, parasol, button boots. Mary as I knew her, with the ladies of her various clubs, hard-eyed minks draped over her vast front, hair tinted mauve.

I gave myself up to the process of going through those photo boxes. Like a new lover, I stayed up with them all night. It was almost dawn when, coming across a photo of Nancy and me that my mother had apparently sent to Grandmother Matson—the two of us on bikes in front of the ranch-style—it occurred to me that I now sat in my own living room on the same love seat that my mother and I had sat upon so many years before:

folding laundry, watching *Queen for a Day*, talking to Archie and my father.

I looked up from the photo to a dawn of moist billows of fog. Through the window, the trees were scary in the way that half-hidden things often are, and I felt doubly disoriented by my next realization: I'd somehow become older than my mother had been on that distant afternoon.

In the Matson box, the only family photograph that included my mother was one in which she wasn't even the subject. The subject was a fat man with a checked tablecloth tied about his middle. My grandfather. He leaned over a barbecue grill—his mouth open barbarously wide, ready to bite a piece of hot meat—while my mother, eleven or twelve, stood in the hazy background, hoisting a striped cat. Before I recognized her, I took her for some neighborhood kid sneaking her kitty into the picture.

Toward the end of her life, lying in a nursing-home bed, my Grandmother Matson told me more than once: "Your mother wasn't pretty. Not like me! I was a *beauty*! But I got her up in nice clothes. I could whip up anything we saw in the shop!" With her perfect false teeth, my grandmother drew in her lower lip: a sensual, flirtatious gesture that suited her, despite her balding head, despite the way her flesh puddled around her bones as she lay in her crib-like bed. "The boys were crazy about me! Always trying for a peek when I stepped up on the trolley!"

In the nursing home, my grandmother had little to occupy herself with, beyond a transistor radio and memories. Some days, she grabbed my hands and, teary-eyed, begged: "Find a way to slip me some pills, can't you, darling?" By then, it was too late to wish she hadn't been so vain, that she'd been a better mother; and I comforted myself with the fact that, supposedly, my grandfather had been my mother's champion. He encouraged her to apply for the Griffin Scholarship, which she won. He disapproved of her leaving college at nineteen to marry my thirty-one-year-old father. More than once, my mother told Nancy and me, "*My* daddy thought *your* daddy was cocky, and too much the man-about-town!" She'd draw a sharp breath, smile. "All the girls were crazy about him! But he chose me! I was the lucky one!"

Pompadour, bedroom eyes. From the Powell photos, I know what the young man who courted my mother looked like. I know him also as a tiny boy in military cape and hat, saluting the photographer. My father was one of those terribly handsome children who, with a furrow of the brow, makes sorrow appear infinitely more beautiful than joy. Now on a scooter. Now on a high-school stage, dressed-up as the king of the pirates. Young again, and holding the rope to a brindled pony. Home from the army. With his big sister and little brother in a field of poppies, the trio almost invisible, the effect like one of those children's picture games: can you find the faces in the field of flowers?

"THERE'S A Welsh forehead for you!" So Archie Jones cried when he first saw boyhood photos of my father. That was late in the summer of '59, the day we finished packing for our move to Meander. While the rest of us ate tuna sandwiches, Archie walked from the ranch-style's tiny dining room to the living room, back and forth. Though very fat, Archie was grace-ful, and, like some gorgeous ocean liner, gave the impression of being simply too *large* for small, unsightly gestures. We were proud of Archie. Despite his own hard times, he seemed absolutely competent. Even his clothes suggested he knew about the world: a chalk-striped suit of a fabric variegated and softly gray as pigeon feathers, a shirt my mother whispered was silk, gray socks clocked with a second gray, darker, smokier.

"Ah," said Archie, and read aloud the naive, adoring phrases my grandparents had written on the backs of certain pho-tographs: "'Our little soldier! My, my! Doesn't he stand tall!' 'Here with his Sneezy! Such pals!'"

In one photo, my father and his brother and sister stood before a boxy frame house. The wood had never been painted, and it appeared almost charred, a pearly mix of silver and black. His grandmother's boarding house, my father explained to Archie:

"That's southern Iowa. A lot of Welsh settled there, to work the mines. Dad's mother—she had a lot of miners for boarders. When Dad was just a tiny"—my grandfather's phrase: "a tiny"—"his dad ran off. He was a terrible drunk, apparently. She had to make her way alone."

I raised my eyes above some instant flood of sad surprise to peek at Nancy. Had she ever heard any of this? Our great-grandmother had been abandoned? Our great-grandfather had been a drunk? Such things had happened in our family? Nancy, however, was lost in the world of her newly shaven calves, so entranced by the creamy, dreamy smoothness she'd achieved with our dad's Schick razor that she'd missed out entirely on this piece of history.

His voice grave, Archie said, "A strong woman, I'm sure."

My father cleared his throat. "That she was."

"And your father—to have accomplished so much!"

"A hell of a guy. He had to leave school at ten or eleven, something like that, to help his mother. They had next to nothing, and today—well, he probably owns eight hundred acres, plus this little bank of his—"

"Oh, wait!" my mother cried—in a different key altogether. She'd been unusually animated ever since we'd bought the Bishop house. That last day in Dolores, she swept around the house like a dancer, bright-eyed, laughing at everything. Now, nothing would do but that she unpack our electric globe so Archie could show us Wales. "Here!" She flipped a switch, lighting up the bulb that transformed the globe into an object so warm and beautiful that, had I been ruler of the house, I would've kept it always burning, like the candle above the altar at our church.

While Archie trailed his fingers over the globe, my father smiled at Nancy and me in a special way, every muscle of his face working toward a picture of delight: Make no mistake about my mood! I'm happy! Aren't you girls happy, too?

"Here we are!" Archie looked up with a smile. Illuminated from within, Wales appeared warm and yellow as the butter brought in tiny cups with restaurant lobster. Mexico was pink on the globe. Because it had been the site of my parents' honeymoon, Mexico was magical; as, indeed, were the Bahamas, the pre-Castro Cuba of blazing floor shows, Puerto Rico, Jamaica, Florida—any place my parents *had* been was more magical to me than anywhere anyone else dreamed of going.

"A man can scarcely cross a Welsh lane without jostling a Powell," Archie said. "My own family"—he broke off then, and, as if he merely meant to check the time, took out the pocket watch he always carried in his vest.

We sat quiet. We understood that some family rift had caused Archie to leave Wales, that it was a matter Archie found too painful to discuss.

"Two-fifteen." He pocketed the watch, looked up with a small smile. "If you visited, Robert, you'd surely find many relations only too glad to welcome you into their homes."

My mother nodded, and, in a soft voice, while she wrote "SALVATION ARMY" across a box of jelly glasses, allowed how she'd love to go, see the choirs and sheepdog trials and all.

My father raised his eyebrows in amused skepticism. He hadn't been around her enough that summer to know her new mood. In the car that morning, driving Nancy and me from the cottage on Lake Bascomb to the ranch-style in Dolores, she'd gaily announced, "I'm going to lose weight in Meander! And take classes at the junior college, too! Learn French! What do you think of that, girls? We'll all go to France some summer!"

She stacked the box of jelly glasses with the other boxes by the door. "So, Archie, what's the proper way to say it? Great Britain? The British Isles? My aunt has records showing my side of the family descended from some—lord?—something English."

Archie spread his fingers out across his knees. He stared at the backs of his hands, flipped them over and considered the fronts. "An *English* lord?" He looked up, grinning. "Well, I won't tell if you won't, Dotty!"

My father laughed at this—Ho, ho, Dotty!—and, then, taking a playful swat at him, my mother began to laugh, too.

Still, it made sense to me that my mother had royal blood. Now and again, when my father tore out his hair over some business deal or other—we were going down the tubes! straight to the poorhouse!—she'd say, quite regally, that she didn't need a fortune, as long as they were together, why, they could always move on the farm, she'd be perfectly satisfied to live there.

"The farm" was the two hundred and eighty acres my parents had received from Grandpa Powell as a wedding gift. When my mother brought up living there, however, my father shook his head, said, "Don't be ridiculous, dear."

I remember my mother on one of those occasions, sitting in candlelight at her end of the dining-room table. We must have still lived in the colonial, then, because at the ranch-style we'd only had room for our kitchen set, and I remember the way the light pooled on the wood as my parents talked.

"I'm not being ridiculous." My mother closed her eyes and turned her face up—as if to bask in some delicious ray of sunshine. Her lips curved in a smile. "We'd have a garden, and—instead of going to beauty parlors, I'd just sit on the porch in the morning and brush my hair dry in the breeze."

My father clapped his hands together: "Aha!" he crowed. "But there *isn't* a porch, Dotty!"

I grinned at their exchange. Despite his objections, my father often told us stories about the years he'd spent managing his father's farms, and even when the stories told of collapsed barns and pet cows that had to be slaughtered, they made farming life sound appealing. "If we do it," I said, "can we have chickens? And lambs?"

Nancy made a screeching noise, fast tires coming to a halt. "We're not moving to any old farm!"

"We certainly aren't," my father said. "Now lower your voice this instant."

II

CHAPTER 3

On the afternoon that the last big flatbed from my father's asphalt plant arrived in Meander, I was in the front hall, unpacking Halloween costumes. My mother stepped out into the foyer. "Oh, boy," she said. "I can hardly bear to look." As a little joke—for my benefit—she peeked out from between her fingers at the truck. Our living-room furniture had been stacked every which way on the flatbed, then roped in like a herd that might bolt.

"I hope I don't have to go out." She hiked my father's work shorts, cinched in to fit about her waist. "I look like an Okie."

The drivers were Hughie Mayfield and George Gross, men I thought of as my friends. "Look at them clodhoppers in our path!" Hughie cried while he and George huffed past me with a sofa. George made an indignant noise: "Watch yourself, Mayfield! That's my honeybun's feet you're talking about, there!"

"*Your* honeybun?" Hughie's face was red with effort, but he still managed to give me an injured look over the sofa back: "What's this, Penny? Ain't you my girl no more?"

As a kid I didn't give the matter much thought, but, apart from my father, of the men I knew growing up, I knew Hughie and George best. They'd been working at the asphalt plant before I was born. Also, whenever my father had a project around Lake Bascomb, he'd send George and Hughie to do the job, which meant they stayed in our cottage guest room while the summer girl moved in with Nancy and me. An imposition on my mother, who had to make the men three meals a day, do their laundry, and so on. And, no doubt, George and Hughie would have preferred a motel room. I, however, loved having them around. They were big, rangy men, who, after work, put on flannel shirts worn soft as dust and sat joking with me and drinking beer. While my mother and Nancy and the summer girl went upstairs for privacy, I stayed to watch TV with the men. George would let me jump on the foot he'd frostbitten in Korea. Hughie would give me his skinny comb so I could arrange his Vitalised hair into bangs and goofy crests.

Our Dolores furniture fit in the Bishop living room with room to spare. The love seat we'd used for a couch in the ranch-style sat in the front hall, the dining-room set was laid out as in the colonial—though the table had gotten scratched when one of my father's file cabinets had come unmoored during the trip.

"Sorry about that," Hughie said, and George too. My mother looked up from spreading scratch cover on the wood. She nodded, "Thanks, anyway, fellows."

In the hall I gave them sideways hugs, which they accepted with awkward but good-natured laughs. I'd never hugged them before. Maybe I guessed—correctly—that I'd never see them again. Then I walked them to the truck and, after they got inside, I sang them a chorus of "Happy Trails to You." They were more comfortable with this, and both made appreciative yipping noises and coyote howls as they drove away.

After that, I went back to my job in the hall. And spying on my mother in the living room. Forehead wrinkled, eyes squinted, she seemed to be trying to blur her view of our Dolores furniture: Early American, but with the fins of the fifties.

While I watched her move about the room, I slipped into a pumpkin costume I hadn't worn since kindergarten. Its stays were sprung and a broad wing of mildew spread across its front, but I found the thing intriguing as a measure of my growth. There had been a hat to the outfit, too, a little pumpkin lid hat. I was rooting around in the boxes for that hat when the doorbell rang.

Through the front hall's gauzy curtains: a tall and extremely thin woman, and, by her side, a sour-looking girl about my age, maybe younger. Both were tanned a deep brown, and wore shoes with rope soles, toreador pants in shocking pink, acid green—colors that implied a degree of daring, even danger.

"Mom!" I ran to the living room. "Somebody's here!"

"I know." She was inspecting herself in the big mirror that would eventually go over the fireplace, but now sat propped against a wall. The mirror's odd angle distorted her image, made her head look too small for her body. "I'm a mess," she said. She sounded short of breath. She made a mean grab at the flesh exposed by her sleeveless shirt.

"Could you get the door?" she pleaded. "*Please?*"

The woman let loose a little bark of laughter as I approached the screen. "Hi, neighbor!" she called, at the same time giving a hug to the girl at her side.

The women we had known in Dolores wore their hair in buns or poodle perms. This woman's pitch-black hair was shoulder-length and turned under in something like a pageboy—yet the effect was more Egyptian than collegiate. Her lipstick was pink, not red, and there was the matter of her nose, too. Though her nose spread oddly where it attached to her forehead, and ended in a snub broad and flat as a hammerhead, through sheer confidence this woman managed to make such a nose seem—enviable.

"Penny?" My mother—somehow she'd gathered her courage—arrived behind me in the hall, and, smiling, poking at her hairpins, said, "For heaven's sake, invite them in, Penny!"

"You must be Dotty! I'm Margret Woolum, and this is Eleanor!" The woman smiled broadly while her daughter stared at us with disdain. We could have been a dusty exhibit at a natural history museum, a badly stuffed pair of emus, say, glass eyes fogged by time, stitching come undone.

I wanted to protect my mother against such stares—partly because I loved her, partly because I believed that if I could protect her, then she could protect me.

"As you can see"—my mother gestured towards our unpacked boxes, our clothes—"we're all a mess!"

Margret Woolum broke in: "We don't see a thing!" Then added in her pleasantly buzzing voice, "Oh, Eleanor, how nice to have a new friend!"

As Margret Woolum chatted away, she gave the girl a little back rub, smoothed the parting in her waist-length ringlets, then planted a kiss on the spot. I glanced at my mother. She was, like me, watching the Woolums hungrily. The rule at our house was that the important love was the love of man and wife. Still, my mother often stared at other grown-ups enjoying their children. "Look at what good times they're having!" she'd cry. "Why can't we have fun like that?" She believed, I'm quite sure, that other people's children attracted love from their parents by some magnetism that Nancy and I lacked, that Nancy and I must understand that she couldn't be expected to love *us* that way.

Still, it did seem possible to me that day, standing in the front hall with the Woolums, that I could lean against my mother a little; that she might want to imitate the Woolums, too—

"Oh, no, you don't! There's mildew all over you, Penny!"

Eleanor laughed at this, tipping her head backwards to look up at her own mother. To my amazement, her mother laughed, too. Then Eleanor assured me her brothers were monsters, I'd hate them, and her mother laughed again, and told my mother perhaps they ought to arrange a betrothal between her thirteen-year-old, David, and our Nancy.

Eleanor. What kind of name was Eleanor? A crimped name, I thought, something out of the days of corkscrew curls and pantaloons; also, a name that immediately began to gather a perverse glow, sound as if it might have been used by centuries of nobility. A bow-down-and-worship-me sort of name. Princess Eleanor. Queen Eleanor. There was a name like that—Eleanor of Aquitaine. Had there ever been a queen named Penny?

Margret Woolum took out a cigarette and lit it with a silver lighter.

My mother, who had always told us smoking was unladylike, smiled and went on chatting. But when she noticed the cigarette ash beginning to droop, she said, "Let me see if I can find you an ashtray in this mess!"

"Oh, I'm fine," Margret Woolum said, and tapped the ash into her cupped hand.

What did my mother think of *that*?

Margret Woolum said "Hell" and "Oh, Lord!" and "My Gawd!" Of course, she didn't fascinate her own daughter the way she fascinated me, and while she told my mother about something called the Turnkey Club, how we'd *absolutely* want to join, Eleanor wandered off towards the kitchen.

"Penny," said my mother—her voice sounded so oddly musical, I started—"aren't you going to go with your guest?"

In the kitchen, I found Eleanor leafing through my mother's address book, an invasion that shocked me so thoroughly that I think I would have backed into the hall had she not lifted her face, giving me no recourse but to say: "That's personal."

Eleanor dropped the book in mock horror, her fingers flew up as if burned. Then she laughed and drifted on into the dining room, there to pick at the corner of one of the room's demure, peach-toned panels of life on the plantation.

"Your furniture's ugly," she said. "Also, our house is lots more famous than yours. Your house was just built by one of the *disciples*."

The only disciples I'd ever heard of were the ones who traveled with Jesus, but I got Eleanor's drift, and hoped my mother—just then entering the kitchen—hadn't overheard.

"He's the best orthodontist we've got, Dotty." Margret

Woolum said, which meant, I understood, that she and my mother had already discussed my buck teeth.

"A-hem." Eleanor tapped the toe of one of her rope-soled shoes on the toe of my oatmeal-colored oxford. "If you're wondering where you can get clothes like mine, you can't." Before I could think of a reply, she explained her outfit came from Chan Bishop; that "Uncle Chan" had bought it for her on a trip to New York: "The espadrilles are from Spain, *via* Saks."

I nodded, and, then, as if nothing could have interested me more, headed back into the kitchen where Margret Woolum held forth on the merits of public education—which you might as well love, ha, ha, since it *is* the only game in town!

Espadrilles. *Via.* While I struggled out of the pumpkin costume, Eleanor drew close to whisper, "Uncle Chan's best friends with my parents. He's at our house all the time. He says my mother's the only truly civilized person in Meander."

As if this struck me as terribly funny, but I was too polite to laugh, I smiled and turned away and stared out a kitchen window to the ivy-covered house next door. Not the Woolums' house. The Woolums lived to the east, beyond gravel terraces. The ivied house belonged to the older lady we'd seen on our first visit to Meander. Mrs. Krause. A garden pot holding the remains of a mostly dead geranium lay tipped over in the dirt beside one of the Krause downspouts, and, in my head, I played out a remote, miniature drama in which I rescued the plant, put it back in its pot, brought forth radiant red blooms from the one green leaf now curled in towards the stem.

"Oh, my Lord!" Margret Woolum reached into the kitchen pantry, left open during our unpacking. "These *can't* be Queen

Anne cherries, Dotty! I haven't even *seen* a can of Queen Anne cherries since I was a girl!" She closed her eyes and licked her lips, then smiled at Eleanor and me. "Pop them in the fridge and eat ice cold on a hot summer day!"

Margret Woolum's flashing eyes, her enunciation, made me shy, but, to my surprise, my mother jumped right in. "Oh, yes!" She moved towards the pantry, and as she passed Eleanor, she ran a finger along one of Eleanor's ringlets. "How about with a dash of cream on top?"

Margret Woolum placed her hands on her cheeks and wagged her head back and forth. "Wonderfully decadent, Dotty!"

I wanted to protest: my mother's hand on Eleanor, the chummy, drummed-up enthusiasm over the cherries. The label on that can was pale with time and incident, scratched up by years of use in games of "store." That can had traveled with us from the colonial pantry to the basement of the ranch-style to the custom-made pantry shelves in Meander. Along with a foggy jar of plum pudding, the cherries had always seemed like emergency rations, things not good enough to eat under normal circumstances, but available for energy-producing calories in case of disaster.

Now I wondered: *Were* Queen Anne cherries wonderful? If so, why had we never eaten them? Because of my father? I knew we didn't eat squash or rhubarb or salmon loaf because my father didn't like them. But perhaps my mother had been saving the cherries for a moment just like this, so she might insist, her cheeks bright with pleasure, "Take them home with you, Margret: a treat for you and Eleanor later this afternoon"?

Sophisticated. That was the word that popped into my head

when Margret Woolum laughed. She was nothing like my mother's friends in Dolores, women who wore sprung cardigan sweaters and pleated skirts, tucked a few tomato plants in among their zinnias each spring, gathered at one another's homes in the winter to play bridge or make craft items for church and school bazaars.

"Careful, Dotty! You offer me something, I'm inclined to take you at your word!" Margret said, and my mother replied— almost girlish, flirtatious—"I want you to take me at my word!"

I was relieved when they moved on to talk of cleaning ladies: My mother ought to give Chan Bishop's gal a call, she knew the house already. Eleanor, however, sighed in noisy boredom. "So is your father a professional?" she asked me.

"A 'professional'?" The only thing the term brought to my mind was boxing.

"Like, my dad's a *lawyer*. Carrie Hobart's dad's a doctor. They live down beyond Uncle Chan's new place. Things you have to *learn* how to be: that's professional."

In a rush of protective feelings for my father, I stuttered, "My dad was *almost* a doctor. He'd bought his cadaver and every- thing, but then *his* dad needed him to manage the farms. My grandpa's a banker, but he owns farms, too. Well, we own *one* of them. My grandpa gave one to each of his kids—"

My mother seemed to be picking at her nail polish in a point- ed way, and so I broke off. Maybe she believed our owning a farm made us sound like hicks? Or did she think I bragged?

"Anyway, he's real smart, isn't he, Mom? He had the highest IQ of anyone who ever went through the army, right?"

"Of anyone who went through that particular *camp*, honey,"

she said with a laugh; and then—to my shame—she winked at *Eleanor*, the way one adult will wink at another when a child makes a childish error.

"In answer to your question, Eleanor," Margret Woolum said, "Penny's father is a businessman, like Uncle Chan."

Eleanor shrugged. "Anyway, my father's *brilliant*."

Margret Woolum sucked in her cheeks, drawled, "*Everyone's* father is brilliant, darling" and then—her ears must have been sharper than ours—she turned to the hallway, where my sister appeared, carrying an open magazine in her hand.

"You must be Nancy! So do you like Suzy Parker, Nancy?"

Nancy looked down at the magazine, the pretty model swirling across the page in a red coat. That was Suzy Parker, Margret Woolum explained; then proceeded to tell us the wage Suzy Parker made for each hour's work—the sort of figure so wildly inappropriate to the task that later, trying to recall it, you could easily be several times off the mark in either direction.

"Nancy, Penny, Dotty! All those 'y' endings!" Margret shook a finger at my mother. "*I* simply *cannot* call you 'Dotty,' Dotty! I *know* at heart you're a 'Dorothy'! Tell me I'm right! Aren't you a *Dorothy*?"

My mother looked away from Nancy and me as if she wished she might be alone with Margret in order to answer, then said, "No one calls me Dorothy, but that is my real name."

Margret snapped her fingers: "And that's what *I'm* going to call you!"

I looked over at Nancy to see what she thought of this amazing series of events. "I like it better, too," she said firmly. "I wish I had a different name, too."

Margret set a finger to her temple. "Maybe you're just thinking wrong! Think of Nancy in the Champagne district of France! Think of yourself as some delightful French *ingénue!*"

We all stared at Nancy. *Nancy.* The experience was a little like looking at those trick pictures: do you see the beautiful young lady or the hag? The children kissing or the chalice? I felt unnerved, and I think my mother and Nancy did, too. Even after Margret Woolum left, they behaved a little differently, their faces had a shine to them, as if they'd been exposed to some chemical or light.

If my returning father noticed any of this, however, he didn't mention it. He was in a terrific mood. Up he came from the basement garage, singing "Barnacle Bill," and my mother—who rarely sang at all—did the rejoinder in the funny squeaking voice of Olive Oyl: "Who's that knocking on my door?"

That evening, after an early supper, my father took us on a tour of the town. We drove to a Piggly Wiggly supermarket that sold what were, for us, exotica: caramel-colored loaves labeled "Russian Black Bread," cans of smoked oysters, waxy buttons of Edam cheese. We bought roasted peanuts at a sprawling brick store bearing the neon-green, celebrity-style autograph of Sears Roebuck. All of us chatted excitedly, pointing out this and that as we sped along under shadowy arches of big elms, into neighborhoods and out again, into areas of gas stations and tennis courts and churches.

"Man, oh, man, looky here!" My father pointed to a coin-operated laundromat done up with Corinthian columns. "Look at all the cars!" Equal burdens of hurt and admiration squeezed his voice thin as a knife that we knew he was bound to turn on himself. There had been a period when he'd experimented with coin-ops himself. An old army buddy, Dusty McMichael, had assured him that all you did was set the operation humming—Dusty's phrase, "set it humming"—and rake in the money.

"That's not so many cars," I said, and Nancy added, "There's a dentist next door, too. Some people are probably going there."

Our father snorted. "At this hour? I doubt it, honey." But as we bumped over a series of railroad tracks—they were everywhere in Meander, hauling in steers and hogs for Bishop Meat—he seemed to brighten once more. "Any-hoo, things for the door plant are going along *dandy*!"

Oh, good, the three of us chimed. Good, great!

"So, how about I buy you ladies Dairy Queens?"

My mother smiled over the back seat at Nancy and me. For the tour, she'd put on a dress, high heels, and a hat with a little blue veil attached to its brim. She looked the way she looked when she served coffee in the parish hall after church. Dignified, if frumpy, a little like Mrs. Eisenhower, or Queen Elizabeth. "Best offer we've had all day, right, girls?"

Then, while we sat in the car, waiting for my father to fetch us cones, she read aloud from a fact sheet put out by the Chamber of Commerce: Meander was a leading producer of cement, phosphate fertilizers, and processed meat products. Though corn and soybeans formed the agricultural base of the community, sugar beets were grown and refined in the area as well—

"Say!" Grinning, passing around cones, my father climbed

into the car. "I just got to thinking, watching them make up a malt: we might have a malt machine at the warehouse!" He grinned at Nancy and me in the rearview mirror. "Maybe you girls'd like me to haul up some tables and chairs left from the pizza parlor. I think they're stored there too. You could have that rec room all to yourselves. What do you say? We could even stick a pizza oven down there! Have your friends over for pizza!"

"Mmm," Nancy murmured, "neat."

And I: "Wow. Yeah, neat."

My mother flapped her free hand behind the seat in an effort to stir us to a noisier display of gratitude, but Nancy and I knew that the pizza tables and so on would be forgotten in the crush of my father's other responsibilities. If we showed too much excitement today, he might feel bad later, remembering. My mother knew this, too. It was from her we'd learned to season our enthusiasm with distance, an air of ambivalence. Still, she gave us a sharp look before my father told her to take his cone until we got to the site of the door factory.

All those family strictures we had to master. All those jokes we had to applaud. We were in the Buick that night; my mother's car, but my father drove because—as he said—he got too nervous when she did. Laughing, he often told people stories of how she'd almost gotten the two of them killed through some misjudgment or other—the width of a bridge, the speed of oncoming traffic—and oh, it'd been lucky he'd been able to grab the steering wheel, step on the brake! During these stories, I sometimes wondered why no one pointed out that my mother drove Nancy and me and herself everywhere—to piano lessons, the grocery store, Lake Bascomb and back; that if my father's stories were to be believed, we lived in daily peril.

Did we live in peril? It was true, my mother sometimes pulled out on a road a little too soon, or waited too long and missed an opportunity. She always seemed willing to let my father drive, but were we better off with him behind the wheel? He was a speeder. Several times in my childhood he had to drive us down into ditches after miscalculating the slower speed of cars traveling ahead of us.

Even that evening, on our way to the factory site, he drove well over the limit, and this on a day when he'd already been stopped once by the highway patrol. ("Mother, you've got a migraine," he'd whispered as he pulled onto the gravel shoulder. The officer wrote in his book as he made his way to our car. "You've got a migraine, and I was rushing you to your doctor." He was polite. He was charming. His worry over the ticket made his voice sound exactly like it sounded when my mother really did have a migraine. The officer let him off with a warning.)

My mother always said, "Your father is the best driver in the world." Now, as we whizzed along towards the factory site, she didn't seem to notice the speeds that made Nancy and I hold onto our armrests. Voice merry, she said, "Wait till you meet that Margret Woolum, Bob! She's so interesting!"

"I liked her style," Nancy said. "She had cool hair."

Knowing my mother would feel slighted by such a remark— Nancy had never said such a thing about *her* hair—I sat forward in my seat, I blurted, "Could we have the radio on, Dad?"

"Cool hair!" My mother laughed, then gave my father a sideways look that suggested Nancy was terribly naive. "Her hair was straight out of a box, Nan!"

Nancy shrugged. "I don't care."

"You don't care!" My mother tried to make her voice light and teasing, but I could hear what she felt: hurt, betrayed by praise of someone else's charms. "Now the little girl, Eleanor, *she* was a beauty, and smart to boot!"

Nancy made an incredulous face for my benefit, but I was busy steeling myself for what would come next: my father's lecture on how, though Nan and I would never be beauties, never be Miss Americas, we ought to be *happy!* Gad, we weren't deaf or blind or spastic! We hadn't been crippled up with polio like our poor mama.

"Think about that!" He thumped his hand on the steering wheel, even laughed a little. "Gad! When you think of everything that could have gone wrong, we were darned lucky!"

Growing up in Illinois, you learned that if you heard the approach of a train from a place where there couldn't be a train, a tornado was headed your way, drop to the ground, quick. Growing up in my family, you learned that any discussion of female charms led to yours being automatically held up for dismissal. First my father cut Nancy and me from the race. Then my mother jumped in to cancel herself from the running, too. "That's right!" she said, with painful good cheer, tears clouding her words, "I was never pretty, and I had that darned brace on my leg, but I always wore a smile, I was always friendly to everyone!"

My father reached over to give her a little pat and then the nod of approval that always made me both happy and panicky, the emotions smearing into one another. By way of protest, I said, "I'd like to have clothes like that Eleanor. Mr. Bishop gave her those clothes."

"Bishop." My father sighed. "I ran into him downtown this morning. Poor fellow. I tell you, had any wife of mine behaved like such a whore, I'd have taken her over my knee and blistered her fanny!"

"*Bob*." My mother's eyes darted towards the back seat.

He brought up his shoulders—"Sorry, girls"—then took a whistling sip of air, added, "Any-hoo, he seems real nice. He said he'd take me up in his plane sometime." My father laughed. "I had to set him straight on one thing, though! He had the idea *Archie* owned the plant, that I worked for Archie!"

We'd been driving for quite a while by then—we were on the far outskirts of Meander, and dusk had begun to fall—but I could still make out the worried look that passed over my mother's face before she asked, "How'd he get that idea?"

My father lifted his shoulders again.

Nancy said, "Eleanor Woolum calls him 'Uncle Chan.'"

And I—in a preposterous voice, a voice that sounded nothing like the voice of Eleanor Woolum, who was, after all, just a midwestern kid like myself: "Of course, dah-ling, you realize that dah-ling Uncle Chan considers Mrs. Woolum the *only* civilized woman in Meander?"

My father whooped a laugh, then turned down a gravel ramp and into the cornfield he'd purchased as the site for the door factory. "Well, here 'tis!"

My mother leaned forward a little, hesitated. Looking for the right thing to say, I suppose. What she came up with was "*Voilà!*"

"Ha! Watch out, goils! Mother's starting to sound like Arthur Godfrey!"

"Oh, poo!" She gave him a playful swat. "Once I start learning French, *you* watch out! With all these cosmopolitan influences, if you're not careful, you might come home someday and find me—wearing a beret!"

My father was still laughing as he struck out across the mud and shattered cornstalks that remained from the land's last crop.

"Oh, boy, and it's starting to mist, too." My mother began to pull the pins from her hat—long, fascinating pins with their teardrops of plastic pearl at one end. I watched carefully, endlessly charmed by feminine paraphernalia and their little burdens: the tightening and loosening of screw-on earrings, the insertion and removal of hairpins and hatpins, the small pinches at the fingertips necessary for the removal of gloves. Such were the occupations I imagined for my grown-up self—each one a prelude to kisses, romance, male admiration.

"Do we have to get out of the car?" Nancy asked.

Our mother turned. "That man is your father. He's the kindest, smartest man you'll ever meet, and he'll be heartsick if we don't get out!" And so Nancy and I followed behind as, in high heels, she made her wobbly way across the field to Dad, his backdrop the screen of the nearby drive-in theater—just then beginning to play its enriched peach and blue version of life across the dusky sky:

A woman mixes a drink for a man. He is tan, with the sort of crisply amused blue eyes that spell danger and attraction as surely and compactly as street lights signal both stop and go. She—her dress is matte black against the blaze of her white skin. Her hair is the pale yellow of school chalk, and drawn high on her head, teased and sprayed into a cornucopia. The man seizes her shoulders. The drink is spilling, the woman resisting. She raises her forearms hard against his chest, but what good does it do? Oh, she is in his thrall and it is terrible and thrilling! His kisses feed upon her lips. From her lips it isn't far to her neck, and by the time he reaches her neck, she seems to have joined his struggle, abandoned her own—

I turned to Nancy, but before I could even whisper a word, my father began to run towards us, waving his arms: "Take them back! Turn around, Dotty! Gad! Don't you see?"

As if we hadn't registered a thing—were primitives who couldn't even read a photograph, imagine depth in the two-dimensional—Nancy and I blandly followed Mother toward the car.

"Remember, girls," my father called in the tolling voice he used for quoting Shakespeare, Ben Franklin, Proverbs, "no man buys a cow if he can get the milk for free!"

I'd never heard that saying before, but it made me queasy, and hoping, at least, to change the subject—I cried, "Pheasant!"

Not exactly a lie. I *had* seen something at the dusky edge of the cornfield; but by the time I had said "pheasant" I knew it was only an old paper bag, brown, torn. Which didn't matter anyway since no one asked "Where?" or even looked.

"It's starting to rain, Mom!" Nancy said, "I'm freezing!" And I—panicky, feeling we might never make it back to the car, be safe and warm again—I blurted, "Me, too!"

"You can't be that cold!" my mother said, but as we drew

alongside her, she wrapped an arm around each of us, rubbed at our gooseflesh—so nice, until she whispered, "Please, don't ruin things for Dad by complaining!"

And Dad, catching up to us, demanded: "What seems to be the problem here?"

"No problem!" Her voice was bright. "Everyone's fine!"

In the car, on the way back across the cornfield, I had to remove my glasses to wipe off the mist, and as I stole a last look at the movie, I myopically mistook what I saw on the screen for a candle, burning; then I put my glasses back on, and the candle resolved into the woman I'd seen before, only now she wore nothing but a white slip, and stood, eyes open wide, both hands clutching a gun to her chest.

The car hit the gravel ramp, then we were on the highway again. I craned my neck for a last view of the woman. The camera made an erratic, downward movement—something meant to imply dizziness—then it pulled steadily back until the frame held not just the woman's high-heeled feet, but the blood-stained carpet where she stood, and, then, the feet and the carpet and the body of the man who, only moments before, had bent down, and struggled for her kiss.

CHAPTER 4

The morning light in my new bedroom was not so different from the light in Nancy's and my room on Lake Bascomb, but Meander's morning smell was a shock. The live steers and hogs waiting for the move to Bishop Meat fouled the Meander stockyards, and the others—rendered, cooked— filled the air with an astringent smell so far from anything I imagined about death that it took me back to death again.

Side by side in the bathroom mirror, girding ourselves for the first day at our new schools, both Nancy and I took tentative sniffs. Nancy, looking pale, announced, "I think I'm going to be sick." With her rattail comb, she wanly teased a little flag of hair into shape. "Plus I couldn't sleep last night. All those trains!"

I didn't tell her how the trains' creaks and booms—the coupling of cars in the night—had terrified me, delivered me into a feverish world colored by Disney's *Darby O'Gill and the Little People*. In *Darby O'Gill*, the banshee came at night. A blue fog riding out of the sky in a coach drawn by enormous blinkered horses, the Shee carried off people to Death—and the sound of her coming and going was the sound I heard in Meander's trains.

I stopped on the landing on my way downstairs. Out in the street, Archie Jones was pulling his big car up to the curb.

"I'm not eating, Mom," Nancy called, which, coupled with her stylized progress down the stairs, struck me as excruciatingly glamorous. Over the summer, through repeated trips down the cottage steps, Nancy had perfected a movie star's descent, something to do with the slow extension of each foot in its pointy-toed flat.

In the kitchen, Nancy leaned languidly against the counter, and demanded, "How can you possibly eat with that smell out there?"

My father laughed. He and Archie Jones sat in the breakfast nook, my mother worked at the stove. "Better get used to it, Nan! The slaughterhouse is the biggest employer around!"

"That's true, Robert," Archie said. He'd spent Labor Day out of town, and his face—usually so ashy pale it made me think of the man in the moon—his poor face had the wet and hammy look of a day-old sunburn. Even so, he seemed dignified. And when he spoke, he sounded brave, the way—in movies—generals sounded as they spoke to soldiers in hospital beds. "But, perhaps, one day you and I will change all of that."

"Robert," Archie called my father, never "Bob," which made all of their conversations seem to occur in a private place, apart from whatever else went on around them.

Robert. Dorothy.

I don't think I ever knew how Archie and my father met. My father was always striking up conversations in garages and coffee shops. He'd come home to dinner, tell us how he'd stopped for some girl, hitchhiking out in the middle of nowhere with a sick baby, and he'd ended up hunting down a doctor in a little town he'd never even stopped in before. Or, say, he'd met quite a fellow—a Texas oilman—at Rotary Club! Or look here: he drew from his wallet a butterfly of signature produced by a pig farmer who could, using both hands, write his name both backwards and forwards at the same time!

I *did* know that Archie had worked his way up through big door and window outfits in the East. Archie's only mistake, my father said, had been taking that job at St. Louis Door. (Archie, however, said of St. Louis, "All's well that ends well, Robert! If things had worked out for me there, we'd never have met!")

"Say, Archie"—my father held up his empty cup to my mother so she might bring more coffee—"you know that little ditty, the one: 'My heart leaps up,' and so on?"

"The Romantics." Archie cocked his head to one side. "Lovely. 'The child is father to the man,' and so on?"

My father nodded, began:

> My heart leaps up when I behold
> A sparrow in the sky—

He broke off with a laugh. "But it's not *sparrow*—"

Archie brought up his big shoulders in a slow show of regret that he didn't know the word either. My father began again:

> My heart leaps up when I behold
> A *something* in the sky.

So was it when I was a child.
So is it now I am a man.
So let it be when I grow old
Or let me die.

Archie nodded, then added, his forehead wrinkling:

The child is father to the man—

While I set my dishes in the sink, I whispered to my mother, "Archie sounds like that butler from the ads on TV! The little butler under the table, and he picks up napkins people drop?"

"A *butler* under the table?" My mother smiled and ran a spoon around the eggcups, then transferred the eggs to plates. I loved to watch her hands: the long fingers, the backs criss-crossed with veins of a turquoise so soft it looked like trails of powder, like something you could blow away with a breath.

"Nan," said my father. Nancy looked up from sharpening her pencils over the wastebasket. My father smiled a pained smile common to his family: a squint, cheeks bunched up as if someone had stepped on his toes but he wasn't going to let on. "Close your mouth there, sweetie, can't you? Nobody wants to see a gal go around with her mouth hung open like a barn door."

"Dad!" Nancy cried, then hurried from the room.

He shook his head. "Didn't mean to hurt her feelings, but a girl needs all the help she can get, doesn't she, Archie?"

Archie smiled, then went on to say how there was all kinds of potential for growth in a town such as Meander; truly, Robert, what can stop us but a limit to our imaginations?

"Wouldn't that be something, though?" My father pulled his hand down across his mouth, as if shy of the smile that blossomed there. "To be bigger than the slaughterhouse! Man!"

"But, you know, Bob"—my mother set the eggcups in the sink, they rattled beneath the tap—"you shouldn't call it the 'slaughterhouse,' honey. You should call it the 'pack.'"

"What's this?" My father grinned and wiggled his tongue around in his cheek. "The 'pack'?"

"People in Meander—they call it the 'pack,' not the 'slaughterhouse.' You know that, honey."

He pretended to be in a huff, drew in his chin, puffed out his cheeks. "But a *slaughterhouse* is what it *is*, dear!"

In some soundless imitation of laughter, Archie opened his mouth, bobbed his head. Blue eyes crinkling, he said, "Perhaps the good townspeople would be amenable to *abattoir*, Robert."

"Dotty'd like that," my father said, and, as I set his eggs before him, he asked, "What do you think, Pen? You think *abattoir* might suit the delicate feelings of the people of Meander?"

I didn't know the meaning of *abattoir*, but I was happy to be allowed into the charmed world of men, and so I laughed, too.

"We're teasing your mother awfully, aren't we, though?" Archie said, and smiled at her, and shifted the conversation to certain sick rosebushes lining his front deck. Hadn't he noticed roses at our house in Dolores? "Can you offer an old bachelor a little aid, Dotty?"

My mother had just been bringing her own plate to the nook,

but she did not sit after placing the dish on the table, instead heading through the door to the dining room and beyond. "It could be borers," she called. "Let me look. Everything's a mess, but I've unpacked a lot of books—"

My father smiled fondly as she moved off, then he leaned across the table to Archie, whispered, "We always get rosebushes for Dotty on Mother's Day. If you get my drift. *Replacements*?"

"*Ah*," said Archie, and, in a low voice, went on to offer financial information he believed my father might like to know—the rates at certain banks in Meander were such and such, and elsewhere thus and so. "Of course"—Archie looked apologetic—"your *father's* bank—"

"No, no." My father waved away such talk. He prided himself on never having gone to his father for money. "I'll get financing, as long as you're sure we'll get a return."

Archie straightened in his seat. "And here comes your lovely wife, now," he murmured.

My father gave me a wink, then raised his voice to a more normal conversational level: "So! Maybe Dotty can fix your plants up, hm?"

"What about this, Archie?" My mother opened a glossy gardening book to a spot held by her thumb. There, a series of black-and-white photographs illustrated the advance of some borer, the last picture a shot of a bisected rose, the creature within wagging its blind head at the viewer.

"That's the fellow, Dotty!" Archie said. "Now what do we do to wipe him out?"

HEADING FOR school that first day, I tried to look—*jaunty, intrigued*, qualities I associated with the bright young heroines in books I'd read. On a "trial run" the day before, my mother had pointed out several landmarks that could help me find my way: an umbrella-style clothesline like the one we had at our cottage, a grape arbor, a huge white house with a lawn jockey near the curb.

The walled neighborhood of famous houses disappeared behind me more quickly than I remembered. Beyond the neighborhood, Meander appeared more normal: bungalows interspersed with big old frame things and the occasional brick apartment building. Eventually I spotted the grape arbor, and then the clothesline, now sagging with a weekend's worth of wet swimsuits. There would be a trestle just beyond the house with the lawn jockey—the trestle had a pedestrian walkway along one side, and I would use that to cross the creek. But I couldn't make out much of anything in the patchwork of sunshine and foliage and shadow that lay ahead of me. Had I somehow passed the big house without realizing it? Drymouthed, panicky, I set my hands on my hips in what I thought of as a pioneering posture and pretended interest in a purple and silver pigeon pecking at the flattened remains of a box of popcorn.

"Hey, ding-dong!" Whooping and hollering, Eleanor Woolum and her little brother, the seven-year-old Teddy, came running out from between an identical pair of brick houses. "You're lost, aren't you?" Eleanor crowed. Teddy—a towhead with pretty blue eyes and shockingly close-bitten nails—zoomed in close, smiling, then pelted me with acorns.

"So which way do you think you go, Penny?"

I looked after Teddy, already running up the street. "That way."

Eleanor sighed, then—as if she'd remembered something delightful—cried, "Oh!" and grabbed my glasses from my face, and refused to return them until she'd tested my vision on several street signs.

"Guy, Penny! You're blind!" she exclaimed, and did I know her own eyes were "twenty-ten," which meant that what people with *perfect* vision could see at ten feet, she could see from twenty?

I didn't suffer her comparison easily, but, just then I was desperate for a friend, and so I offered only a lame, "When I'm a teenager I'll get contact lenses."

"But what'll you do till then? Glasses, and your teeth—even when you get braces, braces are bad, too."

In Dolores, my best friend had been a chubby, kindly girl by the name of Jan Halverson. What if I never saw her again? What if all the girls in Meander were privileged characters like Eleanor, and wore empire-waist dresses and shoes soft as glove leather, satin ribbons in carefully curled hair? My own hair had been cut by my father's barber, Fred, who whooshed his shaver up the back of my head the way he would have on any boy. My dress was my cousin's hand-me-down, my shoes "Girl Scout" oxfords.

By the time the trestle came into view—a drippy "Class of '58" painted on its side—I was sick and scared. I'd felt uneasy about trestles ever since my father—in a funk over the failure of his housing subdivision—pointed one out, and announced in the *so* happy voice he generally saved for his darkest moments, "Now there's a dandy!" We were on a back road at the time, a dusty, narrow road we often used for visits to our relatives in Lamont. "I tell you, many's the time I've thought of driving into that trestle! Step on the gas and—poof!—your troubles are over. The boobs that shoot themselves in the head and mess up their insurance—somebody ought to take them out here, open their eyes!" Both Nancy and I had tried to pretend we hadn't heard—I think neither of us could believe he'd meant us to hear—but our mother, riding up front, gave us a look, and so we had no choice but to acknowledge his pain, to make our own painful protests: *No, no, Dad, don't say that, Dad, please, we love you, Dad.*

Eleanor said, "You have three wishes, Penny. What's number one? Straight teeth, or that you don't have to wear glasses?"

Number one? I looked off at Teddy Woolum, now on the trestle, dropping acorns into the tiny creek below. Number one would have been—a prayer, not a wish: Please, God, let things go all right for us in Meander. Still, I knew enough not to tell Eleanor much of anything, and so I said, "First, I'd wish for a million dollars—"

"Ha!" She clapped her hands in triumph. "I knew you'd get it wrong. The right answer is *infinite* wishes!"

I wanted to protest: she'd thrown me with her suggestions about my teeth and eyes! Instead, I crouched down, read the imprint pressed into the side of the trestle. I was always doing that sort of thing: pretending interest in things I had no interest in—believing this gave me an appearance of normalcy when, instead, it probably made me seem odder than ever.

"MOTT CONSTRUCTION" read the concrete. "That's the man Chan Bishop's wife ran off with, isn't it?" I said.

Eleanor looked away from me. "That's gossip."

My skin prickled at the reprimand. "Anyway, wishing for a wish might not really be a wish," I said. "It's like using a nickel to get another nickel."

Eleanor gave me a long, greedy stare, as if I were a puzzle she'd been told she had to solve without using her hands. "Using one nickel to get a *million* nickels," she said; and then, "You've got a lot of fillings, don't you?"

"Fillings?"

"In your teeth. Your family must eat too many sweets. That's probably why your mom's fat."

Temporarily, the world turned upside down. The trees and houses took on the watery look of their reflections in the creek below. I'd never hit a person in my life, but I wanted to punch Eleanor in the face, make her nose bleed—so much so that I trembled. "My mom's not *fat*! Even if she were, you don't call somebody's mom fat! Don't you know anything about anything?"

Eleanor laughed an adult, throaty laugh, but she kept her eyes on me as if she knew I was a little dangerous. "Pleasantly plump," she said. "Is that better?"

ARRIVING HOME after that first day of school, I startled a painter at work in the basement. "They're upstairs," he grunted, and, eventually, I found my father in the office he'd set up in the former maid's room. He was forty-six by then, but looked young for his age, and, that day, in a short-sleeved shirt, his heels hooked around the rung of his chair, at a distance he could have almost passed for a college student. He turned, smiling, when I came in for a kiss.

"Well, hello there, toots!" He shone his love on me like a spotlight, making sure I could feel it, know it. Still, he was impatient to get back to work. No sooner had he explained that my mother was "off" with Margret Woolum, and Nancy downtown with some schoolmates, than he began to tap his fingers on the paperwork on his desk, and so I quickly left for my own room, where I made some halfhearted attempt to set my collection of china dogs gamboling across my dresser.

"The nursery," my mother called my room, because that had been its function for the Bishops. Some sort of no-nonsense, no-color carpet covered the floor, and, on the walls, pairs of zebras, elephants, lions, and turtles traipsed past palm trees and onto their respective arks.

From the basement, the painter's music drifted up the laundry chute, and I went to the hall, poked my head into the chute to listen. Country music, the music Hughie and George and the other men from my father's road crews favored. I recognized a sweet, sad song that had been a favorite of Hughie's:

> I go on wishing on you
> 'Cuz you're my lucky star.

Eventually, I wound up in my parents' room, which felt comfortingly familiar. I lay down on the bed. Its spread was a glazed and quilted chintz, gray with maroon flowers. Where the material had worn through, the cotton batting was soft and white. My mother's usual hand lotion sat on the nightstand. The nurse on the label wore a cheerful smile. She reminded me of Nurse June in "Rex Morgan, MD." My mother had recently declared she wouldn't read "Rex Morgan, MD" anymore, she was so darned fed up with the way the cartoonists never let June and Rex get together!

(Still, suppose Rex didn't really love June? He never *said* that he loved her. Suppose, during his hours away from the comic strip, Rex Morgan actually loved someone else?)

I took my mother's bathrobe from the post of the big cherry-wood bed, and, after wrapping myself in its yeasty world, shuffled across the room to peek into the top drawer of my father's dresser. Everything there (socks, cufflinks, the tube of Lip-Ivo) was the same as it had been in Dolores, but now Archie Jones' gold pocket watch sat in the drawer, too. My father's response to the gift had taken me by surprise: he cried, and then, of course, the rest of us did, too. We understood the watch was the only thing Archie had of his father. "Archie, gad, I couldn't take it," my father said. But, in the end, he did, because he could also see that Archie—standing with head bowed, hands folded behind his back—Archie needed to give it.

That pocket watch—it was so unlike the sturdy expandable band wristwatches my father wore. Still, out of respect, he carried the thing with him to church, or to the business meetings he and Archie kept with bankers and so on. He made a point of taking it out, showing it around as a prized possession.

I was smearing on a little of my father's vanilla-sweet Lip-Ivo when an abrupt grinding noise of tabulation from his adding machine recalled me to myself. Carefully, I slid closed the drawer, shuffled over to the window.

An enormous crew was spreading gravel on the roof of Chan Bishop's new house. "The hog shed" was what my father always called the place. "The boob's a millionaire, and he sticks a hog shed in this lovely neighborhood! A man with everything!" Then he would pause. "Of course, he lost his wife and kiddies, so you can't help but feel sorry for him, too."

To me, Chan Bishop's brick pentagon looked like the model fallout shelter that loomed in the middle of the Piggly Wiggly parking lot, like an enormous—*foundation*, something meant to be sunk in the ground.

While I stood looking out my parents' window, Chan Bishop swung his fancy car (a Jaguar, according to Eleanor Woolum) into his new carport. I thought of him as a character out of a book or a movie. That summer, when our Powell relatives had come to Lake Bascomb for a Fourth-of-July picnic, my grandfather had offered us an account of the Bishop fortune. Supposedly, Chan's grandfather—just a boy running errands, sweeping up for a law firm—had made a deal with the lawyers: he'd collect their bills for a percentage. With that money, he bought land. Eventually he started the bank, and built what my grandfather said may have been the grandest private estate in Illinois—outside of the big places in Chicago, of course. Chan Bishop's *father* had started the packinghouse, which was important, yes, but the real killing—at least according to my banker grandfather—the real killing had been made when the Bishops' bank foreclosed on farm after farm in the thirties.

His brilliant blue eyes blazing beneath the brim of his fedora, my grandfather said, "We always tried to be Christian in our dealings."

My father and his brother and sister put down their ears of sweet corn and nodded in one accord and said, "You darn betcha," and

"We know that, Dad"—though there was, in fact, plenty of unchristian tension between *them*. My Uncle Roy and Aunt Fran had never left Lamont. Roy—and Fran's husband, too—worked in my grandfather's bank. Roy and Fran had also made my grandparents happy by signing the White Pledge of the Women's Christian Temperance Union, a pledge never to touch alcohol. Together, they sang in the choir of my grandparents' church. Still, my father remained my grandfather's pride and joy.

What would my grandfather have thought of Chan Bishop and his fancy car? I watched as Chan and a workman stepped through an opening onto a porch overlooking the creek and old mill, then I stuck my hand behind the bedroom's curtain. Haldis Bishop's sunlamp guards still hung there, alongside a garter of pale blue satin, tiny bells stitched to the wadding. From the Bishop wedding, I supposed, and felt a moment of sadness before I became drunk on the garter's sexy aura of Gay Paree and barmaids out of the Old West.

In my mother's dressing room, in front of the mirrors, I slipped on the garter. If I avoided looking at the whole of my ten-year-old self, and squinted so I didn't see the sun-bleached fuzz on my calves, the garter looked thrilling, didn't it? And things were even better when I removed my glasses. For her birthday the week before, my father had given my mother an exercise cot, and I seated myself on the thing, swinging one leg back and forth the way the barmaids did on *Gunsmoke*. *Tantalizing* the men.

I turned off the lights in the dressing room and lay down on the exercise cot. According to its makers, the machine could rock and jiggle away "even the most stubborn fat from buttocks, stomach and thighs." After my father had set up the thing, Nancy and I had each taken a turn on it. Mother, however, stayed in the master bedroom, sitting on her bed, reading the accompanying literature. "I'll do it without an audience," she had said when my father called her to come take a turn.

I switched on the machine and considered: If things went wrong in Meander, we could move into the dressing room and master bath, rent out the rest of the house. A balcony let off the bath. We could sit on the balcony and drink lemonade and sing old songs, evolve a home along the lines of Anne Frank's family hideout, a wonderful improvisation from impoverishment.

Downstairs, someone began to call, and I switched off the cot, ran out into the hall. My father stood at the top of the stairs, frowning: "What the devil?"

"Hallooo! Hallooo, y'all!"

"Mrs. Woolum," I whispered to him.

The two of us descended to the living room where Margret Woolum stood with my mother—who was shyly smiling, all decked out in a scoop-necked dress of parrot colors: blinking blues and pinks, black, green, a wild gasoline swirl.

"Oh, Mom!" I cried, and Margret raised an imaginary trumpet to her lips: "Ta-ta!"

"But don't touch, Penny!" my mother cried. "It's real silk!"

I backed away, murmuring praise, while she fixed her eyes on my father's face. "It's only on approval, to see what Daddy thinks," she said.

Margret Woolum's laugh ran about the room like some frisky little dog who then curled up at my father's feet. "So what *does* 'Daddy' think?"

"Well!" My father raised his hands to cover his eyes. "It's—
colorful!"

"Oh, men!" Margret shook her fist at my father. "She looks
wonderful, Bob!" she said, then poked her head through an
open window, hollered, "Chan! Chan Bishop! Come over here!
We need your expert opinion!"

My mother protested; my father protested. They exchanged
nervous looks while Chan Bishop hollered back "What the hell
are you up to now, Margret?"

Margret grinned, then we heard shoes popping the hackberries on the Woolums' redwood deck, followed by the crunch-
ing noise of steps on the gravel terraces.

"Don't you think it might be painful, seeing us in his house?"
my mother murmured, but Margret rolled her eyes:

"Nonsense!"

The front door swung open, shut. Chan Bishop cantered into
the living room just as he'd left the house that first day: his long
legs loose, moving so fast that he actually seemed to have to
rein himself in before he stopped. A smile flickered somewhere
in the lower half of his big terra-cotta face as he bent to kiss
Margret Woolum's cheek, but then he frowned, asked—teas-
ingly proprietary—"Do I smell *paint*?"

"Don't worry," Margret said. "It's just the basement. Now
listen—"

Arms stiff at her sides, my mother began: "Really—"

"Oh, shh! Now, Chan, isn't Dorothy wonderful in that dress?"

Chan Bishop's big teeth flashed white. He might have come
from another land entirely, been a Hawaiian islander, a Spanish
lord. "Dorothy is wonderful in that dress," he said. He seemed

to mean what he said, but, at the same time, he delivered the lines like a reluctant boy, and the adults laughed at the effect.

"I *think* that was a compliment," my mother said. Smiling, she started to smooth her fingers down the skirt fabric, then stopped herself and moved off toward the little tea cart she'd set up in the corner of the room. Whenever she worried her limp might be noticed, my mother tended to use an odd, controlled step that actually made the limp *more* noticeable instead of less, and this was true now. "Can I offer anyone a drink?" she asked.

The question gave me a shiver. My parents' having a drink on a weeknight was exceptional, and the added presence of glamorously abandoned Chan Bishop made the event dazzling. Also, this would be the debut of my mother's decanter. That summer, she had made many worried trips to antique stores around Lake Bascomb, certain that entertaining in the Bishop house called for a sherry decanter. Her final nerve-wracked decision had been something English, etched with lilies. It was "papered," she had explained to Nancy and me, showing us documents that testified as to whom the decanter had previously belonged, where it had been made, and so on.

Chan Bishop made a little groaning noise. "Don't make me drink sherry! I'll feel like I'm at my mother's!"

"Chan." Margret bared her teeth at him. "Sherry would be *lovely*, Dorothy."

Fascinating: the way she bullied and teased him, seemed to flirt with him so outrageously that the flirtation was canceled out. "Lovely," Chan drawled. My parents both smiled, but looked a little awkward, as if they weren't sure of their parts.

Beer was what Chan Bishop wanted, and my mother sent me off to fetch a can from our old refrigerator, now relegated to the basement garage—which was where I found Nancy, busily scrubbing lipstick from her lips with a Kleenex.

She had gone downtown with twins named Marlys and Tracy. A high-school boy had tried to pick her up. "This beautiful guy! Randy Scarlas. A Greek, Penny. *Greeks* live in Meander!" She sounded so amazed that, for a moment, I imagined Meander with its own pocket of milky blue waters, white houses that climbed hillsides silvery with olives—

"I kept walking, of course, but we're going back tomorrow! And there's this newsstand, too. The old man that runs it sells pop that's only a nickel and it tastes like it has alcohol in it. El Toro—it's *delicious*. And he sells dirty magazines—you could see guys reading them—and a newspaper for *Communists*."

The idea of a high-school boy trying to pick up Nancy alarmed me but I also exulted in her triumph. I could picture her exactly, swinging down the main street, cheeks sucked in, looking absolutely uninterested in the hoots of those exciting boys.

All I had to offer Nancy was the presence of Mr. Bishop in our living room, the silk dress, the adults' having drinks. But maybe this was enough—-or Nancy pitied me—because she said, "Let's go in there! We'll say we're looking at the art books."

The art books on the living room shelves were leftovers from certain classes my mother had taken at Murray College for Young Women (*Beloved Works of American Painters*; *European Masters*; *The Impressionists*; *Dutch Engravings*) and Nancy and I actually did look at them fairly often. Both of us liked well-stuffed paintings. Velázquez's "Las Meninas" was my favorite.

Nancy preferred the detailed hell of Bosch. That day, however, we opened the books at random—Gauguin, Remington—then whispered over possible evidence of Chan Bishop's heartbreak, and analyzed his blue oxford cloth shirt with its button-down collar, his brand of cigarettes, the way he held his cigarette deep in the fork of his second and third fingers, and covered most of the lower third of his face when he took a puff—nothing like Margret Woolum, who positioned her cigarette at the lady-like tips of her fingers.

In its earliest incarnation, Chan explained to my parents, the house's walnut moldings were finished wood, unpainted. The house hadn't had any "picture windows" at all, just rectangular panes separated by muntins.

Nancy whispered, "Do you think—the way Mrs. Woolum dresses—do you think she's trying to look like a teenager?"

I considered Margret's spaghetti-strap dress, her pale lipstick, and careful hairdo. I knew no teenager who dressed or carried herself with such confidence. Still, I sensed that criticizing Margret somehow fortified our own mother's wobbly position in this new world, and so I said, "Sure."

Nancy nodded, then turned to her book's next page, a picture I hated but always found seductive: a cartoonish farmer leering at a voluptuous young woman asleep under a tree. What I hated most about that painting—not a good painting I understood instinctively, akin to the "girly" pictures men put up at the asphalt plant—what I hated most about it was the way the artist, Thomas Hart Benton, seemed to be on the side of the man. I felt certain that he meant for the viewer to laugh at the painting, but I could only imagine some moment beyond what we saw: the man pressing his hand over the terrified woman's mouth, touching her in a private place. To make matters worse, the way the painting ogled the woman stirred something deep in my gut. Despite my revulsion for the farmer, I wanted to be the woman. I couldn't stop myself from wanting to be her, flimsy dress outlining my thighs, breasts. I couldn't resist the fantasy of being so admired—not by *the farmer*, no, but by the audience to whom the woman was so clearly offered.

Nancy turned the page, whispered, "You think Mr. Bishop minds our living here?"

I looked over at the adults. My mother and Margret were examining some detail of the fireplace while my father spoke to Chan Bishop. I couldn't hear what my father said, but while he talked, Chan Bishop rolled the can of beer in his hand back and forth across his forehead. Was he sad, or just thinking? I could tell by the way my father held himself—without devices, showing all his frowns and grins—that he liked Chan Bishop.

As if he knew we watched, he called over to us, "Come here, girls! Mr. Bishop's got a picture of his kiddies, here!"

A girl, a boy, both of them blue-eyed and blond and got up in vaguely nautical outfits, little hats. Margret and my mother came to look, too, Margret making a little noise—*uh*!—that suggested she missed the children. "Such darlings!" she said.

Chan Bishop grinned. "Obviously, they take after their mother. This is an old picture, anyway." He glanced at me. "I suppose Grace is about this one's age. But taller. She's getting to be a real beauty. Here—she was only six, maybe five. Even Mike's seven now."

Nancy and I exchanged a glance as our parents started in—

what handsome children!—and I was more than happy to answer the ringing doorbell.

Beyond the screen door stood a man with picture perfect posture. He was whistling "String of Pearls," but he stopped when he saw me. "I understand my wife's here!" A handsome, hairy man—black hair puffing out between his loosened collar and tie, its furry flames climbing the base of his neck.

I opened the door. "Mr. Woolum?"

He nodded, then bounded past me, giving me a glance that suggested he thought it both funny and—presumptuous?— that I meant to show him in.

"Roger!" Margret gave her husband the sort of full-toothed smile beauty contestants provide their judges. Clearly proud, he stepped to her side while she made the introductions.

One thing I learned in Meander: all I had to do was keep quiet and the adults would begin to think of me as no more worrisome than the coffee table. While I'd been out of the living room, Nancy had gone elsewhere, but no one seemed to notice at all when I sat down by the bookcase again. My father began to chat with Roger Woolum about his little door factory on the edge of Meander. "Little door factory" was my father's phrase. I'd heard him use it any number of times when talking about the plant—the phrase made him sound both modest, and as if he were a man who understood what "big" really meant. Even I understood that only a man who understood "big" could ever expect to *be* "big." Still, the conversation that afternoon left him looking slightly feverish. Talk of the economy turned to talk of President Eisenhower, about whom Chan spoke familiarly because he actually knew him.

"Well, it's my dad that's his pal, not I," Chan said. "I've just had dinner with him a few times."

"Still," my mother murmured. "The president. Did you meet Mrs. Eisenhower, too? Was she nice?"

Chan, it turned out, had gone to Harvard, a place that sounded to us as distant and exotic as Buckingham Palace or—Oz.

Rolling her eyes, Margret said, "Chan was there at the same time as that Bobby Kennedy," and Chan nodded sourly:

"That's a family that doesn't have political ambitions. They'd just as soon we named them monarchs, and stopped all the fuss."

"That's certainly true of Jack," Margret said. "Too much profile and not enough courage."

The other adults began to laugh, but Margret lifted her hands in the air to stop them. "No, don't anybody think I made that up. That's Eleanor Roosevelt's line. Even his own party's wise to *him*."

In the lively and thoroughly Republican conversation that followed, my father did manage to say, "You got it, Chan! This playing fast and loose with union thugs is for the birds!" My mother, however, seemed to have a hard time even controlling her smile. It took on an odd, jumpy look, like a needle on a seismograph. She glanced from Margret to Chan to Roger to my father with an intensity that suggested she hoped to memorize something the others did or said.

Whup, whup, whup! Margret rapped a fresh package of cigarettes on the kitchen table. The welfare system, she declared, was a sop. "What the fools don't see is that every time they put out their hands, they dig that hole they're stuck in a little deeper.

They make themselves less than human!" She shook her head, then added with a little gulping laugh, "They're turning back into Neanderthals. No, that sounds too evolved, doesn't it? Maybe they're just creeping back to the sea!"

None of my mothers' friends in Dolores spoke up during political discussions; and while Margret talked, my father held his eyes open wide and looked like a person who'd just taken a whiff of something startling—ammonia, Limburger cheese. Chan Bishop was the first of the adults to spot this, and he began to laugh.

"Margret!" Chan pointed at my father. "Look! Look at your effect on Bob!"

My father drew his hand across his mouth. "Was I staring? Excuse me, Margret! Your—*eloquence* took me by surprise!"

All of the adults laughed at this, except my mother. My mother turned away with a keen look on her face—almost as if some noise had distracted her, she hadn't even heard what my father said. In turning, however, her gaze fell on me. She took me by surprise, and I, her. From her expression, it seemed to me quite clear that she'd forgotten I sat there, and I remember wishing—the mind can move so fast sometimes—*wishing* I hadn't shown I'd heard my father's praise of Margret Woolum. Too late. We were both unguarded, and though I'll never know what she saw in my face, what I saw in hers was terrible: that she viewed me—simply because I sat as witness—as also her enemy and her judge.

CHAPTER 5

According to the Meander newspaper's "Newcomers" column, my family's favorite activities were hikes in the woods and "water sports at their summer home." I look at this clipping today and wonder.

Hikes? Water sports? Did water sports mean playing chicken on inner tubes? Did my parents say "water sports" or was that something dreamed up by the newspaper man? Both reporter and photographer, he *had* been a bossy guy. My mother should stand beside the kitchen's barbecue. No, not *there*, *here*. What's the little girl's name? Somebody comb her hair, why don't you?

My mother had a migraine that night, and each time the camera flashed, she winced. I can see the migraine in my copy of that picture, the way her right eye looks a little bigger than the left. The migraine had to do with an argument about the man painting our basement. A *barn* painter, my mother discovered, after he brushed over the famous architect's famous light fixtures as if they were mere impediments to the progress of color. ("Can't you at least stop him?" she'd pleaded with my father, who had replied: "You want to stop him, go ahead! I'm sure as hell not *paying* for that mess!")

"Here." With his knee, the photographer nudged Nancy closer to my father on the breakfast nook's banquette. "Close your mouth, there," he said—Nancy turned bright pink—then he asked my mother, "What're we saying you got in the pan, there, Mrs.?"

Frijoles, read the caption in the newspaper:

> Mrs. Robert Powell stirs *frijoles*, a vital part
> of the international theme dinners enjoyed
> by the family of four.

International theme dinners?

In the photograph, Nancy and I and our father sit in the breakfast nook, while, spoon in hand, our mother pretends to cook at the never-quite-functional but exceptionally handsome barbecue. Our postures are bad. I show all my big buck teeth. My father wears white socks. Still, we look happy in a way that sophisticated people, for all their handsome arrangements of limb and lips, rarely manage to look. One reason I married my first husband: when he saw that photograph he said, sounding like some old softy looking into a pet shop window, "Aw, and you can even see your mom's not stirring anything in that pan, can't you?"

THE AFTERNOON that the photograph appeared, Chan Bishop came by to drop off a copy he'd torn from his own newspaper. When I answered the door, he pretended to be shocked.

"What's this, Patty? Taking time off from your study of art history to fraternize with the neighbors?"

I understood that he teased me, and that I shouldn't act too impressed by his manner; it alarmed me, though, that someone who didn't even know my name felt free to look into, and comment upon, my character.

"Actually, my name's Penny," I said. I sensed my mother coming up behind me, and wished she'd go back. My father had just called to say he'd be waylaid in Dolores another day or two, and even though my mother wore her glasses, you could see her eyes were red from crying. Also, whatever the ambitions of her shirtwaist—the fabric blue and white and depicting gardens and pavilions, men in powdered wigs down on their knees in front of women of small, upthrust bosoms—it seemed to me to look like a bedspread, and I was, I'm sorry to admit, shamefully miserable about the fact. I wanted Chan Bishop to admire my mother. I wanted him to have the sort of teasing friendship with her that he had with Margret Woolum, something that would define my mother as welcome in that world, too.

"Don't worry!" Chan nodded at the record album and six-pack of beer—one already punched open—that he carried in his arms. "I'm not descending upon you, Dotty. I was on my way to the Krauses' for dinner, and just thought I'd drop by with this—" He maneuvered his clipping of the "Newcomer" article from his pocket.

"Oh. Well, thanks." As if counting the pulses in her artery, my mother held her free hand upon her neck. The Woolums and Chan made her nervous. I'd heard her say so to my father.

"Of course"—Chan grinned—"you girls *could* let me come in and drink a beer, and thus spare me a good half an hour of listening to Ruby and Tom explain how they knew Haldis and I had troubles, but hadn't wanted to interfere—"

I flushed at the name of his ex-wife. I thought of her as a criminal, an outcast; my mother, however, just smiled and said "Ah," and invited him in.

As Chan went into the living room—he insisted my mother must hear his record album—Nancy arrived home. Supposedly, she'd been at the library, but her whole being radiated with the marvelous, adult odors of cigarette smoke and the perfumes she and her friends tried on downtown. Since moving to Meander, Nancy had figured out how to approximate the hairdo worn by Elizabeth Taylor in *Cat on a Hot Tin Roof* (combed back from the brow, then forward onto her cheeks). She now owned a tube of pale lipstick and a compact of Cream Beige powder for chin and nose.

"How humiliating!" she cried when my mother handed her the "Newcomers" clipping. "Anyone can see there's nothing in the pan!"

"Oh, poo," said my mother, as if *she* saw beans, plain as day. Chan's cleaning lady, Bea Dart, now cleaned for us, too, and as she walked through the hall with the vacuum, my mother called, "Bea, do you think this pan looks empty or not?"

Bea Dart set down the vacuum, then stepped into the kitchen. She was probably no older than my mother—she may even have been younger—but she was worn, huge, her calves above her anklets thick with bulging veins, the skin beneath her eyes a wrinkly, velvet brown that made me think of the gills of mushrooms.

Out in the living room, the stereo needle made a little skip. Then a song, sung in French by some husky-voiced chanteuse, filled the downstairs.

"Mr. Bishop, right?" Bea said as she picked up the newspaper photo. "He likes that foreign stuff. Hmm!" She handed the article back to my mother. "You look real pretty there, Mrs. Powell."

I nodded: happy, grateful.

"Oh, pht!" said my mother. "I mean, thank you, but—look at this pan, Bea. Do you think people would know it's empty?"

"Well." Bea cocked her head to one side. "There's no reason somebody might not think you got a little bit of something in there." Then she and my mother went out into the hall so my mother could locate her purse and write out Bea's paycheck.

A letter from my Grandmother Matson sat on the counter, unopened. Sometimes my mother read those letters immediately; sometimes they sat unopened for weeks. The letters told how much my grandmother had paid for various food items, how she'd saved a neighbor's fruit from rotting by putting it up as jam, what was up with her various ladies' clubs. Often she included glowing references to my mother's cousin, Merle, whom my grandmother clearly felt ought to have been her own daughter. I had noticed the letters about Merle often left my mother cranky, and, in June, when my grandmother had visited Lake Bascomb—my grandfather had died three years before—I sensed that my mother could hardly wait to see her go.

"I look ugly!" Nancy seized up the clipping again. "I don't even look like this now, but everyone will remember what a dork I was when school started!"

Chan, entering the kitchen, placed his hands over his ears, his eyes, his mouth: the three monkeys of discretion. I was pleased that he assumed we'd understand what he meant, but Nancy stomped from the room, and up the stairs.

"What do you think, Penny?" Chan picked up the clipping. "Do *you* think it's a good picture?"

I hesitated. If I said, yes, I might appear vain; if I said no, then he might search out some flaw that would otherwise have gone unnoticed.

"It would have been better if they'd gotten more of the kitchen in," I said. "Maybe people will think the only thing we have to cook on is the barbecue."

Laughing, Chan took a seat on the kitchen nook's banquette pulled me down on his knee. Which meant I immediately pegged him as the type who showed his friendship for adults by acting friendly towards their sons and daughters. Still, I stayed put. I didn't respect myself for it, but I seemed unable to resist even what I took to be fake affection.

When my mother returned to the kitchen, Chan explained to her that he'd been in France that summer, he'd heard the woman on the record album while in Paris.

She smiled and nodded. She was working on dinner, a meat loaf of hamburger seasoned with Lipton's onion soup and catsup and extended with oatmeal and eggs.

I pointed to the empty record cover Chan had set on the table: a tousle-haired young blond, clad in only a man's pajama top, throwing open her shutters on a view of the Eiffel tower. "Is that the singer?"

He laughed. "Afraid not, Penny. This is—what we *pretend* the singer looks like while we listen to her." He tapped the cover with a fingernail that was pale as shell against his tanned skin. Then he murmured, "But Haldis had legs like this gal."

I glanced over at my mother, now busy working the soup mix into the meat. On behalf of her and a host of others, including, perhaps, my future self, I said—imagining myself clever and opaque—"But don't you think that name, 'Haldis,' sounds like a mineral, or, maybe some kind of fish?"

Chan laughed, then looked back at the photo. "Haldis *loved* having her picture taken."

My mother glanced up from her work with a droll smile. According to our lights, Chan had told us something that put his ex-wife in the wrong, revealed her conceit, and this meant that we were all becoming friends. Chan, however, didn't return my mother's smile. He stood, abruptly tipping me from his knee; and while my mother quickly looked down, abashed, he walked to the refrigerator, opened it and took out one of the beers he'd stashed there.

"Haldis." He stared into the blank face of the refrigerator— his old refrigerator, Haldis's and his refrigerator. "Haldis was a *true* beauty," he said, and then he *did* look to my mother for a reaction, his face a little sly, like the face of a boy who watches to see if his parents will reprimand him for some minor, but dirty bit of business.

With a quick stroke, my mother cracked an egg on the rim of her metal bowl, tossed the shell into the sink.

A true beauty. The words reverberated in my head, like the last words of a quarrel, and with all my heart, I wished Chan would say, "*You're* a true beauty, too, of course, Dotty!"

I didn't, however, expect to look up and see him moving towards her, reaching an arm around her—and I shrieked in alarm, "Mom!"

Instinctively, she shrieked, too.

"Hey!" Chan turned, hands up in the air. "This *is* all I was after, ladies." Slowly, like a criminal showing his weapon to the police, he brought forth a can opener from behind a curtain over the sink. "See? My old church key."

"For heaven's sake, Penny!" Red-faced, my mother stared back into the bowl of meat. "For heaven's sake! You half-scared me out of my skin! Just—go find something to do!"

"That's right!" Chan grinned. "Go gargle with peanut butter, kid! Go play in traffic!"

My mother started to protest, then stopped herself and laughed instead. To show I was a good sport, I smiled, too, but Chan was done with me. He turned toward my mother and began to tell her how Haldis had bought the material for the kitchen curtains on one of their trips to Bali. "Do you know Bali, Dorothy?"

Dotty. Dorothy. I noticed he went back and forth.

"The people in Bali say they don't have art, Dorothy. They say no matter what they do, they do it as well as they can."

My mother looked up from patting the meat into a loaf pan. "That's nice. So everything's art, then?"

"Everything or nothing." Chan took a long drink from his can of beer. "So—where's the boss today? Off making roads?"

She nodded, then a little teary-eyed, bit her lip.

"She—misses him," I murmured.

Chan studied her for a second, then tipped the last of his beer into his mouth. "Of course she does. He's a lucky guy."

I liked Chan Bishop for saying that, and, later, after he'd gone on to the Krauses' for dinner, and Margret Woolum came by, I tried to think of a way I might repeat his praise. I'd settled myself in the breakfast nook with colored pencils. It seemed a legitimate occupation. The meat loaf was baking alongside three big potatoes, and I was drawing a jay with black eyes made extra bright by the squares of "reflection" I'd included on each pupil.

Chan had given Haldis a Mercedes Benz *after* she left him, Margret Woolum told my mother: "Can you imagine?"

"Mercedes Benz," I mouthed, just as I mouthed the words my mother had written on an index card pinned to the bulletin board: *dialectical, sangfroid, etiolate*. I'd never heard of a Mercedes Benz. I pictured a wild animal—wild, furry, made up into a coat of unimaginable splendor. Just recently, I'd learned about chinchillas when Margret Woolum brought home hers from the cleaner's cold storage. Each fall, according to Eleanor, Margret installed the chinchilla and a blue fox in the cool closet of the family guest room. One afternoon, home alone, Eleanor and I had become so intoxicated by the furs' glamour that we'd stripped naked in order to take in more of those lofty coats, the cool slip of their satin linings.

"Chan said he'd take us out to his parents' home sometime," my mother told Margret. "Is it really as grand as people say?"

"Oh!" Margret emitted a regal blast of cigarette smoke. "It's— impossible! Really, they live in just a fraction of it." Then she went on to tell my mother how the senior Bishops were charming, really, but they'd marched Chan and his brother off to schools in the East at some awful age. "Six, I think. They were hardly home until they came back to run the pack." Margret stretched her mouth wide to dramatize her horror, then let loose her throaty, exasperated laugh. "Who understands men? As soon as Chan and Haldis had Mike, Chan started talking about sending him off! They fought about that, believe me!"

In a quiet, careful voice, my mother asked, "Did you like her? Haldis?"

Oh, Haldis was wonderful. The two couples had wonderful times together. Season tickets for the opera in Chicago, some terrific vacations, plus the kids were friends.

My mother nodded. "I suppose you were shocked. About what happened?"

Margret tilted her head to one side, looked my mother over a bit. "*Well*," she drawled, "no, honey, I wasn't *shocked*. Everyone else seemed to be, but, no, I wasn't."

My mother glanced my way, then said, her voice lowered, "I guess he's having a hard time of it. I didn't mean to count but he had an open beer when he arrived, and he finished two more while he talked to me!"

Margret tapped a teasing finger on my mother's arm. "Maybe *you* made him nervous! He usually comes over for coffee in the morning before he leaves for the office and, from what I gather, he thinks you and Bob are Mr. and Mrs. Wholesome Americana."

My mother eyed the clipping on the counter. "I certainly look wholesome in that. Positively *corn-fed*."

Margret laced her fingers in a girdle across her flat belly, and explained that she'd just spent a week on unflavored gelatin mixed with bouillon. She knew all kinds of tricks: cigarettes

helped, of course, and sit-ups, and—she half-whispered—
"Haldis and I used Ex-Lax once!"

"Ex-Lax?" My mother's eyes opened wide.

I felt an outrageous excitement at the idea of my mother
changing into someone like Margret Woolum, and, without
thinking, I blurted, "You know, Mom! *Grandma* uses Ex-Lax."

The women looked over at me; then, without a word, they
walked into the living room.

A little while later, on my way upstairs, I heard them discussing the replacement of our living-room furniture, my
mother doing her best not to appear to ask advice, Margret
doing her best to appear not to offer it. And what about classes at the junior college? My mother explained she wanted to
learn French.

Margret said something that I supposed must be French, and
my mother—sounding shy and grateful and a little impatient,
too—asked, "What'd you say?"

Margret laughed, then translated in a sexy voice: "'Have you
a room for two?'"

I found Nancy in the upstairs hall. She was scowling, and
wore only underpants and a shirt decorated with a design of
blue American coins. On the floor in front of the hall mirror a
fashion magazine lay open to an article entitled "Do you have
great legs?" Knees touching, Nancy bent from the waist, inserted a pencil between the fleshiest part of her thighs. According
to the magazine, she explained, if she could do this without the
pencil's touching flesh, then her thighs were not too fat.

It must have been October by then. Nancy had acquired a
boyfriend. Not the Greek of her dreams, but a classmate short-

er than herself, with a high, squeaking telephone voice. An unremarkable boy, but enviable all the same. The entire world seemed to be in sharper focus for Nancy now that she had a boyfriend to escort her through it.

I lay down on my stomach to consider the legs of the model in Nancy's magazine. They were like the legs of the woman on the cover of Chan's record: long, slim. Supposedly like the legs of Haldis. I thought of what Chan had said about Bali, and then I thought about the photographs of fat Russian women that the newspapers ran now and again: enormous women shovelling snow from city streets, or—without what Westerners would have considered requisite shame—spreading their great selves across crowded beaches. Those photographs—they always struck me as some sort of encoded warning to females who might aspire towards equality.

I rolled onto my back. "Nancy," I said, "did you ever think, what if everyone were beautiful? Would nobody be beautiful then?"

"Impossible. Also dumb."

"But what if it *were* possible? And how do you know? Look at dogs, how dogs look alike. All cocker spaniels, all German shepherds. Maybe they've evolved that way. Maybe someday we'll all just be—types."

Nancy didn't pay attention. Her voice dreamy, distracted, she said, "I'm going to buy a raincoat like the one on the cover. That's the same kind of raincoat Audrey Hepburn wore in *Love in the Afternoon*."

I considered a brown spot on the hall ceiling. Squirrel nests, my father had said. "But what if everyone had the same amount of money and clothes and food, Nan? Would you like that?

Suppose it was given out even, and we never had to worry about those things?"

Forehead wrinkling, Nancy bent with her school ruler to measure the fold of flesh that formed when she executed a knee bend. She made a notation on a piece of paper, then fixed her bright eyes upon me, and announced, "Mrs. Woolum says Haldis Bishop was so skinny her hipbones stuck out in front of her stomach!"

Haldis Bishop? Why did everyone talk about Haldis Bishop? "Some people don't have food and clothes!" I said. "What if we didn't have food or clothes or a place to live?"

"Penny"—Nancy hung her face over me; all of a sudden, she was grinning —"promise you won't tell?"

"Tell what?"

"I overheard Archie tell Dad they'll clear over a million dollars the first two years the plant's in operation!"

The blissful feeling of release that spread through me almost immediately turned to suspicion. "How'd you hear that?"

"Listening in on the phone!" She raised one full hand of fingers, and a thumb from the other hand, wiggled them in the air. "*Six* zeroes."

I rolled onto my stomach. Six zeroes formed in my head. Zeroes with stick legs and arms, fat men tumbling into one another like something out of a math book, a drawing meant to make children laugh while they learn. "But wait," I said. "Six zeroes is nothing."

Nancy frowned. "Well. A *one* and six zeroes."

I tapped my finger against the three-prong outlet on the wall beside me. "You know those masks where one's laughing, and one's crying? This thing looks like the crying one."

Nancy glanced my way. In a flat voice, she said, "Tragedy."

I pushed myself up onto my knees. Near the electrical outlet a small metal flap led to what I knew was one of many tiny tunnels belonging to the house's obsolete vacuuming system. I lifted the flap, pressed my ear to the opening. In stories, when a person located a spot like that, she'd end up hearing everything she wanted to hear, or didn't want to hear; and it seemed unfair to me that the tunnels in our house had nothing to say, all they gave back was the dull murmur you found inside seashells, the tiny roar your blood made as it moved about inside your head.

CHAPTER 6

| ELEANOR | He speaks French and German. |
| MYSELF | He stays tan like that by lying under a sunlamp fifteen minutes every day. |

Where we were: lounging on the bottom steps of the staircase that led to rooms in which our subject had once bathed, slept, presumably tucked in his children at night. The afternoon light in the hallway was dim, submarine, but Eleanor and I were used to the neighborhood's green gloom, and too absorbed in our competition to turn on a light.

| MYSELF | He smokes Tareytons. |
| ELEANOR | He'll only buy shirts from Brooks. |

Out in the kitchen, my father began to laugh. Was he on the phone? Talking to my mother? He sounded happy, though just before Eleanor had arrived, there had been two distressing phone calls: the first, a complaint from his own father about some standing water he'd noticed on a drive by my father's farm; the second, something about a mess in Dolores, gad, he'd have to get back there first thing Monday morning.

Was it trouble at the Dolores Ballroom? Did I mention my father owned the ballroom? It was a battered old place with scarred wooden booths hemming the edges, but it was tinged with romance, too: star lights, a ceiling covered with puffy clouds. My father and a man named Bill Rail had hoped to polish the place up, get it going like back in the Big Band days. Bill Rail himself had played a clarinet back in the forties. He'd met Artie Shaw when Artie was married to Ava Gardner. He'd known Benny Goodman and Glenn Miller. Bill Rail had enthusiasm to burn. He could whistle "Rhapsody in Blue," *in toto*, and entertain guests at parties with excellent boogie-woogie piano. Unfortunately, too late, Bill Rail and my father had learned that they had exactly two audiences to draw upon, kids interested in rock-and-roll bands and tearing doors off the restroom stalls, and old people who wanted to step out to the polka.

Eleanor looked in the direction of my father's laughter, licked her fingertips—red and wrinkled from the pistachios we were sharing. "No offense, but don't you think it's weird Chan spends almost as much time with your parents as mine?"

I laughed. "You don't even know when you insult somebody, do you, Eleanor?" Doing my best impression of merriment, I sucked on the shell in my mouth, cracked it with my teeth.

ELEANOR	His mom had an operation to make her elbows look young. And—he's the same age as my mom.
MYSELF	Your mom is the same age as my

	mom. Okay. He uses Vademecum toothpaste.
ELEANOR	My *mom* gave him Vademecum, dummy. How can you expect points for that?

Eleanor, of course, had the advantage in the game. She had known Chan Bishop since the day she was born. Chan had come to the hospital and looked in on Eleanor through the nursery window and declared she looked like a squirrel monkey kept by his college roommate. Miss Vassar, the monkey had been called, and sometimes Chan called Eleanor "Miss Vassar," and, of course, there was nothing like a nickname to show intimacy.

"Oh," Eleanor said, "and he had a cyst removed on his neck last year! I saw the stitches. Also, he doesn't go to church."

"Actually, he's going to start going to church with us!"

Eleanor's upper lip puckered in a way that showed I'd taken her too much by surprise. This scared me a little. "You've got chunks of nuts stuck in your braces," she said, then brushed pistachio skins off her Bermudas and onto the carpet, and stepped over to the wall where she began a grim inspection of my mother's print of Audubon's pileated woodpeckers.

"Okay, okay." She turned back to me. "Now, don't tell I told, but he's *dating* a lady who does *pastel* portraits."

I peered into the bag of pistachios to hide my surprise and disappointment. I still hoped Haldis and the children would return. Also, my parents didn't seem to know about the portrait artist. They felt so sorry for Chan, the deserted husband who needed to be fed and cosseted, urged to find a nice girl.

But maybe my mother *did* know. One night, when I'd stepped into the living room, flicked on a lamp, I'd discovered her by the window. "Turn that light off!" she'd snapped, and immediately she'd ducked beneath the sill.

I'd hurried across the darkened living room to crouch beside her. Had she seen a deer from the woods? A raccoon?

The moonstruck views of our new neighborhood—white crack of creek, luminous cliffs—those views always moved me, but that night there was something new in the picture.

Only days before, Chan had moved into the new house, and, now from a large central skylight there rose a lavender glow that bleached the underside of the branches that arched over the pale gravel of his roof. The branches made a second roof to a purplish cloud that seemed ready to house some substantial drama: a crèche scene, a murder. A beautiful, mysterious thing to see, that light, one more piece of magic in the magical neighborhood.

As if she read my mind, knew I half thought of the light as Chan's own, strange emission, my mother said, "It's just an ultraviolet lamp, Penny. What he's doing—he's *sunbathing*! So he'll be pretty for the girls!" Her laugh had been filled with both tolerance and disdain. "Personally, I never thought it behooved a man to be vain of his looks."

| Eleanor | You run out, Penny? You give up? |
| Myself | He won't eat cabbage, but he *loves* Brussels sprouts. |

That fall, when the Woolums and Chan came by for dinner, my mother often served Brussels sprouts because

Margret Woolum had told her that fall was Brussels sprouts season.

"Fall or not, they taste like turpentine to me," my father said, but he smiled down the table to Margret—her black hood of hair glimmered like the candlesticks—and Margret groaned, "Oh, *Bob!*" drawing out his name as if it were a delightful curse.

Why was I there? That fall, I'd reinstituted the puppyish habits I'd given up years before. I took to sneaking into dinner parties—often on hands and knees—and lying over my father's lap, beneath the table. He'd give me a little back rub while he chatted with guests who often didn't even realize I was there.

That fall, Margret Woolum taught my mother that *au gratin* did *not* mean "with cheese," and showed her how to brown bread crumbs in butter, sprinkle them over Brussels sprouts. Sprouts were good with lemon juice, sprouts tasted fine with rice wine vinegar purchased at the oriental shops in Chicago. Margret "whipped" my mother into those shops one day when my father was in Dolores. In addition to rice wine vinegar, my mother bought oyster sauce and shrimp chips and rice candy in edible paper wrappers. She and Margret went to a Chinese restaurant that was all lit up with paper lanterns; and, that evening, instead of the hamburger patties and wedges of iceberg lettuce she usually prepared when my father was gone, my mother cooked rice, set Nancy to cutting carrots and celery on a slant, and, me, to toasting almonds.

"We're going to eat Chinese!" she said, humming, looking cheerful. Still, she'd also seemed pretty cheerful the week before. Then she'd discovered that Nancy and I had neglected to wash our ice-cream bowls, and—bang!—eyeglasses tipped eerily on her nose, she'd come to the den where we sat watching TV, and she had pelted the two of us with the contents of a bowl of wax fruit. "You sit there with your smug little faces! Both of you! I have to stay here all alone, and—you don't appreciate a thing I do! You don't appreciate your dad's out there *killing* himself for you!"

Afterwards, while I'd picked up the chipped and broken wax fruit, Nancy had sat in a chair, stone-faced, despising me for my sniveling promises: we'll be better, we'll be tidy and polite, Mom, please, we love you, we appreciate you.

"Girls"—now, dashing soy sauce into the vegetables, my mother smiled, and said in a voice full of pleasant mischief— "you won't tell Daddy what I'm about to do, will you?"

I tried to laugh. A little chittering noise came from my mouth—something like the sound made by a squirrel on a branch. I wanted to encourage my mother's playfulness, but was her question a trick? Something meant to test our loyalty to Dad? She wouldn't ask us to hide something *bad*, surely, but if what she meant to do *wasn't* bad, why be afraid of his finding it out?

Wary, giddy, I looked to Nancy. Maybe she'd give me some sign if she knew disaster were about to hit. Nancy, however, only frowned at the carrot peels on the butcher block. As if she had not even heard our mother's question.

The counters in that custom kitchen were eerily sleek. I ran my finger along the hairline where the top and side pieces had been so perfectly fitted together. Everything that the Bishops had done to the kitchen was perfect: white tiles near the stove, butcher block near the sink, rabbeted benches in the breakfast nook. Which meant, sometimes, that I felt the kitchen belonged to the Bishops still.

"So?" My mother drew out the word, made it a little challenge. *Soooo*?

"So, come on, Mom," Nancy said. "What's the big secret?"

She grinned and walked on tiptoe to the pantry. Plain white paper covered the can she took from the shelves, and the words on the paper appeared to have been written by hand, in India ink, just for us: a label fancy as a wedding invitation. On tiptoe still, she carried the oddly elegant can across the kitchen to the electric opener. "Margret has this fellow from Chicago. Fancy foods! I guess Chan's wife hardly bought a thing that didn't come from him!" She laughed, her eyes filling with happy tears. "Really, I bought this for *company,* but I think we ought to have special things together, sometimes, don't you?"

For her sake, I tried to look expectant, excited, but not to a degree that would open me up for later criticism from Nancy.

"See!" She held out the open can. Whole legs of crab meat pressed one against the other, pink, white, arranged like petals on a flower.

"Pretty!" I said.

Nancy backed away. "It smells."

"It does *not* smell!" My mother's eyes flashed. "You are *not* to say it smells, Nan! It's seafood." Then she laughed, an emotional quick-change that made me think of my father downshifting as he caught sight of cops. She wanted to be happy. To be our happy friend, not some grouch. "This noon," she said, "Margret kept trying to figure out what was in our shrimp dish. I told her 'sherry,' but she didn't believe me. She assumed *I* wouldn't know if *she* didn't know! But"—up flew my mother's hands in a gesture of triumph —"*voilà*! When the boy brought our bill, I said, 'Could you possibly tell us what that lovely taste was in the shrimp? I thought it might be sherry.' He smiles at me, and what do you suppose? Believe it or not, I was right!"

CHAPTER 7

By November, my parents owned not just sherry and Scotch, but bourbon—for Roger and Margret Woolum—and three bottles of wine: Taylor's Sauterne, Rufino, and Mateus. My mother wanted the Rufino for its raffia-covered bottle, which she hoped to someday use as a romantically wax-dripped candle-holder. I favored the Mateus, its label's dreamy, golden architecture. I assumed our wines were fine and expensive, and weighed their glamour and promise against certain items I'd taken to hiding away—almost without consulting myself—in the far shoe drawer of my closet: packets of restaurant sugar, a bag of dried lima beans, a can of Nestle's Quik, a box of spaghetti, a courtesy pack of needles and thread my mother had brought home from a hotel, plus a number of cheerful articles that explained how people on limited incomes could make do, transform a pair of men's pants into a woman's skirt, say, or obtain protein from peanut butter and dried milk.

On the Saturday that Chan Bishop invited us to make our official tour of his new house, my father carried along the Mateus. He was in a rotten mood, I could see. *Bang!* he closed the liquor cabinet door. It rebounded. Bang! The door flung itself open again. Bang. Open!

"Goddamn it," he muttered, and left it as it stood. All of which had something to do with a question my mother had asked about the door factory: if he didn't understand something Archie had done, why didn't my father just ask Archie to *explain*?

My stomach ached as, single file—Dad at the lead, heels popping like firecrackers against the metal stair treads—we trooped down the basement stairs to the garage.

"I don't even want to see Chan's house," Nancy wailed. "I'm going to miss Scott's call!"

"Ho!" My father threw open the basement door. "You want to keep this Scott interested, you better make sure you *aren't* always home when he calls!"

We filed past him, into the open garage, and then the sunny day. A long, chilly rain had fallen the night before, leaving the ground and the masonry of the houses dark with wet, and this, plus the fall sunshine, gave the entire neighborhood all the sparkle and variety of a clear stream, the sort of beauty you might register even at a time like that, when all you could feel toward it was a species of shame.

Nancy sniffed the air. Her face registered revulsion. "Blood," she said, then tipped her nose in my direction. "It's you, Penny. Whenever you're outside, you smell like blood."

"I do not!" I protested.

"Gad!" My father let loose a corrosive little laugh as he brought up the rear. "Don't you get it, Dot? Starting up any business, certain things have to be done! Building! Financing!

People to see! We've got very specialized machinery coming in here. Even installing it's going to take time!" He didn't wait for a response, but started off down the drive, faster than the rest of us, as if he meant to leave us behind.

"Hell!" He spun around. "You think you can do a better job, Mother, take over! Nothing would delight me and Archie more!"

Well, of course she didn't think she could do a better job! She'd said no such thing! He put words in her mouth! She simply thought—if he were unhappy that things were coming along so slowly—after all, it *was* his money that was being sunk in the factory, not Archie's. He certainly had a right to ask a few questions, didn't he?

My father waved to Chan, already waiting for us on the high brick porch of the new house; then he murmured, "Archie's *supposed* to know what he's doing, Mother! If I ask him if he knows what he's doing, what do you think he'll tell me?" With a jaunty little move, he bent to scoop up and pocket a rusty nail from the drive. "And, just for the record, let me say, I sincerely regret that I *ever* mentioned any of this to you! You see, I had the impression you might be able to understand a thing or two about the fix I'm in! I *imagined* you might shut your mouth long enough to listen, but, apparently, that isn't possible—"

"Mr. and Mrs. Krause," Nancy whispered.

I felt sick, wobbly, as if all four of us rocked in a leaky boat on a rough sea. Still, like the others, I waved to the silver-haired Krauses as they drove past in their Cadillac. My father called out friendly things about the beautiful day. The Krauses nodded genially. Their car topped the hill, disappeared.

Pale-faced, distressed, my mother murmured, "I finished making up the meatballs for the party, Bob. I used ground pork and my own spices instead of buying store sausage. Margret didn't think it was worth the effort, but I bet we saved three dollars!"

"Ahoy there, matey!" my father called ahead to Chan.

"*Bob*?" my mother said.

"I *heard* you, dear! You're a good little shopper, all right? Now let's just hush!"

Chan leaned over the rail of his porch, smiled down upon us. "Have you come bearing gifts, Powell?" he called.

"Gift," said my father, "singular," and, then he rushed the last few feet towards the porch, drew back his arm, and, with a great *crack*, brought the bottle of wine against the bricks.

Had this been his plan all along—a christening? After a startled second, my mother recovered enough to cry, "Hurrah!" and then Chan cried "Hurrah!" too, and started down the steps.

I crouched beside my father to help him pick up the shards of glass. His cheeks were glossy from his just having shaved, and, at that moment, they looked very pink, too. He muttered, "Gad, I guess that's kind of an idiotic custom, isn't it, Pen?"

I tried to smile, look encouraging. I could smell his garlicky breath over the smell of the broken bottle of wine. He was so much on the road now that the meals he ate were not the meals we ate, and when he did come home—usually he was gone Tuesday through Friday—his breath was alien.

For our tour, Chan wanted to take us in the front door. "To get the full effect," he said, and led us alongside the house, past the new little trees, the piles of leftover construction materials. "Sorry about the mess here."

"Mess?" My father allowed that he'd have considered himself *lucky* if the door plant had gone up half as fast. "The way that crew laid our footings, you'd think we lived in the Middle Ages!"

Whenever my father complained about his business to someone outside the family, my mother smiled at the person, gave a little wink: Things aren't really so bad. People always seemed relieved by her smiles and winks, and, now—no matter how upset she'd been in the drive—she recovered enough to give Chan such a smile, and he quickly returned it.

From the start, Chan had liked my parents. I can hardly remember a time I saw him when he didn't tell me what good people they were, salt of the earth. I suppose that was one reason why it took him so long to get around to giving them a tour of his new house: I think he wanted their approval.

At the front door, he hesitated, tapped his fingertips against the knob—some big brass thing done up to look like coiled rope. "Here goes."

That house—it was all artistry. Several varieties of sunshine occurred beyond the theatrical overhangs of the roof. There were stained-glass windows, skylights. There were windows as long and narrow as those TV cavalrymen used while shooting at the Apaches, and, through one of them, a pencil of yellow light fell on the brick floor of a small bedroom, climbed the side and top of a little bed, then rose again, bright as flame, on the brick wall.

But why had he devoted so much space to the living room and dining room? Two bedrooms! Where would he put his wife and children if they came back?

"Look at this, Dotty!" My father pointed out the way in which the handsome herringbone pattern of the brick floors had been echoed in the beamed ceilings and cedar cabinets. "This is really something, Chan! Real craftsmanship!"

"I give a lot of credit to the architect," Chan said. "And Margret, too. Hell, half the ideas were Margret's."

My father nodded affably. "I *bet* she'd be good at that!"

I watched my mother for her response: Margret was now her friend, and, yes, my mother did manage a smile. But I *understood* envy, and I could *hear* my mother's envy expand, rustle inside my ear like a creature emerging from a chrysalis, drying its wings before flight. I had—I don't exaggerate—such a panicky sense she might hurt herself with some abrupt word or movement, that I began applying whispers I imagined might work as some sort of perverse salve: "Weird chairs!" "Strange colors!" "Is that *supposed* to look like that?"

After a few moments of this, she smiled at me, hard, then gave my hand a fierce squeeze. "Stop, okay?" she said, as Nancy, skimming past, whispered, "Look over by the fireplace."

A pastel portrait mounted on oak tag leaned against a pile of logs. A pretty woman: light hair, light eyes made startling by black makeup. "Portraits by Abbey James," said the lettering beneath the picture.

In a teasing voice, my mother asked, "You bringing Abbey James to Margret's and my party tonight, Chan?"

He bared his teeth, which I'd come to see were not really so white, only looked white because of the darkness of his skin: "I'm sure you and Margret would have a field day with that!"

My father laughed merrily, then added in an undertone, his

signal for Nancy and me to pretend not to hear: "So, Bishop, I guess that's your bedroom in the middle of the house? Does that make it the Holy of Holies, or what?"

Chan grinned. "You two give me a hard time, you know that? Now tell me, Dotty: what's the Holy of Holies?"

She lifted her hands in the air to signal blissful ignorance.

"You see, Powell, your own wife's a heathen, too!"

Pretending to be aggrieved, my father cried, "Why, Mother! The Holy of Holies is the inner sanctum! Only the high priest may enter, and"—he switched his voice into an unctuous imitation of our priest, Father Leo, and lifted a finger in the air— "he but once a year, on the Day of Atonement!"

Chan pulled a long face. "*Once* a year?"

My parents' cheeks turned a little pink at this, which made Chan laugh. "*Anyway*, Father Leo's having enough trouble teaching me the names of the disciples, so let's not get esoteric, Bob."

"Ah, the good Father Leo!" my father said. I think, like me, my father still found it delightfully improbable that Chan went to church with us each Sunday. "But, Chan, hasn't Father L. taught you the little ditty about Fifty-Two Mab Street?"

"What's 'Fifty-Two Mab Street'?" Nancy asked.

"I didn't teach you girls 'Fifty-Two Mab Street'?" Our father's voice was full of amazement. Though he hadn't raised us as he had been raised—church four times a week, no liquor, no cigarettes—he always seemed shocked that we didn't have his background; hadn't spent our summers at Bible school, and Wednesday nights in cold or hot halls, sitting on our hands while someone from the WCTU delivered a lecture on hell-fire and damnation.

"Well!" He took a scratch at the bridge of his nose, then began: "The 'five' in 'fifty-two' stands for the five Js: James and John, sons of Zebedee; James, son of Alpheus; Judas, called Thaddeus, and Judas Iscariot. The 'two' in 'fifty-two' is for the two Ps: Philip of Bethsaida, and Peter, who was Simon called Peter." He hesitated. Smiling, but shy in his pleasure in the trick, he looked at no one as he went on: "'Mab' is Matthew, Andrew, Bartholomew. And 'Street,' which can be abbreviated 'St': Simon and Thomas. 'Fifty-Two Mab Street'!" He finished with a clap of his hands, a wink.

"*That's* a mnemonic device?" Chan asked.

"Ah-hah! We'll make a good churchgoer of this heathen yet, won't we, Mother?"

She smiled. "At least we'll feed him Sunday breakfast."

"There you go!" Chan dropped into one of the canvas chairs he had ordered from New York. He put his feet up on the coffee table. "Leo might not support this dairy-case proselytizing," he said—stretching, yawning—"but, I'll be damned if real bacon and eggs aren't more seductive than storybook fish and loaves!"

Bacon and eggs. Fish and loaves. I'll be damned. Such conversation provided me with little jolts of confused delight. To think a person might set a miracle right alongside something my mother cooked up in the Sunbeam skillet!

While the adults talked on, Nancy sidled up alongside me and, making eyes at the portrait of Abbey James, whispered, "I bet he does it with her."

Thanks to a conversation Eleanor Woolum had had with her big brother, David, I knew that "it" was a penis going inside the hole that existed somewhere—where?—beneath a woman's underpants. Quickly, I glanced at my mother to see if she'd heard Nancy. No, she was smiling, listening intently to some banter between my father and Chan.

"Oh, hell! Hell, at least *they* know how to enjoy their money, Powell! Look at my dad! Look at you! You've got enough to live comfortably, but, you're gone most of the week—" Chan broke off at my mother's mild hum of objections. "You know it's true, Dotty! He's working too damned hard!"

I turned back to Nancy. I wanted to know what she knew about Abbey James, but Nancy was shaking her head at Chan. "If it weren't for Dad, Mr. Jones wouldn't even have a job!" she said.

"Right," murmured my mother, though with some ambivalence.

Whether he heard the ambivalence or not, Chan wet his index finger on his tongue, held it up, as if to judge the direction of a wind. "Ah, the loyal troops! I'm going to have to talk with this Jones, find out what he's done to inspire you all so!"

Voice wavering, my mother said, "It's *Bob* that inspires us, Chan."

My father smiled. "That's sweet of you, Dotty, but let's not forget why I got involved in the first place. Nan's right. That group at St. Louis Door treated Archie shabbily. That's the main thing. And, *damn* it, if all goes well, this door plant ought to provide something nice for when the girls grow up!"

Chan leaned forward in his seat, gave my father a sly grin. "Nothing in it for you, Powell?"

He laughed. "Oh, hell, I guess I just like to work, Chan!"

Since he was so fond of serving, Chan teased, maybe my father ought to be a politician. Mayor? Governor?

The idea made my father laugh, but my mother looked solemn, and as soon as she opened her mouth, I knew what she would say: "What he really wanted to be, Chan, was a doctor."

Chan pinched his lower lip as he considered this. "Is that right, Powell?"

My father grinned. "Dotty always forgets I fainted the first time I viewed a surgery!"

"You would have been terrific," she said firmly, then stood, excused herself: Margret would be at the house soon, and the two had lots to do before their party.

Nancy followed my mother home, but I stayed on. While the men split a beer, Chan told my father how he'd like to leave the packinghouse, start up a charter plane business on his own. Bored, I looked at an art book on the coffee table. The men's conversation was of the sort I heard all the time at my own house.

What did Chan's father think about the idea? my father wanted to know. Was this something he could swing on his own?

Chan bent forward, strung his sentences together like an eager boy. He seemed happy. But I wanted him to talk to my father the way he talked with the Woolums. Often, when I went to pick up Eleanor Woolum for school, I walked in on spirited discussions of art, history, politics: smiling a little maniacally over some neatly defended opinion, his tie not yet pulled tight for the office, Roger Woolum might be reading something to Chan and Margret. Chan usually sat with feet up on the den table, and offered his opinions to the ceiling. Margret—alternately pouring coffee, gulping laughter—made statements the men couldn't help but respond to: "Oh, well, if someone accidentally shoots a—what do you call it? one of those ceramic lawn deers—that doesn't mean we're obliged to eat it, Chan, much less pretend it tastes like venison!"

Chan's art book featured Arshile Gorky. Whose luck had been awful. No one liked his work. He was in a car accident and broke his neck. His studio burned down. His depression was so great his wife left him, and took the kids. He hung himself.

I looked up from the book at the sound of my father setting down his beer glass with a definite click. Something in his conversation with Chan had changed while I read. Now he and Chan grinned at each other as if a gauntlet had been thrown.

"But, Powell, surely you can see power's more interesting than money!" said Chan.

In a teasing, breathy voice, my father answered, "But, Chan, don't you know, Chan? Money *is* power!"

Chan laughed. "That's why my wife ran off, I s'pose?"

My father flushed. "That—that was a darn shame, Chan. But, say, you're probably better off without her! Any gal that'd do such a thing—"

Chan walked over by the porch windows and squinted off at the cliffs' damp gold. "Penny," his voice was low, slow, "did your dad ever tell you 'Fox and Grapes' as a bedtime story?"

I glanced to my father for help. "Chan," he said, "I spoke out of turn. Forgive me."

Without a moment's hesitation, Chan replied, "Forgiven! Forgiven! As long as you offer me a beer when we get to your place! And, listen, let me give *you* some advice, chum." He pointed out the window in the direction of our yard. "You know what kind of birds you've got at your feeder, there?"

My father and I walked to the window, though we both knew what we'd see: pigeons. Lavender and white and gray and cinnamon and tan, flapping up and down. Birds that carried a patch of nacreous midnight, cracks of lightning. Birds banded black and purple and rust, padding about in dumb dignity upon cracked corn and droppings.

My father glanced over at me, winked. "Oh, let's see: there's a cardinal, and a—junco, isn't that a junco there, too, Penny, next to the downy woodpeckers?"

He meant for me to laugh at this, and so I did. It was funny, wasn't it? How, in September, my mother had sent him out to buy birdseed, and, instead, he'd come home with a trash barrel full of cracked corn? One-tenth the price, he said when my mother objected that it would only attract pigeons and squirrels. In imitation of prissy womanhood, he'd put his hands on his hips: "Wait and see! If there's nothing else, I bet they'll eat corn!"

Chan said, "Those are crap machines, Powell. You got to tell Dotty she's using the wrong feed."

To distance myself a little, I ran through my head a song I'd learned at school:

> When a pupil to his school goes
> He is dressed up in his best clothes
> And his mother does her best to
> See his clothes are clean and pressed, too.

It was the way the sentences were skewed: that was what made the song funny.

The three of us left Chan's after that. As we crossed the main drive, passed by the feeder, my father gave me a wink. "Guess that darned corn does attract pigeons!" he whispered.

I felt partly responsible because I'd *wanted* him to be right. I'd wanted to believe the birds might change their minds about what they'd eat in a pinch, and so I said, "Still, they *are* beautiful, Dad."

He gave me a grateful smile. "I guess they are, aren't they, sweetie?"

"Common as sparrows," said Chan.

I blinked in the foyer's dark. The design of the wallpaper swam in and out of focus. My mother had told me it was *fleur de lis*, and sometimes I thrilled at the idea that French words could summon up a picture in my head. That day, though, I felt gloomy that my father hadn't told Chan about the corn. And I felt sorry for pigeons and sparrows, whatever needed defense for being ordinary.

"Bob?" Margret Woolum stuck her head out into the hallway. "Telephone for you!"

"It's Archie," my mother called. "Long distance."

While my father went for the phone, Chan pulled Margret into the hall, gave her a hug and a kiss. He kissed my mother, too, but only at parties, and I supposed it would be a sign that we were really part of the neighborhood when he did it at midday, before Sunday breakfast, and so on.

"Hi, Penny!" Margret said, then turned back to Chan. "Please, *please* talk to Dorothy!" Her voice squeaked with exasperation, she poked a fingernail into his chest. "She's leaving mushrooms out of the sauce because *you* don't like them!"

"Ah, yes," Chan barked—comically loud, so my mother would be sure to hear—"that Dotty's a sweet girl, Margret!"

Giggling, my mother called from the kitchen: "You see, Margret? There's my reward!"

Chan bent Margret's arm behind her back; some imitation of playground torture. He grinned, she grinned. "You know, Margret, *Haldis* always insisted on giving me sauce with mushrooms. Haldis considered it a point of honor to give me mushrooms. I don't know that she even *liked* mushrooms herself!" He released Margret, winked at me. "Why should it bother you if Penny's mother wants to accommodate a fellow?"

"Oh, shoo!" Wriggling away from him, laughing, Margret gave me the sort of look she often gave my mother when they were in Chan's company—a look that suggested all females had to be in cahoots against the likes of him. Then she cupped her hands to her mouth, as if calling from a long ways off: "Dorothy! I thought you and Bob were going to reform this Bishop fellow, make him go and sin no more!"

I started to laugh, but Chan raised a finger to his lips, signaling I should be silent so he could hear my mother's response—which came from the kitchen, clear as bells:

"Margret, after that old poop takes down the Ping-Pong table, he can go to h-e-l-l for all I care!"

Chan and Margret exchanged a delighted glance. My own response was pure shock, but my shock—the tingle of it— turned out to be something I could transform into a different response. It was energy. It could make me laugh—

Chan clapped a hand over my mouth, then pivoted my head

in the direction of the stairs. "Up you go!" he whispered. "You don't want her embarrassed 'cause you heard that, do you?"

That hand over my mouth startled me—the smoky smell of Chan's fingers. I glanced at Margret, my eyes filling with tears, but she only nodded. "Hurry, Penny! Go on!"

I took the stairs three at a time, then stopped at the top, shaky and confused. A bar of light let out into the hall from beneath the master bath door. Nancy. I wanted to knock, tell her about our mother saying "hell." I'd make it funny, I'd tell how Chan and Margret had laughed. But a noise sounded in the master bath: the medicine cabinet door rumbling like a train on the tracks. I had a pretty good idea of what that signaled: Nancy stealing my mother's diet pills.

A week before, I'd come into the kitchen and found Nancy neatly refilling the capsules of amphetamine with hay fever medicine. She made no effort to hide what she did, just said in an eerily blunted voice, "Tell, and I'll kill you."

I didn't believe that she would really *kill* me; still, I knew I'd suffer for telling. "But, Nan," I'd asked, "how's Mom supposed to lose weight if she's just taking antihistamines?"

Nancy had lowered her eyelids, rested her fingertips on the kitchen counter. She looked all knowing, as if, at that moment, she received divine messages. "Don't you get it, Penny? Mom can lose weight because she *thinks* she's got the real thing. But if I took the antihistamine, I'd *know* it was antihistamine, and it would never help me."

I was helpless in the face of such arguments. So I didn't bother, now, to knock on the bathroom door, but sat on the hall's top step, poised for Nancy's exit, ready to look her way in what

I imagined would be the most natural sort of surprise. I read the titles of the books my mother had left on the broad railing of the upstairs balcony. Several of them, I knew, had been suggested by Chan and Margret. *A Brief History of Persian Rugs*, *Brave New World*, a biography of Queen Victoria, *Lolita*, *Touring the Champagne District*.

Downstairs, Margret erupted in gulping laughter, and then, an unfamiliar female voice cooed: "John."

Seemingly in response, a man sighed, "Marsha."

I scrambled to the balcony railing just as my mother and Margret and Chan hurried into the hall in a clump as noisy and giggly as the junior-high girls Nancy sometimes brought home.

"John."

"*Marsha.*"

"Mom?" I called.

She tipped her head back, gave me a startled look: "Just—stay there, Penny. We're playing a trick on Daddy."

John and Marsha seemed to be in the living room. Back and forth, they called to one another, in variations of longing and excitement that made me shiver. In the past, the only person who had ever indicated to me that a woman might like sex was Bea Dart's daughter, Paula, who, while baby-sitting me one evening, had related a tale in which a boy and girl went to the drive-in movies, and, after the boy returned from buying popcorn at the snack stand, he found his girlfriend having sex with the gear shift.

"John!" "Marsha!" Faster and faster. "MarshaMarshaMarsha!" Building to a crescendo: "JOHN, JOHN, JOHN!" Then dropping, finally, back to the languorous tones of the beginning: "John." "Marsha." "John."

"What the devil?" Laughing, my father came into the front hall. "Gad! I'm talking to Archie, and it sounds like there's an orgy going on! Where in the devil"—"divil," he said, just like his dad—"did you find that thing?"

A record. I was both disappointed and pleased. Disappointed at the artifice, pleased it could be endlessly repeated.

THAT NIGHT, at the party, the record was started up again and again. Each time, lying on my bed, I heard the guests' laughter swell, I felt a little injured on behalf of John and Marsha. Maybe they *were* funny, but it seemed perfectly logical to me that what could make adults laugh could make goosebumps rise on my arms, and this was the fact that the record imitated some version of what the adults knew truly did exist in their world.

At any rate, the record rarely made it all the way through before someone lifted the needle—certain guests groaning while others cheered.

I fell asleep to dance music—the old Tommy Dorsey records my father loved—and woke up cold, still in my clothes and shoes, stretched out on top of the bedspread. My little radio alarm showed after two, but I could hear the faint sound of my father running totals on his adding machine.

Quietly, I went down the hall. I stood outside his office, and watched him work. His whiskers were grown out, and grayer than I remembered them. As always, he looked both vulnerable and strong. I wanted to sit in his lap, tell him I missed him. But suppose I gave him a start? Suppose I frightened him, and then—embarrassed at being frightened—he turned angry? And then I tried to apologize, but felt overwhelmed by the injustice of what came from loving him; and he saw that, too, and was apologetic, but resented having to apologize to a kid who'd sneaked up on him in the night, scared him out of his skin?

In the near distance, the trains began to creak and boom. By then I knew where the train couplings took place: a piece of high ground several blocks to the west. Strange weeds grew there, and sumac, the leaves bright red and pink and yellow and even blue with the autumn. The tracks met and parted in complicated arcs. You could easily imagine catching a foot there, dying under a crush of cars. Still, it was not the trains that frightened me in the night. In the night, the trains were not trains, but the Banshee in her terrible coach, coming to haul me off to Death, and I hurried back down the hall, desperate to yank a pile of covers over my head.

CHAPTER 8

In the house of my father's sister, Fran, family photographs stood or hung everywhere: on the window sills, dressers, the top of the piano, and, especially, the walls of the stairwell that led to the second floor. At the base of the stairwell were black-and-whites of Fran and her husband, Lloyd, as bride and groom. Newlyweds planting a garden. Fran pregnant; then pushing my cousin Rust in a stroller as cousin Janet toddled alongside. Rust and Janet played in the sand in front of my grandparents' cottage on Lake Elaine; they were tiny Christmas angels, student council members, junior choir members, and high-school graduates.

Because my family didn't display photographs, I assumed my aunt's displays were wrong, crass, like her purple couch and lavender bathroom. Still, I envied the photographs. They impressed me, and not just because they proved that people I knew now had existed in the past, been alive before I'd been alive. No. What I felt most strongly—most poignantly—was their assertion that what happened in your past *did* matter, it was *not* canceled out by every forward step, while at my house the past was a broom constantly sweeping away evidence of itself.

Nancy and I had always made a tour of our aunt's house together, but that first Thanksgiving after our move to Meander, Nancy declared herself "totally uninterested." She stayed in the kitchen, reading, and I went alone to visit the stairwell, the pear-sweet storage space under the eaves, the lavender bathroom where water turned tiny mint-like pillows into a handful of soap bubbles.

Fran had lived in the same house since before we were born—a white frame, spic-and-span clean—and, even with my cousins off at the homes of their college sweethearts, the house was unchanged: the photos, the pheasant-feather lamp shades, the magazine-like examples of boy and girl rooms (wood and wall pennants; flounces and collectible dolls). If Nancy had been with me, though, she would have made the house new all over again, made me snort with laughter over Janet's private photo documentation of her angelic ways: helping old folks to cups of punch, modeling a skirt and jacket made in Home-Ec, passing out cookies at a blood drive.

Down in the darkened basement, the men watched the football games. My uncles and an adult cousin sat on a blanket-covered couch at the back of the room. My father and my grandfather—dress pants, wool hunting shirt, fedora—had drawn folding chairs close to the TV screen, and there, identical noses and cheekbones lit up like masks by the light from the black-and-white set, they hollered instructions to players, coaches, referees:

"Go, go, go, go, get him, *get him, GET HIM!*"

John. Marsha.

In the living room again, I tried to pick out a few songs on the piano. I could overhear my aunts, out in the kitchen, telling my mother the latest news of their church. Oh, the most marvelous sermon! Oh, the lovely hymn at Wednesday night service! And what did Dotty think of the route the church bus meant to use when the ladies group got together with their sister church in Springfield?

A few days before, I had overheard my mother tell Margret Woolum that my Aunt Lee, wife of my father's brother, Roy, made her think of those trees that had been pruned to only a few branches, made to grow flat against a wall. "An *espaliered* tree," she said, pleased at both remembering the term and making Margret laugh.

My mother was never seduced by her sisters-in-law's talk of Bible Club, choir, and bandage rolling. She looked upon visits to Lamont as a kind of torture. All four of us used to laugh when, before getting in the car, she'd check her purse for her bottle of tranquilizers, then annouce, "Okay, I'm equipped!"

"Penny." Drying a piece of silver with a towel, she came to stand in the doorway between the kitchen and the living room. "How're you doing?" she asked, then rolled her eyes to let me know she was bored out of her mind.

I grinned. From behind her, Nancy called, "Oh, is Penny there, Mom?" Her voice was syrupy-sweet, a parody that made my mother and me grin. "Do come sit with Grandma and me, Penny!"

In the kitchen, my grandmother had plopped a magazine down on top of Nancy's novel. Grandmother's magazine contained stories and poems of happy sacrifice and good country people, and lavish illustrations: praying hands superimposed over a blossoming apple tree, raw blue skies above pumpkin-colored shocks of corn. My grandmother (pink cheeks, silver bun, china-blue eyes) could have been in that magazine, a glowing image of senior citizenry. In fact, she suffered from what I suppose must have been Alzheimer's. Earlier that morning, she had not been able to remember the word for the potatoes in the sink. She'd tried "socks" and "bricks" before giving up in bewilderment and despair.

When I sat down beside her at the table, she scooted away from me, no doubt assuming I was a stranger. Aunt Fran, however, peeking at Grandma, Nancy, and me over her lunch counter, cried, "Isn't that sweet? Grandma and granddaughters on Thanksgiving Day!"

My mother and Aunt Lee—both of them got up in Fran's bibbed aprons—came to take a peek. "Awww," said Aunt Lee, and my mother, wryly, "regular little angels."

"Well, they are!" Fran said. In the photographs on the stairs, Fran was beautiful, but no one ever said she was beautiful, perhaps because, in life, her face continually wrenched itself back and forth between sweet and sour. As a kid, I concluded that this was the way a person looked who was a "Goody Two-Shoes." Now, I see her expressions as a family curse, one I didn't recognize in my father because I knew him too well.

"We'll get Roy to take a picture," Fran said, and called down the basement stairs to my uncle.

At home, my father sometimes referred to Roy as "Sad Sack." Roy was younger than my father, but looked like a bloated, older version of him—a big blow-up toy that had lost air. My father considered Roy a burdensome toady at their father's bank. "Roy's too scared to do anything much but sit on Mom's sofa and whine about what a mean world it is out there!"

Still, Roy had a playful side—especially when my father and grandfather weren't around. While he lined us up that afternoon—the aunts and my mother were called to pose, too—he did a little hula to show how far apart to stand. Then he pretended he couldn't stop himself. He made up silly hand movements until he had us all giggling—even my grandmother.

When he finally had us the way he wanted, however, Roy stopped and stared—open-mouthed, dramatizing surprise—at my mother and aunts. "You three could pass for sisters!"

Fran liked this, but she was fourteen years older than my mother and seven years older than Lee—neither of whom said much, just smiled tightly.

Nancy made a little snarling noise. She set her jaw hard to one side, fanned the pages of her novel. Nancy was continually irritated with our mother for not being thin and fashionable. "Doesn't she have any *pride*?" she hissed in my ear, and, to my confusion, I felt ashamed and sorry for not just my mother but myself, too.

Roy's comparison had been superficial—a matter of costuming—but not insignificant. All three women wore dark hair held back in buns; dark, belted shirtwaists; shoes with high, grandmotherly vamps and thick heels.

Nancy whispered, "If Grandma didn't have white hair, she'd look like one of them, too!"

I stared at my grandmother, now humming to herself, stroking a picture of a little girl: blond hair, blue eyes uplifted beneath her Sunday school hat. "Isn't that something?" she whispered to no one in particular.

"It's not too forlorn here, is it?" Fran asked as we began carrying the food out to the dining room. "Without Rust and Janet?" She smiled at Nancy and me and—just coming up the stairs—our cousin, Roy, Jr.

"Forlorn?" Roy, Jr., said. "No, ma'am. There'll be more walnut pie for us, right, girls?" Roy, Jr., was in his late twenties, tall, big-boned, a weight lifter with a soft, fatty face.

My mother smiled at Roy, Jr., while she poured ice water into the fancy glasses on the table. Roy, Jr., had recently become an FBI agent, and she seemed to believe this gave our family some measure of honor, and even extra safety.

"Those pies do look good, don't they, Roy?" she said.

Walnut pie was his favorite, Roy, Jr., said, and explained he'd gathered the pie nuts at "The Eighty"—The Eighty being a small farm my grandfather had bought when my father and his brother and sister were still young.

While he talked, Roy, Jr., removed the gun and holster that were part of his new job—a little show that made Nancy and me roll our eyes in disdain. Then, just as Roy, Jr., set his gun and holster on top of Fran's china closet, my father entered the room, and, with a wink at those of us gathering around the table, he reached up, tapped the gun out of sight. "No need to spoil somebody's appetite!" he said with a laugh.

Roy, Jr., regarded my father with a cool gaze. "I was just telling Aunt Dotty how I'd gathered pie nuts at The Eighty. Maybe I'll save you some next year."

My grandmother was trying to scoot her chair up to the table, and as my father moved to help her, he said, "Nice of you to offer, Roy, but don't put yourself out."

Roy, Jr., nodded. "Okay, but I'll be over there more often now. Did Gramps tell you he signed The Eighty over to me this fall?"

My father's mouth opened, closed. He glanced at my mother, then away. I tried not to look at any of them, especially not him, his face all red—like a wet, red sock, so saturated with color it seemed you could have wrung out red. With much effort, he managed to say, "Is that right?" then he declared my aunt's table needed a shim, and he disappeared under the table with the book of matches my aunt had used for lighting the candles.

"What's this?" My grandfather stopped in the doorway from the living room, grinned at the sight of my father's rear end sticking out from beneath the table. "What's going on down there, son?" he called. "Has Fran got rats again?"

"Rats?" Fran gave an awkward laugh, while Lee—face white with embarrassment at her son's announcement—Lee explained to my grandfather, "Bob thought the table wasn't quite level, Ed."

"So, Aunt Dotty"—Roy, Jr., leaned back in his seat, tucked his hands into his armpits—"how're things going over in Meander? How's this door thing coming?"

"Why, absolutely *fine*," she said, and gave him a look—oh, she could be tough when someone affronted my father! That look was a brick heaved at Roy, Jr.'s big chin. She turned to smile at my grandfather as he took a seat. "We're enjoying Meander so much. This Archie Jones who works for Bob—he's a Welshman. He's told us lots of interesting things about Wales. Bob and I think it might be fun to go there."

My grandfather gave a pinch to the front and back of the brim of his fedora. "A land of poverty-stricken, drunken miners," he muttered—at which, face wrinkling in alarm and pain, my grandmother cried, "Who's drunk? Who?"

The others rushed in, no, no, while she fixed her eyes on Nancy and me. "If the good Lord wanted us to drink or smoke, he'd have made us born with a bottle and pipe in our mouths!"

"That's a sensible view," my father murmured. "I suppose God must not want us to eat then, either, Mother, since we weren't born with a steady supply of food in our mouths?" He turned to his father as if he'd completely forgotten Roy, Jr.'s news. "You ought to meet this Welshman of mine, Dad. Not only is he a crackerjack salesman, he's a real *gentleman*."

Roy, Jr., made a soft nickering noise, rolled his dune of a neck: pop, pop, pop.

"Junior!" his mother protested. "Please!"

Roy, Jr., smiled. "But, Uncle Bob, how the heck do you check out a person like that? Someone from a foreign country?"

"Why, heavens, the same way you check out any man." My father stared evenly into Roy, Jr.'s eyes. "You talk to him. You judge his character by what he says and does."

Roy, Jr., stretched his big arms high, yawned. "All that's going to change, you know. Before long, even the private citizen's going to be able to tap into the sort of information we've got at the Bureau. With computers, we're going to be able to find out just about anything about anybody"—he snapped his fingers— "and that fast. You ever want me to look into the background of this Jones, let me know, Uncle Bob. I could do it"—he winked—"not on the taxpayer's time, of course."

My grandfather turned to my father, smiling. "That'd be something, wouldn't it, Bob? That'd be dandy, wouldn't it?"

"Why, it'd be a nightmare, Dad!" My father's eyes stood so wide open the irises looked odd, like blueberries bobbing in tiny cups of milk. "Heavens, I don't want somebody checking up on my partner! This is a man in whom I've put my trust! And—we're going great guns over there! This Archie's already got so many advance orders, he could keep us busy for the next two years!"

I glanced at my mother, busily tracing her fingernail through the cut glass pattern of her water goblet. How could he say "great guns"? The plant wasn't even running yet.

My grandfather smiled at my father's pronouncement, then turned to Roy. "You see? I told you Bob had things under control!"

"That's good news," said Roy, though he lifted his eyebrows a little in the direction of Roy, Jr., just then making much of holding up a napkin to cover his smirk.

Fran, still standing, set her hands on the back of her chair. "I hope our dinner isn't being spoiled," she murmured.

And Lee: "Yes! Please! Let's eat!"

We forgot to sing the Doxology that day. We sat, we ate. My grandmother periodically looked around the tense table, studying our faces. She sensed something was wrong. "What is it?" she asked my grandfather.

"Just hush, Mother," my grandfather said. "Hush."

ON OUR way back to Meander that evening, I woke up from a nap as my father cried out: "That little pip-squeak!

And Dad—giving him The Eighty! What about our kids? Does he think I'm doing so well he doesn't have to give our kids anything?"

"Let's forget all that, honey! Just—look how beautiful it is out!" My mother pressed her forehead against the window, as if to absorb more of the twilight. "This is my absolute favorite time of day: 'L'heure bleu.'"

I didn't know French, but I knew what this meant because I'd seen those words myself, no doubt in the same place she had. The fashion magazines that now came to our house included dreamy, beautiful ads for a perfume named 'L'heure bleu': blue pigeons flew up from a blue plaza into the Parisian dusk. In script, the advertiser had written: *The French have a name for the hour between daylight and evening, the hour when lovers meet—*

My father was silent for the rest of the trip home, but I could feel him stewing, and, so, on our way up the stairs from the garage, I was careful to whisper when I asked, "Mom, did Dad mean that about the factory going great guns?"

Behind me, Nancy made a shushing noise. Mother didn't respond at all. She walked ahead of the two of us, carrying a big bowl, a pair of salad tongs rattling against its sides. With a defiant, backwards glance at Nancy, I repeated, louder now: "When Dad told Grandpa things were going great, was that true, Mom?"

She stopped. A swatch of hair had come undone from her bun, leaving the mesh doughnut beneath exposed. "Oh, honey!" She turned to me. Her face was so drawn and weary it seemed as if we might have been trudging through a forest for hours, we'd come through a battlefield, we'd fallen out of the world of romance into a world flat as slate and with no more design than the silty residue of the last chalked message. "What do you *think*?" she asked, then continued up the stairs as if what I thought would provide me with the right answer—a dizzying notion, really.

By the time my mother reached the top step, my father had already found Chan at the front door, let him in. The two were in the kitchen, Chan relating his *own* Thanksgiving fiascos with his *own* family.

My mother stopped at the sound of Chan's voice. "Oh, brother," she muttered, and let her shoulders sag. I waited behind her on the stairs, not saying anything, but Nancy said, "Move, you guys!" and finally my mother stepped forward, and into the kitchen.

Not I. I knew my father was too fiercely loyal to his family to even dream of telling Chan about our visit to Lamont, and, that night, I didn't care what Chan had to say. With Nancy on my heels—snorting in impatience—I kept to the hall, then climbed to the second story and the dark of my bedroom. There, like a heroine in a horror tale, I locked my door, leaned against it.

Here and there—on the tusk of an elephant, the prow of the ark, the Flood's many waves—the room's Noah's ark wallpaper had been coated with a silver material. No doubt, this was meant to glow cheerfully in the dark. Instead, the silver always looked ominous, like charred slime, those "snakes" that puffed up from the black pellets we set fire to on the Fourth of July.

I'd begun saving money once we moved to Meander. In the light from my bedside lamp, I counted what I had: twelve dollars and eighteen cents. My emergency supplies were stored in the closet shoe drawer: the budget articles, a pair of socks, the needle pack, my food—which now included a penny candy bag I'd filled with oatmeal, and a can of peas. I put these things in a circle around me, a fire meant to keep back the wolves, a talisman, but I was no primitive. The way I saw things, there were no safe places left in the world.

CHAPTER 9

This was, I suppose, the reason that, after Thanksgiving, I asked my classmate Ginger Conroy if she would take me to the cafeteria ladies, and help me to ask them if I might get free lunch leftovers, too. Ginger laughed at my request, but not unkindly. She was a tall and gawky girl with a grand beak of nose that gave her an aristocratic air. I liked her, and, early on, asked if we couldn't sit together at lunch. That was when she explained that she didn't eat in the cafeteria, she'd worked out a deal where the cafeteria ladies gave her leftovers to eat in the furnace room.

The day that Ginger and I stood at the end of the line to make my request, a heavy snow fell. The sky outside the cafeteria's basement window wells was white as the snow, seemed incapable of holding air. I was nervous, but the cafeteria ladies didn't even question me. Kindly, older women with fake corsages pinned to their fronts, they said, Oh, sure, why not? And from that day forward, while the other kids trooped into the cafeteria, Ginger and I went to the furnace room, where two napkins and two spoons and two soup bowls of something—

maybe macaroni and cheese or apple crisp with squares of corn bread—awaited us.

Ginger's mother was a widow and a cocktail waitress who supported her own mother plus three children. On the one hand, I understood the world of difference between the finances of Ginger's family and my own; on the other hand, though, I had my own scale of fear, and I think it made me feel at least as deprived as Ginger. The day after Christmas break, when Ginger told me her family had twenty-eight cents to live on for the rest of the week, I saw the numbers done up in rich, velvety blue; numbers of an old style, the "2" dangling a kind of harem girl's forehead pendant. All that my father owned— the farm, the shell of a grocery store, the beginnings of the door factory, the ballroom, the asphalt plant—all of that seemed ominously vague, a kind of cloud that might suddenly turn out to be solid rock falling from the sky to crush us. Or, then again, suppose it broke up, floated away, then where would we be? The person who knew she had only twenty-eight cents—well, that person could decide not to spend it; that was one thing she could do. Or, she *could* spend it. Or, she could call a meeting, like the plucky characters in books I loved best, and set each member of the family in search of some fine, cheap—or even free!—bit of vegetable to contribute to a pot of soup. Who knew? On his merry way, a person might find a milk cow on the loose, or pass through an abandoned orchard where plenty of apples hung on the branches, ripe and ready for picking.

"Well?" Ginger said. She was a dramatic girl. While she waited for me to respond to her announcement, she held her face close to my own. Three chicken-pox scars of various sizes sat above one of her fine eyebrows, and, without really thinking about it, I was forever trying to rearrange the scars, put them in order, from smaller to largest.

I looked into the dish of spaghetti before me—something left over from before Christmas. It had a definite "off" taste, but I didn't want to say so for fear Ginger might take the comment personally. I took another bite of the stuff, chewed. Then I smiled.

"I'll buy you some lentils," I said. The idea of buying lentils— a definite staple and a clear necessity—this made me happy. "Lentils yield more than twice their weight when cooked."

Ginger pushed a scab of burned topping to one side of her bowl. She gave me a skeptical look. "What are lentils?"

"Oh, they're good! You cook them with a ham bone and an onion and that makes lentil soup. My mother makes lentil soup almost every Sunday. It's a real money-saver, and it's high in protein, too. All beans are high in protein. Especially combined with dairy products."

Ginger laughed. "Where'd you get that?"

I looked over my shoulder towards the door to see if anyone listened. "From the newspaper. You know, like, they tell how you need carrots to see at night, and if your jacket sleeves get too short, you can cut the ankles off socks and use them for cuffs. Articles like that."

"You're crazy," Ginger said, but in her usual friendly way, as if whatever were negative about me were okay, too.

"Girls?" Marie from the cafeteria stuck her head into the furnace room. "I still got some wienies and beans from today. You want those, too?"

"Yes, ma'am!" Ginger cried. "Mm-hm! Bring 'em on, doll!"

Of course they liked her better than me. Of course I resented it, and envied her, and considered myself her superior because I took with a little please and thank you what she won with tail-wagging enthusiasm.

It might be prettier to hear that I didn't eat at all in those days, grew nauseated at the sight of even a dry cracker, but, in fact, I ate anything I could put my hands on. After church, in the social hall, when the cookies ran out, I ate sugar cubes dunked in the cream set out for coffee. My parents had bought a bottle of pickled onions for some Christmas party, and, one afternoon, alone in the house, I devoured that almost full jar with a side of six or seven stale Milk Bone biscuits left in the broom closet since the era of the Bishop poodle, Mr. Rocket.

"Ginger," I said, after Marie had brought our "seconds" to the furnace room, "do you ever think how we could live in here? If we painted it and all?"

Ginger gave a prickly look to the furnace room's old rock walls and pipes and flues. "Well. But who'd pay for the paint?"

"I'm sure we could afford *paint*, Ginger."

She shrugged. "Paint's expensive. Anyway, why would you want to live in a furnace room, Powell? You're *rich*!"

How thrilling that someone considered me rich! And yet how distressing, too. "We're not *rich*, Ginger! When my dad's in Dolores, he doesn't even have a bed! All he's got in our old house, there, is a foam pad."

Ginger sat back in her chair. "You have *two* houses? *And* a summer place?"

I pushed my glasses up my nose, squinted off towards the

corner of a window well not yet covered by snow. "But the house in Dolores, it's just—" I had the good sense to stop myself, to stare out the door toward the lunchroom proper, where children carried trays and empty milk bottles to workers lined up behind tubs and garbage pails. What a relief it was, then, when the fourth grade's Mrs. Utne flung herself into the furnace room.

"Got to have a cigarette!" she cried, and smiling broadly, took the chair next to Ginger, scooped the little ashtray on the table close. "What a day I've had!"

Ginger and I both smiled at Mrs. Utne. I envied Ginger for having had Mrs. Utne for Fourth. When Mrs. Utne saw her old students, she gave them hugs. During playground duty—all wrapped up in a big old raccoon coat, smoking cigarettes—she stood in a constant ring of children. While the other teachers had wearily given over their appearances to what was serviceable—flats and, at most, a powdered nose and lipstick in the morning—Mrs. Utne wore her hair around her shoulders in soft curls, and always bought some special breed of stockings that caught pools of opalescent light on her long legs. After meeting her at PTA, my mother had pronounced Mrs. Utne "striking," and said she felt sorry for her, a divorcee, a single mom: "That's a tough life."

Mrs. Utne's cigarettes thickened the air in the little furnace room. I felt nauseated—no doubt from the spaghetti—but I wanted to stay. What if something happened? Somehow, the furnace-room door got locked, and Mrs. Utne and Ginger and I were able to spend the whole afternoon together?

Mrs. Utne asked Ginger about her mother. She'd so enjoyed

meeting her, Mrs. Utne said. (Did she remember meeting my mom?) She talked about her son, a third-grader at a school across town. She meant to show some of his artwork to her class next week. If we liked, we could stop in and take a look, he was very talented.

"Of course"—she made a point of catching both Ginger's eye and mine, giving us each a wink—"I'm prejudiced!"

That was the first time I realized that someone might use the word "prejudiced" to mean unfairly *in favor of* instead of *against*. Unfairly in favor of her son. So I would never have a chance with Mrs. Utne either. A dark, oily feeling took up residence in my stomach, which shimmied like a failing engine.

Dizzily, I watched Mrs. Utne remove a gold-and-black filigree lipstick from her shoulder bag, reapply her bright mouth with an ingenious brush brought forth—click—like a stiletto knife from a second tube. The world—the world began to pull back from me like a wave. I felt the way I'd felt at the seashore on trips to my grandmother's. The surf pushed and pulled the thinnest possible skeins of water around and under my feet—and the next thing I knew, I was sick, vomiting into a big green trash can that sat beside the furnace.

INEVITABLY, A call was made. The assistant secretary came into the nurse's office to tell me that my mother was at a meeting, but she guessed "a Bea Dart" was coming.

When I supposed I was done vomiting, I went out into the snowy day to wait for Bea. Eventually, her old turquoise Chevy came dragging up the street, listing to one side as if Bea's great size unbalanced it. I hurried down the walk, eager not to keep her waiting, irritate her in any way.

"Thanks for coming."

Bea gave me a weary look through the haze from her Lucky Strikes, then put the car into gear with a terrible jolt. "I didn't mind," she said. "At your place, I'd be doing floors."

Like so many things Bea said, this made sense. Of course, nobody wanted to "do floors." Still, I felt shocked that she'd admitted she didn't enjoy the work she did for my family. And because there was nothing I could say to make things better, the two of us rode home in silence.

We found my father and Archie Jones in the kitchen, looking down at the breakfast nook table, both of them still wearing their winter coats.

My father grinned when he saw Bea and me in the doorway. "Guess the jig's up now!" he said with a laugh. "These gals have caught us red-handed, Archie!"

Two decks of playing cards lay on the table. One featured a charming blond lady in a yellow dress and yellow hat, the other an identical lady with red hair and green clothes. I knew those cards; they were the cards Nancy and I used for Concentration and Oh, Hell and Rummy.

Archie hardly looked up to say hello, just tapped a finger on the card my father had turned up as we walked in the door: nine of hearts.

It didn't seem to occur to my father that I shouldn't have been home from school. Perhaps he imagined that I'd come for lunch? That school had already let out for the day?

"I got sick, Dad. At school. Bea came and got me."

"Good heavens, sweetie!" His face instantly long with concern, he helped me out of my coat, set me down at the breakfast nook table.

"What she needs," Archie said, "is a cup of ginger tea. Where might I find a bit of ginger, Robert?"

While Archie rummaged through my mother's spice jars, and Bea went off to wax the bathroom floor, my father explained that Archie had been teaching him to "count" cards. "Quite a trick! A good mental exercise!" He looked across the kitchen to Archie, recited some lesson or other.

"That's right, Robert," Archie said, and, shaking the little jar of crystallized ginger he'd found, smiled at me. "Your father is a brilliant man, Penny."

"Ho, ho!" My father quickly swept up the cards, gave me a wink. "It's fun, but I'm no gambler! Now why don't you go lie down, Pen, while Archie fixes your drink?"

I lay down on the couch in the den. The den had windows on three sides, and stuck out from the house like a peninsula. With the garage directly beneath it, it was a cold room. I would have liked to pull the curtains closed, shut out the world, but my father insisted we keep the curtains open while the sun shone. This helped keep down our heat bills.

"Here you go!" Into the den my father came, bearing a coffee cup. On the saucer, he had set a little gift, an ingenious pen that featured a tiny truck and tree encapsulated in a thick liquid. When the pen tipped into writing position, the truck ran down towards the nib, and into the tree. "Accidents don't happen," read the legend on the side of the pen, "they are caused." Frightening, reassuring: it was your fault if something went wrong, but apparently you could prevent just about everything. Not acts of God, I guessed, but anything else.

Like everyone in my family, my father looked a little shy when doing a kindness. "Somebody left it at the plant. I thought maybe you'd get a kick out of it."

"I love it," I said. "It's great."

Shortly after, I listened as his car backed out the garage beneath me, chugged up the hill. Not much later, Bea—already in her coat—came to tell me she'd be going, too. "You be all right here alone?"

I nodded, sure.

She glanced out the window over the couch where I lay. "Hmm!" she said, and then, "What do you know about that?" Her words were slow and almost as quiet as words a person might mutter to herself, but she kept looking out the window, then back at me, until, finally—more from my sense that Bea expected me to look than from my own curiosity—I raised myself up.

Chan and Margret. The two of them standing on Chan's snowy porch, chatting. Neither wore a coat. Both stood straight and tall as owners of the world, the hero and heroine of some old movie. I thought of a conversation between my parents one night over dinner: my mother had told my father how she'd suggested to Margret that they might try introducing Chan to a lady from our church—an attractive nurse—and Margret had whooped, "Chan with some Florence Nightingale! You can't be serious!"

In response to my mother's story—laughing, shaking his head—my father had said, "Well, who knows? I sometimes wonder if Margret doesn't enjoy keeping Chan's attentions to herself!"

My mother had nodded stiffly, then murmured, "Yes. Well, I never wanted to say so."

Bea Dart pulled a plaid scarf from her pocket, smoothed it across her chest, then folded it into a fat woolly triangle. "I don't suppose you ever met Mrs. Bishop. *They* were a pair, all right. I used to help out at parties sometimes. Not where you'd see me, or nothing." She snorted a laugh. "She didn't think *I* was good enough to show, but I took care of washing up. There was plenty of liquor at *those* parties, believe you me, kid."

I nodded as I stared out the window. Margret's cardigan had slipped off one shoulder, and Chan—with one of those perfectly unconscious gestures that movies use to convince you absolutely of intimacy—Chan hitched the cardigan up again. He was Cary Grant, Margret was Katherine Hepburn. Their romance had cooled, yes—in an old romantic comedy from "PM Matinee," they would be broken up or on the verge of divorce, but the story's events would conspire to bring them together again.

As if to make the story more perfect, a third person stepped through Chan's door, and out onto the porch: the minor character. A springy little redheaded man in tweed sports jacket and ear muffs, camera slung around his neck, he began snapping pictures of the neighborhood. For a while, I worried because he didn't point his lens at our house; but then both Margret and Chan began to point at our roof—some high feature, and then some low—and the little man began to snap in my direction, and then Margret and Chan slipped into their own lives, became themselves again.

Bea Dart lowered herself heavily onto the couch to strap on the metal traction devices she wore over the soles of her shoes on icy days.

"So what was she like?" I asked. "Mrs. Bishop?"

"Oh, don't suppose I know!" said Bea. "Once, after Paula and me'd been here cleaning, she said money was missing—she made out like Paula'd took it. I never liked her much after that, and it wasn't long till she run off with Mr. Mott."

Bea looked out the window again. Chan held the porch door open. Margret and the little redheaded man passed under his arm and into the house. "You don't ever want to start drinking alcohol," Bea said. Her voice was bland, nothing like the voices of my Powell relatives when they talked the sins of liquor. "Alcohol's what killed my husband, you know."

"No," I said, then added, uncertainly, "I'm sorry."

Like some lovely tracery of leaves at the bottom of a pond, something you didn't see at first because of the reflections on the pond's surface, a girl's smile materialized in Bea's heavy face. "It wasn't your fault, kid, so what's to be sorry for? Me? You start feeling sorry for me, I'll be in trouble, I won't even be able to get up on my feet and head over to Mrs. Branden's."

She extended her hands in front of herself, then, held them out as if waiting for someone to help her rise, and—with some misgivings, a sense that all I really did was send her off to work again—I pulled Bea to her feet.

THAT AFTERNOON'S "PM Matinee" turned out to be *With a Song in My Heart*. In *With a Song in My Heart*, singer Jane Froman

(Susan Hayward) marries the wrong man (David Wayne), but in the end—much to my surprise—she not only gets to divorce him, but to go on to a wonderful new life with a much handsomer man (Rory Calhoun).

Nancy wandered into the den as the credits began to roll. She squinted at the TV set. In an effort to coerce my parents to buy her contact lenses, she'd completely given up wearing her glasses, and the last time my mother had tried complaining about it, Nancy had pointed out that Mother, too, now went without her glasses plenty of the time.

Had I noticed this? I'd never thought of Nancy and my mother as looking at all alike, but, since moving to Meander, by the end of the day, all of their squinting gave them identical creases, pink as paper cuts, across the bridge of their noses.

Something never dealt with in those movies where the mousy secretary took off her glasses and became the sexy babe: How was it that she was still able to see? Did she no longer need to see now that she was seen?

"Nancy, you wouldn't believe the happy ending this movie had!" I cried. "This singer, Jane Froman—"

Nancy waved an impatient hand in the air. "I've seen it. It's a true story, Penny; that's how come they couldn't change it much. Plus she's a cripple at the end. I figure it's because she's crippled they let her be happy."

CHAPTER 10

That winter, each time a truck passed me on my way
to and from downtown or school, I wondered if it might be the
truck carrying the furniture my parents had ordered in
Chicago: the pier cabinets with their very own lights inside, the
gold-leafed credenza, and other marvels that promised to settle
us more solidly into the neighborhood.

My mother often looked out the window over the kitchen
sink as if she imagined the truck might pull up at any moment.
"Remember, it'll be a Bekins truck," she'd say, "so if you see a
Bekins truck go by, let me know. We don't want it taking our
things to the wrong place!"

This made Nancy snort in derision.

Didn't anyone else notice the changes in Nancy? I could only
guess where she spent her afternoons and evenings based upon
the smells she brought home, the look of her flats (so dry she'd
had to have spent the afternoon in a car; or mud-caked; or soaked
to a slimy wetness, then cured to something hard and salty as
sausage rind). Her breath smelled like nail polish remover: a
symptom of the ketosis she assured me was a good sign.

"The smell means I'm burning fat."

"What fat?" The absence of all cushion had transformed Nancy's face to something almost reptilian. She had stopped eating with us when my father was out of town—a practice my mother consented to since all meals with Nancy ended in a fight—and now she ate whatever she liked: a Pop Tart for breakfast, nothing for lunch, a half-cup of carefully measured cottage cheese and one canned peach for dinner. On Christmas morning, she had led me into the bathroom to look at the scale. "Ninety-one pounds!" she announced proudly. "Twelve pounds less than when we moved!"

Often, late at night, I woke up, aware that lights shone in the main hall. I'd hear the hum and click I associated with my father's adding machine and think he'd returned from Dolores unexpectedly. But the light belonged to Nancy, trying on heaps of clothing in front of the hall mirror; the noise, to my mother, rocking away on the exercise cot.

"That machine!" my mother complained to Margret Woolum. "I get on it every day. And those darn pills do nothing but dry out my nose! Three months, and I've lost a measly six pounds!"

I sat in the breakfast nook, just home from school. I watched as my mother gave a mean pinch to the flesh above her waist: "Fifteen pounds, and I'd be happy as a clam, darn it!"

Margret laughed. "Aw, kid!" She lay her slender hand on my mother's still well-rounded arm. "But maybe you're just meant to be the weight you're at! Maybe that's the attitude!"

My mother's own laugh was harshly jolly. "As if *you'd* accept that!"

Alarmed at this outburst, I blurted, "Can I have money to buy glue, Mom? I need glue for tomorrow."

Without a yes or no, she walked into the hall. I smiled at Margret while I slipped back into my school coat, still lying on the breakfast nook's banquette. Margret blinked, wiggled her mouth back and forth as if she held a candy drop, and so couldn't speak.

Sometimes, I imagined disasters befalling the Woolums, and my own family becoming heir to whatever the Woolums had that we didn't. But, no, that isn't quite it: I didn't imagine us taking possession of their house or clothes. Instead, the absence of the Woolums made whatever it was we lacked— invisible, no longer a concern. Suddenly, we were acceptable just as we were. Chan Bishop, for example, came to *our* house for morning coffee.

In the hall, my mother handed me a five from her wallet, then whispered: "What she said isn't true. I *can* be thin."

I nodded. "Sure. Thanks, Mom."

I pretended not to hear when Margret called after me that I ought to see if Eleanor wanted to go, too. I liked to shop alone. I liked my dreamy walks up the hill. When I was alone, the fat lady ironing in the window of her apartment house wasn't funny but fascinating. "WILL WE BE NEIGHBORS IN HEAVEN?" read the message board on the evangelical church at the top of the hill, and, cryptically, "TIME ENDS ETERNITY WHEN?" Then came the dull little shingled house whose yard contained a patch of pure enchantment: a community of tiny clay figures and buildings so discreet I hadn't noticed them until frost had killed off the camouflaging snow-on-the-mountain and lily of the valley. There were clay sheep and elves and a tiny wishing well. Walking towards a miniature clay cottage with an agate roof were a clay man with a clay cane—its lower half gone—and a tiny clay lady with a scarved head and a basket on her arm.

I made my way past a mom-and-pop grocery, and the gas station where Eleanor and I sometimes stopped to take a voyeuristic peek into the cars and trucks towed in from accidents. A store that sold business machines. A dry-cleaners. McLellan's, I knew, would have the glue I needed, and after I'd made that dull purchase, I'd be free to go to Dana's Department Store. Dana's was an old high-ceilinged place with pneumatic billing tubes whirring across the ceiling. On the third floor was Children's, and there, most importantly, was a cream beret with a navy and cream striped ribbon that ran around the brim and criss-crossed in back. The label of the beret read: "100% Virgin Wool," and "Made in France." France, I knew from the library filmstrip our mother had taken Nancy and me to see, was a charming place of happy families and art lovers, twinkling leaves, old buildings that cast deep shadows on sunlit streets.

From the first time I saw that beret, I knew it was meant for a younger child, but I believed it would make me appear beloved; and *appearing* beloved, I might become beloved, and by this miracle lift my family into the enchanted Meander that seemed still to lie out of reach.

The saleslady in Children's was a limping older woman with the grizzled hair of an ancient Scottie. She watched me approach the hat display. Since my last visit, someone—I assumed she—had put the beret in a plastic bag, taped shut.

I didn't think to ask for an explanation, but she gave one. "We have to keep it covered. Because it's white. We can't have it getting dirty with handling." She began straightening the gloves and mittens on a nearby counter. "You come in here a lot," she said, darting looks at me while I pretended interest in a coin purse made up with the face of a clown. "Where's your mother, that she lets you shop so much?"

I glanced up, my eyes wide. Where did I get that expression? That fake surprise? "Probably she's down the basement, looking at cross-stitch kits."

When the clerk smiled I felt the way I'd felt at the school's Dad–Daughter Date Night. I'd had to take Chan Bishop because my own dad was out of town. Which was a little embarrassing, but bearable until the principal took a look at the bakery cake sent by my mother, and said, "Oh, I guess Mom didn't have time to cook, hmm?"

His first job as a principal. Probably not a terribly smart man. Probably nervous at meeting Chan Bishop, and imagining that his observation passed for wit.

The cake was a thing all done up in blue roses and piping; I was proud of it. My mother had let me pick it out. Still, I understood that the principal saw a bakery cake as a sign of deficiency, and so I said, "Oh, no, my mother *made* that cake."

The principal winked at Chan—who said, firmly, "Yes, Penny's mom is quite a pastry chef." He held his hands above the cake, mimicked someone squirting tube icing in great swags, tiny florets. "All those gadgets." He shook his head as if in the face of some gift impossible for mere mortals to comprehend.

I was grateful, of course, but the principal still smiled in that awful way, as if he saw a need in me that I couldn't hide, and that was the same smile that the department store saleslady smiled as she asked, "Does your mother have an account here?" She straightened a tiny sweater, then folded it over her arm. "Maybe she'd like to see the hat? Though it's probably too small for you. It's really meant for a younger girl, you know."

"I meant it for my little sister," I said. "Her head's smaller." Then I turned away and, letting my fingers trail over other items, started towards the elevator. There was plenty, I told myself, *plenty* that saleslady didn't know: my father was building a door factory and we lived in a famous house and my parents were friends with all kinds of people, one of the richest men in town ate breakfast with us every Sunday, went to church with us, ate Sunday dinner with us at the Turnkey Club, and my mother wore a watch made out of diamonds and platinum—

"Down?" said the elevator lady.

I shook my head. I made my way back to the clerk, now vigorously turning, hook out, those hangers switched around by careless shoppers.

"I want the beret," I said.

She looked away from me, her lips pursed in some private grin. "Gift-wrapped?" she asked.

I nodded. I even selected one of those tiny cards offered in children's departments—mine featured a duckling carrying a baby blue umbrella—and I borrowed the clerk's pen and I wrote on the inside without a moment's hesitation, "Happy Birthday, Grace!"

OF COURSE, there was no way that hat could fulfill what I'd hoped it might. My mother said it was much too small,

Nancy roared, "Hey, you want to look like Donald Duck, you're all set!"

Still, the next Sunday, when we all stood in the Turnkey Club coatroom, stomping our feet and laughing at how cold we'd gotten in the drive over from church, Chan Bishop said, "That's a new hat, isn't it, Penny? Very nice!"

I gave my mother a look, but she was peeking in the coatroom mirror, nervously touching the back of the twist that had recently replaced her bun.

"Not a strand out of place, Dotty!" Chan said.

"I guess I'm getting used to it, but, gad"—my father winked at Chan—"these gals with their darn hairstyles! Sometimes, I don't recognize them from one week to the next!"

My family was invariably in good spirits at the Turnkey Club. We were proud that we had the right to walk across the black tile floors and Persian rugs, keep liquor in their lockers, look out the town's highest windows, sit in the library's big red-leather chairs.

Chan called out some foreign greeting to the club's manager, who wrinkled his forehead a little, then smiled as he led us to our table.

"He's a terrible teaser, isn't he?" my father said to the manager, then turned to Chan, "Was that German? Hell, I know *eins, zwei, drei, vier . . .*"

We were all laughing when the manager left us. "Now Dotty, here"—my father smoothed one of the club's big napkins across his lap, then looked up, his eyes full of happy mischief—"Dotty wants to learn French, Chan. You know French, don't you? Speak some French and see if the old girl picks it up."

Chan shrugged: "*Je n'en sais rien.*"

"What's that mean?" I asked.

My mother, who had bought herself a little French grammar, laughed: "Oh, something about *rien*."

"There you go!" Chan opened his eyes in delight. "Dotty's learning to make jokes in another language, Powell! You better watch out!" Then he dropped a shoulder, bent toward my father to whisper, "The fellow coming this way, that's Judge Leonard. I'll introduce you. Judge—"

Chan knew everyone at the club, and always made a point of calling people over to introduce them to my parents.

"These are the people who are directing my salvation," he told the judge and his wife. "They're going to get me a whole new outlook, and find me some sweet young thing in the bargain. Where's she going to turn up, Dotty?"

Smiling, my mother made a helpless gesture, and the judge and his wife laughed before moving on to their own table.

"I *suspect* this paragon's supposed to appear in the church social hall after Sunday services," Chan continued. "Right, Dotty? She'll hand me a cup of bad coffee, our eyes will meet—" Chan broke off. "Don't look now, but when you can—discreetly—by the foyer."

A redheaded woman, pretty and slim, stood in the cool light coming through the club's tinted windows.

"Watch how she acts when she passes by!"

Nancy and I smiled at one another in anticipation of a minor drama. Was this one of Chan's girlfriends? Like our parents, we fussed with our napkins, poked at the meat and potatoes on our plates.

"Gloria!" Chan called out.

The woman nodded curtly: "Chan."

"Brr!" my father whispered as she moved off.

All of us watched, then, as the manager seated the woman and several redheaded children at a table by the windows.

"Gloria Mott," Chan said. "*That's* what my old pal Danny left. Which ought to give you some idea of what a knock-out Haldis was!"

I could hardly help stealing a look at the Mott children. Had anyone ever mentioned them or this Gloria before? They were normal enough looking kids, I'm sure, but I observed them through a filter that made them freaks, cripples, skin too pale, bodies lumpish—

Fingers pressed together in something like an attitude of prayer, Chan stared across the room at the woman.

Both my father and mother seemed stunned by such rudeness. They exchanged a helpless glance, then scanned the room as if for distractions. "Oh! Bob"—relief flooded my mother's face—"there's Archie!"

Elaborately—almost as if he had a stiff neck—my father turned his entire upper torso in his chair: "Ah!" He raised a hand to salute Archie, who, in the handsome gloomy light of the club looked like someone important: a famous moviemaker, a plantation owner, the premier of some distant country. Eyes mild under salt-and-pepper brows, Archie nodded in our direction, and the gesture made it appear we were all equally known—or unknown—to him. Which gave me a funny feeling, as if we might be in disguise: royalty, criminals, spies. Slowly, he crossed the adjoining dining room, moved out of our sight.

My father tipped forward in his chair, watching him go, then he tapped out a rueful laugh. "The man who will either make my fortune or ruin me forever!"

"Why don't you ask him which it will be, Bob?" my mother said. "We're all dying of curiosity." She was teasing, but they'd argued over this same issue just the day before. My grandfather had telephoned, and apparently said the wrong thing about the door factory. Not long after, I'd heard my father shout, "No, I *don't* know what I'm going to do about it, Dotty, but I sure as hell can't believe my brother knows more about the door business than Archie!"

Chan stretched—so theatrically it seemed almost as if he wanted us not to notice something: the grin on his face? "Listen, Bob, try to find out for me who the hell Archie's tailor is!" he said.

My father grinned, too, though warily. "What's up, Bishop? You look like the cat that swallowed the canary."

"Oh, nothing, but, you know, I see Archie pretty often, playing poker with the lunch crowd. I had to laugh, the other day. He always looks so dignified, but here he was, showing all the old boys a picture of a woman with her dress cut down to"— Chan made a slashing movement across his chest—"and he implied she was his, shall we say, *paramour*?"

My father gave my mother a quick glance to show her his surprise, then he laughed in the way that a person will laugh upon discovering, in public, that he stands outside of an event to which everyone assumes him to be privy: a widening of the eyes, a blushing recovery, the fuel behind the chuckle a little too rich. "Is that right? That's not the sort of thing Archie and I talk about, but I had some impression he had a lady friend—a schoolteacher—in St. Louis."

Chan grinned. "You ever heard of a school called something like the Hot-Shot Club? The Hot-to-Trot Club?"

"You're serious?" My father laughed again. "Maybe he keeps a schoolteacher here, a va-va-voom girl there!"

"You two," my mother said, but it was a comic scolding, and she added in a light voice, "Chan, maybe you and your artist friend could double-date with Archie and his va-va-voom girl?"

Chan wagged his finger at her. "That's all over, so you can't tease me there, Dotty!"

She put a little pout on her face. The men laughed at this, but Nancy, looking clammy, stood and rushed from the table.

I glanced at my mother for permission to leave the table— maybe Nancy was sick—but when I caught up to Nancy, she was in the library, flipping through a *Town and Country*.

"What happened?" I asked.

"*Her*." Nancy shivered. "When she starts acting cute—it's repulsive!"

The tinting on the library windows turned the sky the color of raw oysters. Below us sat car lots decorated with bright plastic flags, and there were snow-steeped rooftops pocked by the heat of furnace pipes. In the distance: a park filled with leafless trees, the skeletons of playground equipment.

"Do you mean *Mom*?" I asked, finally.

Nancy set down her magazine with a sigh. "She's too *old*."

"Too old?" I followed her out into the foyer.

"Stand guard." Nancy began to pull chunks of prime rib and baked potato from her pockets, deposit them beneath the sand-filled dish in the foyer ashtray. I didn't mind. I might pretend to be her guard, but I actually enjoyed my fake task:

admiring the Persian miniatures that hung in the hall, jewel-box dramas which never even hinted there might be a division between the domestic and the divine.

THAT WAS the day Chan decided we all ought to go to Quarry Farm, the Bishop estate. His parents were in Europe, so it would be a good time for a tour.

Nancy didn't object at the table, but when the five of us reached the cloakroom she tugged on my mother's coat. "I can't go," she said, "I've got to meet Marlys at the library."

I plopped down in a chair while they whispered back and forth. My father and Chan were talking about horses, there was nothing more beautiful than a beautiful horse, my father said—so enthusiastic he didn't even notice Archie Jones coming our way.

"Here comes Archie," I said, and then, gloved hand over my mouth, I giggled—loud—imagining this would somehow put me in league with my parents, their earlier remarks about Archie.

"What on earth!" My father grabbed my hand and squeezed my fingers hard. "We are never rude!" he said through gritted teeth, then called out in a friendly voice, "Archie, say, did they feed you all right in there?"

"Ah." Chan saw the tears in my eyes and began to pat me on the back. "Something went down the wrong track," he said to the others, then explained to Archie that we were headed to his parents' place to take a tour, that we'd love to have Archie come too.

ON THE way to the cars, the adults acted festive, laughed about the drizzle. "Shave-and-a-haircut," my father honked as Archie climbed into Chan's car; and Chan honked back, "Two bits!"

"I don't see why I have to come," Nancy said.

My parents didn't respond to that. A couple of blocks later, however, while we sat behind the Jaguar, waiting for a train to pass—steers, destined for Bishop Meat—my father said, "I can't see what the idea was, Chan inviting Archie!"

"Oh, well." My mother settled into her seat like a bird in a nest. "It'll be fine." She was happy that we were finally going to see Quarry Farm. She turned and smiled at Nancy and me over the seat back. "This will be a real experience!"

My father caught my eye in the rearview mirror. "Sorry if I got a little rough with you back there, Pen, but you know—"

"That's okay," I mumbled. "I'm sorry, too."

"So!" The car started forward once more. "How big of a place do you think it'll be?"

"Who cares?" asked Nancy.

"Big as—Mulfords?" I suggested.

My mother laughed. "Oh, bigger than that!"

"Big as—the library? I mean, in Dolores?"

My father laughed. "Well, not that big, surely!"

The route to Quarry Farm was all snowy fields broken by the occasional windbreak, nothing very interesting. But then Chan turned onto a road between two bare fields and we suddenly saw, simultaneously—as if it sprang from nowhere, like some shaggy gray beast—a great wooded area, and, then, as we drew closer, a high iron fence surrounding the woods, and, in the distance, an astonishing length of rooftop.

"And there's a gatehouse!" I said. "A real gatehouse!"

At the gate, my father brought us to a stop behind Chan and

Archie. An elderly man—a folded newspaper protecting his head from the drizzle—hurried out of the gatehouse and around to Chan's side of the Jaguar.

"Gatekeeper," my mother said, turning to smile at me.

"Whoop-de-doo," said Nancy, but she looked, too. "Guess he doesn't want to let Chan in."

The gatekeeper looked back at us and frowned.

My father tapped his foot against the brake pedal. "Think I should get out?" he asked my mother, but then the gatekeeper hurried back inside the cottage, and, eerily, as if moved by a ghost, the big gate began to swing open.

While my mother and father and I made little noises of satisfaction and relief, Nancy pretended to snore.

NOT LONG ago, a composer friend of mine showed me a brochure for the arts colony where she had spent a month at work on her compositions. The colony's main building and grounds looked familiar, and when I opened the brochure, I discovered the colony was, in fact, the old Quarry Farm, donated by the Bishops sometime in the eighties. Remarkably enough, I recognized the director— her photograph appeared on the back of the brochure—as the woman who had ushered us into the mansion all those years before:

"If you'd called first, Chan—Mr. Bishop—I would have put down mats." I remember the woman as dressed all in pink, even pink stockings and shoes, as if pink were a condition of her employment, like black for a nun. "Your mother would be terribly upset if the rugs—"

Chan closed his eyes, smiled forbearingly. "We're going to keep our shoes on today, Peggy," he said in a singsong voice. "We all know how to wipe our feet."

Peggy pursed her lips, and left the hall.

"She's acquired my mother's habit of thinking of me as a kid," Chan said. "Which makes all of you my messy playmates."

My parents smiled, but I blurted what had welled up inside me ever since I'd spied the house: "This place is like a castle!"

Chan and my parents smiled, but Archie raised a finger in the air. "Ah, but, Penny, a castle isn't just a home! It's a place in which business is conducted, and wars fought."

With a laugh, my father said, "Sounds pretty much like home to me!" Which caused my mother to give him a withering look—one that had enough playfulness to it that it made everyone laugh.

"We should start with the upstairs. Keep your coats on for now, the heat isn't on in this wing."

Two ballrooms—wooden floors gleaming, spotlessly clean. Cavernous bedrooms with marble fireplaces, high ceilings, heavy drapes. "Like *Jane Eyre*," Nancy whispered to me.

Beyond a long hallway, and a rear staircase, we came to the servants' quarters. Eighteen tiny rooms, each papered in some dim old pattern, each with its own tiny sink on one wall.

"I've stayed in many a spot like *this*," Archie said, stepping through a doorway, trying a faucet.

"Water's off," Chan said.

Archie sniffed the air. "Even the smell of this old wallpaper makes me nostalgic!"

My father wanted to know all about the estate's construction, of course. How long had it taken to put up the buildings? Were the walls out front native stone? My mother, on the other hand, seemed mostly interested in the ways in which Quarry Farm resembled our own house. As we made our way through the downstairs, she whispered to Nancy and me, "Did you see how that carpet matched the carpet in our living room and the dining-room wallpaper's almost identical to ours?"

I wondered why she whispered. Maybe she thought Chan would feel insulted by any suggestion that he'd imitated his parents' house. Or, that by *our* buying *his* house, we'd acquired a special relationship to him. As a family, we were always sensitive about giving the appearance of laying claim on anyone, anything. At any rate, Chan noticed her whispering, and he sang out—we were starting to go into the playroom just then— "Hey, Dotty, you think you're still in church?"

She laughed. "It's so grand, I guess I'm a little cowed!"

I thought Chan's eyebrows went up a little at her pronunciation. "*Cooed*," she had said, for she'd read this was the preferred pronunciation; yet everyone we knew said "cow," to rhyme with "how," and what was the good of saying things right if they only made a person sound wrong?

The playroom featured a faded mural of fairy-tale characters—Puss-in-Boots, Snow White and the dwarves, Hansel and Gretel, Cinderella—and the Bishop children. The artist had captured to perfection the fairy-tale figures, but botched the kids. Chan and his little brother and sister seemed crude, hulking mutants in an otherwise beautiful world, the boys' arms were pestles in the mortars of their short-sleeved shirts, the little girl's head would have immediately snapped off its stick of a stem had she stepped into the world of three dimensions.

Still, I was enchanted by the playroom. The old toys of paint-ed metal and wood, and the way they lay scattered about the room, suggested a story in which the children had been called away from play in some long-lost time, and never come back.

"You see this, Penny?" My mother held up a metal bank, a pig with a blue hat, on its side the words "BISHOP MEATS."

In a window seat, Chan was nursing a beer he'd grabbed during our tour of the kitchen, but he got up, and brought over a handful of change, and we took turns inserting coins in the bank's slot, the action causing the pig's hat to rise as if tipped.

"How'd you do?" said my mother as Chan held out the pig to her and the little hat tipped.

"How'd you do-do-do?" Chan said, then took a long pull of beer—I think his playfulness had embarrassed him. "You know, Matson"—he frowned as he looked around the slightly dusty room—"sometimes I wonder if I remember playing with the toys in here, or just seeing my kids play with them." "Matson" was what he'd taken to calling my mother—her maiden name—and even my father and Margret and Roger Woolum sometimes called her this, too.

My mother gave the bank a shake, grinned. "Oh, but this *must* be yours, Chan! It's almost an antique!"

She was teasing, but Chan didn't laugh. He said, sounding injured, "I meant—I don't remember. I was off at school a lot."

"Well, I know that, Chan," she said, and gave him the con-solatory smile—closed lips, lots of eye contact—that she offered Nancy and me when we felt snubbed by a friend. Then she stepped to a nearby window and peered out. "This is my favorite time of day. Especially in winter, when the snow looks blue"—she hesitated, then added a quiet—"in the dying light."

Maybe Chan had been a little angry with her before, but he seemed to understand what it cost her to say something that verged toward the poetic. He squeezed my shoulder, and walked me over beside her. "I agree with you there, Matson. This is the best," he said.

Archie and my father went on talking over by another window, but the three of us stood quiet. I stroked the playroom curtains: tan and patterned with tiny red apples topped by sprigs of green leaf. I felt awkward, and wished that Nancy would look up from whatever it was she'd found to read, that she would join us, that she would say something to break the spell that held Chan and my mother and me.

"Chan," my father called out, "what's the story with those big boulders out by the pool? Were they hauled in or are they natural?"

Chan turned away from the window, tapped a photograph on the wall: a great team of horses pulling a boulder on a sled, the action followed by a group of men in high white collars and bowlers.

My father nodded genially, but he stood with his shoulders hunched—almost as if he carried a pack. Clearly, socializing with Archie weighed him down, and Archie must have felt his own or my father's strain, for both men jumped a little when a knock sounded from behind what had, until that moment, appeared to be only a closet door.

"Two entrances," Chan explained as he opened the door, and there stood Peggy from the front hall, now backed by a room as gold and dark and lovely as the wing of a Monarch butterfly. This turned out to be the library, where Peggy left us with a full tea service and lots of little sandwiches and fancy cookies and—as if not to imply that other adults might have different habits from a son of the house—four cans of beer.

My mother set about pouring tea, a task that made her both radiant and nervous. After she'd served Archie and my father—Chan had grabbed one of the beers—she leaned toward Nancy and me, and asked in a teasing, Britishy sort of voice, "One lump or two, ladies?" Unfamiliar with the Bishop pot, however, this time she tipped it too far, the tea *swooped* from the long spout, overshooting the cup and splashing onto the tray.

"Oh!" She looked around, fast. Chan had turned the other way, Archie and my father stood before the fire. "Shh," she said, as if she imagined Nancy and I might tell on her. Then, ignoring the tray's fan of fancy napkins, she pulled her handkerchief from her purse and mopped up the spill.

"*So.*" She plunked the sopping handkerchief into her purse, then gave us a wink. "So. Did you see the paintings Daddy and Archie are looking at? That's Chan's mother and dad."

I hurried across the room to stand with the men, neck craned upwards. Both portraits had been painted by the same hand, with brush strokes smooth as something poured from a pitcher, and handsome pearly grounds that darkened to olive and umber at the edges. Mrs. Bishop, however, was all pink cheeks and kindness while Mr. Bishop wore steel gray and looked as if he might bite.

"To the finest examples of collusion between the artist and his subjects that it's ever been my privilege to witness!"

My father and Archie and I turned. Chan stood with his beer raised to the portraits. "Don't you see it?" he asked. "The serene mother, the captain of industry. Captured for all time."

In the low voice of an adult trying to talk a child out of a dangerous situation—away from a power line, down off a ledge—my mother said, "I've heard they're lovely people, Chan."

And Archie: "There's no denying they've provided you many things, the likes of which most folks never see in a lifetime!"

Chan bowed at the waist. "Ah, yes! I am what I am no doubt in great part due to my parents!" He hesitated—something in his breathing and posture suggested he might say more. "Bob"—he grabbed the unopened beers from the tea tray, and, looking like an athlete with a football, grinning, he clutched them to his chest and trotted towards the playroom door—"Bob, you can give Archie a ride back to town, can't you?" he said. "You can find your way out of this old barn, right?"

"Chan"—my father took a step towards him—"are you okay?"

"Fit as a fiddle," Chan said, and stepped into the playroom, and quietly closed the door behind him.

We left immediately, none of us saying much of anything until we were past the gatekeeper.

"I'll tell you, Robert," Archie said—his voice low, as if he imagined the keeper might hear him still—"I had the distinct impression that fellow had orders not to let Chan in."

At this, my father *raised* his voice, as if defying someone to tell him to be quiet. "Old man Bishop must be a bastard. From what I've heard, Chan's had a raw deal from day one."

My mother was sitting with Nancy and me in the back while Archie rode up front with my father. She didn't say a word, but she kicked at the back of my father's seat, as if warning him to watch what he said in Archie's company.

CHAPTER 11

"We thought you'd call ahead," my mother told the men who brought the new furniture. "My husband's out of town."

In their quilted coveralls and hooded sweatshirts, the men looked like terrible teddy bears—mutilated teddy bears, ears lopped off above bright vinyl faces.

"We never call ahead," said the taller of the two.

"Never," repeated the other.

They shoved our old furniture into the den—which became, piled high with chairs, couches, and tables, a kind of Ali Baba's Cave, almost as exciting as the rooms holding the new pieces. Even before the men left, Eleanor Woolum and I climbed into chairs set on top of the old dining table, and from that pleasantly unfamiliar perch, watched "Popeye" on *Fred's Clubhouse*.

Bulging, swaggering Bluto—bigger than life, bearded—hammered Popeye into the ground like a nail into a rotting apple. Olive Oyl wrung her hands. "Ohhhhhhh, Popeyyyyyyyeeee!"

"I don't see what Olive sees in Popeye," I said.

Eleanor looked startled. "What's *Olive* see in Bluto?"

"Let that can of spinach roll away!" I cried. "Come on! Keep that spinach away from Popeye!"

Eleanor pinched my arm. "Popeye's the hero, idiot!"

But maybe in Olive's arms Bluto would change?

Couldn't Bluto change? Of course, if Bluto changed, he might not be Bluto anymore. He might become Popeye, who didn't know how to appreciate Olive.

Popeye would never change. All Popeye could do was suffer moments of heroic muscle. And here it came: Popeye sucked his spinach up with his sailor's pipe. KLANG! went his muscles, solid iron weight!

The dull revenge began.

I couldn't bear to watch, or not to watch: Popeye sending Bluto up to the top of the flagpole—DING! Popeye whirling Bluto over his head like a helicopter blade. Popeye letting Bluto loose, and there he goes, CRASH!, through a post office wall, and, after more noise, here he comes on a conveyer belt, now all tied up with paper and string, stars and bluebirds in flight around his head, a shipping label plastered over his mouth:

SHIP TO THE END OF THE LINE.

"Penny." My mother stood in the doorway to the dining room. Her face was white, slick as a just-opened jar of cold cream, the way it looked when she got her migraines. I jumped off the table and ran to her side. "Eleanor's going to have to go home," she whispered. In one hand, she held a series of pink, crisp sheets of paper. With the other—woozily, trying to steady herself—she reached out for the top of the TV.

Eleanor hopped down from the table top immediately. "Goodbye," she called, and exited left as my mother began to wave her sheets of paper in my direction, to ramble on about things I didn't understand, how Margret had acted as if they had to buy their furniture through the Furniture Mart in Chicago, how Dad would have a heart attack when he saw the bill—

I began to tremble. "But he was with you when you picked things out, wasn't he?"

She nodded. "But he never saw the *total*."

"Why don't you get in bed? I'll make you ginger tea. Archie showed us—"

"Ginger tea." She whispered, as if her normal voice might knock something loose inside her head. "No. I left a message at the asphalt plant. They're supposed to tell Daddy I'm sick. When he comes home, see he gets some supper, okay?"

Alone in the kitchen, I examined the refrigerator and cupboards. We would have fish. There was the haddock my mother had bought for its low-cal properties. Broiled fish, Minute Rice, a salad.

How could it have been that cooking this simple meal took forever, and what I ended up with was a mess?

Nancy poked through the food with the tip of a knife—not eating, of course, only making faces, commenting on textures. "This is the sort of meal—you shouldn't have made it till he got here."

Nancy was the one who answered my father's telephone call that night. I could tell by her end of the conversation that he wouldn't be coming home, something had gone wrong with the ballroom furnaces, the pipes were freezing.

"No," Nancy said. "Mr. Pringle called, but not Archie. Not

since I've been home. You want me to ask Mom?" She listened for a while, her face growing increasingly miserable.

"Mom listened in," she whispered to me after she set the receiver back in the cradle. "She didn't *say* anything, though, so I guess I have to pretend—and give her the messages."

I stared at a *New Yorker* cartoon Chan Bishop had given my parents. My mother had stuck it on the bulletin board: a dancing woman, her enormous hairdo made out of what appeared to be cats and dogs and flowers. "Salome," read the caption. What was funny about that?

From over our heads came the squeak of a toilet seat being raised. We looked at each other, knowing that noise signaled the fact that our mother would soon begin to vomit, and once she began to vomit with a migraine, she would vomit all night.

We were right. In fact, things were so bad on that occasion that she was still in bed when Dad returned three days later.

He perched on the edge of the mattress, tipping the mixing bowl she kept with her in case she couldn't make it to the bathroom. "Say, the new furniture looks *lovely*, sweetie!" he said.

Her lips trembled. The pale skin of one cheek was creased pink from long contact with the tangle of sheets. Had she been well enough to get out of bed, I think she would have already arranged to send the furniture back. "The bill—" she began.

"Oh, hell! Let's not worry about that!" He looked tired, but pleasantly surprised; like some racer who'd discovered that the grueling event in which he'd placed so poorly was only a trial run, he still had months left in which to practice. He licked his lips, gave me a quick glance, then said he wanted Mother to know he and Archie had had a real heart-to-heart.

Archie had admitted he'd been slow getting the plant going. He'd admitted things hadn't always gone as hoped. Hell, this part of the business was new for Archie, you know, his strong suit was sales. And apparently his last trip to Chicago had been a real success! Things looked promising in Chicago, and the supplier in St. Louis had assured Archie that equipment was on its way!

My mother looked a little confused, but, for the first time in days, she sat up, and, within the hour, she was pulling her sour bedding from the mattress, pushing it down the clothes chute. Later that afternoon, Margret Woolum came by, and—though my mother looked pale—the two of them began pushing the new furniture here and there, establishing what Margret called "focus," and talking all the while about what sort of party they should have to show off the house.

A *calypso* party, Margret insisted. She could spray my mother's hair black, and they could both wear those wrap dresses. Wouldn't that be fun? And if Roger and Bob wanted to be party poopers, fine, they could just come as tourists!

I DON'T remember any other time when my mother was as happy as she was while planning that calypso party. For weeks, she and Margret got together almost every morning to do their party work. They painted palm trees on invitation cards, and scouted for perfect record albums and for a source for mangoes and papayas and plenty of fresh coconuts. They *had* to get tan, Margret said, so each morning, after Chan left for work, they let themselves into his house and, in bras and underwear, lay under his tanning lamp—a source of all sorts of teasing (Chan had come home and found them with the milkman or the gas-man, that kind of thing).

The night of the party, they worked on their get-ups over at Woolums while, down in our kitchen, my father juiced oranges. My mother had hired Paula Dart to keep me out of the way. We had been assigned to TV in the master bedroom.

"Kid stuff," Paula said of my choice of shows, *Leave It to Beaver*. Really, I would have preferred even the sitter who had spent the evening telling me the golf scores of the father of some boy she liked. I was sitting on the floor, at the foot of the bed. I had given up any claim on the mattress. Paula was so big, so redolent of something like bean soup—and since I didn't have to see her when she spoke, I didn't feel I had to answer her either.

"This is pretty much how that Haldis had this room set up, too," Paula said. "Same place for the bed and all."

"Hmm," I said.

I could feel Paula climb off the bed, her big feet hitting the floor. "I'm going to the john," she said. "Don't bother thinking I'll want to have you tell me how things turn out."

On *Leave It to Beaver*, bad-boy Eddie Haskell was being his usual saccharine self while talking to Beaver's parents, and I suffered my usual worry that I might somehow be not just dumb like Beaver, but also two-faced like Eddie. And vain like Beaver's big brother, Wally. And gluttonous like their friend, Lumpy Rutherford. And shrill and unattractive like Lumpy's bald and obnoxious Dad. Which meant I felt sorry for—and often defended—all those characters I didn't really like much myself.

L'heure bleu. I could smell it—the perfume we'd given my mother for Christmas—and then, at my back, the bed shifted. I wanted to look, to see what my mother had done to transform herself for the party, but I felt shy, and so I kept my eyes on the TV as I called, "Hi, Mom!"

"*Mom?*" It was Paula Dart, who rapped hard on the back of my head with her knuckles. "Hey, kid, you know what a hickey is?"

I moved a little out of Paula's reach, then turned to look at her: in addition to the perfume, she had applied twin hot spots of my mother's rouge, a liberal buttering of her red lipstick. "You better wipe that off," I said, trying to avoid the question of hickeys altogether. "My mom'll know you got in her stuff."

Paula grabbed a tissue from the nightstand and, while rubbing at her face, asked, "So how about giving me a hickey?"

I shook my head. Nancy had told me about hickeys.

"Come on. While the ad's on, before the next show starts." Paula pulled on my arm, not hard, but insistent. "I'll wash my neck first and everything."

I made a face. "Why would you want me to do that?"

Paula walked over to the television and turned it off. Keeping her back to me, she said, "'Cause nobody at school thinks a boy's ever even kissed me. How would you like that, if that was you?" Her big shoulders began to leap convulsively. Were her tears genuine? It hardly seemed to matter. I knew how desperate Nancy had been for a boyfriend, and Paula was older than Nancy. I felt sorry for her. I pushed back my revulsion, and followed her into the bathroom.

"This is good soap," I said, and demurely handed her the antibacterial bar Nancy used for pimples.

Paula's tears—or maybe it was *my* acquiescence—had revitalized her. Her pink-rimmed eyes had a fresh sparkle. She gave a damp little laugh, then gave the soap a look of contempt before using it to lather a washcloth.

"And you should use rubbing alcohol, too," I murmured. "That's what we use on thermometers before we put them in our mouths."

"Ha!" Paula flipped her ponytail back behind her shoulder. "You think everybody in America uses *rubbing alcohol* when they give a hickey?" But she took the bottle I held out to her, and she scrubbed at her neck until it shone pink.

From the hall below, Roger Woolum was calling, "Bob, I'm here. The girls are still fussing away!"

The alcohol tasted bitter, and its smell irritated my nose, but I appreciated this antiseptic barrier while I sucked on a little square of skin beneath Paula's jaw. She is the victim of a venomous snake bite, I told myself. You are drawing out poison to save this person's life.

"Did it work?" she asked when I drew back.

A purplish mark, a halo of red. "Yeah."

She craned her neck before the mirror. "Yeah. Good." She gave me a fierce look. "But don't you tell."

And I, almost in tears—lips fragrant with alcohol and tingling from the job—I said, "Don't *you* tell!" and ran straight downstairs to the powder room so Paula would not see me wash my mouth out with soapy water, spit and spit.

When I finally came out again, Harry Belafonte was playing on the stereo. Harry Belafonte hushed his voice, he was so sad to leave that little girl behind in Kingston town.

In the kitchen, I found Paula complimenting my father on his pirate getup, which included ripped trousers, a cardboard sword, a red scarf borrowed from my mother, and his own teeth—very realistically blackened for the evening. "Thank you, Paula." He grinned, showing the teeth. "Of course, you realize I'd have made you walk the plank if you'd said otherwise!"

From the front hall, Margret Woolum called, "Here we are!" and into the kitchen she spun, tossing her chinchilla into the breakfast nook, planting on my father's lips a kiss that seemed, at one and the same time, very flirtatious, all in fun.

She looked pretty wonderful—bare middle tanned as a nut, blue eyes shining like miners' lamps out of that brown skin. We were all admiring her when my mother entered, and began quietly unloading a bag of fruit into the refrigerator.

"Wow, Mrs. Powell!" Paula said.

My father laughed. "Good heavens, Mrs. Powell!" he cried. "Is that you—beneath all that?"

She stuck out her tongue at him. The other adults laughed, Margret loudest of all. I felt dazzled and confused. The Gauguin extravagance of what my mother had achieved with the dime store's black hair spray and poppy-colored lipstick, the sprig of Christmas poinsettia tucked into hair that hung in soft curls around her shoulders—weren't we allowed to believe in it?

I stepped to her side as she shut the refrigerator door and began folding the paper bag. "You look pretty!" I whispered, though that wasn't the right word, she knew I'd short-changed her, and so she didn't look my way when she asked, "Do I?"

"Quite a getup," my dad said, giving her a pat on the hip as he headed for the garbage with an empty bottle of lime juice.

"Apparently," Roger Woolum said—everyone turned towards him immediately, all of us eager to be distracted from the presence of my mother—"apparently Chan spent the day with a car dealer in Chicago." Roger made a delicately disdainful face. "He's ordered something new. *Bronze*, I think, he said."

My father shook his head. "Gad! If you ask me, all Chan needs is a nice gal! You and Margret surely know some nice gal in town he could get hooked up with!"

"Oh, Bob! I think Chan will find his own girl when he's good and ready!" Margret said.

"He's thirty-four years old!" My father added a splash of Cointreau to the blender pitcher. "He's throwing himself away, mooning over that what's-her-name. He could do anything he liked with his money, but—ach!" He waved a hand in the air at the folly of his friend.

My mother cleared her throat. Everyone looked at her, then away, discomfited all over again. "Margret's right, though, Bob," she said. "Chan told me what he'd really like to do, right now, is try his hand at writing."

Margret made a little squeaking noise, raised her Caribbean eyebrows towards Roger. "He *told* you that, Dorothy?"

My father slapped his forehead. "Last I heard, he was going to be a pilot! Writing! Gad! He's got a wonderful job, he's sitting on top of the heap—"

"I don't see what's so awful about his wanting to try something artistic," my mother said.

"Aw, Dorothy." Margret nuzzled my mother's cheek—carefully, so as not to smear their brown complexions—"That's because you're sweet! I suppose if I had some crazy scheme in my head, you'd be the first person I'd share it with, too. But Chan can't go around being the *enfant terrible* all the rest of his days!"

My father agreed with Margret: Chan ought to put his nose to the grindstone, get ready to take over the reins! "Gad, if I'd been fortunate enough to be born into a dynasty like that—"

Roger Woolum raised a silencing finger as several guests called their hellos from the front hall, and my father broke off what he'd been saying to shout, "Hey, who's out there?"

A pirate and two more bronzed ladies poked their heads in the door, followed by several men in Bermuda shorts and Hawaiian shirts, binoculars and cameras slung around their necks, and Chan—shoeless, shirtless—identifying his role as "beach bum."

"What a kook!" my father said. "Gad, don't tell me you walked through the snow like that, Bishop!"

"Powell, you're entirely too staid," Chan said. "Mustn't be too staid, old man."

Margret fidgeted while Chan and Roger and my father talked about Chan's new car, the trip to Chicago and so on. She folded her arms across her bare belly, sighed, went over to peek into the sink where my mother was running citrus rinds down the garbage disposer, temporarily drowning out the sweet, splashy music of the steel drum band on the stereo.

"*Chan.*" Margret grabbed my mother's hand and, pulling her after herself, stepped out into the center of the kitchen, "Come on, what do you think? Do we look quasi-authentic, or what?"

He didn't answer for a moment, then he smiled, and said, "Matson, what big white teeth you have!" Which made my mother grin—though with her mouth closed—and lower her eyes.

Margret tapped her foot. "What about me?"

My mother moved back a few steps, made herself a spectator as Chan walked in a little circle around Margret, who—to the amusement of the guests—continued to tap her foot.

Roger Woolum crossed his arms over his chest and looked on these proceedings proudly. "She's been doing fifty sit-ups every morning and fifty more every night, that's how come her stomach's so flat," he told the group.

Margret protested, but Chan nodded solemnly. "Is that what it is?" He stepped behind her, then reached out, set his hands on either side of her bare waist.

"Chan," she yelped, "your hands are like ice!"

"Oh, hell! Are you going to dance or not? We'll do that dance we did in Tobago!" He looked over his shoulder at my mother. "You, too, Matson! Come on, it's a line dance!"

"Brr!" Margret said, but began to dance forward, lifting her arms in the air. She smiled at my mother. "Come on, Dorothy! It's easy!"

Because of her limp, my mother didn't often dance, but that night she stepped forward, gingerly placed her fingertips on Chan's waist.

"All right!" said Chan, and he and Margret began to pull her forward with their own progress. "Head us toward the living room, Margret!"

Laughing, moving along in a bumpy but happy way, my mother turned to my father: "Come on, Bob!" Her teeth *were* big, a startling white against her dark skin. But they were pretty. Wasn't that what Chan meant? The way he'd said it, you couldn't quite tell. Did he mean she looked like a wolf, or pretty?

"What a bunch of kooks!" my father said, as he wiped up the counter with a sponge. "Gad."

"Some pirate you are!" Margret cried. "But see if we care!" and to the thump of the music, the line, now including six or seven guests, began to snake and shake toward the dining room.

"Mambo!" somebody shouted, and someone else, "Cha-cha-cha!"

Over her shoulder, eyes a little worried, my mother smiled at my father. I expected to see him smile back. Instead, he made his face a blank so forceful it stopped my heart, and made my mother drop her hands from Chan's waist, and step out of the line as the guests moved off into the rooms beyond.

I wished Paula would disappear, but there she stood, dreamily drawing fried pepitas up the side of a bowl, popping them, one by one, into her mouth. "So, Mrs. Powell, hey," she said, "why'd you stop dancing?"

My mother licked her lips. Maybe she meant to answer, but before she could, my father said, "Oh, I suppose she didn't want to look foolish." He smiled his black-toothed smile at my mother. "Isn't that about right, Mother?"

"*No*, that is not about right."

"Well, then!" He chuckled. "Let's just say that's why she *should* have stopped!"

Her fingers trembled as she adjusted the poinsettia in her hair. "I quit," she said, "because the look on your face had already spoiled things for me."

I felt hot, horrified that Paula was a witness to this, but my father didn't seem at all bothered. "Aha!" he said and merrily clicked his heels together and smiled at Paula and me. "But isn't that pretty much what I said, girls?"

"Bob"—just then, in my mother's mouth, his name didn't seem to be his name, it was a plea. My father, however, responded as if he had heard nothing special, "Yes, dear?"

She closed her heavily made-up eyes for just a moment, then took off, running, towards the hall.

"Ay, gad." My father picked up a sponge and wiped chips of ice off the counter and into the palm of his hand, flicked them into the sink. For a moment, I stood there like Paula, as if nothing had happened. But then I knew I had to go after my mother, and I whispered to Paula—sounding as fierce in my whisper as I could—"I'll be back. You stay here."

MY MOTHER had locked herself in her dressing room. From the master bedroom, looking through a keyhole left over from the days before the house had switched to modern locksets, I could see her. She sat on a corner of the exercise machine, her chin resting on the window sill.

"Mom? Are you okay?"

She didn't answer, and I could imagine only the worst sort of reasons why: she'd gone deaf, she'd swallowed poison, she hated her life so much that she'd cut out her tongue—

"She in there, Penny?"

Heart pounding from the scare of that voice coming up behind me, I leapt into the air as my pirate father came around the side of the bed, his cardboard sword raising a whispery burr as it swept against the puffy, floral spread.

"Is it locked?" He asked the question in the sort of matter-of-fact voice he would have used, say, had the two of us sat at breakfast, discussing whether or not anyone needed more bread put down in the toaster. I nodded.

"Unlock the door, Dotty." A different voice, but I recognized this one, too: the voice a father uses when giving orders to a kid.

Almost immediately, the lock clicked.

He turned toward me, working hard to arrive at something like a smile. "You can go, Penny. Everything's fine."

I wanted to believe that he could see what I couldn't: Everything was fine. I also didn't want to leave her alone with him, and this was something new and awful.

"Go on now. We'll be down in two shakes." His voice had grown bigger, more cheerful, but in an ossified way, almost as if it played on the wrong speed. "Go on."

I stepped out into the hall. To discourage people from wandering through the house, my parents always kept the lights at the top of the stairs turned off during parties, but I could see Paula out there, dancing in the dark to the music that floated up the stairs. Like the people down below—many of them laughing, making noisy hoots and hollers—she was doing the line dance, her hands held out before herself, resting on some imaginary waist. I didn't interrupt. I felt I mustn't let her know I'd seen her sad and lonely dance, and so I stayed in the dark until the song ended and she stopped moving—which was just about the time that my parents came out of the dressing room and, without so much as a word to me or Paula, returned to their party.

CHAPTER 12

In early spring, Chan Bishop went out to Quarry Farm and cut armfuls of pussy willows for my mother and Margret Woolum. The buds were tight on their red twigs, but after a few days in the warm houses, they opened into the softest gray bits of fur imaginable, so sweet and tempting that Teddy Woolum inserted several up his nose and had to be carried, weeping, down the sidewalk to the Hobarts' so that Dr. Hobart could extract the things.

Eleanor was sure that the bouquet Chan had given her mother was bigger than the one he'd given mine. "Seventeen branches for my mom, fifteen for yours," she said.

We were on our way home from school at the time. The melted snow had made the sidewalks long, narrow puddles, forced us to walk in the streets.

"Part of my mom's bouquet is in our den," I said. "She split hers in two." Which made it appear that I knew my mother had more than fifteen twigs, when, in fact, I didn't know if she'd split a group of *fifteen* in two, or if *fifteen* remained in the front hall's brass container, or what. And then I remembered something, and felt guilty and sorry for being so mean-spirited:

Margret Woolum had been sick. Margret had had to go to the hospital because her gelatin diet made her lose all of her potassium. Roger had found her passed-out in the laundry room.

"Look," Eleanor said. That morning, Teddy had thrown several good-sized chunks of limestone over the side of the trestle's walkway, and we'd watched them skitter dully across the thinning creek ice; now, the rocks were gone, sunk in holes where the creek's dark water showed through.

"Spring," I said, and though it wasn't warm enough for us to go without coats, I slipped out of mine, buttoned it at the neck, and wore it like a cape, my beret stuffed up one sleeve.

That beret had been the cause of plenty of jokes, and as I moved along that afternoon, kicking my legs out to the side, singing little bits from *West Side Story*, I pretended not to notice when the beret slipped down the silky lining of my coat sleeve, and parachuted into a pile of slush.

My heart beat hard while I waited for Eleanor to notice, to tell me to pick it up, but something else had caught her eye: a car backing out of Chan's drive. "God!" Eleanor yelped. "Look!" and stood stock still.

Blond hair, the big black sunglasses of that era's glamour pusses: unreasonable happiness suffused me. "Haldis!" I said.

The woman drove past, her face so grim it seemed she must know we watched. Then Eleanor turned to me and hooted, "It wasn't *Haldis*! It was some *girlfriend,* booby!"

Because of her mother's being sick, I didn't snap back at

Eleanor. Still, I didn't go to her house that afternoon, or ask her to mine.

I found my own mother at work in the kitchen. She'd spent the day at the Red Cross, and still wore her gray volunteer's uniform, which meant she looked like a nurse, but better: like a nurse from out of the past, with long sleeves and starched white collar and cuffs.

She smiled when I came into the kitchen. Every once in a while, my mother would come up with a really twinkling, expectant smile, a smile that suggested she felt just fine in the world, and she smiled several of those smiles that afternoon. My father had been with Archie in Chicago all week, trying to convince some of Archie's contacts to become backers for the door plant, and she was making a special meal to celebrate his return.

"A beautiful pork roast and baked potatoes and green bean casserole. You can do the fruit salad if you like, Pen. He said five-thirty at the latest, so I'm planning on six!"

We both smiled. Just then, it seemed whatever was a problem about my father (his habitual tardiness, for instance) was also a treat to be shared.

After I'd finished making the fruit salad I went out to the den to watch *Fred's Clubhouse*. At five—now wearing her own clothes—my mother joined me on the couch for Walter Cronkite and the news.

"Nancy should be home now," she said at five-forty-five.

"Y-Teens. She won't be here till six."

At six, the timer on the oven began to buzz, and—lips in a moue—my mother got up to shut it off.

"Everything's done," she said when she came back. "Everything looks great." She hesitated in the doorway, then walked past me to the window that overlooked the drive.

"I'll do my piano till they get here," I said—some imitation of a model kid, though my mother was too distracted to notice.

At six-thirty, when I went out to the kitchen, she was adding water to the pans in the oven, and looking teary-eyed.

"It's all ruined now," she said at quarter of. By then, she looked more mad than sad. "Didn't I tell you to unload the dish washer before you watched TV?" Her voice swooped with emotion. "What am I going to do with you girls? What am I going to do, period? If I'd ever treated my mother with such contempt, I'd have gotten slapped silly!"

From the front hallway, Nancy called, "Sorry, I know I'm late."

I sneaked a peek at her as I put the silverware away. She wasn't only late, she was a mess, her face pink and puffed, especially around her mouth and chin.

My mother looked dazed. "For goodness sake, Nan." She leaned back against the counter. "What—take off your jacket this instant!"

If Nancy hadn't been so emaciated, it wouldn't have been so easy to see that she'd stuffed the cups of her bra. As it was, her "breasts" looked stitched on, like the arms of a teddy bear.

"Take whatever you've got in there, out!" my mother said.

Nancy opened the refrigerator, sighed, closed it again before turning to Mother, asking, "*What*?"

Embarrassed and scared, I went back to unloading the dishwasher.

"I'm not stupid, Nan. Take—whatever it is, out!"

Behind me, something physical occurred, a distinct rustle of human movement, and, by the time I turned, the two of them were struggling against each other, Mother yanking tissues from the neck of Nancy's sweater.

"Mom," I cried, "stop!" She got Nancy down on the tiles. She sat on her while she finished removing the tissues.

"Mom, please!" I pulled at her arms—not hard, I was too scared for that—but hard enough that she turned to cry:

"You want me to sit by while your sister turns into a whore?"

"*Whore*?" Nancy hesitated, but only for one moment, before she pulled one of her hands free and gave my mother's cheek a resounding slap.

That slap. My mother gasped and backed off Nancy with a scuttling movement. She was frantic, she looked around herself. I don't know what she had in mind, but when she saw the pile of lunch plates I'd just removed from the washer, she reached out a hand, swept the whole bunch of them across the counter—a *zing* of pottery on Formica— and onto the floor, where they broke with an organized sort of clatter.

"That's it! I'm leaving!" she sobbed, and headed for the stairs.

While I helped Nancy to her feet—how cold and dry her hand was!—I called out, "Mother! Come back!"

AGAIN, SHE had locked herself in the dressing room. I could hear her in there, the sound of her pulling suitcases from the big cupboards above the mirrored closets.

"Other people's children love them! What did I do wrong?"

"We love you, Mom! Don't say we don't love you!" I cried. Some glue of terror clotted my tongue. Everything was coming to an end, sucking down the drain. "Wait! Just wait, Mom!"

"Nancy!" I ran through the house calling, "Nancy!"

She didn't answer until I was on my second trip through the basement, and tripped over a box of paint cans in the laundry room.

"Here." Nancy sat in the chair of the enormous mangle our mother used for ironing sheets and table cloths. She was reading *Green Mansions*.

Out of breath, crying—though I knew it would be better not to cry in front of Nancy, I said, "Apologize to her, and— I'll pay you."

She rested her chin on the handle of the mangle press. "How much?" she said. Coolly. But her face was a dead white.

"Five dollars—come on! She's *packing*, Nancy!"

Nancy looked back at the book, seemed to take up her reading again. I tried to be patient and wait quietly, but I was too worried, on edge from listening for the sound of my mother's suitcases in the hall above. "*Nancy!*"

She looked up. She said, "I won't do it for less than ten."

WHEN MY father finally did arrive home that night—we'd forgotten about *him* for a time—the three of us had to scramble to assemble ourselves in likely positions in the kitchen. He was singing, "'I'm home from sea, my love it's me: Barnacle Bill the Sailor!'" and, trying to sound chipper, I called down the basement stairs, "Hi, Dad!"

"Well, hello, Pen!" he called back. "Say, go let Archie in, will you? He's parking out front."

"Archie!" my mother murmured. She looked a wreck, we all did—pale, porous, as if we'd been pickled. While I hurried for the front door, she called to my father, "*You* sound cheerful, Bob. So, how'd things go?"

He didn't answer, but said in a big voice—after the brief pause in which I knew he would have kissed her cheek— "We've got enough to feed Archie, too, don't we?"

I couldn't hear her response, but, as I let Archie inside, he made it clear he didn't want to impose. Truly, he said, tilting into the hall to call out that he had only stopped by to deliver gifts.

Archie smiled at me while we waited for some response from the kitchen. Archie wore a white silk muffler, loose, hanging down on either side of his collar, like a liturgical tippet. I was thinking he looked like our priest in Dolores, when he leaned close to whisper: "Supper burn?"

The alcohol on his breath singed my nose. And there was a powerful odor of alcohol on my father's breath, too, when he stepped into the hall. I recognized that smell from Chan Bishop, and knew that it came not of having just a drink or two, but of numerous drinks—consumed both recently and over a long haul.

"Wait till you see what Archie's brought you!" My father's grin was too big. His mouth must have been cottony because his upper lip snagged on his gums, and he actually had to use his fingers to release it. "Ha-a-a-a-h," he said, a queer, happy little moan that he immediately seemed to regret—it made his condition too obvious—and yet, the unstoppable grin said, he just couldn't help himself.

"Look at this!" he cried when he had my mother and Nancy and me assembled in the hall. On the bureau sat three chubby-cheeked, scant-haired boy dolls that, to my mind, looked quite a bit like Archie. Archie in different lives. Each doll was identical to the other, but one wore the clothes of a cowboy, one the suit of a railroad engineer, one a farmer's overalls.

"He got one for each of you!" my father said. As if it were quite normal for my thirty-four-year-old mother to receive a doll.

Nancy said a terse thank you for her engineer while I examined the careful stitches of my cowboy's neckerchief. My father fingered the miniature shoulder straps on the overalls of my mother's farmer. "Aren't they something?" he said. She nodded politely, then hurried back to the kitchen.

Archie was welcome to stay to dinner, my father said. "You don't want to go back to that big old empty house! And Dotty'll want to hear all about our trip, you know." He hesitated, then gave Archie a wink. "I could use some help in that regard!"

"Dinner," my mother called—"or should I say what once was dinner?—is served."

In compensation for her coolness—with much grinning and laughter—my father launched into stories of the German shepherd, Koenig, he and my mother had owned before Nancy and I were born. One of these I'd heard plenty of times: Koenig gobbling down a carpenter's finger, accidentally sawed off while the carpenter made my parents a set of bookshelves. Still, I laughed along with Archie, and winced again at my father's imitation of old Al Duncum's hollering "I'm dripping on your carpet here, Mrs. Powell!" and then, "Oh! Oh! Damn it! Somebody catch that dog!"

Usually, when she bothered to eat dinner with us, Nancy sat across from me at the table; that night, because of the presence of Archie, we sat side by side, and, while my father told his story, Nancy didn't laugh, but leaned close to whisper in my ear, "They're *drunk*."

I saw, then, that my mother knew this, too. While Dad rambled on, she whacked a serving spoon against her plate, made a point of how difficult it was to serve her dried-out casserole.

"Old Al and I headed over to the hospital. He had a towel around his hand, and of course I felt awful, I'm apologizing all the way, and finally he looks at me and—oh, he looked like the devil, all white in the face!—but he says, 'Tell you what, Mr. Powell, if it'd make you feel better—since this is probably going to lay me up for a bit—maybe you could tell my wife you want me to do a little work up at your summer place, and then me and my girlfriend could spend some time over there.'"

I'd never heard *that* ending to the story before, and I glanced at my mother to see if she had either.

My mother had been gazing at the dining room's plantation panels as if she found them full of new and interesting information, but, suddenly, she stood. "We have ice cream," she said briskly. "Would you care to stay for ice cream, Archie?"

It seemed to me that anybody would have seen that her asking Archie if he wanted to stay meant that he ought to leave. Maybe the drinks had made him dull. Anyway, he didn't go while the going was good, and once everyone sat behind a dish of butter pecan, my mother said, "So, Archie, how are things with the factory?"

Archie looked to my father, who made a dramatic gesture— bolted forward a little in his chair, as if to suggest my mother had rudely stepped on the brakes of decent life, come close to hurling us through some perilous windshield. "Mother," he said, "let's not bother Archie with that while he's our dinner guest. I think you know the score. If we don't go broke before we get things off the ground, well, then we're—doing dandy!"

Archie blinked. He folded his hands in his lap and, for the first time since I'd known him, he looked helpless—like one of those cartoon characters who knows his rowboat is sinking, and there's not a thing he can do about it.

My mother, on the other hand, gasped and pressed her napkin against her lip. Had you entered the room at that moment, you would certainly have guessed someone had struck her, and she now staunched the flow of blood. Not moving the cloth, she turned to my father to ask, "What do you mean?"

"I mean"—he took a spoonful of ice cream into his mouth, then held his jaw to one side while he waited for the lump to melt before he swallowed. "I mean we'll be fine if we don't go broke."

With great deliberation—as if it might shatter—my mother set her napkin down on the table. "So—what happened on this trip, then? Did you get your loan?"

"Oh, hell!" Laughing, my father rested his elbows on the table, his forehead on his fists. "*That* was an experience, believe you me! I don't know exactly what sort of *business* those fellows were in, but, all of a sudden, Archie and I looked at each other—we were in this nice big office—and it dawns on both of us at just the same time: hell, we're dealing with mafiosos!"

My mother gave Archie a sharp look. "How on earth do you know mafiosos?"

The name truly did sound odd in her mouth; but I don't think it was this that made my father laugh, and drum on the tabletop, like a man impatient for his waiter to bring the bill. "Don't get all excited, Mother," he said out of the corner of his mouth. "We were too small-time for those fellows!"

"Thank the Lord for small favors!"

"Oh?" Bright-eyed, head cocked to one side, my father looked like some scary bird. "I'm out there *killing* myself for you, breaking my *back*, and you have the gall to say 'Thank the Lord for small favors'?"

She pressed her fingertips to the thin skin of her eyelids. "Bob, whether or not you understand this, I don't *want* you out there killing yourself for me. Just—take the loss." Her voice was quiet. She looked at my father with an intensity that rendered Archie almost invisible. "We could move back to Dolores, Bob. At least you'd get off the road. We could spend time together. The girls and I—none of this"—she wagged her hands in the direction of the chandelier, the wainscotting, Archie—"none of this matters, as long as we have each other."

Was that true? I sensed that if my father believed it were true, it would be true, which struck me as both wonderful and terrible. Our salvation or destruction was totally in his hands, and, somehow, she had put it there.

"I've said it a hundred times." Her voice now sounded more

desperate. "We could move to the farm. I don't need to go to beauty parlors or wear fancy clothes."

I nodded hard, eager to forget every ambition, to move us along to some other sort of existence altogether. "And Nancy and I could save money, Dad. We could eat popcorn instead—"

"*What?*" My father spun in my direction, his index finger a kind of pivot on the table. "*Popcorn?*" he shrilled. "Ye gods! You see what a bunch of boobs I'm dealing with, here, Archie!"

"Now, Robert." Archie's voice was low, soothing, "now—"

"The fact of the matter is, Archie and I would have been damned *lucky* to get money from those crooks! If things are bad now, it'd make your head swim to see where we'd be if I tried to get out! Whether you comprehend this or not, ladies"—his voice grew almost luxurious, creamy, as if he meant to enjoy what came next—"whether or not you understand, we're talking over a million dollars here! We're talking ruin, ladies, as in—*kaput!*"

My mother sat back, hard, in her chair. Nancy's face looked waxy, the way it always looked before her faints.

"But, Robert," Archie said, "let's not be unduly alarming. You still have the asphalt plant and—"

"*Kaput!*" My father jumped up from the table, ran to the kitchen and back again, the notepad my mother used for shopping lists and messages in his hand. "Here!" Standing at my mother's elbow, he wrote down a series of numbers, toted them up, scooted this here, that there. "You see what we stand to gain if this works out?" he demanded. "You see what we stand to *lose?*"

Like an accident victim who wanders away from a wreck, my mother stood, veered off toward the kitchen.

"Oh, hell!" He dropped down in her chair. He threw the pencil at the wallpaper, where it left a gray check on a peach hoop skirt. "Everything I've done, I've done for you three!" he shouted towards the kitchen. "And what do I get? Kicked in the teeth! *Kicked* in the teeth!"

"Don't say that," I pleaded. "We love you more than anything!"

And Nancy, her voice panicky, spiraling higher and higher: "What's this mean? Does this mean I won't get to go to college?"

"For God's sake!" My father grabbed my mother's abandoned ice-cream dish and angrily scraped up its last spoonful. "Mother!" he called into the kitchen. With a clatter, he dropped the spoon into the now empty bowl. "Mother!" He hurried through the door to the kitchen, then we could hear his shoes pounding on the basement stairs, as he called over his shoulder, "You started this, Mother! Now you fix it!"

Doors slammed. Silence pooled, then convulsed as the garage door rose on its tracks. A moment later, the car started up, and backed out the drive.

In despair, Nancy and I grabbed one another, howled, "Mom! Where's he going? What'll we do?"

She didn't answer. She stayed out in the kitchen, slamming things into the dishwasher.

Archie folded his napkin tight over his index finger and, like a mother cleaning grime from a child's chin, rubbed at the corners of his mouth. After, he set the napkin on the table, and patted it comfortingly. "It will all be fine," he said. "Your father—loves you dearly. Dearly." He continued to pat the napkin. "Family is the most important treasure. Blood is—"

He hesitated. Nancy and I—sniffling, shuddering—waited

for him to finish the line, and when he didn't, in one quaking voice, we offered "'thicker than water.'"

"Thicker than water." He nodded and took a deep drink from his glass of water. "We just have to trust that—all will turn out well."

My mother had come to stand in the dining-room doorway as Archie spoke. In deference to her fury, Archie didn't quite look at her, but merely canted his head in her direction.

"I'm aware of my part. I came—it was your father, of course, who risked his capital. I feel the responsibility—"

Did we care what Archie had to say? Not a bit. We shuffled towards our mother. It seemed to me that if we could huddle together, we could somehow make ourselves into a shelter.

Our mother accepted our embraces hungrily, but murmured into our hair, "Something terrible's going to happen. I know it."

"You'll excuse me," Archie said. He pushed his chair back from the table. "I thank you—a lovely dinner, Dotty. I'll just see myself to the door."

"No." Hot-eyed, she pulled away from Nancy and me. "No."

We followed her as she followed Archie through the French doors to the living room and out into the hall. She wasn't being hospitable. Far from it. She walked close on Archie's heels and didn't speak. I understood exactly what she meant to convey: her opinion that he might be capable of sticking something in his pocket before he went out the door. This was a little mean, yes, and I doubt she even believed it. The gesture itself was the important thing. The gesture made her stand tall, and move quickly, and look as if she were convinced that she still had the power to be on guard in her life.

CHAPTER 13

I have no idea how my parents patched things up after the Chicago blow-up. They talked to each other at breakfast the next morning—though with the wan apologetic air of people who'd just come through a bout of flu together. They went out to dinner with the Woolums and Chan that night, a Friday night.

Does it make sense that we believed our troubles were—at one and the same time—not worth mentioning and so dark and terrible that no one on earth could have been trusted to keep them secret or help us bear their weight?

Saturday noon—our first meal all together since the quarrels—our mother said to Nancy and me, "Dad's got enough to do without worrying about us, so let's make things as pleasant as possible."

She was serving out grilled cheese sandwiches just then—on dinner plates, since the lunch plates had all been smashed on Thursday. When he entered the room, she looked up smiling: "Lunch?"

He took a seat at the table, but after one bite of his sandwich, he got to his feet, and dialed out on the wall phone.

"Aren't you hungry, honey?" my mother whispered.

"Shh." He tilted his chin into the air while he waited for an answer. I'd seen his father do the same thing; both of them unfocused their gazes while waiting for answers to telephone calls or questions. A cool gesture, but it didn't hide the fact that nothing mattered more than the answer to come.

That day, there was no answer, and, hanging up, my father raised his free hand in a gesture of defeat. Still, the expression on his face suggested satisfaction, the way the face of a moviegoer or reader will when the story carries him forward to a terrible but inevitable conclusion. "Gad!" he said. "You'd think he'd be available today!"

Then he returned to the table. Sat down. Stared in the direction of my mother's aspic molds, antique butter paddles, and Mexican chocolate mixers—though I don't suppose he saw them. "*Tk!*" He made a little noise with his mouth—a noise I knew he sometimes made while alone, at work in his office. My mother set a basket of chips on the table, and he looked up at her with a start.

"You remember everybody's coming for chili tonight, Bob?" Her voice sounded odd, as if anxiety had spun webs in her throat, and now she had to speak through them. "We've got three bottles of Chianti, but there's no pop for the kids or beer for Chan."

"Fine." He slid out of the nook and headed into the hall. "I wanted to run out to the plant anyway, see how they got the new equipment set up."

"But you're not going now." My mother looked crushed. "I wanted to talk to you—about hiring a summer girl. I've got some possibilities, but I don't know how much to offer—"

He reappeared, already slipping on his coat. "Offer what you did last year—plus twenty, twenty-five."

"But, Bob"—she hesitated—"take the girls with you, why don't you? That way you'd at least have a chance to visit."

"Dotty!" As if suddenly blinded by headache, he stuck the ham of his palm into his eye. "Is this *necessary*?"

I lowered my head. I didn't want to show either anticipation or disappointment, anything that might cause further distress.

"Gad," he muttered. "Well, tell them to hurry up, then!"

Nancy sniggered. "Hey, Dad, we *can* still hear, you know?"

He reared back, made big eyes. "What's this smart-aleck stuff, Mother?"

Nancy raised the back of her hand to her nose, pretending to cover her laugh. "I said we can *hear*. Anyway, I have plans for this afternoon."

He smiled with all of his teeth. When did he ever smile like that except when he was furious? "You have plans? Then the hell with you, babe!" Still smiling, his step positively elastic, he left the kitchen.

My mother gasped, "Nancy Powell! What on earth could be more important than spending a little time with your dad?"

Nancy carried her plate to the sink. The song she hummed to shut out our mother's words came from *Mighty Mouse* cartoons. It was the song that the fair maiden mouse always sang while—deep in a trance—she lay tied to the railroad tracks, or chained to a log that drew closer and closer to the mill saw that would rip her in half if Mighty Mouse didn't appear, and soon—

"Mom," Nancy said as she turned to leave the room, "your

husband doesn't want to spend time with us. Why should we want to spend time with him?"

"He doesn't want to spend time with you! Everything that man does, he does so you can have a better life than he's had!"

Nervously, I pinched up the last bits of potato chips from the straw basket, and, in the process, ate a few shards of straw. I knew my mother believed what she said. I also sensed that her words were intended not so much for Nancy as for my father, out there in the hall; that they were meant to gain his approval.

I, too, wanted his approval. His approval was one of my hopeless ambitions. And so I was the one who went to the factory with him that Saturday; and, as we drove past fields still soggy with melted snow, pigs standing stiff-legged in their muddy lots, I was the one who asked him the sort of questions I would later ask the boys who became my boyfriends and husbands:

How do you do this or that and how is such and such a thing working out—

He bit into my questions with weary relish. He sighed, he grimaced, he told me about his tenant, Hanson, who'd apparently fouled-up laying the tile on our farm: "What a mess! I'm going to have to get over there and take care of it or we won't even get a crop in!"

I felt like Mortimer Snerd, or Charlie McCarthy, face all wood and strings, waiting to be shifted to its next position by somebody else. "So Hanson's still a headache, huh?" I said.

He smiled. "Oh, heavens, yes!"

I had made him happy, it seemed, and that made a nervous

happiness hum and buzz in my chest. I rolled down my window, felt the velvety fuzz in the tracks. The sky that day was a bright, headachy blue that my father declared beautiful, beautiful. He rolled down his window too, and as we drove along the highway, he began to sing:

"Oh, Danny Boy, the pipes, the pipes are calling—"

He broke off. "Do you know 'Danny Boy,' Pen? When I was just a tiny, Dad used to have Fran and Roy and me sing when visitors came by. 'Danny Boy' was one of his favorites, and 'The Old Lamplighter.' You know those two?"

I nodded uncertainly. "Not the lamp one, but 'Danny Boy'— they use that on the *Danny Thomas Show*."

"Dad was always so proud of my singing!" He laughed, as if this had been foolish in his father, but then he began to sing again, putting his all into the song—in the old way, one arm crooked and working along like a bellows.

He was still singing "Danny Boy" when he tried to insert his key in the door factory's deadbolt, and found it didn't fit.

"Wait here, Pen." Off he trotted around the corner of the building. All corrugated metal, the factory always made me think of an airplane hangar, something chill and windy and uninviting. I kicked at the gravel, jammed my hands down in the pockets of my jacket. What if he didn't come back? How long would I have to wait before I'd know if he wasn't coming back?

Then I heard his feet on the gravel, his noisy sips of air. He was shaking his head. "Gad. Of all the nut deals!"

I joined him at the rear of the car, where he rooted around in the toolbox he kept in his trunk.

"Hm!" He picked up a lug wrench. "Guess this ought to do it," he said, and then, to my amazement, he stepped to the office door, hefted the wrench, and smashed it clean through the window.

He turned to smile at me, so I did my best to smile back as he whipped off his jacket, wrapped his hand in the cloth, and broke out what remained of the glass.

The plant was dark beyond the door, but once we were inside, he began snapping on light switches, the long line of fluorescents pulsing to life like a string of ghosts. Puffing out small clouds of breath into the building's cold air, I ran forward, did a little hop and skip, some imitation of the spunky kid I supposed I might have been in the past but wasn't anymore. Which didn't feel too bad until I turned and saw my father's face: white, rubbery.

"What is it?"

"Last week"—he seemed scarcely able to lift his pointing finger—"that whole end was full of deliveries." Hands pressed to the top of his head, he hurried to the enormous overhead door at the end of the building, tested its lock. "We had almost our whole set-up." He walked to the door at the other end of the building and tested its lock, too. "This is nuts."

On a wall telephone that had been installed near the front door, he tried Archie's number. "No answer." He took a deep nervous breath. "Damn it!" he muttered. "What's the last name of that secretary?"

Baber. I knew it was Baber, but he didn't, and it took me a moment to get up the courage to offer him what he didn't know.

"Baber! That's right!" He looked at me as if amazed. "Thank you, sweetie!"

After much prodding from my father, Shirley Baber finally told my father that Archie had discovered the last order was all wrong, he'd had to send it back.

"Of all the idiot deals!" he cried as he hung up the phone. "How Archie manages to foul up so many things is beyond me! Gad"—he glanced my way—"if he turns out to be a bastard, I kid you not, he'll be sorry he ever messed with me!"

He went to work, then, cutting a piece of plywood for the broken window, and I ate powdered creamer from a jar in the cubby where the coffeepot sat. I couldn't imagine Archie in that building. In his fancy suits. I couldn't even imagine him in the little carpeted office, closed off from the work of the place.

The building echoed with the sound of my father hammering the board into place, then he called, "Come on, sweetie, I'm going to have to run down Archie. We'll grab Chan's beer while I take you home. Chan's got to have his beer, got to drown his sorrows."

I considered the mention of someone other than Archie a lifeline and, as I made my way toward the door, I asked, "Do you think Chan's wife is ever going to come back?"

"*Chan's* wife?" He laughed. "Why, she married that other fellow, honey! That Mott."

This news—my misunderstanding—floored me, but I stumbled on. "The girls from St. Joseph's say people like that—anybody who gets a divorce, like Elizabeth Taylor and Eddie Fisher—they'll go to hell."

My father shrugged, then held open the door for me to pass outside ahead of him. We got in the car. We bumped across the rough lot, then pulled onto the highway. I tried again. "If his wife broke his heart, then Chan shouldn't have to go to hell, right?"

My father snorted. "I grew up with all that nonsense, Pen, but I don't believe in hell!" His free hand took a chop at the air. "And all this talk about broken hearts! Gad, I could have married any of a million gals and been just as happy! The idea there's one person you'll meet—that's for the birds! You remember that before you let anybody go breaking your heart!"

Astonished, my brain working like one of those flip books I'd owned as a child—interchangeable characters perform interchangeable actions in interchangeable places—I sat, silent, as we passed by the soggy fields, some of them seamed with the remains of last year's crops. I tried to imagine my father and mother with other faces, but I couldn't. My mother was my mother was my mother. I tried to imagine my father childless, or with children born of other women, and then, for one anguished moment, saw myself as I supposed he saw me. Not pretty. Not interesting. Just his child. An accident of fate.

Up until that moment, I'd believed that the fact that he and my mother had found one another made me special to him, too. Now, this seemed a pathetic fantasy. My father didn't tell stories about me to his friends. He didn't take my drawings and poems to his office and pin them on the wall. Maybe he wouldn't even remember me from this period of his life. It would be Archie Jones he'd remember, just as in the past he'd had his eras of Leon and Bill and other partners who brought him closest to his dreams and nightmares.

WHEN WE finally stopped in the parking lot of a little grocery on the edge of Meander, he noticed I was crying. From the corner of his eye—as if at a stranger who'd suddenly drawn even to him in a race—he peered at me. "What's this blubbering? All I meant to do was save you some pain down the road! If I said something wrong, excuse me all to pieces! String me up by my thumbs!" With that, he left the car, struck out across the lot.

Even from behind, you could see he had small feet. His heels were no wider than the heels of women heading into the store. I had his small bones and big head, but I wasn't like him. I told myself I'd never be like him. I wouldn't love him anymore. I would love only my mother. I would polish my love for my mother to its full glory.

But a few minutes later he came out of that shabby grocery at a trot, grinning, his arms tight around two big bags, and I didn't hesitate to climb from the car and open a door for him.

"Thanks, sweetie!" He smiled as he put down the bags, then said softly, "Say, forgive me if I sounded rough back there. I shouldn't have blown up like that."

"It's okay," I said, but began to cry again once we were back in the car.

"Here, here, Pen, I bought us a little treat, a box of powdered sugar doughnuts, why don't you open them up while I drive, honey?

WHEN WE finally pulled up in front of the house, my father looked—refreshed, happy in almost the same way that he looked happy when he started in on one of his businesses.

"You hear that?" he said. "Gad, that's the creek making all that noise, the creek rising." He shook his head in a kind of admiration. "Well, you take in the groceries, won't you, honey? Tell Mom I've got to try and run down that damn Archie!"

That damn Archie.

With a little jolt, I realized that this sounded perfectly familiar, that Archie was following his predecessors to a nicety, joining the wonderful but down-on-their-luck fellows who had turned into snakes in the grass, shysters who'd held him up, sold him a bum steer, rigged a rotten deal. Charlie Gill, Leon Cottrell, Bill Rail, Tom Strickland, and all the others. Where were they now? Consigned to my father's bitter museums of thieves, skunks, and crooks.

I found my mother and Margret in the kitchen, making the chili. "So where'd that devil of a father of yours take off for?" Margret asked. And my mother, chopping onions, groaned and laughed, "Oh, Lord, who knows?"

"Oh, Lord," was, for my mother, a new and chic ejaculation. "Oh, Lord!" she said when, later that day, I pulled her to the living-room window to take a look at the rising creek. "Oh, Lord!" when one of that evening's guests changed the record on the stereo from Pete Fountain's clarinet to "John and Marsha."

Most of the invited families had already arrived by then, and my mother was doing her best not to seem disturbed by the fact that my father hadn't returned yet, or even phoned.

"John!"

"Marsha!"

Eleanor and I, serving ourselves from the big pot on the stove, moaned along with the record while Nancy gave us severe looks. She sat in the breakfast nook with fourteen-year-old David Woolum, and the high-school-age Hobart boy—who wore a sports shirt that featured buckled pockets, each one marked with rust stains. Neither boy impressed Nancy in the least. Watching them arrive, she'd laughed about their clothes, their hair, the Hobart boy's body odor. Still, goofed-up on my mother's diet pills, she had begun chattering away at the boys, and they seemed to become better- and better-looking the longer they stayed in her company.

"Oh, John, John, John!"

"Marsha, Marsha, Marsha!"

Chan—sitting on the kitchen counter, talking to Margret and my mother—tossed a celery stick in our direction. "Why don't you two go play in traffic?" he cried.

"That's right!" My mother pushed up the sleeves of her sweater, lifted her big salad bowl. "Go gargle with peanut butter!"

Chan and Margret exchanged a look of delight—almost like proud parents—and then Chan pushed himself off the counter. "Hey, Matson, how about dishing me up some chili before you go outside?"

"Serve yourself, Bishop!" she called over her shoulder, and with a comic bump and grind, headed down to the basement rec room and the patio beyond.

"But, Matson!" Chan brayed to the delight of the guests. "Matson! I'll starve!"

That night, the cold and the damp made our concrete patio feel like ice, but after the long winter, people were happy to be outside, laughing, huddling close to stay warm. We could hear the rising creek, the rough water echoing off the cliffs. The floodwaters added a new, fecund smell to the pack's familiar stink. Margret brought out the turquoise and gold glasses that had been used as candle holders for the calypso party and—lit up, scattered here and there, near feet as well as on tables and benches—they gave the gathering the look of "spontaneous" glamour so often featured in my mother's magazines. I was not only seduced by such glamour, I wanted to shape it, too, and I squeezed my eyes half-shut so that the fringe of my lashes removed the scene a little further into the distance.

The movements of my mother in the rec room, however, caught my eye, threw me out of the magical scene. She was dialing the telephone, waiting. I remembered, then, that we were worried about my father—even Nancy had come up to me, once, to whisper, "Is Dad back yet? Has Mom heard anything?"—and I felt guilty that I'd been swept along by the beauty of the spring night.

A short while later, my mother came out to the party again and settled herself, Indian-style, on a cushion. I could see her mind was elsewhere even while she smiled and nodded at what Roger Woolum had to say about the limestone that had been quarried for the neighborhood's walls. I wanted to interrupt, suggest that maybe Dad was home now. Maybe he'd parked on the street so he could sneak in, take a quick shave. Right now, he stood under the shower, singing "Danny Boy"—

"You realize," Roger said, "the presence of limestone means billions upon billions of tiny sea creatures—"

"Penny!" Chan pulled me down on his knee as I started for the house. He lifted his beer toward our roof. "Did you know your house is fireproof, Penny? All masonry, and a roof made out of asbestos tile?"

Dr. Hobart—the neighborhood doctor, now our doctor, too—Dr. Hobart leaned forward in an old butterfly chair someone had hauled out from the Woolums' basement. A slack-bodied man with a syrupy, charming laugh, he said, "You know, Chan, the real problem with house fires tends to be the stuff inside them."

Chan ignored Dr. Hobart. "That's a good safe house, Penny. Nineteen-twelve that house was built."

I nodded. "The year my dad was born."

"I'm glad it's the bunch of you that lives here now." Smiling, Chan looked towards the house. "Listen to those dedicated lovers! Where does a person find such a dedicated lover?"

For a moment, I didn't understand that he referred to the "John and Marsha" record. Whoever had put "John and Marsha" on the stereo had forgotten to set the arm, and, through the open windows, over and over, the little 45 had continued to play, just audible above the rising creek and party's conversations.

Dr. Hobart turned towards me. "Say," he teased, "a hot young chick like you didn't come on a date to this affair with an old geezer like Bishop, did you, now, Penny?"

I grinned. Chan pretended to protest: "Hell, Doc, all the girls my own age are married!"

"Tut, tut!" Margret stretched out an arm from the director's chair in which she sat, poked Chan in the knee with her soup spoon. "You might do well to remember, Chan, that all the girls your age aren't *girls* anymore!"

Whoaaa! said the nearby adults. Whoaa!

My own mother laughed at this as she rose to her feet, and—

in a voice both playful and indignant, some imitation of Margret, but much more skillful than in the past—she said, "*I've* encouraged him repeatedly to ask out Anita Regan at our church, or Kay Utne from the grade school, now haven't I, Chan?"

As if he tolled a bell, Chan gave a solemn, sustained pull at the hem of her pants leg. "That you have, Matson."

"Well, all right, then!" She leaned down to gather up a few stray napkins and glasses. I knew why: an excuse for going inside. Once inside, she'd call the little downtown office, Archie's house, maybe even the asphalt plant in Dolores.

"I'm sure both ladies are veddy proper," Chan said. "Hook noses, orthopedic shoes, overbites."

I jumped from his lap in protest. "Not Mrs. Utne! Mrs. Utne's really pretty!"

Chan stood, crooking one arm before his face, as if to ward off a shower of stones, then he called out, "Hey, you need some help with the door, there, Matson?"

I caught up to them before they climbed the basement stairs.

"Look, Matson: it's The Shadow!" Chan said. "I was just telling The Shadow here about your fireproof roof." Then he bounded up the stairs, ahead of us, calling over his shoulder, "I assume you ladies won't mind if I change that damn record."

In the kitchen, on her way to the sink, my mother glanced at the list of telephone numbers she kept on the bulletin board.

"You want me to call some place?" I asked.

"Oh, I don't know." She rinsed a bowl under the tap. "I suppose he'll be here when he gets here."

A spin on his answer to the question I'd heard her ask for years: When will you be home, Bob?

Chan pulled a beer from the refrigerator as he entered the kitchen. My mother held out a glass.

"No glass for me," he said, but took it, filled it halfway to the top, and, with a grin, put it into my hand. "You ever tried beer before, Penny?"

"Chan," my mother protested.

"Oh, hell, Dotty, I've been giving Grace beer since she was old enough to drink from a cup.

"Mom?"

She laughed. "I guess it *is* only a tiny bit."

I drank off most of the beer in one swig, the way I'd have taken a dose of medicine, and both of them laughed.

"But, hey," Chan said, "a fireproof roof! Aren't you two a little impressed?" We laughed at this, too, and then he grabbed my free hand and twirled me around the kitchen in a lazy, light-hearted way. This way, then that. The music he'd put on was the sort he was always bringing to dinner parties: Astor Piazzola's light tangos, that sort of thing, music that was an odd but convincing blend of sweetness and suspense.

"To your mother!" Chan lifted his beer to her as we swept past. The three of us laughed. I clinked my glass against Chan's beer can, and my mother, standing with her back against the counter, grinned. She'd pushed her hair back with a soapy hand and left a crest of bubbles there. I almost told her about it, then decided, no, it was pretty.

"Why, hell," Chan said, "come to think of it, you girls have almost got your own *fallout* shelter down the basement!" and, as we danced, he went on to explain that there was an old cistern off our storage room: tight as a drum, nine by nine, with the eighteen-inch walls of the rest of the house.

Nobody had ever danced with me before. I felt awkward, but also happy. Maybe I was a little drunk? Could a kid get drunk on half a can of beer? At the end of the song, Chan bowed to me, then stepped over to my mother and held up his hand the way people did in movies where the dance would be—a minuet? A waltz?

"Oh, I don't really dance, Chan."

"Well, of course you do!" Chan said, and then she smiled and let him take her hand.

The dancing they did that night was the same sort of dancing he and I had done, playful stuff, an easy movement around the room, almost a promenade. When their song stopped, I danced with Chan again, and then Mother did, and Chan took out another beer so we could all drink a toast to the house—wasn't it a terrific place? he couldn't think of any family he'd rather have live in it than us—and then we all danced together, making little loops around the kitchen, bowing to one another and laughing.

None of us heard my father come in the front door, or noticed him at all until he stepped into the kitchen:

"Say, this looks like a happy bunch!"

Chan grinned. My mother grinned, too, but took a shy step backward, while I—without warning—flew across the room and threw myself, crying, into his arms.

"All hail the conquering hero!" Chan said. My father laughed a little, patted me on the back. Sounding slightly bewildered, he asked, "What's all this about, sweetie?"

"I thought maybe you'd got in an accident!"

"For someone who thought I might have been in an accident, you seemed to be having an awful good time!" he said with a laugh. "Anyway, haven't I told you I don't get in accidents?" He rubbed at his eyes, yawned. A fake yawn, I thought, and felt a little chill.

"So"—my mother edged her way to the sink, sunk her hands back in soapy water before she spoke—"so did you get hold of Archie, Bob?"

"Yes, yes." He waved his hands in the air over his head. "It's—complicated. Apparently these idiots sent us the wrong equipment and Archie had to send back three-quarters of it. Gad!" He laughed. "I don't know why they don't just take a gun and blow my brains out. Put me out of my misery!"

"Whoa, there," said Chan, and set to work getting my father a beer, punching it open, pouring it, all the while telling him what he'd told us about the cistern.

"Penny." From the kitchen doorway, Eleanor Woolum gestured to me, come on.

"What is it?" I asked when I'd joined her in the hall. She didn't answer, but pointed toward the front door, and so I followed her outside.

The moon was full, the light lovely. Eleanor started in the direction of her house, and I trotted along behind without much thought until she turned to whisper, "We're going into Chan's!"

It still strikes me as odd that I didn't resist the suggestion. Maybe it was the beer. Maybe the fact that I'd never really thought of Chan's place—so new it still smelled of builder's supplies—as something *personal*. Chan's house was—a stylish container. Other people's houses seemed almost like their bodies, but Chan's was just an attractive thing he owned, like the Jaguar, or his little Piper Cub, and when Eleanor stood beside his front door, and she said, "Go on, Penny, it's unlocked," I put my hand on the knob, and turned it, and entered.

"You did it." Eleanor let out a little breath. "You did it, you're the one, Penny."

I thought she sounded stupid. She didn't seem to realize that in absolving herself from blame, she also cut herself out of credit for the deed.

Beyond the dimly lit central hall, the house fanned out in darkness. We hesitated for a time, then, slowly, our fingertips brushing the rough brick walls, we glided toward the golden glimmer of a bathroom lit by a night-light.

Really, it was no comfort to be in that bathroom. The night-light made our faces spooky, though Eleanor didn't seem to notice. "Look." She pointed to big sheets of brown paper taped to the walls over the tub. "My mom did those."

I had to go closer in order to see the gold enamel on the craft paper. Nude women. Life-sized.

"She painted them for Chan's birthday."

Out of envy, I said, "They're from an art book. They're Matisse's dancers." Had the paintings been given to Chan at a party my parents attended? If so, I wouldn't have minded, but I didn't remember my parents going to a birthday party for Chan.

"I've been here three times so far," Eleanor said. "Twice with Carrie Hobart. She's the one who figured out he never locks his door. Look at this." She pressed a button on a tube of white plastic that sat on the counter. The tube began to hum. "It's an *electric* toothbrush! Watch!" She snapped a small brush into the appliance, squirted on a bit of paste she took—familiarly—from a drawer. She brushed her teeth.

"You're nuts," I said, and slowly moved back into the dark of the hall, away from Eleanor and the chatter of the toothbrush.

Was I drunk? In the perfect pearly dark of the living room, the pale sheepskin on the floor floated like a rough cloud. I made my way around it with the sense of escaping some danger, and, gratefully, lowered myself into one of Chan's canvas chairs. The heart I normally thought of as my own, as firmly fixed in one place, swung in my chest like a kid on a rope in a barn.

A wing of light flapped behind me: Eleanor opening and closing the refrigerator door. "You want some cream cheese, Penny?"

"Quiet!"

A moment later she appeared beside me, sucking at the white wedge of cheese she'd stuck on her finger. "Come on, you've got to see what's in his bedroom!"

Moonshine flooded the skylight over Chan's bed: to my surprise, his blue sheets were unmade, as if he'd just climbed from them. We never left our beds unmade except on days when Bea Dart came to clean, and I thought it both thrilling and awful that a grown-up would leave his room in such disarray.

"Look!" Eleanor pointed to a cigarette butt in the ashtray on Chan's bed. "Lipstick!"

Instantly I thought: her mother's. But, really, it could have been Bea Dart's, Chan's mother's, anyone's, and I said, "The person didn't necessarily smoke it in here, you know."

"Don't you remember how we saw that blond lady leaving his house?" Eleanor opened the top drawer to one of the room's built-in dressers. "Want to know how I can tell if she and Chan did it? Want to know how I keep track?"

Whatever Eleanor meant to tell me, I didn't want to appear to have asked for, and so I pretended interest in the items on Chan's bookcase: the white marble horse with its tail thick and straight as a bundle of spaghetti, a cluster of framed photographs. I tried to lift the stone horse, but it was too heavy. Then I picked up an enlargement of the Easter photo of Chan's children that Chan had shown us the fall before, and I stepped with it under the moon-full skylight.

"What have you got?" Eleanor darted across the room. "What— oh, that's a really old picture. Hey!" She laughed. "I told you that beret of yours was babyish! It's just like the one Grace has on there, and she's—like, only six or something in that picture."

A white beret with a rim made of white and blue ribbon. My hat. Of course. I'd gone out and bought Grace Bishop's hat.

Eleanor tugged on my arm. "Come look in the drawer."

"Wait." I brought a second photograph under the moonlight. "This one's got your mom and dad in it, Eleanor."

Eleanor gave a bored glance to the photograph—a group of adults clustered around a single engine plane. "They all went to some island one spring. Now come over here!"

"That woman next to Chan looks familiar."

She yanked the photograph from my hands. "The lady with the really short hair is Haldis, and the one with the suitcase, that's Gloria Mott. She was the wife of this bald guy—he's the one Haldis ran off with."

I stared at the photograph. Roger, Margret, Chan, and the strangers who had been their friends before my parents ever came along. The woman Eleanor had pointed out was thin, tan, her almost-white hair blown forward as she crouched to pull a block out from under the plane's front wheels. Was *she* the true beauty? "Are you sure that's Haldis?" I asked.

"Of course! I lived next door to her all my life!"

By that point, I felt as if nothing in Chan's dresser would surprise me—I was Dorothy in Oz—and so I let Eleanor lead me to the open drawer, show me the small cardboard box inside. "You know what this is?" She removed a foil packet from the box, carried it out beneath the skylight so I could see the golden soldier's profile on its front.

I hesitated. "I think, once—my dad and mom brought us back mints like that. From a hotel."

"Mints!" Eleanor whooped, then tore open the packet. Its silver insides seemed to give a spark as the foil ripped, and a small circle of white fell—wet, shining—on Chan's blue sheets.

"It's a *rubber*!" Eleanor flashed her perfect-toothed grin, spooky in the dark. "What a man wears on his wiener when he sticks it in a lady's hole!" She wiggled her hips from side to side. "And one more's gone since I last checked!"

Something physical—as sharp as the heat you could bring up on your hand with a magnifying glass—a *burning* began inside my head and, the next thing I knew, I'd grabbed the box of condoms from the drawer, and—playing happy, jubilant—I cried, "There! There!" and scattered the packets over the room.

Like a shot, Eleanor took off, down the hall and out the front door. I followed close behind. Our eyes were used to the dark by then and we moved swiftly, we didn't bump into a thing.

"Stupid," Eleanor breathed at me as we ran, crouched, along the neighborhood's outer walls. "We'll never be able to sneak in there again!"

LATER THAT night, I woke to the sound of the trains and the rush and the bang of the flooding creek. The light in my room seemed odd, of a different order—silver, metallic, like the glow-in-the-dark waves on my Noah's ark wallpaper. I closed my eyes against that light and whatever it meant to reveal. I knew, however, that I felt guilty—I thought it had something to do with sneaking into Chan Bishop's house, but the idea of dancing in the kitchen kept coming into my head, too, all the laughing and smiling and dancing.

God, I promised, I will never again drink beer, and then I said the Lord's Prayer, the Nicene Creed, the Apostles' Creed, not once each, but several times. Then I imagined the things we would need to take with us into our bomb shelter. I mentally constructed shelves for the cistern and stocked them deep with cheering cans of fruits and vegetables and Boston Brown Bread. I'd never tasted Boston Brown Bread, but always believed it would be fortifying and sweet. Corn, shoe-string potatoes, pork and beans, corned beef. Peaches. My father liked canned peaches. His family rarely had fruit when he was a boy, and he still considered canned peaches a treat.

"Penny?" Slowly, my mother opened my bedroom door. "Are you awake?" she whispered.

Without my glasses on, I saw her as a moth-like creature in

her long, blue nightgown. "I couldn't sleep," she said, but she sounded pleased, excited. "It's this crazy light. Did you notice the light? Come over here by the window. It's the flood."

I put on my glasses, and crossed to her, looked out at the glen. It was molten, and I needed a moment to understand what had happened: the flooding creek had split in two and now rushed over both the dam and the grass, leaving the hulk of the old mill a gray eye in a silver needle.

I smiled up at my mother to show my appreciation of the moment, of her waking me. She laid her arm across my shoulders and gave me a little hug. A perfect moment. I wanted to *fix* it, have the flood stay, running so wild, to have that *amazement* remain. Her cheek on top of my head, she whispered, "You and I are alike, aren't we? We understand each other, right?"

I smiled at her as if her question pleased me. Earlier, when she and Chan and I had been dancing in the kitchen, I'd felt proud of her, and myself, too. But I knew other moments in both of our lives, and as we stood there in the moonlight, our moment of camaraderie began to weigh upon me. I felt the way I suppose a person feels when the drowning victim he means to rescue starts to thrash about, drag him down. I wanted to cut loose from her. But, really, had she truly been drowning— to prevent my mother from *knowing* that what I wanted most of all was to save myself—well, then I would have been willing to go down, too.

III

CHAPTER 14

After that spring's flood subsided, a number of fish remained on the lawns, one upright, held—as if still swimming—by the canes of a rosebush in the Hobarts' lower yard. For a week or so, the broad swath of grass over which the creek had run lay slick and muddy. The next rains, however, washed the grass clean. Only the minuscule shells of river creatures remained behind, and even they had disappeared by the time we left for our summer cottage.

Though the cottage on Lake Bascomb had been built before I was born, I knew a story or two about its construction. How there had never been a blueprint, how the doors hadn't fit. How it had taken some worker's girlfriend, a former WAC, to point out that what the men had built—still carrying around tender memories of the armed services—was a barracks. A two-story rectangle with windows placed for cross ventilation. Two doors on the east, one for entrance, one for exit.

The cottage sat in a woods atop a bank, the lake fifty feet below. The town of Lake Bascomb was several miles away. Closer to farms than shops, we had only to walk up the road for fresh eggs, while a week's laundry meant loading up the car twice for the trip into town and back. That June, we discovered that, in our absence, someone with a BB gun had shot out the big mercury lamp over our drive, and a family of skunks had taken up residence in the pump house.

I was always happy to return to Lake Bascomb, and that year in particular I liked the idea that we could turn our backs on Meander. Despite its pleasures, Meander had been one unfamiliar thing after another. I *knew* how life went at Lake Bascomb, or at least how it had gone in the past.

My father would join us at the cottage on weekends. Nancy and I would run out to welcome him home, and, by the time we'd gotten our hugs, our mother would be there, too, smiling, giving him a kiss. The Carnation man would come in his step van Monday, Wednesday, and Friday. Twice a week, Mr. Ruan would drive by with his nags to pick up hard trash. There would be a summer girl, usually the daughter of family friends, and she would keep Nancy and me partly out of our mother's hair. We would spend most of our day playing in the lake, which was the same silty green as the government-issue blanket my father had brought home from the army.

That summer, however, things were different. It turned out that my father's business duties in Dolores and Meander meant he wouldn't be in Lake Bascomb much at all.

"Lord, I don't see why we didn't just stay in Meander!" my mother said in one of her regular long-distance calls to Margret Woolum. "At least at home I had a washer and dryer!"

That summer, Nancy—who usually let me be her friend from June through August—no longer wanted to ride bikes or build stone huts or listen in on the phone calls of Lake Bascomb's antiquated party-line system. That summer, everything bored Nancy to death. She spent as much time as possible writing letters to her boyfriend and tending to her hair—waxing, shaving, plucking, curling, washing, drying.

"July 1st," she chanted, muttered, sang, whenever she found our company too oppressive. "July 1st." The day she would leave for two months of horse camp with her Meander friends.

To make matters worse, one morning in early June, I turned away from my dreamy study of blue jays screeching outside the picture window and received a terrible message from my mother. After a fruitless search for a summer girl, she had placed a call to Paula Dart. Paula would arrive that afternoon, and my mother didn't want to hear a word of complaint about the matter, thank you.

Nancy whinnied in disgust. "She's—horrible, Mom! And it's not like we need a summer girl anymore."

Woozily, I sat up on the divan. Paula watching me! Every hour of the day!

Mother hiked her swimsuit—she sunbathed with the straps undone so her shoulders wouldn't bear white marks. "Look, kids," she said, "*I'm* the one who needs a summer girl. I've *always* been the one who needed the summer girl."

THE DUSTY Coca-Cola clock in the bus station window said that we were on time, but the lady at the counter explained that the bus had been early. We'd missed Paula's arrival, and she was not in any of the old movie-house seats the bus company had set up in the waiting room. My mother frowned, then went to the filmy plate glass windows and stared out at the parking lot.

"Maybe she didn't come," I said. "Our lucky day."

My mother held up her finger. No more jokes. "You girls check the bathroom. And for goodness sakes, make her feel welcome! I'll see if she's out back."

The bus station ladies' room was typical: a lot of balled-up paper towels, suspicious-looking puddles creeping out from the stalls, a mirror so smudged the reflections it gave back resembled something out of TV dream sequences. I looked to Nancy to see what she meant to do. Nancy leaned against the bathroom wall as if she'd just come to use the toilet. I wanted to call "Paula," see if someone in the stalls answered, then leave—fast. But I felt self-conscious. There were other people in the bathroom: an old lady carefully brushing her teeth at the sink; a very large young woman in a shockingly short pair of cut-off jeans touching up her makeup before the cloudy mirror.

Like Nancy, I took a spot against the tiled walls. Nancy made a face in the direction of the young woman at the mirror. "Prostitute," she whispered.

Were there prostitutes in Lake Bascomb? Maybe, but when the young woman began to sing, "Love Potion No. 9," I knew immediately that we had found Paula Dart.

Hair dyed to the same flat blond as the pine boards my father had bought for replacing planks in our dock. Eyebrows shaved off and drawn in again in lines thin as scuttled parentheses. The eyes themselves were rimmed with a lizardly cerulean, the lashes so stiff and black with mascara that I thought immediately of Haldis Bishop's old sunlamp guards.

"That's Paula," I whispered to Nancy, at just the moment that Paula turned, began to laugh uproariously at Nancy's look of surprise.

"You didn't know it was me, did you? Where's your mom? Out there?" With a last delighted glance in the mirror, Paula started for the door. "She's going to die, right? You two need to use the john, or you coming?

Nancy gave me a kick as we went out the door. I knew what she meant: Paula was the Bizzaro World's version of the B-movie tough girl who folds her arms under her breasts and refuses all kisses until her honey agrees to drive his hot rod in the big race.

"Mrs. P! What d'you think?" Paula called ahead of herself as the three of us—Nancy and I lagging behind—made our way across the waiting room to my mother.

My mother raised a hand to her mouth, asked, "Paula?"

"Surprised you, right?" Paula laughed. "I did it all in the bus station, after Mom dropped me off. This real nice lady, there—she come in the rest room while I did the bleach part and she helped with the timing. You got to do the timing just right." She looked around herself happily. With a wan motion, my mother indicated we should start for the parking lot.

"Larry!" A tall boy in a denim jacket turned as Paula called out to him, "Hey! Gone but not forgotten, right?"

The boy smiled, lifted his hand in a kind of salute. His skin was bad, and he had a queer rolling walk that I supposed he'd mistakenly developed on purpose. Still, he was a good-looking boy, even Nancy registered his good looks.

"Air Force," Paula said to us—not lowering her voice a bit—"on leave."

"This is a small town, Paula," my mother murmured. "People here tend to be quiet."

Paula nodded. Then, quickly, while our mother was lifting the trunk lid, she yanked back the collar of her shirt to show Nancy and me a purplish splotch on her neck. "See?"

Maybe she gave me a conspirator's wink, but I don't think so. I think she'd basically abandoned her past in the Meander bus station—a notion that, back then, seemed perfectly possible to me.

As we drove to the cottage, I pointed out certain landmarks—the water tower, Elders' State Park, the Dairy Queen—but Paula didn't seem interested. She switched on the radio—she rode up front with my mother—and she started telling a story about a Mrs. White for whom her mother also cleaned. "And you know the Hubbels?" It seemed that at the Whites' last party, there had been some mix-up in invitations—

My mother cut this story off. "We certainly wouldn't want you carrying tales about *us* to other people. 'Do unto others—'"

"Before them others do it unto you," Paula finished with a laugh, and then, the tip of one tennis shoe pressed to the dashboard, her heel bouncing in time to Domenico Modugno's "Volaré," she explained that she preferred the instrumental version over Modugno's because with the instrumental she could be the singer.

Nancy kicked me. I kicked back. My mother glanced into the rearview mirror, gave her head a quick shake.

Of course, there was no way my mother could be happy with Paula. Hiring Paula had been an act of desperation. She didn't like Paula any more than Nancy or I did. As it turned out, however, her bad opinion of Paula made a difference in my mother's life: once Paula moved in, my mother hid her amphetamines.

Hiding the amphetamines meant, of course, that—for the first time—my mother actually got the effects she paid for. Also, that she suddenly spent a lot of her time walking around the cottage with her jaw clenched tight, looking like actors in race car movies when the camera zooms in to show them speeding around the track at hundreds of miles an hour.

On the telephone to Margret: "All I can think is that the pharmacy here has fresher pills. In one week I've lost seven pounds! Food"—she was a little breathless, doing waist twists—"for the first time I really see you only need it to survive."

During this phone call, Nancy and I read on opposite ends of the divan. (The *divan*: a cottage name. In Meander, we had a *couch*.) At mention of the pills, Nancy had lifted her head, hoping, I suppose, for some clue to their hiding place. She had torn apart the cottage one afternoon but never discovered the spot. Since Paula's arrival, Nancy had *gained* seven pounds in a mad dive into the potato chips, cookies, and ice cream she'd denied herself for most of the last year. She was, of course, still very thin, but her face, especially her eyelids, had the swollen, transparent quality of blisters.

While our mother talked to Margret—the two of them now practicing French phrases from the set of foreign language records they'd each bought before we left for the summer— Paula stood out by the trash barrel, watching the fire, and singing a full-throated "My Funny Valentine." A depressing song. What kind of lover spent a whole song telling his sweetheart how deficient he found her looks? Wasn't love supposed to make the beloved beautiful? To distract myself from the weight of the song's lyrics, the seduction of the tune, I traced

the design on the divan slipcover with my tongue: otherworld-
ly flowers and vines in green and gold and red, all unfurled
across a field of cream. Who was I to know that the cloth
aspired to anything higher than itself? I loved for themselves
the printed-on stitches that the designer dreamed might make
the stuff look like the crewelwork it imitated.

My mother pushed the telephone further under her jaw so
she could do deep knee bends. "*Je suis—ennui*," she said uncertainly, and then, "Tell me things, Margret. Tell me funny things
people said at the club. Gossip at me, why don't you?"

"Mrs. Powell." The screen door slammed as Paula came in
with the trash basket. "Get off the phone. You got company."

Lorraine Bergreen—a little partridge of a woman, short
curls the silvery-brown of streusel topping—and her daughter Jeannie. Jeannie and I grinned at each other while our
mothers exchanged awkward hugs and Nancy sunk lower on
the divan, keeping herself out of sight. Paula was introduced
and there was some discussion of the Bergreens' trip from
Dekalb, how long it had taken, and had they found the cottage in good shape?

Oh, the Bergreens were full of a story: unlocking the cottage
door, they'd been forced to one side as a woman and two kids
rushed past, and disappeared into the woods, leaving in their
wake, dirty sheets, bags full of trash.

"It smelled in there," Jeannie said, and stuck out her tongue,
held her nose. She looked just like her mother, except that her
hair hung down her back in a very straight ponytail that she
was forever drawing to a moist point between her lips.

"Did you call the police, Lorraine?" my mother asked.

"Oh, yes, yes, but they were gone with the wind! Say, Dot, you're getting to be a skinny Minnie!"

My mother swatted in her direction. "I swear, I never see you, Lorraine, but you say I've lost weight! If I'd lost all the weight you've said I'd lost, I'd have—vanished years ago!"

Paula grinned at Lorraine Bergreen. "Mrs. Powell's taking diet pills now. That's how come she's losing weight so good."

"Paula." My mother did a comical throat-clearing to suggest she didn't appreciate Paula's remark. "Maybe you'd like to go upstairs and relax while we visit?"

After Paula had gone upstairs—"I wish I had a tape recorder! The things she says!" my mother whispered—Lorraine brought out a package of Oreos from her big purse.

"I hope you won't kill me, Dotty, if you're dieting?"

Laughing, my mother wagged a finger at her old friend. "Damn you, Lorraine!"

Lorraine looked surprised by "damn," but tickled, too. "Well, we've got to keep up our energy to tame these wild Indians," she said, batting her eyes at Jeannie and me as she tore open the package with her teeth.

"Mother," Nancy called from the main room, "are you eating cookies?"

"No, dear," Mother called back in a musical, we-have-company voice. "Why don't you come say hello to Jeannie and Lorraine?"

A finger stuck in her copy of *The Catcher in the Rye*, Nancy came to the door of the kitchen. By then, Nancy had surely read *The Catcher in the Rye* a good five times. It was, she assured me, a book I was too immature to understand, a book that reflected her thoughts on the world precisely.

"Oreos," she said, and gave the cookies a lover's furious, passionate glance before hurrying upstairs.

"Apparently our dear *Paula* said something to Nan about her ankle bones being thick," my mother whispered to Lorraine. "I, of course, have to join Paula for *Fit and Trim* every morning if—and I quote—I ever hope to get rid of my 'flabby butt.'"

Lorraine stared with gratifying outrage in the direction of the upstairs tub, now thundering over our heads as Paula ran a bath. "You're not serious!"

"Oh, yes"—my mother snapped her mouth shut, like a fish taking a worm—"and, damn it, Lorraine, I go along! I get out a chair and put my legs on it for the sit-ups—the whole nine yards—otherwise the little snip thinks she's better than me!"

Lorraine laughed. My mother's own glee was different, hot and shiny and mutable as glass on the pipe. She stayed on her feet while the rest of us sat, eating cookies. She used a wooden match stick to remove a line of grime that had built up along the metal strip fronting the counter tops. Since the arrival of Paula, and gaining access to the true amphetamines, she had stripped the wax from the wooden floors, reapplied it, buffed it; painted the dock and pump house; alphabetized the linen cabinet and the pantry. Asparagus, beans, beets, corn—

"Oh!" My mother looked towards the stairs, held her finger up to her lips, a signal that we should be quiet. "Get this," she said softly, "the other day, she was sashaying about with two neckerchiefs tied across her front—which she calls, get this, 'The Boobsey Twins'—and who should come by but the Fuller Brush man? Now—isn't this interesting?—the Fuller Brush man, who, last year, came maybe once a month, who I used to have to *hint* about samples to, he's here every couple days with free lipstick for all!"

"Maybe he likes *you*, Dotty! Did you ever think of that?" Lorraine smiled, then looked down as if what she had said embarrassed her. "You're pretty sexy with that new hairdo and all!"

"Oh, stop!" My mother covered her face with her hands, then, blindly grabbed for the cookie bag, and popped an Oreo, whole, into her mouth. "Woof, woof!" she said, making a point of the grand bulge of cookie in her cheek. "Woof, woof, woof!"

Lorraine laughed, but I supposed—because I sometimes felt the same way—that what she really wanted was some sort of reassurance from my mother: *Yes, you're right, I am different, you're not imagining it.* Lorraine and my mother had been friends for a long time, and though—in my company—they mostly talked about the bugs in their tomato plants or the shapes of their rear ends, I knew they often put a pleat in their private conversations when Jeannie and I entered the room. They'd certainly shared at least some of the facts of their lives.

At any rate, what my mother *did* go on to say to Lorraine that morning—while pouring glasses of milk for Jeannie and me— was that the people in Meander could be terrible snobs. With a swooping movement, she snatched up a grapefruit spoon someone had left on the kitchen table, and, pretending it was a long and fancy cigarette holder—though I'd never seen any-one in Meander use a cigarette holder—she gave it an elegant tap. She straightened her glasses and peered through them as if through some dowager's lorgnette. "'Now *what* did you say your husband does, dear?'" she creaked.

The Bergreens laughed, but I could see they were surprised by such dramatics. Clearly, instead of proving she was the same old Dotty, my mother's impersonations showed she'd changed; and, to distract the Bergreens from those changes, I rushed in:

"There's this girl I play with, Eleanor Woolum, she goes around all the time acting like she's Queen of Sheba." I tossed my head back, and swished around the cottage kitchen. A little statue of a cedar waxwing sat on the fireplace mantel, and I gave its base a haughty glance. "Of course, you realize, Penny, that *my* father's brilliant! And my *mother* has a twenty-four-inch waist! Furthermore, the richest man in town, darling Channing Bishop—*you* know Bishop Meat, don't you?—darling Uncle Chan says my mother's the only truly civilized woman he knows. And you *do* understand, don't you, that he could never be best friends with *your* parents!"

Lorraine and Jeannie stopped laughing when they realized my mother hadn't joined in, that she'd put down the grapefruit spoon and now stared at me with a fierce light.

"My goodness, Penny!" Her lips twitched as if in some private amusement, though only an idiot would have thought she was amused. She rearranged a few hair pins in her twist. "My goodness gracious!"

UNLIKE MY mother, I felt disconnected from Meander. A week or so later, when my father laughingly reported he'd discovered a collection of empty scotch bottles behind the furnace, I found myself on a kind of swiftly moving pinwheel of furnace rooms, basements. The colonial, the pink ranch, the house in Meander. Before I regained my bearings, I had to set myself down on an imaginary compass rose, face north, and fix in my head the base of the elm that grew in front of the window well outside the furnace room in Meander.

"Scotch bottles?" my mother said. "Who on earth?"

"Our painter, I guess," my father said with a laugh, and she laughed, too, as if the painter's mess were now just a jolly memory.

At the time of this conversation, we'd all just returned from a drive around the lake in a new, blue convertible my father had brought to the cottage as a surprise for my mother. "Can we afford this?" my mother had murmured as she and Nancy and Paula and I climbed into the car.

My father laughed. "Honey, Archie's got a deal cooking right now. He's hooked up with some people who build government housing. Thousands and thousands of doors!"

Still, it was clear my mother felt uncomfortable with the car, and over dinner, my father said, "I don't know, I give Mother a new car, girls, but I don't think she likes it!"

She demurred. Of course she liked it.

"I love it to pieces!" Paula crowed. "Hand it over, babe!"

My mother cringed, then asked my father—who looked aghast at almost everything Paula said—if he'd seen Margret or anyone while in Meander.

Well, he'd had dinner, once, at the Woolums'. "Chan was mowing his lawn, and I was giving some water to that little piece of privet. Margret came out and invited us in for lamb chops! Chan"—he glanced at Paula, then broke off whatever story he had meant to share—"I guess his kiddies are coming to visit soon."

Paula grinned. "So, did Mr. Bishop have his shirt on?"

My parents exchanged a glance. "What?" said my father.

"Remember that party of yours when he came without his shirt? I was thinking"—she wiggled the stripes of Maybelline Black that had taken the place of her eyebrows—"some people mow their yards without their shirts on."

After dinner, when Paula went out back to burn the trash, my father winked at Nancy and me, busily washing dishes, then whispered with a glance out the window and in the direction of the ash can, "Mother, what hast thou wrought, dear?"

She laughed. "So what were you starting to say about Chan?"

He glanced at Nancy, me. He said, "Oh, later."

THE NEXT Monday, not long after my father left for the week, Lorraine and Jeannie Bergreen came by. "Hey, Dotty," Lorraine called through the screen door, "I brought over that recipe for lasagna where you don't have to cook the noodles first! Kind of crummy, but, man, is it easy!"

As I let the Bergreens in, I rolled my eyes. In the shower, Paula was singing Connie Francis's "Who's Sorry Now?" The Bergreens rolled their eyes, too, and, giggling, the three of us headed towards the kitchen and my mother.

Actually, we hadn't seen as much of the Bergreens as usual. The last time they'd been by, Jeannie and I had gotten into an argument. "You think your family's better than mine," she'd said in parting. Which was absolutely true. Whatever troubles I had with my family, I assumed it was the best family to belong to. On the other hand, I assumed everyone felt this way about their own family, and that what Jeannie really wanted was for me to consider *her* family better than mine.

"Dotty, you got a new car!" Lorraine called. "I guess things must be going well for Bob after all?"

I waited anxiously for the answer as my mother took a last swipe at the kitchen counters. The smile she turned on Lorraine had a cautionary but unemotional quality, like one of those little signs that indicate the fence in front of you is electrified. "Oh, who knows, Lor!" She pressed hard on *knows*, as if all of us would be just *so* relieved to change the subject. "Say, did you meet those new people—the Cranes—from St. Louis?"

Lorraine smiled as if she, too, were half-relieved my mother had found a way not to answer her question. "Mr. Corn Futures Genius and the pretty young thing? They were out on their porch last night, *holding hands*."

"Ha!" said my mother. "Well, she's pregnant, so that ought to last about—" She broke off after a glance at Jeannie and me. "Bob met him—Dave—before, I guess. They're going sailing next weekend."

"'Scuse me, Mrs. Powell! 'Scuse me!" In the doorway stood Paula, head wrapped in one towel, body another. "I just got to thinking the kids might like to go to the drive-in for lunch."

"Ah." My mother turned to wink at Lorraine. "You were thinking *they* might like to go to the drive-in, Paula?"

"Yeah."

"Then you must have forgotten I've got a luncheon?"

"Oh"—Paula raised her absent eyebrows into the bland reaches of her forehead—"I guess I thought you'd changed your mind. I mean, you haven't done yourself up—"

In Meander, my mother had acquired—though only for special occasions—an odd, barking little laugh, which she used now. "Well, excuse me, Paula! Next time you tell me well in advance what I ought to do before I expose myself to the world! Maybe plastic surgery? Or will a trip to the beauty parlor suffice?"

Paula grinned. "You're teasing, Mrs. Powell, but if you want me to do a makeover sometime, I got plenty of ideas."

"Oh, Paula"—my mother fanned the fingers of one hand at the base of her neck, some arch gesture meant to make Lorraine laugh—"do tell!"

"So, Dotty," Lorraine interrupted, "where you off to?"

"Number one, dye your hair blond. I bet you were blond as a kid, and that's what your coloring's best for." Paula grinned. "You dye your hair blond, Mr. Powell might stay home more often!"

My mother gave Lorraine a vivacious wink. "Dye my hair blond." Her voice was creamy as my piano teacher's when she wanted to give me the idea of *legato*. "Well, that'd be a change all right."

Lorraine and Jeannie and I laughed, and then my mother joined us, and we all went on laughing. I would, however, have been happy to forget the incident, but, a few days later, Jeannie insisted on telling a girl named Mary Frances Schwab all of the details.

At the time, I was reading an old *Saturday Evening Post* I'd found on the Schwabs' front porch—actually the Crosleys' porch, for the Schwabs were just renting the Crosley cottage. Even the magazine belonged to the Crosleys. "How one man learned the secret of handling girls who insist on having their way." That was the caption to the *Post's* story, "The Lady and the Brute," in which the hero has trouble controlling his fiancée until, on a hunting trip, he dreams that he meets a wild cave girl and subdues her with a good crack to the jaw. Thereafter, the hero discovers he has only to threaten a spanking in order to make his fiancée toe the line. Thus both the modern woman and cave woman are made happy by the hero's measured brutality.

I was wondering over this, and the feeling of both despair and excitement the story aroused in me, when Jeannie told Mary Frances Schwab about Paula's "makeover" offer, and worse, about a drive we had taken in my mother's new convertible.

"All these boys were out in front of the snack stand by the park, and Penny's mom is driving by—feeling real cool in her new car—and one of the boys whistles, and *she* thinks he's whistling at *her*, but he goes, like, "'Not you, lady! The *car!*'"

Mary Frances Schwab was Jeannie's and my age, but a semi-invalid—arthritic, asthmatic. Arthritis had baked her hands pink and shiny as rose quartz, and her voice came out a kind of wheeze. I didn't feel I could get angry at Mary Frances for laughing at the story, but I shouted at Jeannie, "My mom didn't think they were whistling at her! She never thought that! Don't be nuts! That's why she and your mom laughed about it so much—because the boys *thought* that's what she'd think!"

Jeannie smiled at Mary Frances. "Well, yeah, I didn't mean she thought—*necessarily*—they were whistling at her. Anyway, it was *funny*. What he shouted and all."

"Some boy *insulting* my mom is funny?"

Mrs. Schwab inserted her head into the porch. Worry over Mary Frances had worn her down, made her edgy. She never looked as if she got enough sleep, enough to eat. She never went anywhere, and her hair stuck up like frayed rope. "Girls?" She set her hands on the spoons of her hips. "Problems?"

According to my mother, the Schwabs were in Lake Bascomb because of Mary Frances. Lake Bascomb had the New Hope Clinic, which we, and everyone else that we knew, understood to be a place of quackery, its "doctor" charging desperate patients outrageous fees to send them—through their home faucets and stoves—special healing currents. "Still," my mother always said, "we don't make fun of him to his believers, Penny. He may be the only thing some people have to hang onto."

When Mrs. Schwab left the room, Mary Frances leaned close to Jeannie, whispered, "Want to come to my room and see my horse collection, *Jeannie*?"

Jeannie poked the damp point of her ponytail into her cheek and looked at me. "Well," she said—neither of us particularly liked Mary Frances; we thought of our visits to her as good deeds—"maybe Penny wants to see, too."

I pinched at the couch's rough fabric, a familiar banana leaf print of gray and maroon and green. Out in the road, a tall girl in the distance was slowly resolving into Paula Dart. "No. My summer girl's out there," I said, "I've got to go."

"*Penny*!" Jeannie protested. "You know I think your mom's *pretty*!"

I was startled by this admission but said, only, "Do I?" Quite cool, my gaze seemingly elsewhere, though I spied how Jeannie's eyes trembled as if the pupils were pretty pebbles someone had just dropped into a stream. Feeling both sick and triumphant, I made my way toward the door, and down the steps.

Paula was *not* looking for me, but for a boy she'd bumped into at the pharmacy the day before. With a broad wink, she informed me he was a "hunk of tuna."

"Did my mom leave for the laundry?"

She nodded. "Let's go back to the house. He might show up there. We can watch *The Day Breaks*."

A soap opera. Something my mother would have considered trash. On *The Day Breaks* a well-coiffed brunette struggled against the embrace of a beefy blond in what—from its whiteness of cupboard and costumes—appeared to be a hospital setting. Paula explained, "That's Nurse Ruth, and the guy kissing her's Dr. Rob Davis. I don't know what's going on since your mom don't let me watch, but I guess they been to a party. He's English. You'll see. Women can't resist Dr. Davis. I been watching since I was littler than you, and, I kid you not, that guy's bedded down every babe on the show."

I glanced across the main room to Nancy. Over in the far corner, she held *The Catcher in the Rye* in her lap. She appeared to be reading, but her grin implied that she, too, listened to Paula.

"Our mom would have a fit if she knew we watched this," I said.

Paula laughed. "Your mom don't let you breathe! My mom and me watch *The Day Breaks* together! When she's doing her ironing, she always watches, so she really knows the soaps. Dr. Rob—he's the kind she warns me against. The guy she's crazy about is Vincent Parnell from *Heart in Hand*. 'Scuse me"—Paula suddenly started for the door—"this'll be for me."

"What'll be for her?" I whispered to Nancy.

She pointed her novel at a big, good-looking boy just then

loping across the lawn in front of the picture window. "Him, I guess."

Eldon. Beautiful Eldon whose thick hair was brown where the sun didn't reach, but mostly a sweet straw color. Eldon had just come off work, Paula said, as she seated him on the couch. "Eldon works for the Highway." She tapped an index finger against one of the boy's biceps as if checking for ripeness.

Eldon nodded, then gave our cottage a sour look. "Me and a buddy come through this neighborhood last spring and ruined his whole undercarriage on them speed bumps out there. Paula told me your old man put them in."

Without looking up, Nancy said, "You must have been speeding. Also, we don't refer to my father as 'the old man.'" Then she laughed a little, though whether at her book or Eldon I couldn't tell. I could tell, however, that she felt good in her worst way, and might soon say something mean—which had to do with the fact that she had managed to not eat anything at all for the last two days, and that her hairset had turned out perfectly, the ends of her new "flip" just so.

"Also"—she stared at Paula—"you know the rule. No boys in the house when Mom's not here."

Paula ran her bare instep down Eldon's calf, something I'd never seen a person do in my life. Eldon didn't seem to notice. He looked around the main room, up at the ceiling, out to the kitchen: a prospective buyer, a robber casing the joint.

Voice buttery, Paula tilted her head towards Nancy. "Don't mind that one, Eldon. That's Nancy, and she's a pain in the-you-know-where. None of them thinks how it is for me, being here, without no privacy. The mom got me so's she can go out and do whatever her heart desires, but when do I do what I want?"

Eldon stood. From the pockets of his blue jeans he extracted a good deal of change, a half-stick of Juicy Fruit gum, a pair of nail clippers, and a square foil package identical to the ones I'd seen in Chan Bishop's bedroom.

"Let's see here"—he palmed the package, slipped it back into his pocket—"let's see." He handed Paula a fifty-cent piece. "Have them walk to the Odd Fellows Park for ice cream, why don't you?"

Nancy protested, "I'm not five years old, you know!"

Eldon grinned. "So buy yourself a pack of cigarettes, then." When he stretched, a crescent of his brown belly showed between his blue jeans and tee shirt. All three of us girls looked. He saw us look. He stretched a little higher. Nancy and I looked away in embarrassment.

"Christ almighty!" He eased himself back on the couch once more. "Have a beer, Nancy, you're so god-damned mature!"

Once we were outside, on our way, Nancy smiled up at the sky. I didn't see why. The sun was hot; the light, once entered, not nearly so pleasant as it had appeared from indoors.

"What is it?" I said.

"I could get him away from her in—oh, about five minutes."

"Why'd you want to do that?" I asked. "Except he's cute?"

Nancy didn't answer, just pulled her rat tail comb from the pocket of her shorts, carefully ran the comb through her flip. I decided not to tell her about Eldon's rubber. Chances were she'd say I was disgusting, I shouldn't even know about such things.

THE ODD Fellows Park sat a mile or so up the road. We'd just started back for the cottage with our ice cream when my mother's convertible rolled to a stop ahead of us on the shoulder.

"Uh-oh," I said as we ran toward the car. "What are you going to say, Nan?"

"The truth."

My mother frowned as we climbed in. "Where's Paula?"

Demurely, Nancy replied. "Well, this boy came over. He gave us money to go for ice cream."

"Paula sent you *away* from the house?"

Nancy gave a bland nod. "I guess you said you weren't going to be back till four?"

My mother stepped on the gas, sent the shoulder gravel flying. "I had a *feeling* I should come home. I just had a feeling." She never slowed until we screeched to a stop in our drive.

The screen door was hooked shut.

"Open up, in there! Pronto!"

From upstairs, Paula called she'd be right down, she'd just been getting ready to take a bath.

"Good Lord!" My mother gave the hooked door a series of little yanks, then turned her frown on Nancy. "You should have known better than to leave!"

"Coming, coming!" Paula called.

"I told her no boys," Nancy said.

The sidewalk outside the door held our footprints: Penny, Nancy, Dotty, Bob, 1950. Someone had held me for the print of

my own baby foot—so vague, so tiny it looked like an enlargement of one of those gelatinous creatures viewed under a
microscope.

"Lord," my mother said.

Behind the screen door stood Paula, wrapped in her beach
towel. That beach towel was a thing of wonder to me, with its
life-size blond in black bikini and straw hat, transistor radio
perched beside the flip hairdo. Paula's face had a funny, puffy
look, but she was smiling, showing all her terrible teeth. "Sorry
I ain't dressed, but I didn't want to keep you waiting!"

"What on earth!" My mother pushed past Paula, hurried up
the stairs. "You send the girls up the road all alone so you can
do who-knows-what?"

Paula gave Nancy and me a severe glance before calling,
"Eldon left, Mrs. Powell, right after he was nice enough to give
money to your girls for cones." She sounded prim. "I was going
to take a bath just now. That's why the door was locked."

Nancy snorted, "Yeah, right," and hurried after our mother.

Their going upstairs was what made the two of them miss the
sight of a pair of bare feet trembling at the top of the frame of
our picture window, and then the whole of naked Eldon dropping down into the purple and yellow pansies in my mother's
brick planter.

Paula looked at Eldon, then me, then, very casually, out the
screen door, as if everything she saw were of equal interest.

Maybe if she hadn't stood there beside me, I would have
called, "Mom! He just went out the window!" But I kept my
mouth shut, and, actually, felt only relief as Eldon bundled his
clothes under his arm and vanished down the bank.

"Okay!" My mother's heels tapped the stairs as she descended. "I don't know just what went on here, but I've got a pretty good idea."

Paula sighed. She inspected the ends of a bundle of her hair. "So, are you saying I'm *fired*?"

My mother seemed baffled. She must have expected an argument or tears. "If it weren't for your mother—well, just don't you ever pull anything like this again!" She glared at Paula, then banged out the screen door and started across the lawn in the direction of the Bergreens' cottage. Brisk, attentive, like a person making her way through heavy traffic—that was how she looked.

From the top of the steps, Nancy called down, "You don't fool me, Paula."

Paula laughed. "I didn't fool her neither," she said, "but I'm still here!"

CHAPTER 15

Dave Crane thought he'd met Archie Jones back when both of them worked in New York! Wasn't that something? "This would have been back when Archie was selling for Andersen."

Waiting for her response to this information, my father smiled up at my mother.

She slid a poached egg onto his plate, wet her lips, murmured, "Did you ask what he *thought* of Archie?"

My father gave an indignant laugh. "Why, he considered him quite a guy! What on earth, Mother?" With the flat of his palm, he reasserted the crease in the morning newspaper. "Any-hoo, I can't eat this now! I've got to get over to Dave's. They moved up the first race this morning."

After he left, my mother stood staring out the kitchen window. Blades of mown grass stuck to her feet and ankles from her trip outside for the morning paper.

"Can I go swimming, Mom? Is it long enough since I ate?"

"Probably."

Probably? "Maybe I'll wait a little longer," I offered.

"I don't know what he's doing with that Crane," she murmured. "One more wheeler-dealer."

I was glad when the phone rang—one long, two short, our signal on the party line—and she hurried to answer it.

Paula—in the bathroom, bleaching her hair—yelled, "Somebody going to get that?"

"It's for me," my mother yelled back, then repeated, quietly, "it's for me."

Margret Woolum.

Recently, my father had complained about all the long-distance calls my mother was making. I'd even heard grumbling from Mary Frances Schwab, whose family shared our party line:

"Your mom's always on the phone! We can hardly make a call!"

"How do you know it's *my* mom?"

Mary Frances and Jeannie Bergreen and I were in the Bergreens' boat house at the time. Mary Frances tipped her head back as if reading something off the rafters and said, "'Oh, Lord, Margret, when Bob saw that last book you sent, he about had kittens!'" Mary Frances lowered her gaze, then let it shift to where I sat on a pile of life jackets. She was no dummy, she knew she had me. "They speak foreign sometimes, and there's a man, too, sometimes, a foreign guy."

"A *man*?" Jeannie said. She turned to look at me. "Who?"

I made a big deal of laughing, bent over at the waist, ho, ho, ho. "It's a *record*! She and this friend of hers have French language records they practice with! That's what you heard!"

Now, on the telephone with Margret, my mother cried out with gusto: "*Tant pis!* You poor thing."

The bathroom door gave its usual pop, and out stepped Paula in a bath towel. "So what do you think, Penny?" She bowed in front of me where I sat on the divan, presented me with her newly bleached hair. "Did I miss anything?"

"Looks okay to me."

"Maybe someday you'll be helping *her* do this," Paula whispered, widening her eyes in my mother's direction.

"Oh, well," I muttered. My mother's bleaching her hair struck me as pretty unlikely. But once, on a trip to the drugstore, Paula had convinced me that we should use the change left over from buying Nancy's ear medicine to buy my mother a box of hair dye.

"Definitely blond," Paula had said. "And bold. She's got strong bones, you know."

A banner across the drugstore shelf had been emblazoned with the familiar logo: "If I have only one life, let me live it as a blonde!" Dozens of blonds, but I had made a quick choice: "Snow Queen," a color that looked as if it would be pure white in the sunlight, and have the luster of pearls.

"I know!" Paula stood, adjusted her bath towel, pulled me to my feet. "Let's show Nancy!"

"Show her what?"

"Snow Queen!"

Upstairs, seated on her bed, Nancy studied the box of hair dye we presented for her inspection. She pulled out the crinkly sheet of instructions from the box and, chewing her lip, read them over. My cheeks warmed, the way they did at a birthday party when someone was opening my gift, and I didn't yet know whether they liked it or not.

"God!" Nancy pushed the box back at Paula. "You two are disgusting. Just—go away! I want to get back to my book."

I didn't go swimming that morning. Swimming wasn't much fun without Nancy, and I didn't want to see Jeannie. I lay in the hammock in the far corner of the yard, a pair of ancient binoculars resting on my chest. From time to time, I used them to pick out Dave Crane's sail number in that distant flock. I worried about my father sailing with Dave Crane. I followed the course of the boat through the race and home again—Dave Crane making numerous nervous tacks in his efforts to reach his dock. For a time, I even watched the two of them as they bailed the boat, spread the jib and mainsheet out across the Crane's lawn. But what good did my watching do? Eventually, the two disappeared into the Crane cottage. When my father finally did arrive home, he was singing "Barnacle Bill." He was pink with sunburn and Bloody Marys and admiration for Dave.

"Hello, girls!" He paused above us—I'd coaxed Nancy and Paula into playing a game of Monopoly on the main room's floor—then he called merrily into the kitchen, "I tell you, Dotty, this Crane can't be more than thirty-two, three, but, the way he tells it, he's already socked away millions!" He dropped down on the divan to remove his canvas shoes. His feet were water-wrinkled, the toenails broad and tinged with amber.

"Man, oh, man, there aren't enough hours in the day, are there?" He carried his shoes to the cold furnace grate where he set them upside down to dry. He was full of gusto. That evening, over dinner, he quoted one of his old standbys—punctuating his words with the knife in his hand—"There are men in the ranks who will always stay in the ranks. Why? I'll tell you why: simply because they haven't got the ability to get things done!"

This was shortly before he stood and explained that he was sorry to eat and run but he needed to take a gander at Dave's portfolio. "But don't let me rush the rest of you!" He rubbed at the tip of his nose, the same gesture he always made—falsely nonchalant—whenever he realized he'd just sped past a patrol car.

My mother considered the food on her plate with widened eyes. "Bob." She glanced at Paula, as if weighing the wisdom of speaking in front of her. "Bob, does it seem like a good idea to you to get involved in new investments right now? This Dave—"

"Why, Mother,"—in the light, almost gay, voice that could signal either his bitterest anger or his truest happiness, my father said—"surely I can *look*, can't I, Mother?"

She didn't take the bait. She said, "Let's talk about something else. Who'd you see last week in Meander?"

Like a swimmer attempting to clear his ears—do I *hear* you right?—my father thumped his head a little, then winked at Nancy and me; I don't know about Nancy, but I—unable to stop betraying my mother—smiled back.

"Well, let's see. I talked Bishop into a game of Ping-Pong one afternoon. Apparently his kids had just gone back to Arizona, or wherever."

My mother nodded. "Margret said something about that. I talked to her on the phone today. Actually, Chan was there, too. At her house. I talked to Chan, too. Briefly."

"I trust *you* didn't call *her* long distance?"

She bit her lip. "She called me, Bob."

"Glad to hear it!"

"Maybe we should check that last phone bill, Bob. The little you're here, half the time you're calling Archie—"

My father raised a hand, lowered his eyes in Paula's direction. Without a word, Nancy left the table. She took her fork with her, and used it to eat pie straight from the pan on the counter. My parents didn't seem to notice, and to keep them distracted I said, "Dad, I didn't know you could play Ping-Pong!"

"*What*?" He laughed. "Any fool can play Ping-Pong, dear!"

Dryly, my mother said, "I can't play Ping-Pong," and then added, in a little whistling breath, "So, tell us, Bob, who *won*?"

"Who *won*?" My father laid his palms on the table, bent forward over his plate, opened his mouth wide in comic injury. "Who won? Why, *Matson*! I won. Who on earth did you think?"

CHAPTER 16

The day my mother and I took Nancy to Meander to catch her camp train, we stopped at our house: sunk as deep in green as Sleeping Beauty's castle in its thorns, more gloomy and beautiful than ever. I already missed Nancy. Missing her— looking for something to fill me up—I drifted through the rooms, opening cupboards and drawers, fingering my mother's old collection of tiny tea cups, her little box of glass drink stirrers topped by tiny birds: glass roosters and robins and cardinals. Stay away from something long enough—especially if you're a child—and that thing gains power. Open a long-closed drawer and even a gnawed-upon pencil, eraser worn to slick black, possesses a secret: unfamiliarity overlaying the familiar. It doesn't last, of course—it burns off like haze in the morning—but I knew the charm of that effect. I even looked in the refrigerator. The foods my father kept for his stays in Meander were salami, ring bologna, sharp cheddar, fat and spicy and delicious.

"Can I have some?" I asked.

"No, no, Daddy might count on it for his supper!"

I debated going upstairs. I wanted to look at my stash of foods and the little pile of handkerchiefs my Grandma Matson sent each year with my birthday check. I knew the handkerchiefs would smell like wood and spice after a month closed up in my drawer. I also knew that they would be even further behind a veil of strangeness by the end of August, and I decided not to chance the destruction of that veil by looking too soon.

This being the case, while my mother went down to the basement to put in a load of the laundry she'd carted from the cottage, I carried a box of Ritz crackers into the den and turned on *The Day Breaks*. I looked out at the gray sky while the TV warmed up. Maybe Paula would be watching the show at the cottage. Or maybe she'd gone off with one of the amazing number of people she seemed to meet on her days off. We had asked if Paula wanted to come with us to Meander. To our relief, she'd said, "Heck no!"

"Penny." My mother crossed the den with a stack of magazines, dropped them on the coffee table with a little slap. She'd begun to walk a little differently that summer, a change that was most obvious when she was barefoot. She moved on her toes, which transformed her limp into a sway; and walking on her toes made her calf muscles tighten, their definition done up in what could only be described as silver. For the first time in my memory, she gave the impression of inhabiting her body; she'd slipped into it as if it were something previously kept in storage.

"Penny, I thought I'd go visit Margret. The laundry's going to take a while." She drew a five-dollar bill from her skirt pocket. "If you're hungry, you can go downtown and eat, do a little shopping. As long as you're back by, say, five."

I got up and turned off the TV. "I'll ask Eleanor if she wants to come along."

"Eleanor's off at some camp now, too. Art camp. I just talked to Margret on the phone."

As I started off towards town, a fine mist began to fall, and I experienced a kind of thrill: the small clay figures that sat before the little shingled house underwent an enchantment, became— self-possessed, alive in their foggy world. I trembled and grinned as I walked toward the fuzzy reflection of myself that I found in the windows of shops. Perhaps my sense of strangeness was what led me into several stores I'd never visited before, including the army surplus and Daryl's News, where I drank the El Toro that Nancy had sworn contained alcohol, and glimpsed "girly" magazines as I made my way to one of the tiny fountain's three stools.

By the time I arrived home again, I felt—drained. In the front hall I lay my cheek on a basket of warm laundry my mother had set on the bureau, and would have fallen asleep, I'm sure, had I not heard the phone ringing in the kitchen.

"Hello?"

The caller had hung up by the time I answered, but on the counter I found a note. "I'm at Woolums—come get me. Love, Mom."

FINGER RAISED to her lips—like an usher at a theater— Margret Woolum hesitated before opening her front door to me, and then only opened it a crack. "I hate to do this," she whispered, "but do you think you could wait just a minute? Out there?"

I grinned. The request *was* unusual. Behind her, someone said in a loud, overwrought voice—I needed a moment to realize it was Chan Bishop—"I've been through all that, Matson!"

Margret winced as if Chan had shouted right in her ear.

My mother spoke next. I couldn't hear her words, but I recognized the tone of her voice: soothing.

"She's the only one he'll listen to right now," Margret whispered, then slowly closed the door on me.

Almost immediately, however, my mother stepped out. She smiled as if she were truly happy to see me, as if she'd just escaped some ordeal. "Let's go, shall we?" she murmured, and took my hand in hers as we hurried across the yard.

At the rate we packed our baskets of laundry into the car, we might have been evacuees. I wanted to ask why we were hurrying so, but I waited, and then when we were on the highway, her face finally relaxing a little, she told me that she'd been talking to Chan because—well, he'd decided his children weren't really his children, he wouldn't have anything to do with them.

She sighed. "Margret says it's absolutely ridiculous. I don't know. But, the children—I guess they're terribly upset."

I nodded. I felt sorry for the Bishop children, and was gratified my mother spoke to me so openly. I wanted to think of a question or two to ask her, but there didn't seem to be anything she could tell me and so I sat quietly and tried to look mature, and after a few minutes of our driving in silence, she asked about my trip downtown.

Really, we had a nice time on that drive back to Lake Bascomb. Halfway home, we stopped at one of those little drive-in hamburger stands that have mostly disappeared now (festive strings of yellow and blue and red lights over the parking lot, waitresses you could actually get to know if you lived in the town). "A nice girl," my mother said of our waitress, and, then, though she'd already put a tip on the tray, she added the change from the bill.

It must have been eight or nine by the time we got back to the cottage. Paula wasn't home yet, and the house seemed oddly quiet. We went upstairs to get ready for bed and my mother, for the first time in years, came into my room to say goodnight. "It was fun being with you today," she said.

All of this pleased and unsettled me and I couldn't fall asleep right away. I kept thinking about Chan Bishop, and his children, and my mother trying to soothe him. Still, I must have already slept for hours before the telephone rang that night. When I first heard the ringing, and then the sound of my mother hurrying down the stairs, my clock radio showed one-thirty.

"What is it?" I called as, a few minutes later, she started up the stairs.

She came to my doorway. "I need you to get up with me."

Death. My father. My father had driven the car into a trestle. Nancy's train had derailed.

She removed the blue net bonnet that covered her twist while she slept. "There's something outside. Put on a robe."

A wild animal? A robber? Why did we have to go out there? I scrambled down the stairs after her. "Shouldn't we get Dad's shotgun or something?"

"Just come with me and don't talk."

Outside, across the drive, stood Paula, leaning up against a boy, not Eldon, but some squat boy with a turquoise car and upper arms that poured—like liquid metal from a vat—out the cropped sleeves of his sweatshirt. Paula and the boy looked curiously purple in the glow of the driveway's mercury lamp. They both smoked cigarettes, the coals going on and off in the dark like the orange warning lights on radio towers. My mother wouldn't like the smoking, but maybe she wouldn't mind so much just then since Paula and that boy could help with whatever problem lay in wait out there.

"Hey," Paula called, "what're you guys doing up?"

I looked to my mother for an answer. She lay a trembling hand on my shoulder. "Stop," she whispered, and then, raising her voice, called, "Paula, I just got a phone call from Lorraine Bergreen about something she found going on in her motorboat." She swatted at the air in front of her: mosquitoes. That was when I saw the check in her hand. "Go inside, and gather your things. I've got your last week's pay here, plus bus fare."

Paula grinned, as if she thought my mother were teasing. "Come on, now, Mrs. Powell. Let's just simmer down, now. I mean, it's my night off—"

"I assume your friend can give you a ride to the station?"

The boy took Paula's arm, whispered something. Paula pulled away from him, then marched past my mother and me and into the house. We stayed put, under the mercury lights, as if we guarded something.

When Paula returned—she couldn't have taken more than five minutes—she said, "I've got your number, *Dotty*," and snapped the check from my mother's hand. "You're jealous *you* don't have somebody interested in you!"

My mother smiled at this, but I knew she was just being brave, and I picked up a piece of gravel from the edge of the road, and I threw it at Paula—missing, but hitting the car of the boy, who yelped, "Hey!"

"Don't you talk like that to my mother!" I cried. "Don't you dare, you bad girl!"

I was shaking and shivering, and when my mother put an arm around me, I could feel the tremble in her, too.

The boy took Paula's suitcase, threw it in the trunk. "Let's get out of here," he mumbled. He tried to steer Paula into the car, but she seemed to resist, to wait for my mother to say something.

"You know, Paula," my mother threw her head back as if half lost in admiration of the creamy stars, "I brought you into my home because—" She hesitated. What would she say next? "I felt sorry for you. I did my darnedest to treat you like one of my own children."

Behind Paula, the boy turned on his engine, and then his headlights, which shone into the little stand of pines planted by my parents during their first summer in Lake Bascomb, pines that now stood a good twelve feet tall.

Paula looked over at me, shook her head as if what she saw were too pathetic for words. "You think I'd want to be treated the way you treat her?" She laughed, then climbed into the car.

"Say something," I murmured to my mother. "Say something back! Tell her to go to hell!"

She shook her head.

"Just go to hell, you!" I shouted. "Hell!"

"Shh," my mother said, "Penny!" She started to laugh, then, and I did too, but only to keep her company.

Both of us a little shaky, we made our way back to the cottage, where she declared she'd make us cups of "sweet milk" to help us get back to sleep.

"'Sweet milk'?" I asked.

She looked hurt. She'd made me sweet milk before! Didn't I remember? Milk heated up with sugar, then dusted with cinnamon?

"Well, hey!" I said. I made a clown's face. I sounded, I suppose, disconcertingly like Paula, "So maybe I forgot!"

CHAPTER 17

I'd never given much thought to how my mother
spent her days, but, after Paula's departure, I felt responsible
for her. I knew I restricted her life, and—though it seems illog-
ical to me today—I thought I ought to spend *more* time with
her, *entertain* her, since she couldn't really go anywhere.

What a burden I must have been! She tried to get me out to
play with other children. She even went so far as to arrange
afternoon visits for me with Jeannie and Mary Frances Schwab.
Oh, no, I said, I had a stomach ache, a headache, I felt dizzy—
and my fake illnesses drove her to desperate measures.

"You want to say you're sick, all right, but you stay in bed.
No TV. No games."

So I stayed in bed. I mostly enjoyed my sense of invalidism.
I read and, every now and then, looked up when I heard her
go in or out the screen door, or talk on the telephone. Thick
oak leaves rustled outside my window. The lake glittered and
snapped against the rocky shore. The cottage had few books,
but I read most of them that summer. The boring story of a
cowboy that I'd read at least once every summer since I was

four or five. Nancy's *Catcher in the Rye* and a copy of Dale Carnegie's *Lincoln the Unknown* inscribed to my father for "Best Extemporaneous Speech." A two-volume set of Hans Christian Andersen with nice illustrations, and a big *Brothers Grimm* with no pictures, but all of the stories.

Poor Holden Caulfield. Poor Abraham Lincoln. Poor women in *Brothers Grimm*. Those women—I felt sorry for them in the same way that I felt sorry for female cardinals. People said the female cardinal wasn't as pretty as the male since the female's coat was olive instead of red, but who had decided olive wasn't as pretty as red? Who made up a story like "Hansel and Gretel" in which neither Hansel nor Gretel— nor the storyteller—held the father responsible for anything? And how was it that the mother of Hansel and Gretel could force the father to abandon the children in the woods, any- way? Was she as powerful, then, as the God who demanded the sacrifice of Isaac?

My mother made a mournful but amused noise when I asked her about the fairy tales: Didn't she think they were kind of mean to women and all?

At the time, we were gathering some supper for ourselves, working in the half-light that filled that north-facing kitchen at dusk. With a newly sharpened knife, my mother cut tomatoes into clean, perfect rounds. When she finally answered, she said, "Oh, when you grow up, Penny, you find out that *now* the world thinks you're the witch, even though you know you *used to be* the princess."

This was more of an answer than I'd hoped to get, or knew how to use, but she looked at me, head cocked to one side, as if she waited for me to say I understood. All I could do was grin as if she'd told a little joke. She shrugged, smiled, then went back to cutting the tomatoes—big, beautiful beefsteaks that she'd grown along the cottage's south wall. That was when I noticed the fit of her wedding and engagement rings. She'd once taken the rings to a jeweler so he could expand their circumferences. Now, the rings hung loose on her finger, the diamonds not visible, their weight swung down towards her palm as she worked. The narrow backs of the rings exposed a slice of white, untanned skin, and all of this—the red tomato slices, the work of her brown fingers, the soft glow of platinum—it struck me as ineffably beautiful.

In keeping with the elegance I saw in her, I used a wineglass for a bowl when I dished myself up some ice cream. My dinner: ice cream with Rice Krispies on top. Alone all the work-week long, my mother and I had taken to odd habits. Once it had become clear to me that she ate nothing but cottage cheese for both breakfast and lunch, I pointed out that there was no reason, was there, that we had to make meals at all when Dad wasn't around?

"I'd just as soon eat Frosted Flakes or something. That way, we'd only have to clean the kitchen on weekends."

My mother rolled her eyes, as if she found the suggestion preposterous, but gradually our habits fell in line with my philosophy. Not having to clean up after dinner meant more relaxation at night. We read together in the main room, or took bike rides. She went upstairs, early, to read some more, or practice her French. I often stayed up late, downstairs, watching Jack Paar talk to Joey Bishop or Hermione Gingold or some other celebrity. I remembered Hermione Gingold as the grandmother in *Gigi*, and, with his dark, dark tan—only now does it occur to me that his last name surely had something to do with this association—Joey Bishop always made me think of Chan, poor Chan, and his poor kids.

When I'd finally trudge up to bed, my mother would be in her room—usually reading, but sometimes lying under a sunlamp, bra and underpants electric in its lavender glow, Haldis Bishop's eye guards resting on her lids. She repeated the phrases from *French for Beginners* in a whisper that made all of the words seem like secrets:

> *Je suis fatiguée.*
> *J'ai soif.*
> *J'ai faim.*

She was truly thin—*skinny*, as she and Margret Woolum would have said—and, temporarily sightless, propped up on her bedspread with pillows, she looked not just *small*, but undefended, unfamiliar. One day, she came to pick me up at a birthday party I'd reluctantly agreed to attend. She'd bought a big sun hat while I was at the party, and I didn't recognize her at first, and, then, when I did, I thought—and this struck me as a marvel—that a person meeting my mother now would never know that, one year ago, she'd weighed twenty-five pounds more. To a stranger, my mother would be this thin, brown woman in the strappy sandals, the hat with its playful pair of sunglasses stitched right into the brim.

My mother.

All of the birthday party children gathered on an old blanket, watching the birthday girl unwrap her gifts. In my eagerness to reach my mother, claim her before that audience, I stepped on a small package. I felt the gift inside break beneath my heel.

"Hi, Mom!" I shouted and raced across the lawn.

She lifted me up in her arms, so sweet I didn't worry about the acid smell of her breath, the same smell Nancy had exhaled when the diet pills were hers.

And so, that summer, I shut out the past—past summers, past mother—all that behind us. My new mother and I rose at seven. While we ate breakfast, she played her French records, and afterward, I got up, clapped my hands, and said, "*Qu'est-ce que nous ferons aujourd'hui?*" What shall we do today?

The answer was: at eight, get out blankets and exercise with *Fit and Trim*. After *Fit and Trim*, I would play around in the lake while she swam laps between our dock and the neighbor's. Before lunch, we rode Nancy's and my bikes around the asphalt lanes that led to the other cottages—Mother looking very serious, as if she kept track of each revolution of the pedals, and meant to apply them towards paying off some account. Then we ate lunch, and—though we didn't say so—we watched *The Day Breaks*.

Listen: the voice-over of Dr. Tony Sutherland—who appeared merely to inspect a patient's chart—proved that Dr. Sutherland was actually deep in thought about Nurse Haskell, daughter of the show's charming chief of staff: "If only I could get Carl out of Miriam's mind! I know if we were alone for a time, she'd see I'm serious about her. She'd realize I no longer love Donna!"

I appreciated the clarity of the soap opera. Until overhearing Dr. Sutherland's thoughts, I'd been *suspicious* of his overt claims of affection for Nurse Haskell. My mother, however, made a little snorting noise, and said, "So he tells *himself*."

She stood, bent over at the waist, brushing her long hair with snapping strokes—out of the line of sight of anyone who might come to the door. She wouldn't have wanted anyone to see her watch a soap opera. As if to prove that she had only a passing interest in *The Day Breaks*, she never came in at the start of the episode. And when she did arrive, her questions about the story-line were teasing, as if she found it all very silly.

"So you don't think he loves her, Mom?"

"Oh, well." She straightened, picked up a magazine, went out to find a spot in the yard where the big oaks didn't block the sun. That was the way she spent her afternoons, moving my father's old army blanket out of the trees' changing shadows and into the sun, leafing through magazines, worrying about my father. His business dealings were very much on our minds, and to make matters worse, the diet pills set my mother's thoughts racing. For the first time in my life, she said things to me about business errors my father had made in the past.

Oh, she hadn't dared offer a word of advice about Archie or Dad's starting the door plant. He'd just have blown his stack! Even though *she'd* been proved right, back in the days when she told him Bill Rail was a great guy, but not cut out to manage a ballroom. And not just she, but several people had warned him about Leon Cottrell before they'd even started that darned subdivision!

From my bedroom window, I watched her spread the army blanket out over the prickly lawn. You could see the blanket was green—but maybe just because you knew it was green. In the bright summer sun, it seemed to be overlaid by a second blanket of lemony light. My mother untied the straps of her swimsuit and lay down. When she lay down, I went to the guest room to spirit away one of the movie mags and romance comics that Paula Dart had left behind—along with several pairs of balled-up socks, a dirty hairbrush, and the box of Snow Queen hair dye. Actually, I preferred the comics to the magazines. The comics were full of dark nights, close-ups of eyes so brimful of tears it seemed the tears' crests would break like waves. In the comics, things worked out in the end. The cad turned out to not really be a cad, or the girl met someone else who could appreciate her, or she discovered in the boy she'd earlier rejected that he was just what she'd been looking for all along.

The movie magazines were ballast. While I gazed at *Star Town*, I remained in Lake Bascomb. I ran my fingernails over the fine wale of my bedspread, and the bedspread said, "Shh." The cover story featured a ring of photographs: Marilyn Monroe, Clark Gable, Arthur Miller, Montgomery Cliff, and Yves Montand, all of them working on a movie called *The Misfits*. Underneath the ring of photos was the question, in hot red, "WHO'S SORRY NOW?"

"Penny."

I looked up. Hiking her unstrapped swimsuit, my mother stood in my doorway. I tried to push the pulpy magazine under my pillow, but the tucked-in spread blocked my efforts.

She laughed, and came to sit on the edge of my bed. "Let me see." Reluctantly, I handed over the magazine. She flipped through it, then studied the cover. "Did I ever tell you, once I sent away for a picture of Clark Gable, and when I got it, it was signed, 'Best wishes, Errol Flynn'?"

Who was Errol Flynn? I didn't know, but I laughed along with her. That summer was the first time she ever told me much of anything about herself. We'd be standing in the kitchen or lying on the dock, and she'd start talking about, say, the fact that her father's parents were Quakers. "They wouldn't cook on Sundays, so all you'd get if you went there was cold food. Cold oatmeal, everything cold." Another time she told me how she'd gotten in trouble as a kid for sneaking up behind people to scare them. Also, the story I'd heard in the past about a stranger who'd pulled her into his car—that summer she explained to me that the man in the story had exposed his penis to her.

And that day in my bedroom—maybe because of the Marilyn Monroe story in the movie magazine—she told me that she thought her father might have once had a girlfriend. "I'm not sure," she said, "but I heard a terrible fight between my parents once. That house had big wooden doors between our living room and dining room, and I went over by them and listened. From what I could tell, he had—some lady friend!"

My mother didn't seem particularly shocked by her story, so I tried to pretend not to be shocked myself. I think she forgot exactly to whom she spoke. She was on the diet pills, of course, and she was lonely. Not only did she miss my father, but the calls between herself and Margret had suddenly dropped off, and it seemed she and Lorraine Bergreen rarely got together for coffee and chats anymore.

She continued: "My parents never got to be alone. They had a boarder in my room, so I slept in with them, on a cot."

I gave her a stupid nod, as if this didn't scandalize me a bit. Then I got up off my bed and straightened the covers. "Is it time for supper yet?" I asked.

She laughed. "Does it matter?"

Together, we went downstairs. We carried supper—Ritz crackers for me, cottage cheese for her—into the main room, and turned on the news. Our blankets still lay on the floor from that morning's *Fit and Trim* show, and, as if we were picnickers, we sat on them while Walter Cronkite told us what was happening around the world.

"I like Walter Cronkite," my mother said. "He seems like a nice man, doesn't he?"

I nodded. "Like some perfect dad, like Walt Disney." I flushed, thinking I should have said, "Like Dad," but she hadn't noticed, she was getting to her feet, rushing to the window.

"Somebody's here—it's Dad," she said, almost the way Nancy or I would have said it if we'd been up to no good.

Without a word, we hustled into the kitchen where, quick, I stuck my crackers into a cupboard; she, her carton of cottage cheese in the fridge. "Damn!" she said. "I still have on my swimsuit! Oh, and get those blankets off the floor, will you?"

I raced up the stairs with that awkward load, dumped the blankets in my closet. My heart beat so fast, I was sure I looked suspicious, so I made myself sit for a time before going back downstairs.

Not that my father would have noticed anything unusual about me that evening. In the kitchen, he stood with his weight on his hands, leaning into the table. He'd just gotten his hair cut, and now and again he wiggled his shoulders around as if bits of hair had fallen down inside his shirt. "Hi, honey," he murmured, but when I approached to give him a hug, he held up a palm toward me the way a person might if he were contagious, warning you away.

My mother was saying, "But I don't understand."

"Gad, Dotty!" He pulled upwards on his forehead with both hands so that the whites above his pupils were horribly exposed. Did he mean to look so scary? "How many times do you want me to go over this? The upshot is, Roy, Jr.'s going to see if he can use his FBI connections to find out anything about Archie. And Dave Crane's going to ask about his work at St. Louis Door."

My mother had a bright, antic look, an expression I could remember her wearing when we got lost on our way somewhere and she had to stop and ask directions of strangers. "Roy, Jr.! When he mentioned doing this at Thanksgiving, you thought it was a terrible idea! And—why would St. Louis Door tell Dave Crane things they didn't tell you?"

My father wiggled his fingers in the air above his head— some gesture of disgust and dismay. He went to the sink and drew himself a glass of water. "That tastes good," he said. "I've been wanting a glass of water for the last hour—"

"Bob—"

He turned, grinning, rubbing the tender dents in his nose where his driving glasses had rested. Then, as if it were his appointed spot—a lectern—he went back to the place at the table where he'd stood before. "Dotty, why on earth would you suppose that I talked to people at St. Louis Door? From what Archie told me, everybody there was a crook!"

My mother looked over at me, as if trying to decide whether or not to ask me to leave the room. "But"—she took a breath—"you didn't even *know* Archie, Bob!"

The room was so quiet I could hear the little sucking noise my father made—some effort to control his ragged breathing. "Tell me, dear," he said, "how is it you expect you *get* to know people?"

Like a cloud that might have one shape to one person, another to the next, my father's question sat somewhere far over my parents' heads. He shifted his weight from his feet to his hands and back again. He smiled a terrible smile, upper lip hitched a little on his gums. I felt sick that we couldn't comfort him, or make him think better of us, while—with just a kiss, a few kind words—*he* could always make things right, or at least good enough for us to go on.

"But if you're talking about *business,* Bob, about investing money—"

"Mother!" he cried. "You don't understand a thing about business! You have *never* understood a thing about business, and you never will!"

I protested, "That's not nice! Be nice to Mom, Dad!"

He looked startled at my objection. "I think I know how to be nice to your mother!"

She made no response, just lifted the untied straps of her suit, brought them around behind her neck and tied them up tight. A rim of the pale flesh of her breasts showed just below her tan, now so dark it made me think of the nutmeg Margret Woolum had taught her to grate over vanilla ice cream.

"Just kiss her!" I cried.

"*Kiss* her?" My father squinted at me. "For heaven's sake, Penny! You don't kiss someone while you're quarreling!"

"I don't care!"

He turned to my mother. "What's going on here?"

She gave me a wan smile, then said, "Run upstairs, now, honey."

I did as she said, but stopped before I reached the second floor. I could still see my father's graying head when I looked through the banisters. Who was he? Sometimes he seemed to me to be a man who wanted only to do good; sometimes, a man who wanted only to make the jaw of someone—who? his father? some other version of himself?—drop so wide open that he might step inside and take a walk through the wonder; know, for once and all, that he had really and truly left another man impressed.

But he didn't have to do a thing to impress us! We loved him just the way he was.

I beamed messages into the back of his head: Give her a kiss. Tell her you love her. Tell her she's pretty, beautiful, the most beautiful woman in the world.

For a long time my father stayed where he was, head down, the hams of his hands pushed into the edge of the table. The only sound was the sound of his shoes rubbing grit into the floor as he shifted his feet now and again.

Tell her you love her. Tell her.

I didn't see my mother coming across the room toward him until she arrived at his side. I didn't even hear her, in her bare feet. But then a cry rose from my father's throat, she reached out a hand, and in a split second, the two of them were at each other like—wolves, as if they couldn't possibly get close enough, their kisses scary, wilder than anything I'd ever seen on TV, or in Paula's romance magazines, or even at the movies.

CHAPTER 18

Because I didn't want to go back to Meander, I told myself we might just stay on in Lake Bascomb. Summer was beginning to close down. People drove by with crammed station wagons, the Bergreens stopped to say goodbye, the ice-cream stand that served the summer trade closed up. Eventually, even my own mother started packing, and announced that my father was on his way to help us close the cottage for the season, that we had to get back to Meander to pick up Nancy at the train station.

"Why not just sell everything but the cottage, and live here?" I asked. "I don't have to go to school. I could study encyclopedias and things. And you know Clays' apples? They don't pick any of their apples. I could get them for us. We could make applesauce and stuff."

My mother lifted a handful of canned goods into a cardboard box. As she worked, now and then, she'd look off, shiver, seem to forget what she was doing. After one of these lapses, she glanced at me and said, "Here." She unclasped her watch and fastened it around my wrist. "Go play outside for an hour. I've got a million things to do before Dad arrives."

The watch was a dumbly gorgeous thing, all diamonds and platinum, one of those gifts from my father that always confused the issues of looming financial disasters. I looked at the thing on my wrist. I was more intoxicated by its weight than its diamonds: that something so small could weigh so much!

"Couldn't we sell this?"

She looked up from reading the instructions on a box of mouse poison. "What?"

"I bet we could sell your watch, and lots of other stuff."

She shook her head. "Wouldn't make a drop in the bucket," she said, and she wasn't in a mood to chat now, so *scoot*.

Without much enthusiasm, I pedaled my bike onto the road. The neighborhood was very still. In the distance, a motorboat roared, but it was no louder than the noise of those insects that carried on in the browning grass. Sunlight came down through the big oaks and elms, lay on the asphalt like a spell. My spell. Because the road had been built two summers before by George Gross and Hughie Mayfield and my father's company, I felt as tender and possessive toward it as I felt toward the men who'd made it: my road.

Half-relieved that no one could come out of Bergreen cottage and say hello, I dropped my bike in their lawn with the idea that I would revive Lorraine's grand borders of salmon impatiens, gone limp from lack of water. The idea made me feel fine, competent, kind, but after I'd tried two spigots, I realized, of course, the water had been turned off for the season, and so I climbed back on my bike.

A little further down the road, in a broad square of sunlit yard, Mary Frances Schwab sat on a folding chair, pulling the string in the back of the talking doll she had acquired that summer. By way of greeting, Mary Frances waved the doll, then called in a voice both squeaky and stuffy, "We're leaving tomorrow."

I walked my bike across the lawn, steering around a used Kleenex that hadn't made it into the waste-basket beside Mary Frances's chair. "We are, too."

"We hate it here. At home, at least there's air conditioning for my hay fever."

I wanted to be indignant for Lake Bascomb's sake, but how could I be when Mary Frances's eyes looked so painful, the whites all red, and wrinkled up like the skin on a cup of cocoa? I'd never seen anything like it in my life.

"The only reason we came was so I could be near the clinic." Mary Frances looked back at the cottage. Her mother was visible through a kitchen window, apparently scrubbing something in the sink. "I wish she'd go away," Mary Frances murmured. Then her voice resumed its normal volume: "Once Dr. Q's got you started, he can send treatments to you. Through anything metal, I mean. So we don't have to be here anymore. Is that your mom's watch?"

I nodded. "You want to try it on?"

"No way! I'd be too scared. How much does something like that cost, anyway?"

"I don't know. It's not polite to ask what stuff costs."

She made a face. "That's what rich people always say."

"We're not *rich*," I said, and longed to say much more. At that moment, I would have loved to have told someone, *anyone*, about the confusion at our house, our imminent financial ruin. But, then, if I did tell someone, it seemed to me that someone would have to die afterwards so there couldn't be any danger of her telling anyone else. And if that someone died, telling would have done me no good because, once again, there would be no one who knew.

Well, *Nancy* would be home tomorrow. We'd pick her up at the train and—maybe before bed—I'd have a chance to talk to Nancy alone. Nancy would make things all right because she was—a little separate from the rest of the family. And if she were separate, she could see things better. Or she could decide not to be separate, and that would help, too. Anything seemed as if it would help.

"My mom says you're rich." Mary Frances dabbed at her poor, stuffed-up nose with a ball of tissue. Again, she glanced toward the window. This time, her mother was gone. Mary Frances smiled. She leaned close. "So." Her breath smelled horrible, like water left in a vase of marigolds. I had to steel myself not to draw away from her.

"Last night," she whispered, "my mom heard *your* mom talking on the telephone. To a *man*. She let me listen in. You know what he said, Penny?"

While we'd been talking, I'd begun to fashion a little ghost doll out of tissues from the Kleenex box in Mary Frances's lap. Now, I held my doll out at arm's length, as if examining its proportions with a critical eye, as if I were hardly curious about what Mary Frances had to say. With a murmur that what I needed to finish the doll was string, to tie off the head, I started towards my bike.

Mary Frances raised her voice a little—not too much, not so loud her mother could overhear—"He said he wished she were there, and he'd been thinking about her so much, and then your mom got kind of mad, and he said he was sorry."

I tucked the unfinished doll into the waist of my shorts, and climbed on my bike. "Mary Frances," I said, sounding as if I found the whole matter very droll, "in case you don't know, my dad calls my mom long distance all the time."

In some imitation of adult roguishness, Mary Frances wagged her head back and forth. "Well, my *dad* said—"

"Your *dad*! Your dad listened, too?"

She grinned. "No, but my mom told him, and *he* said she— your mom—a woman like her can't help it if men go around falling in love with her."

I looked up after I'd released my kickstand. Very nonchalant, I asked, "Because she's so pretty, you mean?"

Mary Frances shrugged. "I guess. Sure."

WHEN I arrived back at the cottage, I found my mother standing in the driveway, talking to a pregnant woman and a man in Bermuda shorts: Dave Crane and his wife.

My mother's head pivoted in my direction as I called hello, then pivoted back again, the movements smooth and slow and inhuman as something robotic, like the ghostly opening and closing of the electric gate at the Bishop estate.

I got off my bike, coming too close for her to ignore me. "Is Dad here yet?"

She looked at Dave Crane, as if for permission. He shrugged. Mrs. Crane drew in a sharp little breath that I recognized as an expression of sympathy. "Oh, honey," my mother said, "he's—just going to have to meet us in Meander, before we go to meet Nan's train. He can't come. Dave's just talked to him—things are really a mess."

Among the things that Dave Crane had learned from the people at St. Louis Door: it was highly unlikely Archie Jones would know how to set up a door plant. Worse, St. Louis Door claimed they'd *fired* Archie for cheating on his accounts. As far as they could tell, he'd been using their money to pay off debts. Gambling debts, they believed.

In a small voice, my mother added, "The only reason they didn't have him thrown in jail is he's been paying them back."

I went hot. "With our money?"

She ran her tongue back and forth across her teeth, the way she did before going to answer the door, or leaving the car to enter a shop. The afternoon sky buzzed blue, the leaves in the oak trees rattled overhead. Fall. On my bike ride, I'd even seen a few maple leaves in the ditches.

Dave Crane patted my mother on the shoulder. "You're all going to come out of this okay."

She turned to look off toward the lake, empty except for an oil drum buoy someone had stuck in the near distance after years and years of people complaining that they sheared pins on the rocks that lay not far beneath the surface.

"Honest to goodness"—my mother tried to smile—"honestly, I don't need much, but if we lose the house and all—"

"Oh, no!" Dave Crane chuckled. "Bob's got a way of singing the blues, but he and I just did a complete update of your properties and investments—things aren't so grim as he makes out, and we're cooking up a little something right now that'll give you some *real* security for the future."

My mother's face went slack at this last. "You and Bob," she said, then closed her fingers on my arm. "Penny and I have to go in now. To do our packing." She nodded, as if agreeing with someone. "You'll have to excuse us."

I hurried to keep pace with her as she headed to the house. "What do you think Dad's doing with him?" I whispered.

She shut her eyes for a second before opening the door. "Maybe nothing yet—I can't think about it, Penny. If I think about it, I'll scream."

For the next three hours or so, the two of us hauled out old bedspreads and sheets and used them to drape the furniture. We folded the last laundry from the line, punched holes in the boxes of D-Con, and set them out around the house. I didn't complain the way I usually would have: can I quit now? are we done yet?

When she walked into her bedroom, I followed her, assuming another job needed to be done there. Instead, without a word, almost as if she didn't know I were with her, she kicked off her shoes and lay on the bed: flat on her back, hands folded across her stomach. Her hip bones stuck out—that was how thin she'd grown.

"Mom?" I came close to the bed. "Can I lie down, too?"

She didn't open her eyes, just patted the mattress. "You have to be still, though, no wiggling." Then she turned onto her side, brought up her knees. "Here." She smiled. With her eyes closed, she seemed almost as if she spoke in her sleep. "Remember when I used to make you a chair?"

I moved into that crook of legs and chest. Though I no longer fit neatly beneath her chin, I was grateful for her invitation, and tried not to think about her ketosis smell, so sharp it seemed it might blister flesh.

I didn't expect to sleep that afternoon, but sleep I did. I dreamed of people waiting beside a driveway. I became one of the people, waiting. A big black car swung into the drive, its arrival as unavoidable as my next breath. The limousine swung into the drive and I understood, as if someone said the words aloud, that the car was a hearse, that it had come for me. Then I fell over in the driveway and I was dead.

Heart racing, I woke up in the strangled light of dusk. A robin sang its bright, banal song in a tree outside the window. Someone was crying, and, for a moment, I thought it was me— me, so confused that I didn't know where I lay. I jumped up, and ran around the bed, which was, of course, my mother's bed, though my mother was no longer in it.

"Mother?"

From the bathroom—her voice high and panicky—she answered, "Don't come in here!"

Scared, breathing hard, I ran toward the hall. I tripped over something in the doorway—the cardboard box that held the items left behind in Paula's closet—and when its balled-up socks rolled out and across the floor like so many rats, I shrieked.

"Penny?" My mother was still behind the bathroom door, but I could hear that her voice was gauzy with tears. "Are you okay, Penny?"

I sniffled. "Yeah."

"Good. Now, don't say anything. Just come here."

CERTAIN PEOPLE, entering the bathroom, might have first noticed my mother's hair, now snow white, white like taffy, and hacked into sheaves and bundles of wildly different lengths, apparently by the double-edge razor blade between her fingertips. But what I noticed first was blood, and I shrieked again, and covered my eyes.

"Mother!" I pointed blindly to a spot on her temple where I had seen the hair sticking up in slivers of red. "You're bleeding!"

"Don't be silly!" she said.

I peeked at her. Though her own face was wet with tears, she had sounded soothingly rational, the way she used to sound when Nancy and I were younger and frightened by the bad storms that sometimes raged over the lake. "I cut my finger. That's just from my finger."

Long strands of white hair filled the sink, covered the counter top and the empty box of Snow Queen hair dye.

"Oh!" Her composure failed her again, and she cried out, "I was hauling out Paula's stuff, and I found this—I thought I'd just do the color, but then it was so awful! Look at the mess!"

I couldn't quite imitate the rational voice she'd used before. I had to settle for making myself still, the way I would have had a rattlesnake curved in and out around our feet. "It's okay," I whispered. "I can fix it. Really."

"You can fix it?" She laughed, moaned. She rested her forehead against the medicine cabinet mirror. "Oh, Lord, what's your dad going to say?"

Your dad. The phrase made me feel indicted, implicated in his harsher judgments.

"Sit down," I said, "on the toilet."

She flashed wide-eyes at herself in the mirror. "I've had it," she told the reflection. "I have *had* it. He's not getting involved in some other kooky scheme, and that's that! He's put me through enough hell already!"

I opened the drawer beneath the counter, took out a pair of manicure scissors: small, with curved blades. I felt dizzy, as if now we didn't just face rattlesnakes, no, now we perched on a high and narrow bluff, besides. I worked the handles on the scissors. They made a small click. "Come on," I said. "Sit. I'll even things out for you."

She gave the scissors a grim look, but she finally did come, and settle herself on the lid of the toilet. "Can you believe I'm letting you do this?" Her teeth had begun to chatter and she laughed a small, high laugh. "I can't believe I'm letting a *child* cut my hair."

I was too excited to be insulted. I felt absolutely the artist, certain to my toes that no one on earth would try harder than I would; and, at that moment, just how hard a person tried seemed to me the measure of success.

"Just you wait," I said, suddenly full of vague but exciting expectations for us both. "Just wait." Then I moved the scissors towards her hair. As she made a last little ducking motion of protest, I cut the first strand, so wet and heavy that the light-weight scissors seemed to protest, but the blades could not resist the work.

CHAPTER 19

The train carrying Nancy's camp group was to arrive in Meander at seven. My mother and I were to meet my father at the house by five. Seven. Five. All morning long, my mother repeated "five, seven," which made me nervous, made me feel as if she believed we might not make it, or she'd forget our aim, we'd arrive at the house or the station at the wrong time.

And on top of this, of course, there was the matter of her appearance. Though I tried not to be obvious about it, I was pinned to one occupation that morning: looking at her. I sat on the balustrade at the top of the cottage stairs as she went back and forth in the hall, now with a bundle of towels, now a clock radio and heating pad. Her white petals of hair against her nutmeg skin continued to give me little shocks. She might have been the negative of some fair-skinned brunette. And that photo image went further for she seemed shiny and new, too, like the models photographed on the slippery, glossy stock of fashion magazines.

French, I thought, and wished the neighbors hadn't already left for the season, missed out on witnessing my mother's—*translation*.

"Mom, if I wet my hair, do you think you could put some pincurls in? If we had the top down, they'd dry—"

She stopped in front of me, sighed. "No time for that, sweetie." Then, carefully, as if she were a doll on a rotating pedestal, she turned. She wore a new white shell, a white skirt, and a pair of high-heeled sandals I'd been trying to get her to put on all summer. Not meeting my eyes, she asked, "So, really, how do I look?"

"You *know*: fantastic."

One hand on the door jamb, she ducked her head into the guest room to look in the mirror over the dressing table. "Oh," she groaned, but there was pleasure in the groan as well as fear. "What's Dad going to say?"

I wasn't quite myself, or, at least, I wasn't quite as in control of myself as usual, and I answered, "Oh, probably that you look like Brigitte Bardot!"

"*What?*" She stiffened, then hurried off down the hallway and into her bedroom, calling gruffly, "Don't you *dare* say such a thing to anybody, Penny! I mean it!"

I felt so abashed and stupid, then, that I didn't meet her eyes when, shortly after, she announced she had to go pay off the egg lady. Would I check the windows, please?

My father telephoned after she'd only been gone a minute: "Gad! Well, all right, sweetie. Listen, you tell her I can't meet the train with you tonight. This *bastard* Archie—Roy, Jr., got the dope on him." He hesitated, as if giving me a chance to ask for more information, but all I could think of was my mother, dressed-up, waiting for my father to see her. Over my silence, I heard George Gross ask, "Who ate the last glazed doughnut?" which meant my father was at the asphalt plant.

"Can I say hello to George?" I asked.

"What? For goodness sakes, honey! I'm busy here. You understand what I'm saying? Your cousin, Roy, Jr.—he checked Archie out. You tell mother: I've got a meeting with the fellows from St. Louis this afternoon. Tell her I'm going to try to get home tonight, but if I make it, it's going to be late."

I MEANT to write down the message. In fact, I was looking for a pencil when a car horn sounded in the drive. I ran outside. My mother, climbing from the convertible, snapped, "I told you yesterday to coil up that lawn hose and put it in the pump house, Penny!" and, immediately, I started making excuses for myself. I forgot about the message. I began gathering up the hose while my mother packed the car. Soon we were on our way to Meander, and I was thinking about Nancy and whether Nancy would be glad to see me. I became lost in my own thoughts and only came back to the present when we stopped at a truck stop for lunch.

At the truck stop, my mother set her spoon atop her fork, her fork atop her spoon. I didn't understand her fidgeting until I realized that the farmers, the truckers, the men who had left suit jackets in cars and now sat in shirt sleeves drinking ice tea—they were all looking at *her*, all of them. Like the winding sheet of a ghost, that white hair rendered her suddenly *visible*.

She'd taken off her glasses when we got out of the car. Now she reached in her purse, put them back on. Too late. I saw the look that passed between the man running the cash register and one of the customers; a leering grin that seemed to suggest that since they had seen my mother *without* glasses, they knew the glasses as mere disguise, something they could penetrate effortlessly.

"I wish we were home!" she whispered. She lifted her hands to her mouth in a prayerful attitude, blew on them. "Their air conditioner's set too high. I wish we'd already picked up Nan, and this day were—just over!"

It was at that moment that I remembered my father's call, and I gasped, "Oh, Mom! I forgot to tell you!"

As a rule, my mother drove slowly, but after we left the truck stop that afternoon, she whipped the car along without mercy. "This is so damn inconsiderate! Why couldn't he have waited one day to meet with these people?"

I kept quiet, watching the road for slow-moving vehicles ahead, and trying to distract myself by listening to the radio. The sky had gone dark with clouds, but the sun was out, casting a queer and beautiful light on the oat fields, transforming them to the color of lemons and limes. Once, I sneaked a look at the speedometer. Its red thread hovered at ninety-five.

"So, Mom," I said, taking a cue from the radio news, "do you like Nixon?"

"*Nixon*?"

"For president. Do you think he'll be good?"

She gave me a sharp glance. "Who a person votes for is her own business, Penny."

As we drove along, I replayed her answer, trying to make sense of it and the way it made her sound as if she needed a law to protect her from being forced to expose her own opinions.

So maybe she wasn't going to join my father in voting for Nixon? Could that possibly be true?

The roadhouses on the outskirts of Meander appeared. Then the smokestacks of Bishop Meat. We passed the creamery, the Catholic high school. A crew of migrant workers applied turquoise paint to the gizzard-colored building they lived in during the growing season. My mother whizzed by everything, well above the speed limit until a boy on a bike—bending to lick the juice from his Popsicle off the side of his arm—that boy made a heart-stopping wobble into our path, and my mother took a deep breath and slowed down.

MEANDER WAS a deeper, more determined green than when we'd visited earlier in the summer, and as we carried in our boxes and baskets, a wind came up—so strong it seemed to tumble the birds across the sky.

"Now I know what *this* house smells like when you come back to it in the fall!" I said. I meant to sound merry, lighten our moods, but my mother made no response as she carried the cooler into the kitchen. She began to unload food into the refrigerator, then stopped. "Mildew," she said. She jabbed at the refrigerator's mottled gasket, then, like some model of efficiency—as if every day of her life she fought and won battles both big and small—she pulled a pair of blue rubber gloves from a drawer, and, in a bucket in the sink, began to mix up a thunderous batch of bleach and water.

I walked back out to the car. I wished Eleanor Woolum would look from her window, see me lifting out the laundry basket full of breakfast cereals and crackers. "Penny!" she'd cry, and, at least for a time, we'd be happy to see each other.

When I came back in, my mother was tearing paper towels from the roller, mopping up a spill on the floor.

"Should I tell the Woolums we're here?" I asked.

Immediately, vehemently, she answered, "Absolutely not!"

I was surprised, but, then I couldn't recall when Margret had last called the cottage. "Are you mad at Margret about something?" I asked.

Before she could answer, we both looked towards the hall, and the sound of the screen door opening.

"Oh, Lord." My mother crouched down, crossed her gloved hands above the cap of white hair.

Laughing, I hurried for the hall. "Dad? Is that you? Wait'll you see—"

Halfway in the door, halfway out, Chan Bishop was busy maneuvering my bike into the foyer. "Penny." He tapped down the kickstand with his foot, and then, as if it were the most natural thing in the world, opened his arms to me.

I felt it was shameful—how grateful I was for that greeting— but still I hurried into his arms, sank my nose into the collar of his shirt.

"Bob?" my mother called from the kitchen.

"Shh," Chan whispered in my ear. "Let me surprise her."

To be fair—as a compromise—I called, "It's not Dad, Mom," but by then she had stepped into the shadowy hall.

Cautiously, hands pressed to his thighs for balance, Chan leaned forward. He might have been staring into a cave, a possible home to a bear or mountain lion. "Matson?" he asked in a solemn voice.

By the time we'd left Meander for the summer, Chan had taken to kissing my mother hello, just the way he kissed Margret. I was prepared for him to kiss her, but he upset things. Instead of kissing her, he stepped forward and pressed a finger to the brown skin on her cheekbone.

For a moment after he drew his finger away, a white bloodless spot remained on my mother's skin. She seemed to pull back from it—I imagined it hanging in the air like a little cloud.

"Chan!" I tugged hard at the sleeve of his suit jacket. Nothing was going right. "If you wonder about her hair"—a horrible laugh sputtered from my mouth, I sounded like Porky Pig—"it was my fault. Paula Dart and I—"

"Penny," my mother said. "Shh."

Chan looked solemn for another moment or two. Then he laughed, not as if he found something funny. He was just—happy. "God, Matson!" He looked around, as if taking in the hallway, something in the air. He gave himself a shake, like a dog coming out of water. "So. So, where's the boss?"

She didn't answer, just looked down at the rubber gloves on her hands. "These things!" While she struggled to remove the gloves, her shoulders heaved in a recognizable way. "You know Bob!" she said, in the sort of bubbly voice people use to get through a tearful sentence. "Same old thing! Can't make it home tonight!"

With that, she turned, and started to escape towards the kitchen, but Chan said, "Now, Matson," and, with a brief glance at me—a little lift of the eyebrows that I took as a request for permission—he wrapped an arm around her shoulder. "Now,

Matson," he murmured, and gave me a sad little smile, "Pen and I don't want you going off crying alone, do we, Pen?"

At this, of course, I began to cry myself, and Chan motioned for me to come under his other arm, which seemed sort of silly, and soon we were all laughing, me using Chan's handkerchief to wipe my tears, then handing it on to my mother.

We were still laughing a little when a truck rattled to a halt in front of the house, and a man in overalls started up the walk.

"The barn painter," I whispered.

"Oh, boy," my mother sighed. "Oh, dear."

At some time that day, bright blue paint—a *lot* of it—had spilled on the painter's hair, and down his neck, and it seemed he'd never noticed, never even tried to wipe off the second skin of blue that disappeared into the collar of his overalls.

"The effect is pure Matisse," my mother said, making her voice strange, an imitation of haughty authority.

Chan laughed before calling out to the painter, "Hello, there! How can I help you?"

The painter started at Chan's call—really, Chan's voice sounded so big and boomy that even my mother and I exchanged a look.

"You"—the painter arrived at the door, he pressed his nose to the screen. He eyed my mother, then stared at the boxes and suitcases and bicycle in the foyer. He scratched at his blue ear. A strip of the paint peeled off onto his fingernail, and he stared at it for a moment before rubbing it off on his pants leg. "You folks just moving in here?"

My mother began to answer, but Chan held up a hand to silence her. "Who might you be, sir?" he asked. I realized then what voice he used—the voice he used when imitating his father.

The painter closed his eyes, and didn't speak until he opened them again, several trembling seconds later. "I'm the one that painted the basement here last fall. I'm looking for the fellow that hired me and went and never paid."

"Ah." Chan turned to my mother. "Didn't we hear that fellow had gone off somewhere, sweetheart?"

She bit her lip to hold back a smile. "I heard something about him in connection with St. Louis."

"St. Louis." Chan turned to the painter. "Of course, he was awfully unhappy with the job you did. We heard about that." Shaking his head, smiling, Chan reached inside his jacket and removed his wallet. "But, I'm a good sport!"

I could see when he opened the wallet that the panel that had held the old photo of his children was now empty, and that absence gave me a chill. I looked over at my mother to see if she noticed, too, but she was just watching Chan, waiting for cues.

"I'm willing to pay you something to get rid of you!" Chan said—his voice quite friendly, as if he and the painter had reached an amiable agreement that the painter was a pest. "So what do you suppose it would take to finish off this business?"

Again, the painter pressed his face to the screen, this time smashing his nose to one side as he stared at my mother. She smiled lazily, and leaned back onto the little hall bureau. Her hands, propping her up, were set behind her hips, and, while I watched her, she raised her knee, and placed one foot flat against the face of the bureau—a posture I'd never seen her assume in all my life.

I looked back at the painter. I had thought he was trying to identify my mother, but the look in his eyes was the look that Thomas Hart Benton had given the ogling farmer in that painting that I knew from my mother's old art book. The painter had no idea who my mother was. He just was too drunk to be discreet in his gawking.

"Hey, you," Chan said softly, calling the painter back to attention.

"Yeah." The man looked away from my mother. "It was me that supplied the paint, too. The job was supposed to pay two hundred."

Chan quickly counted out all of the bills in his wallet. One hundred and thirteen dollars. He folded the stack in half, opened the screen door, and placed the money in the man's palm. "I think you'll be satisfied with that," he said.

The painter sighed. He took a last look at the three of us, shook his head. I almost wished he wouldn't go. In his eyes— misidentified—I was what he assumed me to be: a princess at home with her mother and father, who were, of course, the king and the queen.

But the painter did go, leaving in his wake a few curls of the blue paint he scratched from his neck on his way to his truck. We all kept quiet. Quiet while he started up his engine. Quiet while he drove away. But after he was a block down the street, I gasped, "Mom, he didn't even know you were the same person!"

Chan opened his jacket and returned his wallet to the slippery inside pocket. "Matson," he said—his downward gaze transfixed on his lapel, the tie he was loosening from his neck—"if you're not too busy, I have something I'd like to show you. Over at the house."

My mother pressed her palms down the sides of her skirt. "Something you wrote?"

Chan looked surprised, then smiled. "Actually, I meant my new car. Remember I ordered that little bronze Jag?"

My mother seemed a little disappointed, and Chan must have noticed this because he added, quickly, "But I do have something I wrote. I haven't shown it to anyone else."

She smiled. "A story?"

"I want to see, too."

They both looked at me. Chan laid his hand on my head, sighed as if he were suddenly tired. "Oh, Penny," he said—not unkindly, just wearily—"there's plenty of time for looking at the car. And this thing I wrote—it's not really for kids."

"That's right." Somehow, my mother managed to step around me, out the screen door and onto the walk. The wind blew her full skirt against her thighs. "And I won't be long, Penny."

So they meant to leave me behind, after all! I wanted to howl. We'd been together, pretending to be a family. I'd gone along with the act. And now they meant to leave me behind!

"We'll stop some place for hamburgers on our way to get Nan." She was already moving. I couldn't stop *her*, that was plain, and so I said, "Chan!" and I grabbed his sleeve.

My mother stopped walking, too, but she already stood on the second tier of the gravel terraces. She looked out across the drive toward Chan's house. She inhabited a story in which I no longer had a part.

"What is it, Penny? Hmm?" Chan's feet didn't move, but I

could feel the grain of the fabric of his jacket as he slowly pulled his arm away. He stared after my mother with a look I'd never seen anyone shine on her before, something so hopeful and earnest and admiring that I wanted both to shield her from it and to deliver her to it.

These warring impulses—and my knowledge of my essential irrelevance to the moment—made me feel as if I were truly two different people, and I found I couldn't say anything at all. I didn't even know which one of me was meant to speak.

"Look." Chan motioned toward my mother. "I got to catch up to Matson, there." Gently, he removed my fingers from his cuff, edged off the lawn and onto the terraces.

I called out, "Chan! What happened to that picture of your boy and girl? From your wallet?"

He made a face, something disapproving, and I felt ashamed in the way that I suppose he meant for me to feel ashamed. Then he said, "Why don't you get me one of your pictures for there, Penny?"

I looked down at my hands with guilty confusion, the horrible pleasure of hearing just the words I wanted to hear and knowing that they almost certainly were a lie.

My mother called out: "*J'ai la bouche sèche, Chan. Allons boire un verre de vin.*"

Did she think I hadn't learned any French that summer, or did she not care what I understood? *Her mouth was dry, she wanted a glass of wine.*

Chan laughed as he hurried towards her: "*C'est ça!*"

THAT AFTERNOON, after my mother left, I went into the kitchen and finished unloading the food from the cooler.

Cottage cheese, skim milk, catsup, butter, minced ham, raspberry jam, Hollywood Bread. Everything was sweaty or sticky. I emptied the laundry basket of its boxes of crackers and cereal and bags of rice. The chores made me feel better, but afterward I was exhausted, it was all I could do to walk upstairs to my parents' bedroom. There, on the great branch of hackberry outside the picture window, squirrels ran across my view of Chan's house. They jumped from the branch to the eaves high above me. My father and mother had a running, teasing debate over that branch. "An ugly old thing," my father always said. And my mother, emphatically, "It's perfectly *gorgeous*! You cut it off over my dead body!"

My mother kept her father's old binoculars in the bedroom bookcase, and I took them out now and focused them on Chan's house. There wasn't much to see. The big window in the kitchen was stained glass. The narrow ones in the living room—designed more for privacy and style than light—were little more than charcoal bands.

What the binoculars *did* pick up, of course, they picked up with accuracy: the curds of concrete that the contractors had failed to clean up along the base of the house, the patina of the eaves' copper flashing. My father had laughed about that flashing: "The point seems to be he paid a fortune to have this green stuff hanging on his house, and everybody who comes by is supposed to say—since they can't say it looks like hell—'How handsome!'"

I couldn't avoid thinking about my father, or Chan, and the way Chan had pressed his finger to my mother's cheek, almost as if to see if she were real, but somehow I managed to steer myself through the white water of such thoughts and into the calm I created in Chan's living room. There, I placed my mother and Chan on opposite sides of the coffee table in Chan's low-slung, hard-to-get-out-of canvas chairs. I fed them cheese on crackers and soda pop. They discussed Chan's story. Chan appreciated my mother's intelligent remarks.

John. Marsha. John.

The insolently happy saplings that bounced their heads alongside Chan's house were ash trees. I knew this from my father. My father knew the names of all trees, could identify with hardly a glance: larch, spruce, ash, willow, cottonwood, basswood, fir, mulberry, various types of oak.

My father probably loved me more than my mother did. I understood this, but also that it would be as unfair to compare those loves as to compare the gift of a rich person with the gift of a poor person. Who, after all, paid more dearly for what they offered?

I swung the binoculars towards Chan's porch, then his carport, and waited for my mother to appear, on her way home. A white station wagon moved sluggishly down the hill above Chan's place. Another minute, and then there was some souped-up car. *Raked*: Paula had told me that was the term for a car with its rear end raised high for racing.

There seemed to be a breeze between my foot and my slapping leather sandal as I descended the stairs. For the first time, I felt the parched grain of the bannister beneath my hand, and sensed the spots on the stairs where the carpet had been compressed by many feet.

In the refrigerator, the food we'd brought from Lake Bascomb sat like dull cousins beside the food purchased by my father. Did I still have to leave his food alone? Forego the Kraft Cracker Barrel Cheese and Bill Bailey Salami?

I resigned myself to a bowl of cereal with skim milk that I carried with me to the den. I turned on the TV to watch the shows my mother would have watched had she been home: the tail end of Walter Cronkite, then local newscasters talking about housing starts, local weather, sports.

Because of all the big trees, dusk fell early in our neighborhood, and those thick-walled houses sucked in the dusk even faster. Outside, Mr. Krause read his newspaper on his patio, but things in our den had already gone blurry. Still, I couldn't bring myself to turn on a lamp. Turning on a lamp would have acknowledged just how much time had passed. Not that I didn't know the time. Once *Masquerade Party* finished, I knew it was seven, the hour for Nancy's train.

I turned off the television and went into the living room. There were no lights on at Chan's either. Maybe he'd taken my mother to the station. Maybe I'd misunderstood.

I knelt backwards on the new couch, watched the headlights of cars swing down the hill. I pinched the cording on the couch, holding myself in place until I couldn't bear it any longer.

At seven-twenty-eight, I began to pray:

> Almighty and most merciful Father,
> we have erred and strayed from thy ways like lost sheep,
> we have followed too much the devices and desires

of our own hearts,
we have offended against thy holy laws,
we have left undone those things we ought to have done,
we have done those things we ought not to have
    done, and there is no help in us.
But thou, O Lord, have mercy upon us, miserable
    offenders.
Spare thou those, O God, who confess their faults,
restore thou those who are penitent,
according to thy promises unto Christ Jesus our Lord;
And grant, O most merciful Father, for His sake,
that we may hereafter live a godly, righteous and
    sober life,
to the glory of thy holy Name. Amen.

Then I declared, aloud: "I'll wait for ten cars to go by."
A Volkswagen bug. A van.

In front of the house, a car door slammed. The sound was dense, cushioned, like a loaf of fresh-baked bread dropped from its pan. I ran to look out a window—understanding, in horror, that if it were my father, I meant to run down through the garage and across the drive to warn my mother and Chan—

Archie Jones. Coming up the walk. I watched him ring the doorbell, then stand, waiting for an answer. "Anyone at home?" he called through the screen door. He looked hot, sweaty. While he waited, he slipped off his suit jacket. I'd never seen him in shirt sleeves, and I felt sorry for him. I couldn't help myself. There he was: old, fat, without a family, living in a foreign country. He smoothed his jacket over his arm; then, with a look about himself, he opened the door, and stepped into the foyer. "Anyone here?" he called.

I had no choice, then, but to step forward: "I am."

Which made him jump, lay his hand on his chest. "Penny! You gave me a start! I—your father isn't by chance home, is he? He said—he'd leave some papers here for me. Probably in his office. If I could step up there—"

In the kitchen, the telephone began to ring. My father had left papers for Archie? It seemed crazy, but maybe the two of them had talked. Maybe Archie was supposed to sign something.

"Run and answer," Archie said, "I'll just head upstairs."

I didn't want to leave him alone, but I *had* to answer: suppose it were my mother, my father, Nancy?

It was Nancy. "Where the hell are you guys?" she demanded. She'd been crying, I could tell. Did that mean she knew something about Chan and our mother? About the door business and Archie?

"Nancy," I said, but then another voice came on the line.

"We'd *appreciate*," this agitated, adult voice said, "your coming for this child immediately! Do not ask *how*, but somewhere between Wisconsin and here she got herself stinko-drunk! Everyone else has been picked up and gone home, and we have no provisions for *baby-sitting* a—"

"Hello?" I said. "Are you talking to me? Is this someone from the camp? I was talking to my sister—"

The caller muttered an aside, then asked, "Is there an *adult* I can speak to?"

"No, but maybe—just a minute! Wait!"

I ran from the kitchen through the dining room and into

the living room. Chan's house still sat dark, looked uninhabited. I circled around, out into the hall and up the stairs to my father's office where Archie was opening and closing the drawers of one of the file cabinets. He turned, gave me a calm look, one eyebrow lifted in curiosity. He didn't look like a man who'd stolen anything. At any rate, without his jacket on, he had no real hiding places.

"Yes? What is it, Penny?"

I blurted something awkward: an adult, she needs an adult on the phone. Archie nodded, then picked up the telephone on my father's desk. While he listened to the camp lady, he glanced over at me. I supposed that the camp lady was telling him that Nancy was drunk. Could that be true? Nancy?

"Well." Archie set the receiver back in the telephone cradle. He wet his lips. He said he would fetch Nancy and, maybe I could do *him* a favor while he was gone. Did I think I could locate the pocket watch he'd given my father?

I must have registered some alarm because Archie immediately laughed. "Not to worry, Penny! It's only that I want to have a watch of the same sort made for myself, so I need to borrow the original. To show the jeweler, don't you know?"

I nodded dully.

"You just look for that watch"—he winked—"and I'll fetch Nancy, and maybe we can keep her little mess a secret, hmm?"

From the landing, I watched to make certain that Archie had actually left before I hurried to my parents' room, and the top drawer of my father's dresser. There, as I knew it would be, sat the pocket watch, and I hurried it into the bathroom, lifted the lid on my mother's box of dusting powder, set the watch on top of the puff.

The next step was for me to call my mother. I would tell her that she didn't need to come home for a while, someone else was giving Nancy a ride home. Then I'd get Nancy in bed as soon as she arrived, and Mother would never know—

SINCE THAT night, I've had many dreams of dialing Chan Bishop's number and not being able to get it right. I hang up. I dial again. Hang up, dial again. Or I'm at a phone booth, and the phone won't take my money. Or I can't find the right change. I don't have my contact lenses in and I can't read the dial, or the dial is made up in a language I don't understand.

That night, however, I dialed Chan's number without a hitch, and when he answered, he sounded perfectly normal. "Oh, sure, Penny! Hold on."

My mother was laughing when she took the receiver. "I guess I wasn't watching the time!" she said. Gay and challenging—as if she dared me to accuse her of anything—and just plain exhilarated by her discovery that she could be so *reckless*.

"Chan says he'll drive me to the station. I'll pick up some chicken or something on the way home."

"But—Nancy called," I said. "Archie was here, and he went to get her. So—you don't need to come home right away, or anything because it's all taken care of."

Whatever had been relaxed in my mother snapped tight. I could hear the change in her breathing even before she spoke. "I'm coming. If Nan calls again, you tell her to wait for *me*!"

I hurried to the living room. I told myself, then—because the confusion seemed to be spiraling—I told myself that all I needed was to see my mother. Once I saw her, the world would be restored to its normal proportions. Or, at least I'd have a better idea of how to defend myself against what headed my way next.

A light flicked on in Chan's kitchen: disconcerting proof that it had been dark in his house, too. Next came the light in his carport, then my mother appeared, her limp pronounced as she ran across the drive in her new high heels.

Quickly, I moved to the den, and switched on the television set. My heart—the way it beat you would have thought I awaited a murderer. The front door opened and closed. I could hear her moving about in the kitchen.

"Penny?"

Now I didn't *want* to see her. Now I had a feeling that if I didn't see her for a while, maybe whatever ripples had been raised by the evening would disappear. "Can I stay here?" I called.

She stepped into the doorway, to the den. She jingled her car keys in her hand. "Can't find my purse," she said.

I kept my eyes on the TV, kept *her* in the cloudier world that surrounded the screen's brilliant black-and-white flicker.

"Come help me look, Penny!" She sounded so much like herself, then, that I followed her into the kitchen.

"Try those boxes. I could have set it in one of them when we came in." She scanned the breakfast nook. "What were you thinking of, sending Archie after Nan? Why didn't you *call* me?"

I didn't defend myself. The more she said, the more it seemed like I'd invented every suspicion.

"Damn it!" She started toward the hall again. That was when she passed close by me, and I smelled on her what I'd often thought of as her "morning smell," and as I turned—startled by that pungent odor—I saw that the knit top she'd put on at the cottage was inside out, the label at the back reading:

Talk of the Town Petites
Size 6

She spun around, as if she felt my eyes on her back. "What are you staring at?"

"Nothing."

She put her hand to the neck of the shirt, felt the tag. Her face blanched. "You mean I've been walking around all day with my shirt inside out and you didn't tell me?"

She was panicky, her eyes too focused on mine. I was angry, then: she shouldn't have pretended that the only problem was an inside-out shirt, and, worse, that I could have fixed everything by being more vigilant.

"It wasn't like that this morning," I said.

A kind of shimmer crossed her face, as if she stood beyond something so hot it distorted the pattern of the air. I thought she might begin to cry, but, then, she started for the hall, ripping off the shirt, turning it right-side-out as she moved. "I'm going," she called over a shoulder. "If Nan phones, tell her to wait."

The front door slammed. I went back to the living room. At the Woolums', the flickering light in the den meant someone watched television. Chan's house was dark again, and I found that a comfort, but, as I watched—like some chill exhalation— the ultraviolet began to pulse in the skylight in his bedroom, and, watching, I shivered so hard that I began to cry.

AT HIS return—probably no more than twenty minutes had passed, though time had slowed to physical pain, time had begun to burn—Archie Jones didn't ring the bell, just called through the screen door in a low voice, "Penny?"

I hurried to the foyer. He was alone. "You didn't find her?" I asked.

"She's out here." He motioned for me to follow him to the street.

"My mom went to get her, too. You didn't see her, I guess?"

He shook his head, then whispered as we neared his car, "I think she fell asleep. In back, there."

I pressed my face to one of the Lincoln's windows. A chubby girl with white-blond hair lay sprawled across the back seat, her heavy arm thrown across her face. I panicked: Archie had picked up the *wrong* girl? But the girl wore clothes I recognized—Nancy's favorite candy-striped top and shorts, one seam split so wide open that it revealed her underpants.

The courtesy light flicked on overhead when Archie opened the door. Something was written on the chubby girl's arm— scratched into the skin—"NANCY + GARY," the letters a fine beading of dried blood, and I was staring, transfixed, at this horrible sign of devotion, when my sister Nancy—located somewhere inside that chubby bleached blonde—Nancy rolled over, and lifted her hand against the light. "Go away," she muttered.

If Nancy knew me that night, she didn't show it. Still, while Archie took the sleeping bag and foot locker from the trunk, I managed to maneuver her out of the car, and into the house.

"Go to hell," she said, wriggling in my grip as I steered her onto the love seat.

"Don't pay her any mind," Archie said. "That's just the liquor talking."

This sounded to me like a line from *Gunsmoke*, but, then, I supposed people in Wales must have said things like that, too. My grandfather's family: It's just the liquor talking.

"Shall we each take a side and get her upstairs?" Archie looked sad and kindly, and I was sorry to have to tell him no: "My mom's going to be here any minute."

He didn't stop smiling at that, but his expression flattened as if he understood my meaning. "Well, I hope you know, I always meant to help your dad, Penny. Whatever I did wrong, if I'd just had more time, I'd have made it right."

I nodded. He looked so earnest that I regretted not bringing down the pocket watch. It had belonged to his father, after all. And he'd even forgotten about it since leaving for the train. It wasn't the foremost thing on his mind.

"By the way," Archie picked up his suit jacket, smiled. "You didn't find that watch, did you? I meant to have a copy made—"

Just like that—all gratitude and forgiveness gone—I shook my head. "It's not where he usually keeps it. In his sock drawer. He must have it with him.

Archie looked down at the floor, he wiped at his mouth. "It was my father's watch, you know. I thought I'd have a copy made—"

"It's not there," I said, now sorry again, half-ready to bound up the stairs, retrieve the thing from the powder box.

Archie lifted his head and nodded in just such a way that I could see he knew that I'd lied. But he smiled at me, too, before he went out the door, as if to say he understood that I meant to do the right thing.

CHAPTER 20

When the police car arrived, I had just finished breathlessly hauling Nancy up the stairs to the landing.

I'd never seen a police car in front of our house before. The pale blue nimbus rode on its roof like the Banshee in *Darby O'Gill*, coiled up, ready to unfurl to some unstoppable enormity. I stood stock-still while the officer got out of the car, put on his hat, and started towards the house. Because of Nancy, I thought. One of the camp counselors had reported her drinking, and now the police meant to arrest her.

Down the stairs I raced, flicking off the lights that shone upon the landing, and revealed the slumped form of Nancy.

The police officer was a young man with dark stiff hair, hairy arms. He didn't meet my eyes, but stared over the top of my head toward the dark hall. "Is there an adult here?"

I shook my head. "My mom's gone to the train to get my sister. My dad's out of town."

He held the bottom edge of a sheet of paper to his clipboard, but the paper lifted, flipped over the top of the board, stuttered in the breeze. The police officer wet his lips a little. "A neighbor?" he asked.

I was half-crazy with anxiety and confusion. I said, "We don't know anybody very well. We haven't lived here long."

"That's all right," he said, then he opened the door, not to come inside, but to signal I should step out.

A BRIGHT red mask held to her face, Margret was the one to answer the Woolums' door. "Penny!" she cried. "You're back!" She held the mask to one side while she gave me a hug. I was on the verge of tears, but she didn't seem to notice. "What do you think of this?" She started to explain that the mask was Japanese—or was it Javanese?—and only then did she see the police officer standing behind me, outside the cone of light thrown by those beautiful but inefficient fixtures favored by the famous architect.

The police officer said things that sounded like the things police officers said on TV: Could he have a word with Margret? Maybe the little girl could have a seat in another room?

Margret glanced at me. My first thought was that she suspected I'd committed a crime; but then I knew that couldn't be so because she stroked her hand down my head and said, her voice very kind, why didn't I go in the den? Teddy and Eleanor were in bed, but David was in the den watching TV.

I did as she said. David didn't give me a second's glance before he turned back to his show, and I didn't ask about the story. My going to the den was an act of compliance, that was all. I went to the window to see if my mother had come home yet, but the house seemed as dark as it had when I'd left.

"I'm going to use your phone," I said to David. Without looking up, he said, "Quiet, Powell."

I watched the door to the Woolums' living room with the sense that I'd be punished if I got caught calling, that I'd be accused of helping the enemy or some such thing. Ten rings, I told myself, then waited through twelve, thirteen.

David gave me a haughty glance when I set down the phone. It was his house. He was at ease. Was I ever as at ease in my house, or anywhere, as David Woolum was? Upstairs, his brother and sister slept, and I envied them their peace, and the fact—I knew this already, though I hadn't consciously admitted it—the fact that tomorrow they would talk about me as a person whose fate had switched tracks, gone down a different line than their own.

"Penny." Roger Woolum stood in the doorway between the living room and den. His face was gray in the light of the television. He asked—sounding both serious and friendly—"Do you know how we might get hold of your dad? Is he supposed to be home tonight, or is he staying in Dolores?"

Margret and the police officer came up behind Roger. I could see that Margret held something—a balled-up tissue or handkerchief—and that her eyes looked sad and puffy. I did my best to ignore these things, but the weight of them began to tilt whatever plane upon which I imagined myself, and I felt myself slip, even as I said in a voice that sounded quite normal to my ears: "He might be in Dolores. He wasn't sure if he'd get home tonight. But he doesn't have a phone. You have to call Mick from the asphalt plant if you want to get him a message."

The police officer and Margret exchanged a look, and even then, despite all of my confusion and worry, I felt a stroke of envy on behalf of my mother: Margret had already charmed the officer into a kind of friendship, hadn't she?

"My mom should be home by now," I announced. "She just went to the station to get Nancy." From beneath lowered lids, I glanced in the direction of the officer. "Well, no—actually, my dad's business partner—he already brought Nancy home. She's asleep. I should be at the house, in case my mom calls. If she wonders if Nancy's home."

The officer raised his chin a couple of times while I spoke—the way a dog will when he smells something he'd like to eat. "So Nancy's your sister, Penny? And she's already at home?"

I tried to find a better place to dig my fingernails into my palms, new and sensitive spots of distraction. I didn't like for the officer to call me "Penny." His "Penny" made me see extraordinary circumstances were bringing him too close, things were worse than I could imagine. I said, "Nancy's asleep. I didn't want to wake her up."

The adults backed away from me for more hushed talk, then Margret said, "What about your grandparents, Penny? Or your dad's brother and sister? Don't they live close to Dolores? Could you find their phone numbers, do you think?"

Had anyone seen me run back to the house for my mother's address book, he would probably have taken me for some happy kid: I was that glad to get away from whatever those adults knew, or wanted to know. Also, though I felt sure, by then, that it wasn't Nancy they wanted, I still knew I needed to get her up to bed before anyone found her on the stairs.

"Mom," I called.

Nancy murmured from the landing. I made my way

through the dark, put my hands under her armpits, yanked her to her feet.

"You have to get in bed!" I hissed in her ear. I didn't shout because I worried my mother might come up the walk or the basement steps at any time.

Nancy was floppy and heavy, and, as a threat, I almost said I heard Mom in the garage, but I stopped myself—

The shape of the truth had begun to emerge, like a ship coming out of the fog, skull and crossbones flying. Superstition closed my mouth, made me rap my knuckles on the little landing table as Nancy stumbled up the stairs and into the dark.

SOMETIME DURING the night, my father and my Aunt Fran arrived at the house. I'd been given a knock-out shot by then, and so missed their arrival. A crazy thing: neither the Woolums nor the officer had wanted to tell me that my mother was dead, and they didn't know what to do with me until I did know.

That night, after I got Nancy into her room, I went down to the den, to my mother's desk. The desk's clear top reminded me that we'd been away all summer, her address book would be in the missing purse.

"Purse, purse," I said to myself, once again rummaging through the boxes and baskets she and I had looked through before. But it turned out that it wasn't at all hard to locate the purse. When I went out into the hall, I saw it immediately: a wicker clutch in plain sight on a cushion of the love seat. Archie Jones had apparently set his jacket down on top of it while he went to the station, then uncovered it again when he left.

I carried the purse into the living room. Because we'd been moving back to Meander that day, my mother had stuffed it with more things than she normally would have. Besides her glasses and billfold, powder compact and lipstick, there were diet pills, a French/English dictionary, her address book, migraine medicine.

The moon streamed in through the living-room windows, making it possible to read the words in the French/English dictionary, the name on the bottom of the new tube of lipstick: Passion Flower.

I took a seat on the couch. I knew I'd have to go back to the Woolums' eventually, but felt I could buy some time, somebody owed me a little time just then, and I carefully wound the lipstick up from its case and, using the mirror attached to my mother's compact, I drew on a pair of Passion Flower lips. I took off my glasses. I couldn't decide: was I really so much prettier without my glasses; or, without my glasses, did my terrible eyesight just make it impossible for me to see my lack of attractions?

My mother's glasses sat in the jumble in my lap, and I slid them on. To my surprise, their correction was so close to my own that when someone opened the front door and switched on a light, everything in the hall beyond me jumped into perfect focus.

"Penny?"

I clawed the frames off my face, smeared the lipstick into my palms. It was Margret, and, behind her, Roger, and Dr. Hobart.

"Hello, Penny." Dr. Hobart stopped at the love seat, opened up his black doctor's bag. "You've gotten taller this summer, sweetie! I bet you must weigh—what? Eighty pounds now?

I didn't understand that Dr. Hobart wanted to calculate how much dope to give me. All I could think of was diets, Mom, Nancy bursting the seams of her clothes. Did he think I was fat?

Behind me, outside, I heard a crash, the sound of breaking glass. For a moment, I thought maybe I'd imagined it—none of the adults seemed to react—but then Roger walked across the living room, and looked out the window behind me.

I looked too and, for a moment, what I saw had the power of a vision: Chan Bishop, lit up, suspended in the night. Then, I understood: I saw Chan through a tremendous hole he had just made in the stained glass window of his kitchen. Below him on the grass lay what he'd thrown through that window: his odd oriental statue of the white horse—apparently still intact.

"I thought I should call him," Margret murmured to Dr. Hobart. "Maybe it was a mistake."

Dr. Hobart advanced upon me with his needle. I knew from the movies that this meant the delay of what a person couldn't bear, and I didn't protest at all.

IN THE morning, I woke up groggy and stupid. I didn't understand much of anything but that I was in my parents' room, the curtains drawn against the daylight. It didn't take long, however, for panic to engulf me, and I sat up, and what did I see? My mother, sleeping beside me, the round heft of her shoulders, her dark chignon flattened against the pillow.

My relief was so great that the next moment's discovery—that the woman was, in fact, my Aunt Fran—ignited me. I exploded from the bed, whatever I knew instantly translated into an inability to stay in that house one moment longer.

Down the hall, the stairs, I flew. My father and Nancy were in the kitchen. Their moans—they sounded like the sirens of ambulances, like no sounds I'd ever heard human beings make before.

I placed both hands on the lock of the front door, working hard to muffle the sounds of its mechanism, but I was as eager for escape as I was for concealment; and, in my hurry, moving off up the street, I could hear the terrible yawn of the screen door, the *thump* of it settling back into its frame.

I didn't have a goal except to run as far and as fast as I could, but even this seemed immediately impossible. I had no energy. The smell of the slaughterhouse, the green of the grass—everything had turned up its essential volume, it was all I could do to pull at the air, like some dream drowner, with everything I had, my lungs, my arms—

"Penny!"

I hadn't even reached the end of the first block.

"Stop, honey!"

In the past, there'd been times when I'd been frightened of my father, but that day I was terrified. I ran from him as if he were a ghost. Blubbering—half on my hands and knees—I scrambled up the little set of steps that led to the house with the clay figures in its yard. I raced past the figures submerged in snow-on-the-mountains, lily of the valley, and ran alongside the house and into its backyard.

My plan was to cut through the backyard, make my way towards the woods and the creek, perhaps hide inside the old mill, but that backyard betrayed me by turning out to be a common stretch of bright grass confined by a wire fence stapled to one side of the house. The way I'd come was also the only escape.

The roar of my father's breathing made my teeth rattle. I turned to see how close he was, then couldn't quite help screaming—as if that grief-stricken husband were madman, murderer—

"What's going on?" A woman rushed from the back door of the house. Hair rollers, aqua housecoat, broom raised over her head. She brought the broom down on my father's back. "What're you doing to that child?" she yelled.

My father clenched his hands at his sides, didn't ward off the woman's blows. "The poor little thing," he cried in a broken voice, "her mama's dead." Then he ran toward me as if I were on fire, he needed to grab me up, roll me in a blanket on the ground.

But he was the fire, wasn't he? Looking into the furnace of his grief and pity—that was when I caught flame. The lineaments of our lives burned into me, and they were too terrible to bear alone. All I could do was give up, hurl myself into his arms, eager to be done with whatever came next.

CHAPTER 21

My mother died driving her car into a tree. An instant death, the hospital told my father. She was on her way to pick up my sister, Nancy, at the railway station. In a hurry. She didn't have her glasses on. I was able to tell my father that. She and I couldn't find the purse that held her glasses. I implied our hunt for the purse was what had made her late, and I got away with it for two reasons:

My father never asked how Nancy got home that night, and Archie Jones had vanished without a trace.

AT THE funeral parlor—a vast room of shadowy green, the floor aswirl with cabbage-colored roses—they laid my mother out in a terrible brunette wig, some dull mat drawn back in what must have been a bun. Years later, when I went to New York and saw my first Hassidim, I thought of that dreary wig and wanted to weep.

"We *had* to have it, Penny," my father whispered to my objections. He and Nancy and I—along with a few close relatives—had arrived at the funeral parlor early. Hollow-eyed, red-nosed, the three of us looked like the drunks we'd used to spy reeling out the taverns on Dolores's main street, fellows you could have knocked over with a tap of your finger.

"She'd done something to her hair," my father went on. "You must have seen it—the people here tried to dye it back, but it just made a worse mess."

"You have to take it off!" I said.

Nancy said nothing. A black scarf covered *her* new hair. She was still stricken with shame that, the night of the accident, my father and his sister had arrived home to find her passed-out in her own vomit; that they had spent a good part of that terrible night holding her up under the spray of the shower while she was sick again and again.

"Oh." My Grandmother Matson approached the casket, then grabbed for its edge to steady herself. She had arrived from California just that morning, and—grieving, exhausted—she appeared so disheveled as to be almost unrecognizable. Her lipstick was lopsided. She wore some sort of pail-shaped hat and her white hair stuck out from beneath it like the frill of a paper plate. She laid her hand on my mother's cheek. "Poor little thing!"

Nancy moaned. We had spent the days since the accident at our Aunt Fran's, where Nancy had refused to eat a single bite of food. Now her face had a pearly glow that I recognized as her sign of an imminent faint, and my father and I each took one of her arms, headed her over to a folding chair.

Grandma Matson said, "Put your head between your knees," and Nancy complied. At Fran's house, in a fit of shame, she'd picked the scabs off the names on her arm, but, of course, they'd scabbed over again. The "Y" of "GARY" stuck out under the edge of her shirt cuff.

"Well," our father said, "here's the Hemenways."

The Hemenways, and then, right behind them, another couple from Dolores, the McMichaels. The Bergreens came, and so did a few other Lake Bascomb neighbors. I'd always known my mother had lots of friends; still, the number of people who came that day startled me. All of the Powell relatives from Lamont, of course, and several Matsons I couldn't remember ever having met. And added to the relatives were couples from Meander and Dolores, and old sorority sisters, and carloads of Dolores women who'd come without their husbands, and Meander women my mother had worked with at the Red Cross and the art museum, or played cards with, served church coffee with, and so on.

As soon as people started to arrive, Nancy and I and Grandma Matson hurried to sit in the front row. I don't know what the two of them were thinking, but it seemed to me that, seated, head lowered, I might be left alone. And, I had a second notion—one I was to harbor for a long time—that if I stayed very quiet, very still, I might not move forward into the next moment of pain. That day, at the funeral, I sat without moving for so long that rims of moisture formed in the crooks of my arms—twin crescents, silver as mercury. Which didn't help. I was haunted. Even at my aunt's, in Lamont, everything contained my mother. When Fran took us with her on a trip to the supermarket, I found my mother in the celery, the adding machine, the linoleum. What she would have said about this or that, what she liked or didn't like. Her voice was in my head: "That's a terrible price for a chuck roast!" "There's nothing wrong with a little rust on the lettuce. The rust has iron in it!" Somehow, she resided in the device that the shoe salesman used to measure my foot, and, too, in the little stool upon which he sat before me. Even places *unlike* any place I'd ever been with my mother were full of her. *She* had never peeked in the windows of the junior college across the road from my aunt and uncle's house, looked at the anatomy charts hanging on the walls there, the cages that held hamsters asleep in a pile of cedar shavings, the aquarium full of frogs with tiny suckers on their fingers. Still, I was acutely aware that, in the past, wherever I'd been, my mother had always been *somewhere*: back at my aunt's, basting a turkey; or covering Fran's table with lacy cloths and candles. Now there was nowhere to look that didn't imply her presence, transformed into absence, a great sucking hole that made me gasp throughout the day, wake up with a shudder in the night.

Only my mother could have comforted me for her loss; and however haunted by her I was, that she could not, or would not, do.

I didn't have to look to know when Chan Bishop and Margret and Roger Woolum arrived at the funeral. Chan and Margret warped the space, the way a step down on a trampoline causes a deformity in the whole mat. The three of them stood apart from everyone else, talking among themselves. In dark mourners' clothes, they looked more elegant than ever, unlike anybody else at the funeral, and they conveyed the impression that they owned a special place at the event: they were family.

Which made me want to scream, tell them to leave—or else, to run to them and throw myself into their arms.

"Penny!" Nancy hissed. "Don't stare!"

She didn't remember the night of the accident, and in all the time since, as close as we've become over the years, I've never told her anything that would change her understanding of what occurred.

Grandma Matson rubbed her hands together: a sound like dry leaves, like paper kicked along in a gutter. Shyly, she reached from her folding chair to mine and patted my hand. We didn't know each other well, but we made an effort. I gave her hand a squeeze. I smiled back.

Bea Dart went up to talk to my father by the casket. Later on, we learned that she'd told him Paula had enlisted in the armed services, become a WAC or something like that.

I was explaining Bea to my grandmother when, behind me, a pair of hands settled heavily upon my shoulders. I looked just long enough to see the pink shell color of Chan's fingernails, then I turned straight forward in my seat again. My grandmother, however, smiled up at Chan, and while he began to introduce himself, I escaped and made my way to a bathroom in the foyer.

That bathroom had a lock on its door, and I used it. I laid out a little square of paper towels on the floor—to keep my dress clean—and then I sat beneath the sink where I could rest my head against the cool pipes. A few people came to the door, knocked, tried the knob, went away. At one point, Margret Woolum came. She called to me, "Let me in, sweetie. Come on now." She even cried a little, but I didn't trust her; I never left that bathroom until my father came to tell me everyone had gone, we'd be leaving, too.

As IT turned out, my father stayed on in Meander after the funeral, holed-up in the house, not answering the telephone. Aunt Fran worried for Nancy's and my sake. When my grandparents came to Aunt Fran's for supper, Aunt Fran said, her voice quiet, that she thought my grandfather and Uncle Lloyd ought to go to Meander, bring my father back to Lamont.

My grandfather made a face—pained or disgusted, I could not tell which. "For goodness sakes," he said, "leave him alone if that's what he wants!"

Fran raised her hand to her cheek, as if slapped, then she got up from the table and went to telephone Margret Woolum, who assured her, yes, she and Roger had seen him coming and going. They'd talked to him that morning. He'd said he was okay, he just had a lot of things to settle.

Four nights later, my father did arrive in Lamont, looking ashen. "Honeys," he said, when Nancy and I went out to the car to welcome him.

For a time, the three of us collapsed against one another on my aunt's couch. We all cried while he tried to talk about what a sweet, sweet mother we'd had, the best mother in the world, and now all we had was each other, we had to take care of each other.

He spoke in an odd, high voice: "keening." When I first encountered that old word in some poetry book in college, I thought of him, I knew the full weight of what the author meant to imply.

I plucked at the loopy fabric of my aunt's couch. Was he finished? The rime at the edge of his left eye suggested he'd cried as he drove to Lamont, that the breeze through his windows had blown dry those tears. "I'm taking care of things," he said.

Nancy and I sneaked a glance at one another.

"So we can be together. Just give me a little time."

My grandparents and my Uncle Roy and Aunt Lee—all of them called to the house by Fran—entered the living room. At sight of my father, my grandmother covered her mouth with her hand.

My grandfather said, "You ought to get in bed, Bob."

He waved this off. "Everyone sit down," he said; and Fran said, yes, she had coffee and cookies, everyone sit down.

My grandmother pointed a finger at her head, trying, I supposed, to indicate to my grandfather that he ought to remove his hat. "Oh, hush, Ida," he said, and then, "So—what's happening with the factory, Bob? Has this Jones disappeared?"

Everyone protested, "Not now, Dad!" But my father only stared at his father; then he got up from the couch, and wearily left the room. We all listened to him climb the stairs. The closing of Rust's bedroom door, the creak of the bed.

That night, I lay awake for a long time, listening, wondering if he might cry out. I didn't hear anything. In the morning, he got up, ate the big breakfast prepared by my aunt and my sister—suddenly responsible, helpful, industrious. Grateful, amazed, I watched as he spread jam on his toast from one corner to the other, just like always, covering every inch of the bread. I was startled to learn that he meant to leave after he'd eaten, but everyone else behaved as if this were to be expected, so I supposed it must be all right.

It was a cool morning, the smell of my aunt's ripening pears sweet in the air as we walked him out to his car. He had just tossed his shaving kit across the seat when my grandfather's turquoise Chevy glided to the curb, stopped.

"Bob." Through his rolled down window, he indicated my father should approach the Chevy. Hesitantly, the rest of us followed. "We could use more rain," my grandfather said, then asked if my father had been out to his farm lately. If he had time, he ought to drive out there, take a look at how that joker of a tenant was letting my father's barn go all to pieces.

Nancy handed Dad a little lunch she'd packed him. During the months to come, she would perfect the role that would stay with her for almost the entire year following our mother's death. I suppose she modeled herself on the image our cousin Janet evinced in those photos on the walls of her abandoned bedroom. Nancy didn't seem to mind—or even notice—that dark roots were steadily pushing at her bleached blond hair. She took to talking in a soft voice, never said anything obscene, and even hung up my towels behind me. I didn't understand any of this, but saw that her new activities gave her an occupation; and, once I understood nobody was getting around to enrolling us in school, I made myself a little day, too.

In the mornings, while Nancy helped Fran around the house, I listened to the old records Fran had saved from Janet and Rust's childhood. I remember particularly Bozo the Clown singing "Frère Jacques," and a recording of certain Mother Goose rhymes that came at me in an all-too-vivid way.

> Georgie Porgie Pudding and Pie
> Kissed the girls and made them cry!

When the boys came out to play
Georgie Porgie ran away!

After that, I'd watch a television show that I'd watched as a smaller kid, a preschool thing hosted by a chubby, sweet-voiced lady who also pitched soap. Then I usually put in a little time down in the basement hitting Rust's maroon-and-gold speed bag, and, outside, shooting his pellet gun at the pears I set up along my aunt's redwood fence.

I was shooting the pellet gun one afternoon when my father surprised me by coming into the yard. After giving me a kiss, he seated himself on top of my aunt's old picnic table, and set down beside him a paper bag he carried in his hands.

"I was just over in Meander," he said. "I had a couple gals give the house a good going over—before I put it on the market." He stopped, wrapped his hand around the folded top of his paper bag. I understood, immediately, that this bag would require a response from me, and I felt frightened; even the thought that it might be a gift gave me a scare.

He smiled—that curious, wincing smile he shared with his sister and brother and father. "The ladies cleaning out your room found a lot of food and things, Penny—coupons and money, too—in the closet, there.

I walked over to the fence, made a show of inspecting the pears for hits.

"They had to throw most of the food away. There were a lot of bugs. But here's what's left. Your money and all." He came up behind me, holding out the bag. He tried to smile, but sadness clouded his face like cold breath on warm glass, and he blurted, "For goodness sakes, what were you doing there, sweetie? Was it—playing store, something like that?"

I felt a child's familiar pain of not knowing whether I was meant to tell the truth or not. I also felt an obligation to honor the memory of my mother, and so I shook my head: no.

"But, Pen"—his voice was a wobbly mix of cajoling, pleading—"you didn't think things were *that* bad, surely?"

"Not always."

"Gad." He shook his lowered head. "Well, come on inside now. I want to talk to you and Nan."

We found Nancy in the dining room, cutting out fabric for some nun-like skirt she and Fran meant to make. My father seated himself in one of the dining room chairs. While he talked, he smoothed his hands over the skirt material—it gave me a chill, made me remember the days when he'd spread out the blueprints for my mother's "dream house," weighed down the curling corners with coffee cups and samples of kitchen and bath tiles.

"This is just between us, kids," he said, "but I wanted you to know. From Mother's life insurance, each of you has fifty thousand dollars." He lay his palms face down, side by side on the cloth, smoothed the fabric again. "That's just for you. I can't even *touch* it. You understand?"

Nancy and I both cried out a bereft: no! We didn't want the insurance money! No! Whatever money there was, we *wanted* Dad to be able to touch it!

He shook his head. "No. It's all yours." He said this almost as if delivering a sentence, yet, at the same time, he raised his hands in the air, like a man being held up, or arrested. His fingers knocked the leaves of a mass of philodendrons growing in the room-divider behind him, and a little ornament our aunt had inserted among the plants—it was a bee made of pink and black pipe cleaners, and it began to bounce up and down, the bead pupils in its tiny plastic eyes jiggling to and fro.

That fall, my father rid himself of property with the smooth, thoughtless strokes of a man scything a field. Whatever he could get for his possessions, he took. By the end of September, he'd sold the Meander house. During the first week in November, someone came forward to begin negotiations for the asphalt plant. The ballroom and the cottage and the grocery and the lot for the dream house went on the market. Not everything sold right away, but he gave the impression of not being concerned, and, then, over Thanksgiving dinner at Aunt Fran's, he announced he'd given packing orders to the tenant on our farm. We'd be moving onto our farm as soon as possible.

Nancy and I gazed at each other in mute surprise. Our grandfather—without looking up—went on stirring cream into his coffee. In old age, he seemed to need to support his right wrist with the fingers of his left hand. Only after an exaggerated pause did he look up as if he'd just caught the drift of things: "The *farm*?" He was pale as Nancy before one of her faints and seemed to urge Roy to some expression of incredulity.

The death of my mother had made everyone polite; it was history that supplied the teasing tone Roy would have taken at any other time. "You're thinking of becoming a *farmer*, Bob?"

"That's a lunatic idea!" my grandfather cried. "By gad! And from what I hear, you're selling everything off at a loss!

Sometimes I wonder if we shouldn't have you locked up for your own good!"

I stared at my food while the others argued. I tried to imagine myself going to school in Rigby, the little town nearest my father's farm. I thought of the way my mother used to talk about the farm. She always made me see a trim white house with green shutters and geraniums instead of the spindly, chipped place that—like some old and starving goose—actually sat in the farm's scrappy yard. Aluminum windows. Used drums of Treflan piled up beside the cellar door. Would I become one of the passel of pale, slippery-looking children with tan hair who always came sliding down the steps to greet my father when he pulled into the lot?

"Now, wait," my grandmother said. She got to her feet. She stared at each one of us in turn. "Wait. Who's this farmer you're all talking about?"

"For heaven's sake!" my grandfather said. "Somebody take her away from the table? Frances, will you do that, please?"

EPILOGUE

I never wished to move back to Meander, but make no mistake: life on the farm was no idyll. The day we arrived, snow fell out of a concrete sky. The farmhouse listed to one side, and looked grimy and miserable despite the efforts of the crew my father had brought in to clean and paint. Like many landowners who didn't live on their farms, my father had cleared the trees right up to the yard so his good soil could yield as much crop as possible. The few trees that had survived his decision were all deciduous, and didn't do much to soften the scene in November. Nancy and I needed only one morning of waiting for the school bus to learn how hard the wind blew across those wide-open fields, how instantly our legs and faces ached with cold, then itched all of the way into town.

Our father wanted to do things right, of course. He just didn't know how. He went deep into his grief, and tying up his affairs kept him busy. If he wasn't working in the little office he'd set up in the farmhouse's smallest bedroom, he was making repairs on buildings and fences and so on. Also, since he'd spent all of his life in homes where females took care of domestic matters, he had the not uncommon idea that a house took care of itself.

Nancy and I tried to be helpful. After school, we hurried off the bus to clean, get dinner going, and so on. Eventually, however, a day came when—it must have been early spring because I remember picking pussy willows while Nancy was inside the doctor's office—Nancy tested positive for a stomach ulcer. One week later, I arrived at the doctor's with boils on my elbows and knees. It was then that the doctor's nurse took our father aside and persuaded him that he really ought to get a lady in to clean and make dinner.

A succession of such ladies came to us for the next two years—at the end of which time the nurse who had first suggested such help became our stepmother.

Sarah Joyce was an English woman who'd married a GI during World War II. Her husband had stayed in the service for twenty years, then retired to his family's farm outside of Rigby—and, shortly afterwards, died in one of those accidents we came to hear of all the time: flipped tractors, limbs caught in augers, suffocation in oat bins and silos.

I think it was a minor farm accident—barbed wire, stitches—that led to my father's first date with Sarah. Nancy and I never heard the details of their courtship, never asked. For a long time, I had the idea that Sarah was too brassy and functional—too earthbound—to be a real threat to the memory of my mother. She was over forty, a blocky-bodied woman with short peach-colored hair worn tightly permed. Just as she had in the doctor's office, she treated Nancy and me with gruff good humor, as if to say, no sense trying that, girls, because I know every trick in the book.

Really, I can't imagine what prepared her for my father. Perhaps she put up with nonsense from that first husband, and didn't mean to do so again. Maybe both she and my father were sadder but wiser. At any rate—unlike my mother—Sarah wasn't hopelessly under the sway of her feelings for him, and, within reason, she never hesitated to tell him what she needed, or wanted.

"Oh, Bob," she'd call if he were driving into Lamont for some chemical or piece of equipment, "be a dear, and get us a pretty bouquet at the florist!"

Or: "I got us tickets to go to that football game over in Champaign. Now won't that be fun?"

After my mother died, my father spoke of her as "Mother." When he began dating Sarah seriously, "Mother" became "you girls' mother." Now, he rarely speaks of her at all, and when he does, he generally addresses his remarks to *Sarah*: "the girls' mother" did this or that, he says—almost as if she were someone he recalls only in connection to Nancy and me, the way he might remember that we once belonged to the Girl Scouts or took tennis lessons.

Which used to bother me a great deal more than it does today. Today, I ask myself, "What else could he do?" Because, of course, like any living soul, my father has had to adjust and adjust, and adjust again, and no doubt that means changing the way he looks at the past, too. In all the years that have gone by since the accident, I'm sure I could count on both hands the number of times I've heard him even mention our days in Meander. Whereas, in the past, he had gone over and over his grievances, after the death of my mother, no, he closed a book on everything up to and including the days of the door plant and Archie Jones and Meander.

There were a couple of years, however, when we did receive beautiful, heavy-stock Christmas cards from the Woolums, and a box of Texas grapefruit from Chan (on top of the pungent fruit, a card with Bishop Meat's greeting and Chan's Rorschach blot signature).

Did my father send *them* greetings in those first years too? I don't know, but I heard him tell Sarah, the Christmas after they married, "Might as well cross everyone from Meander out of that old address book, no need to send cards there anymore."

Given the way he had avoided speaking about the past, I was surprised, then, last Thanksgiving, when he brought up Archie Jones and allowed the conversation to take us back to our time in Meander.

My husband and I and our two kids, and Nancy and her daughter were at the farm. Late in the day, while the kids played outside, and before we started assembling sandwiches from the leftover turkey, we adults gathered in the farmhouse's family room. My father made drinks for himself, Sarah, and my husband, Chris. He made a joke about Nancy and me being teetotalers. Then he told a little story about how, as a tiny kid, I'd once scandalized all of our visiting Powell relatives by greeting my grandfather with a raucous, "What'll it be, Gramps, whiskey or gin?' and, somehow or other, this led to the story of our Great-Grandfather Powell's deserting his family.

That story still has the power to shock me, and though I'd surely told it to Chris at some point in our marriage, I leaned over to him where he sat in one of the family room's big chairs, and I murmured, "They never heard from him again."

Chris began to shake his head in sympathy—he is, like my father, a man full of profound sympathies—but my father objected, "No, no, that's not true, honey! Dad visited him once, out in the Dakotas."

Nancy and I glanced at one another. "Grandpa *found* his dad?" Nancy asked.

My father nodded. "He'd taken up with some woman out there. He was a hell of a stonemason, so it was no trouble for him to find work. Somebody's always got to make up the grave markers. His trouble, back home, was that he'd get drunk, and take it out on the mother, Dad's mother."

I felt myself bristle. "Take *what* out?"

"Ach, honey." My father lifted his hands in the air to signal helplessness. "It was a mean old life for women back then. Granddad—I guess he was sort of a rough character. Dad used to tell how, more than once, the family'd had to sneak out of town in the middle of the night!"

With a start, I realized Nancy and my father and I had all begun to smile. Because distance rendered the historical picturesque? But, no. It was just the three of us who were smiling.

Nancy caught the eye of Chris and Sarah, then added: "Jesse James and his gang went after him once!"

My father laughed. "I imagine Granddad may have told Dad that, Nan, but I suspect, mainly, he just got people riled up."

"But when Grandpa found him, didn't he tell him off?" I asked. "About leaving his mom?"

My father opened his mouth, as if to speak, then stopped.

I thought he looked a little disappointed in me. "Well, this was years and years later, honey, that was all water under the bridge by then. Over time, as you get older"—he lowered his voice, laughed softly—"you can forgive a person for just about anything."

Sarah, who had been quiet during all of this, suddenly smacked her thighs with her palms, and stood. "I got something to show you girls. Everybody just sit tight."

"Pictures, I bet," my father said as she left the room. And, sure enough, Sarah soon returned with a Lord Calvert carton marked "Powell."

"Pictures!" Nancy and I cried.

"We were going through them," Sarah said. "Your great-grandma's in here."

My father grinned. "Well, not *really* your great-grandma. She wasn't a *big* woman, but I don't think she'd fit in there."

"Oh, Bob!" Sarah rolled her eyes, then began to rummage through the box. "What a joker you are!"

"Doesn't look a bit like her," my father said as the picture of my great-grandmother made its way from hand to hand. "Back then—Dad told me—the photographer let them dress up in costumes he had at the studio. Apparently that was a common thing." He shook his head at a thin, startled-looking lady in feathery hat and watered satin. "She never wore anything but an apron that I ever saw her."

"There's a joke there, too, if anyone's got the energy for it," Chris said.

Nancy groaned. "Watch out, Penny. It may be that Christopher's been around Dad too much."

My father laughed and winked at Chris.

"Here's a good one." Sarah held out a shot of my father with his first car. His foot rested on the running board, Roy stood with his foot on the bumper, and there was Fran between the two, her hands lost in a fur muff, her chin in a matching fur collar.

"Look, here: here's your dad in his canoe."

Twelve or thirteen, paddling down the flooded streets of Lamont. "That's Milton Dresser," my father said of the boy in the back of the canoe. "Poor Milton—he died in the war."

"I wish you'd let me have these pictures, Dad," I said. "I'd take care of them, and label them and everything." I turned to Nancy, hoping to forestall any objections. "I'd make everybody copies."

My father shrugged. "There's a box of your mother's side, too. It's been in the attic ever since Sarah moved Grandma Matson back to Illinois."

"Pictures of Mom?" Nancy said in a rush.

"Can we see them? I mean"—I glanced at Sarah—"later?"

Sarah pretended not to have noticed any awkwardness. "Look at these Welsh foreheads!" she said, pointing out to Chris the shiny knobs of my father's family.

"Which reminds me—gosh!" My father was opening a vacuum packed can of nuts and he laughed as it released its little *whoosh* of air. "I never told you girls—the craziest thing!" and, then, he launched into another story:

The year before, while on their winter trip to Hawaii, he and Sarah were just sitting down to dinner one evening when the maître d'hotel came for my father. According to the maître d', my father had a call at the front desk.

"A *call*? Can you imagine that?" Here father set down the can of nuts, looked out the window to the snowy farmyard beyond. "Who would be calling me in Hawaii? I knew it either had to be a mistake, or some disaster, something terrible with the farms, or one of you kiddies." He leaned back in his armchair, covered his eyes with his hands. Sarah reached over from her own chair and rested her hand on his knee, then gave Nancy and me a look that reminded me a little of those looks our mother used to give us when she meant to call our attention to his pain.

"Gad"—he lifted one hand from his eyes, made it into a fist he raised into the air—"gad, my heart was in my mouth when I picked up that phone!"

But there had been no one on the line.

My father imitated the hotel clerk: very humble, "Oh, so sorry, Mr. Powell, but there was someone, an Englishman, I believe."

My children were playing out by the barn, their rag-tag assortment of borrowed snow clothes making them look somehow antique. I missed them. I wished they would come inside, hear this example of their grandfather's gift for mimicry.

"The idea of some *Englishman* calling me in Hawaii"—my father winked at Sarah—"well, I decided it must have been a mistake, I headed back for the dining room."

"A grand lobby they had there," Sarah said.

My father nodded. With a shiver, I noticed that as he stirred his cream into his coffee, he now supported his wrist with his other hand—exactly the way his father used to do.

"A whole wall of palm trees screened off the area where the phone booths sat." He leaned forward, smiled. "That's where I spotted Archie Jones: hiding behind the palm trees!"

Both Nancy and I clapped our hands together. You're kidding! Archie Jones! How bizarre!

"Who's Archie Jones?" Chris asked me, and I explained, "You know, the guy who stole from the door factory. The Welsh guy."

My father flushed as if embarrassed or irritated that I'd ever told Chris about Archie Jones; but then he made a hands-up gesture. "Heavens! I would have been happy to chat with him! I guess he only made the call to find out if I was really Bob Powell. It'd been so many years and I'm such an old goat now." His laugh was low, surprised. I rarely notice the way my father has aged, but I did then: when he laughed, his eyes disappeared in wrinkles and folds. Around the eyes, all Powells develop the smiler's fans of crowsfeet; around the mouth, deep lines of gloom and disapproval. At forty-three and forty, Nancy and I resemble each other more each year. Eventually, I suppose we'll look at photographs of our relatives and find we're as similar as face cards, interchangeable except for what we wear of the fashions of our days.

"Anyway, just to make sure I hadn't made a mistake myself, I checked the hotel register after dinner." My father brought his hands together with a clap! "Sure enough, Archie'd been staying there. He'd checked out while we were finishing our meal."

The story of Archie Jones struck me as a kind of license to speak of the past, and I explained that I'd recently seen a book on the Prairie School architects. "It had pictures of our house in Meander, and"—here, I smiled at my father—"you remember the Lincoln that Archie drove? Archie's Lincoln was in one of the pictures!"

My father grinned: "Great big old Lincoln? Gad, yes. And you kids remember Chan Bishop? The fancy Jags he drove? This Bishop," he said, leaning towards Sarah, "I told you about him, his family was Bishop Meat?"

"The one that wrote that book?" Sarah asked.

My father gave a nonchalant nod, but Nancy and I were all ears: Chan Bishop had written a book?

My father nodded. He'd once run into a fellow he'd known back when he belonged to the Meander Rotary Club, and this fellow had told my father about Chan's book.

"I had a devil of a time getting hold of it! Bishop had used some other name—a pen name, you know—and then I got the title wrong. It was a waste of good money, as I recall, nothing I could have showed you girls, anyway. Full of sex stuff, with a lot of drinking, and so on."

I sat back in my chair. Mention of Chan Bishop made me feel guilty and scared. My heart kicked in my chest very much the way my children had kicked *in utero*. "So what was it called?" I asked. "What was the name he used?"

"Gad, I don't really remember, honey. It was something— *Berlin* something or other, I don't remember."

Dumbly, I began to ramble on, "Well, this Prairie School book—it called our house 'The Zwinger House.' I guess that was the name of the first people who lived there, the ones who had it built."

"Zwinger. I think that's right," my father said, and began to talk about the house, the dam and the mill, and how lovely it had all been. I sat quietly. Didn't say that the book's handsome black and white photos of shadow-cloaked houses had gripped me, made me nervous and delighted and sad—as if I'd met an old lover on the street and stopped to have a drink though I knew better. Didn't say that I'd actually seen the photographer take some of the pictures that appeared in the book (though not the one in which Chan Bishop was shown walking up the gravel terraces, perhaps on his way to visit the Woolums' house, or ours).

Something about that talk—it made me agitated. I wanted to spring from my chair, run outdoors, but I was on guard. I forced myself to stretch slowly before I even stood. Then I went to the window and pushed aside the curtains. "I think I'll go call the kids in. It's starting to get dark out there."

Nancy nodded. "I'll come, too."

As if to say she knew we wanted to be alone, Sarah gave the two of us a feline look, the sort of look she used to give us when we sneaked out to smoke cigarettes in the garage or to meet boys who waited down the road. Sarah's never been one to interfere much, but she's always made sure that we know we don't fool her.

Really, Sarah's been a good wife for my father. She's been able to steer his energy back into the farms—his and the one she brought into the marriage—and they've survived times that have brought ruin to plenty of others. After some thirty years of care and planting, that scrubby farm we moved to in 1960 is now shady and green with a yard full of Scotch pines and blue spruce and rosebushes. Sarah has no interest in books or art, but then neither does my father, really; and she knows about farms, land values, even how to drive a tractor. She's always been a help. When my Grandma Matson broke her hip and couldn't live alone any longer, it was Sarah who flew out to California and brought her back to Illinois; installed her, first in an apartment, and, then, when her health got too bad, in a nursing home. Almost every day until my grandmother's death, Sarah drove into Rigby, visited her in the nursing home. As a matter of fact, more than once—with Sarah present—my grandmother said to me, "Your father was lucky to find this one!"

A remark I always took as a betrayal of my mother. "It's not right," I told my father.

"Don't be silly," he said, but then, hadn't he betrayed her himself?

This past Thanksgiving, when he agreed to ship me the boxes of photographs, I didn't understand what I'd find. As I said before, except for that lone picture of my mother holding her cat, there were no family photos of her in the Matson box; but I did find her, finally, in the high school and college yearbooks that lined the box's bottom:

A lovely girl by the name of Dotty Matson. In cap and gown as her high school's valedictorian. Behind the clichéd test tube as college chemistry student. Award-winning debater caught at an arresting angle behind podium and mike. Classmates wrote fond and admiring remembrances in those yearbooks:

> Dotty,
> If you can't find your dreamboat at the U,
> come back home and I'll be your canoe!
> Les

> Hey, Doc—
> Let me know where you set up your practice,
> and I'll bring you my business!
>   Kent

Dotty Matson meant to be a doctor. Dotty Matson was a smart and accomplished and beautiful college girl when my father met her. And she must have had at least some hint that she was beautiful back then because she'd done the sort of things (hairstyling, makeup, plucked brows) women are expected to do to make their beauty toe the line. Her beauty—I imagine it as a discovery that she made upon escaping home, but didn't have quite enough time to learn to believe in before she ran into my father.

Smart. Accomplished. Beautiful. He must, at least in part, have married her for those reasons, and yet—out of fear? in order to safely box her into the role of wife?—he had proceeded to cast her as something less than what he'd fallen in love with. Sweet Dotty. The crippled girl. The fat lady. The silly. The bad driver. The one who never understood business. Mother.

"KIDS," NANCY and I called out through the open doors of the farmhouse's attached garage, "come on, kids, it's getting dark!"

Neither of us wore a jacket but we didn't go back inside right away; instead, we stood in the cold and dark garage, looking out, hands tucked into armpits. Our father had built that garage while we still lived at home, and because I saw it go up—the insulation between its studs clean and pretty and pink as a baby blanket spied between the slats of a crib—I tend to still think of that garage as new, and more ours than any other part of the farm.

"I believe"—Nancy stepped over to one of the windows, ran her fingers along the top of the framing—"I believe right about here"—and she brought down a dusty box of Marlboro cigarettes.

"Oh, God: antiques," I said.

She laughed. "No, no, I bought a pack last time I was here! It makes me feel young to come out and sneak a smoke when I'm home."

Toward the back of the garage, we shared one of the stale cigarettes, all the while keeping a close watch out the dusty windows so that our children wouldn't catch us in the act. Caught by our father, we'd have been only embarrassed; caught by our children, we'd have been ashamed.

I rubbed my arms, stamped my feet against the cold concrete floor. Through my shivers, I said, "I probably have the only kids in the entire state of Washington who wish they could move to *Illinois*."

Nancy nodded. "Well, what do you think? You at one end of Sarah's place, me at the other?"

"You guys could come over every Sunday for supper." I tried to blow a few smoke rings. "I'd keep goats. And grow raspberries. And asparagus."

We talk like this every time we see each other: oh, to be cozy neighbors! Maybe it's just our way of saying we miss each other. Maybe we'd fight and drive each other nuts. Neither of us is easy to live with. Though it would have helped my husband and me out of a number of tight spots, the trust money I received at twenty-one—plus its interest—remains intact in the names of my unknowing children. Nancy's money, on the other hand, was gone in eighteen months, most of it up her nose. It's true: with hard work, we've both long since left behind our preferred addictions—mine turned out to be booze—but I still make myself ineffective with worry, often bark at my husband and children when they interrupt my work. As if I imagine I can afford to treat my time on earth shabbily! And then I wake in the middle of the night, and remember, in a panic, that I can't, I can't. And Nancy—Nancy's reconciled herself to the fact that, when it comes to men, she's only attracted to con artists. At least until her daughter grows up, Nancy's decided to stay single.

"That story Dad told about Archie Jones"—Nancy stubbed out our cigarette in an old clay flowerpot, blew a cloud of what was no longer smoke, but merely frosty breath—"that was bizarre!" She cleared a circle on the dusty garage window with a moistened fingertip. Dusk was falling, the light growing faintly lavender.

"You know that book I was talking about?" I asked. "It was so strange, Nancy. I actually *saw* that guy taking some of the pictures that were in that book. He took a bunch of them from Chan Bishop's porch. There was one—it's one I didn't see him take—it showed Chan walking up the terrace between our house and Woolums'. It was so strange."

"Chan Bishop." Nancy laughed. "God, I haven't thought of him in years."

"I think about him now and then," I said. "In that picture— he looked so *young*, Nancy. He and Mom, they were younger than we are now! And Margret Woolum. Remember how glamorous we thought she and Chan were?"

Nancy turned toward me. In the gloom of the garage, it was hard to see her expression but for a moment I wondered if she meant to ask me something about Chan and my mother, and I felt frightened—though maybe that was precisely why I'd brought up the photographs again: maybe I hoped she *would* ask.

"Girls?"

My father. Sticking his head into the garage from the boot room. "Aren't you girls chilly out there?"

No, no, Dad, we said, we're just—watching the kids. Then both of us edged away from the smokey flower pot, sidled between my father and Sarah's big cars to look out the wide opening left by the doors on tracks over our heads.

His voice full of pleasure, my father said, "The kiddies have quite a time here, don't they?"

We murmured, oh, yes, and smiled as he came to stand between us. Shrunken by age, these days my father is no longer taller than Nancy and me. Together, the three of us made a little fence toward which the children advanced with sleds and saucers.

"*L'heure bleu.*" My father's voice was quiet, reverent. Nancy and I both turned to look at him.

"Your mom taught me that," he added. "The blue hour."

I thought he was done, but then he laughed a little, the way people in our family always do when they want to go on with something hard to say. "She"—he plunged forward, though his voice scarcely rose above a whisper—"she used to tell me this was her favorite time of day because once it started to get dark, then she'd know, pretty soon, we'd all be together again, safe at home."

I looked away, touched by this recollection of my mother, at the same time that I felt compelled to judge it vaguely counterfeit, tainted. But, of course, my father has his own memories of how things were back in those days. My father knows a different story, and it's one he isn't telling.

THE END

LOOK FOR THESE ALGONQUIN
Front Porch Paperbacks
AT YOUR LOCAL BOOKSTORE:

Daughters of Memory by Janis Arnold
ISBN 1-56512-031-0 $9.95

Losing Eddie by Deborah Joy Corey
ISBN 1-56512-091-4 $8.95

Passing Through by Leon Driskell
ISBN 1-56512-056-6 $8.95

The Cheer Leader by Jill McCorkle
ISBN 1-56512-001-9 $8.95

July 7th by Jill McCorkle
ISBN 1-56512-002-7 $8.95

The Queen of October by Shelley Fraser Mickle
ISBN 1-56512-003-5 $8.95

Music of the Swamp by Lewis Nordan
ISBN 1-56512-016-7 $7.95

Wolf Whistle by Lewis Nordan
ISBN 1-56512-110-4 $9.95

The Hat of My Mother by Max Steele
ISBN 1-56512-076-0 $9.95